BECAUSE YOU LOVE TO HATE ME

13 Tales of Villainy

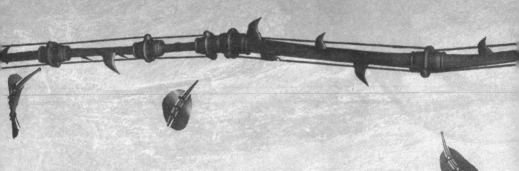

BECAUSE YOU LOVE TO HATE ME

13 Tales of Villainy

EDITED BY

AMERIIE

BLOOMSBURY

NEW YORK   LONDON   OXFORD   NEW DELHI   SYDNEY

This book is a work of fiction. Any references to historical events, real people, or
real locales are used fictitiously. Other names, characters, places, and incidents are products
of the author's imagination, and any resemblance to actual events or locales or persons, living or
dead, is entirely coincidental.

First published in the United States of America in July 2017
by Bloomsbury Children's Books
www.bloomsbury.com

Bloomsbury is a registered trademark of Bloomsbury Publishing Plc

For information about permission to reproduce selections from this book, write to
Permissions, Bloomsbury Children's Books, 1385 Broadway, New York, New York 10018
Bloomsbury books may be purchased for business or promotional use. For information on bulk
purchases please contact Macmillan Corporate and Premium Sales Department at
specialmarkets@macmillan.com

Library of Congress Cataloging-in-Publication Data
available upon request
ISBN 978-1-68119-364-9 (hardcover) • ISBN 978-1-68119-365-6 (e-book)

Book design by Jessie Gang
Typeset by Westchester Publishing Services
Printed and bound in the U.S.A. by Berryville Graphics Inc., Berryville, Virginia
2 4 6 8 10 9 7 5 3 1

All papers used by Bloomsbury Publishing, Inc., are natural, recyclable products
made from wood grown in well-managed forests. The manufacturing processes
conform to the environmental regulations of the country of origin.

To the unapologetically empathetic
and the smiling devil emoji in us all
😈

CONTENTS

BECAUSE YOU LOVE TO HATE ME

13 Tales of Villainy

INTRODUCTION

"You don't have the guts to be what you wanna be. You need people like me. You need people like me so you can point your f@*$!n' fingers and say 'That's the bad guy.'"
—"TONY MONTANA" IN *SCARFACE*

Villains. Stories are nothing without them. Heroes cannot rise to greatness without them. In the absence of an enemy, our beloved protagonists are left kicking rocks in the Shire or taking tea and biscuits in a mind-numbingly cheery Spare Oom. We love villains because they turn their aches into action, their bruises into battering rams. They push through niceties and against societal restraints to propel the story forward. Unlike our lovable protagonists, villains—for better or worse—stop at literally nothing to achieve their goals. It's why we secretly root for them, why we find ourselves hoping they make their grand escape, and it's why our shoulders sag with equal parts relief and disappointment when they are caught. After all, how can you not give it up to someone who works that damned hard for what they want?

For as long as I can remember, I've empathized with the underdog, the misunderstood, the so-called wicked. Perhaps it has much to do with my worldview, which questions the very existence of "good" and "evil" in the first place. Maybe what is considered good today is foolish tomorrow; perhaps the terrible deeds done now will prove themselves necessary evils in a year's time, a hundred years' time. I've always found the concept of good and evil to be wholly complicated, ever since learning as a kid about that conversation God had with Satan regarding Job. It was like seeing your best friend commiserating with your sworn nemesis: *Hold up, you guys are on speaking terms?*

Villains aren't created in a vacuum; they've likely suffered devastations and made the best choices available, never mind that their decisions might differ from our own. They've also had their share of oft-forgotten moments of truth and honor (Jaime Lannister, anyone?). Villains take the risks our heroes can't afford to take and make the choices our heroes are too afraid to make. They live in the Grey, and I, for one, love that sliver of space between light and dark, where things tend to be more interesting, people are more complex, and it's harder to draw clean lines. Look into a villain's eyes long enough and we might find our shadow selves, our uncut *what-ifs* and unchecked ambitions, a blurry line if ever there was one.

Because You Love to Hate Me isn't just about badass villains, it's also about ourselves, in all our horror and glory. Within these pages, you will find thirteen stories of villainy written by some of today's greatest writers and paired with commentary by thirteen of the most influential booktubers and bloggers on YouTube and in the blogosphere. (Unlucky #13, reppin' baddies since 1307.) You'll see nefarious old favorites and new faces, some reimagined, some twisted out of context, but not in the ways you might expect. The perspectives explored in these stories force us to reexamine our most fiercely held notions of good and evil, right and wrong, and what it is to be human. To be alive. Life, death, hate, love, vengeance, heartbreak—it's all here.

Villains, the deliciously wicked. We love to hate them and they hate to be loved, if only because being hated frees them from having to be good.

And we'd have it no other way.

The Blood of Imuriv

BY RENÉE AHDIEH

Everywhere Rhone walked, the nightmares followed.

Colorless creatures slunk at his sides, unseen from all save him. They whispered. Near and around him, their cold breaths pressed against his ear. Sometimes he could understand their mutterings: *Who are you?* Nobody. *What have you achieved?* Nothing. Other times they were the lost language of a faraway galaxy. A language—a world—Rhone only knew of in history lessons. A world his parents spoke of, in hushed tones of their own.

The nightmares often appeared in the shadows. In corners steeped in inky darkness. But he supposed that was to be expected.

After all, nightmares were creatures of the dark.

What Rhone did *not* expect was to feel them—to sense them—creeping silently after him even in broad daylight. Even in fleeting moments of happiness, they writhed through the holes around his heart, wriggling their way into anything and everything.

Until they were all he could see anymore.

His sister's smile was not a smile, but a leer. His father's look was not one of fondness, but of judgment.

And his mother? To his mother, Rhone would never be anything but a reminder.

Of all that had once been.

Of the woman she had once called Mother. The woman Rhone so resembled, in carriage and in character.

Of a monster who had all but destroyed everything she touched.

ᥱ᙭ᥴ

Without a glance back, Rhone left the warmth and merriment of his family's dinner gathering, as he tended to do of late. It was not meant to be a slight to anyone in particular. It was just his way. The parties hosted under the illustrious banner of the Imuriv family were different from many of the celebrations given by other highborn nobles of Oranith; his family's parties were never the garish kind. Instead, they were ones filled with friends and food and laughter, often culminating in tales of his mother's youthful exploits.

As Rhone made his way down the curved corridor, he caught his reflection sneering back at him in the rounded surface of the white wall to his right.

Despite his mother's best efforts, her parties did not deceive him. Though she strove to make them seem inclusive, Rhone knew his presence was—and always would be—unnecessary. Extraneous. The celebrations were tasteful, clearly gatherings meant to reflect their family's status. On the ice planet of Isqandia, in its shining capital of Oranith, there was not a single child who did not know of the Imuriv family.

Most knew of the name fondly. After all, Rhone's mother was quite beloved, despite the whispers of her past. As the sovereign of Oranith, she had brought an era of unprecedented peace to the planet ruled by women.

Others remembered the Imuriv name . . . much less fondly.

A name infamous for murder. Painted by the brush of darkest warcraft.

Colored by ancient, unknowable thaumaturgy.

As Rhone continued walking down the cool, darkened corridors of his family's ice fortress, the familiar hum of droning machines took on a presence of its own. A lulling, hypnotic sort of presence. Lost in its gentle purr, Rhone stopped to wonder what kind of woman his grandmother had been to those she loved.

What kind of woman. What kind of sovereign. What kind of mother she had been before her own daughter executed her for committing war crimes.

Odd how his grandmother seemed to rule Rhone's most recent dreams. Dreams of searing reckoning. Of blood and glory. Dreams of all that could never be.

At least not for him. Or for any man of Isqandia.

The sound of sliding glass whirring open caught Rhone's attention. He turned his head back toward the dinner gathering. A servant in a jauntily patterned smock was bringing his family's guests another round of drinks. Followed by another tray of food. Clinking glasses and cheerful laughter spilled into the hallway, calling Rhone back. Beckoning him to take his rightful place at his mother's side. When he hesitated, the doors snapped quickly shut. The warmth and the cheer faded into memory. Into nothingness.

Rhone turned and resumed his nighttime haunt through the halls of his family's fortress, staying to the curtain of shadows along one side. His hand grazed across the smooth white paladrium wall. The curve of its rounded center, and the soft blue light of its databands, flashing in lines at his shoulders and at his feet. At any moment, Rhone could pause and ask the blue band of light a question. Almost any question. It would respond in less than the blink of an eye. But such a machine could not answer any of Rhone's most pressing questions. No. For now, the blue glow only served to light the path before him.

A small bot no bigger than Rhone's boot careened around a corner, whisking its way to deliver a message contained in the outstretched grip of its metal tongs. A message clearly meant for Rhone's mother. Or perhaps his all-important sister. When the bot spotted Rhone crouching beside the strip of blue light nearest the floor, it stopped with a high-pitched squeal.

The bot lingered, uncertain.

Then the tiny metal creature backed up warily, pausing once more before continuing to chirp its way toward the well-appointed banquet hall at Rhone's back.

Rhone suppressed a wry grin.

Even the brainless bots knew better than to trod in Rhone Imuriv's path. It appeared the tale of his most recent misdeed had already spread to even the lowliest of servants residing within the ice fortress of Oranith.

Perhaps Rhone shouldn't have kicked that cheeky bot out of the way last week. Though he could not recall doing it, his anger had clearly ruled his mind for an instant. A twisted part of him had relished the sight as the small bot had sailed through the air, only to land with a sickening thud against a paladrium wall in the east wing. He'd watched in morbid fascination as the bot slid to the floor with the saddest of chirrups. He might not control much of anything in his life, but at least he had power over these silly metal creatures.

Still, a twinge of guilt knifed through him.

Rhone knitted his brow. Pressed his lips tight.

No. It was not his fault.

The tiny creature without a soul should not have dared to challenge him. And it had been doubly the fool for interrupting him while he was reading, all for the silliest of reasons.

Rhone had not wanted to play d'jaryek with his sister that day. Anymore than the day before that. Or the day after. Altais was a merciless opponent when it came to games of strategy like d'jaryek. And Rhone did not care to fight battles he could not win.

Nor was he in the mood to smile generously through a loss. He was not his father.

No. He would never be his father.

He would never be the kind of fool who happily stood in the shadows of greater women.

As he mused over these and so many other thoughts, Rhone felt his feet carry him toward the game room, unbidden. His steps were smooth and soundless in the elastine soles of his boots. He adjusted the platinum clasp of his navy cloak and straightened its complicated folds. They hung from his left shoulder, in a style nodding to yesteryear. A style hearkening to an imperium lost eons ago.

When Rhone rounded the final corner, he stopped short. The sliding doors to the game room were slightly open, the space between them no bigger than the span of one hand. A white glow emanated from within, its light nothing but a weak ribbon from floor to ceiling.

His curiosity growing, Rhone moved toward the room.

As soon as he brushed his palm across the access panel, the doors slid open fully. The glow inside flashed bright, like lightning cutting across a dark firmament.

Without thinking, Rhone lifted a hand to shield his eyes from the burning light. Once his sight had adjusted, he found himself in the spherical chamber he and his sister had often played in as children. The walls were normally the same shining white as the corridors.

But today a different scene greeted Rhone.

Waves lapped at a holographic shore in the distance. The sun shone high in a clear blue sky. The sand at his feet and along the chamber perimeter was crystalline, glittering all around him like infinitesimal gems. Rhone walked through the room. Birds that had been extinct for millennia—cawing, long-beaked beggars with creamy feathers—drifted above him, their images so clear and crisp Rhone resisted the urge to reach out and offer them a holographic morsel of food.

Even the air smelled briny and sharp and otherworldly.

"This was our favorite," a soft voice emanated from behind him.

Rhone shook his head without turning around. "Yours. Not mine."

"Did you not like it?" Careful footsteps padded closer.

"I preferred the one with the volcano."

Cutting, feminine laughter echoed clear across to the other side of the shore. "Liar."

At that, Rhone glanced over one shoulder, his forehead creasing. "How did you know I was coming here, Altais?"

His sister strolled fully into view, her steps light, her gait precise.

Her smile had upturned all her features. She wore a playful expression. One that Rhone could not mirror, no matter how hard he tried, though so much of their appearances were so similar. Altais shared his dark hair and pale skin. His strong eyebrows and bladed cheekbones.

But while these features appeared severe on Rhone, they managed to look striking on Altais.

With nothing constructive to say, Rhone decided to tease. "You're wearing a dress?" He peaked a brow. "How ridiculous."

"Why is that?" She crossed her arms, the jeweled gauntlet on her left hand sparkling in the light of the holographic sun.

"You look like a fool."

Altais huffed, a gauntleted finger tapping against an elbow. "It doesn't matter if I'm wearing a dress, a suit of armor, or nothing at all. I can still beat anyone who dares to challenge me."

"Dresses are for silly, foolish girls." Rhone grinned mockingly. "I defy you to contradict me."

"Better a silly, foolish girl than a sullen boy like you, skulking in the darkness." She sniffed. "Besides, I like the colors." With a flourish of her skirts, she spun in place. Her dress flashed through a series of rainbows. Rhone recognized the material. It was among the most costly to procure, made of a special cynesilk woven from the strands of many tiny mirrors. Mirrors too small to see with the naked eye. Far too many mirrors for any one person to count.

When Altais was done spinning, she glided nearer to the aquamarine waves. The colors of the ocean rippled across her flowing skirts, deepening until they became a beautiful complementing color, tinged by the rose of a setting sun.

She looked like a girl, for once, instead of the next in line to rule Oranith.

A sudden realization took hold of Rhone. "Are you meant to catch a man at Mother's dinner party with that ridiculous dress?"

"Excuse me?"

"Because you should know it won't work." Despite his best efforts, Rhone could not conceal the petulance in his voice.

Altais's pale brown eyes softened. "Why are you being so hateful tonight, Rho?"

A small pang of remorse flared near his heart. Rhone hated the note of pity in her words. "You've never wanted to marry before. And I can only imagine a dress that hideous to have an equally insidious purpose."

His sister's shoulders sagged for an instant. Then Altais stood taller. "I'm only sixteen. No one is going to force me to marry. Mother wouldn't allow it."

"You say that . . ." Rhone had found a footing. Something to cow his usually confident sister. And he refused to relinquish his hold a moment too soon. "But the matriarchy passes to you—the eldest of the Imuriv daughters. Eventually, you will have to marry to continue the lineage."

"I'm not the eldest Imuriv," Altais grumbled back with a nod to him. "But I am the *only* Imuriv daughter."

"A fact for which I've been constantly reminded my entire life. And . . . a burden I do not want for myself." He tried to sound sympathetic, but the chord he struck did not ring true, even to his own ears.

"Be glad it isn't you, Rhone Valtea Imuriv. Or else you might be the one forced to wear a silly dress."

A ghost of a smile drifted across his lips. "That would indeed be a fate worse than death."

"Or maybe you harbor a secret love of fashion." She grinned back. "Then perhaps you can pray some tragedy befalls me in the near future." Altais stepped closer. "Should that happen, I swear on the fourth star that I will leave you this dress."

Rhone snorted, almost amused. In moments like these, he recalled how close they'd once been. How easily they'd championed each other as children. How much they'd shared. So many memories. "That alone would be reason enough to wish your death."

"Careful, Rho," she whispered, biting back a laugh. "Should anyone overhear you, they might be apt to accuse you of treason." The last word echoed into the holographic blue sky. As the sound ricocheted from the rounded ceiling, a murder of beggar birds scattered in its wake.

Altais's cheeks colored. Her gaze drifted to one side.

Though his sister had pronounced the statement in an unmistakably lighthearted tone, her words nevertheless conjured an entirely different picture.

One of blood and fiery retribution.

Grandmother.

"Careful, Altais," Rhone murmured. "That word spoken by an Imuriv is a promise of impending doom." He took a step back, almost satisfied to see a sudden pallor descend on his sister's face.

Rhone sobered, thoughts of impending doom beginning to take shape. "A bot delivered a message to Mother not long ago. Is there any word on the unrest happening on the planets along the eastern quadrant of the Byzana system?"

Altais took a deep breath. "I have yet to hear anything of substance." Nevertheless, her eyes glittered knowingly.

The sight rankled Rhone. Another sneer formed across his lips. "The Byzana system lacks the resources to mount a proper defense. If they don't pay restitution, then we will simply obliterate what remains of their harvest."

"Mother does not agree with your assessment." Altais frowned. "Neither do I."

"You'd rather levy empty threats at those who defy us?"

She shook her head slowly. "Mother and I would rather meet with the Byzanate leaders and seek a diplomatic solution."

"Then you both are the greatest fools of all."

Dismay flashed first across Altais's features, followed quickly by anger. "How can you say that when Mother sacrificed—"

"Don't offer me a history lesson, little sister. And I've heard quite enough of your lectures on filial devotion."

A groove formed between her brows. "Mother would take you to task for such words, Rho. It's wrong to—"

"Given her lack of filial devotion toward her own mother, I'm not certain I care what she thinks." Rhone turned his back on his sister and focused instead on the small, cylindrical control center near the back of the spherical chamber. It was camouflaged in the trunk of a gently swaying tree with leafy fronds that grazed the shimmering sand.

Rhone watched the leaves dust the holographic surface as a discomfiting silence filled the space between Altais and him. The silence settled into the cracks, bringing them further to light.

A soft touch fell upon his shoulder. "Come . . ." Altais's voice was gentle. "I didn't plan this so that we would bicker about politics. I came because I wished to play a game with you."

Rhone remained silent. For a brief instant, he considered throwing off her touch. But they were standing in the room with the best of his childhood memories. And Altais had been a part of so many happy ones. Before power, family, and responsibility threatened to pull them apart. Before he realized he had no place in his own family. Rhone glanced past his shoulder, his gaze flitting across her gauntlet, its jewels cut to mask intricate dials and gleaming screens no bigger than his thumb. Finally, his eyes paused on her face. "Not d'jaryek," he said curtly.

Her laughter was impish. "You've already turned me down twice. If you turn me down once more, I'll tell everyone you're afraid to play against me."

At that, Rhone did throw off her touch with a disdainful roll of his shoulder. "It has nothing to do with fear."

"Then why won't you play?"

"Why don't we shoot instead?" Rhone walked toward the small white chest near the control console. The box had once gleamed as bright as the bare walls around him. Now it was scored by tiny marks, and its corners were worn smooth.

He pressed the latch, and the cover of the chest rolled back with uneven clicks. Rhone removed two miniature carbines, their surfaces similarly damaged. The silver barrels of the two laser weapons were notched by years of play. When he pressed the switch on one, the muzzle of the carbine sputtered before flashing to life. He aimed it at the wall, then quickly spun in place to shoot one of the squawking beggar birds from the sky. It fell to the sparkling sand with an ear-piercing cry. With a satisfied smirk, Rhone brandished his weapon, watching the tiny sparks and residual smoke curl from its barrel.

"It still works," he mused.

"Of course. Mother made sure we were given only the best."

Rhone tossed the other carbine to Altais. "First one to take down ten birds wins."

"No."

"Then—"

"Why don't we make a deal?" she interrupted. "Play one game of d'jaryek with me, and I'll shoot one round with you."

Though Rhone knew Altais to be a more skilled player of d'jaryek, he knew she would not leave him be if he did not at least try. And he could even the score and then some when it came to a round of carbine shooting.

Altais had never been the best shot. She was a formidable opponent when it came to iceblades, but she'd never mastered using a carbine.

"Fine." He nodded. "But don't cry to our father when you walk away burned."

Altais snorted, and for an instant Rhone recalled her as a child. "Don't cry to Mother when you're left without even a cat's paw on the d'jaryek board."

"I haven't cried to Mother for an age," he retorted, his voice dripping with disdain.

The siblings took position near the back of the room, where the lone console stood waiting. Altais pressed her palm to its surface, and the walls of the chamber flashed from their forestlike splendor back to the subdued dark of the cosmos. She pushed several more buttons, and slowly swirling galaxies blossomed to life in a kaleidoscope of color.

Altais continued sliding her fingers across the console screen and pushing several more buttons. A round table emerged from the smooth floor behind them. Two white chairs followed suit.

The d'jaryek board lay in the table's center. Black and white squares cut at a diagonal across its entire round surface. Along the table's edges were the game's controls. D'jaryek was first and foremost a game of survival.

His sister positioned herself before the controllers on the right. With a sigh, Rhone took his place opposite.

They both struck the switches that brought the board to life. As with the toy carbines, the board flickered, the lights wavering in place before settling on paler, grainier versions of themselves.

When the images finally cleared, a portion of Rhone's pieces on the d'jaryek board fluttered to life. His pawns were sharply curving antlers. His soldiers were gazelles—the craftiest of all the possible avatars. Altais's pawns were cats' paws, her soldiers spotted cheetahs—the swiftest of all the avatars in the game of d'jaryek.

Rhone frowned. He folded his left hand atop his right, taking time to choose his words. "Do you suppose it says something that the game chose a cat as your avatar?"

"No. Unless you believe there's meaning behind the fact that *your* avatar is commonly the food of mine." A mischievous sparkle alighted Altais's gaze.

"Only if they are caught." His frown deepened.

"Then, by all means, let's see who catches whom."

A dial sputtered to life in the center of the d'jaryek board. Both Rhone and Altais struck it.

Rhone won the right to move one of his pieces first—an antler shifted two spaces forward.

Altais mirrored his move.

They played in silence for a time.

When Rhone looked up from the board after his fourth move, he saw his sister staring at him, a thoughtful expression lingering on her face.

"What?" he demanded.

"Are you still very mad at me and Mother?"

Rhone shifted in his seat. "I was never angry in the first place."

"Why do you lie to me so much, Rho? I know you better than any-one else."

"I wasn't angry." His tone was clipped.

Altais sighed. "Would it matter if I told you I was sorry?"

"I was never angry!" Rhone's voice rose in pitch until the final word bordered on a shout.

His sister shot him a pointed glare. "You're a terrible liar, by the way. It was part of the reason why Mother and I thought politics would be trying for you."

Rhone pinched his eyes shut, trying to control his temper.

He attempted to clarify. "I was never—"

"Rhone!"

"Damn it, Altais, let me finish, for once!" His thunderous cry echoed throughout the chamber.

Altais leaned back and waved a hand for him to continue.

"I was never angry," Rhone repeated. "But I was disappointed. You—" He toyed with a d'jaryek piece, his hands flitting across the con-trol screen. The holographic antler spun in place. "You will have the sovereignty of Oranith. It's your birthright. And possibly all of Isqandia. I thought to make a name for myself, too, within our Caucus. I am not certain why you and Mother were so against it."

Altais took a deep breath. "Father did not think it a wise idea, either."

"And why is that?" Rhone's shoulders tightened. He refrained from turning his hands to fists. "Since when did Father ever bother to share his opinion on such matters?"

"We"—she hesitated, chewing on her lower lip—"hoped you would stay on Isqandia and help with everything here."

Anger collected in Rhone's chest. "Do you wish for me to be honest with you?"

"Of course."

"I think you are afraid I will outshine you if I represent our interests in the Caucus."

With that, Altais made a sudden move on the d'jaryek board. Two of Rhone's gazelles were taken down by a single cheetah, the cat lunging for the gazelles' throats, ripping them out with vicious precision.

As the d'jaryek board whisked away the pieces, Rhone and Altais stared at each other in heated silence.

"Now," she began anew, "do you wish for *me* to be honest with *you*?"

"Of course," Rhone said, mocking her earlier response.

Altais rolled her eyes. "The Caucus harbors the best and the worst minds in our corner of the galaxy."

"And you fancy me among the worst?" Rhone sneered as he directed his d'jaryek controllers forward, three into the fray. The move was a gamble. A tactical maneuver meant to lure his opponent into confidence.

He watched as Altais chose her words, almost rolling them in her mouth to see if they tasted right. "We don't want you to be seduced into the wrong side of the Caucus. The side that acts first and thinks later."

Rhone's anger flared even brighter. Even higher. "Am I a silly child in need of guidance?"

"No. But you—you tend to let your emotions rule you. And that serves no one in a place that desperately needs logic and reason. The discussions that take place in the Caucus are often—"

"Enough!" As soon as his anger burst, Rhone tried to take control of it. He refused to prove his younger sister right. "I am not ruled by my emotions." His words were still clipped.

Still forced.

A peal of tight laughter resonated throughout the space. "Even now, you are so angry you want to lash out at something. I can feel it."

"You do not know everything, Altais." Rhone's voice dropped to a dangerous register.

"You're right." She nodded. "I don't know everything." Another move on the d'jaryek board. Three more of Rhone's pieces gone. Lost to the ether.

Altais leaned closer. "But I do know this—"

Rhone's eyes narrowed to slits.

"Mother—Mother doesn't want to lose you, Rhone," she finished. "Not as she lost her father." Altais paused. "And not how we lost our grandmother."

A flash of red blurred across his vision. "Her blood is on Mother's hands. For the last time, I am nothing like our grandmother."

"No," she agreed. "You're not. Grandmother was brash. Quick to judge. Even quicker to act. And when you are quick to levy judgments on others from a place of power, blood often trails behind you." Altais lifted a hand to stay Rhone's rising protests. Her voice turned gentle, the sound mocking him even further. "I'm not saying you alone possess this quality, Rho; that tendency exists in us all." Altais took a deep breath. "But it's not enough for us to hope this quality will remain a mere tendency. We all think it best that—"

Rhone exploded from his seat. "Enough!"

"Rhone—"

"You will not sit around plotting what it is I do with my life, sister." A crimson tinge of fury washed over his vision, coloring everything in his sight. "Not you. Not Father. Not Mother," he continued, his voice filled with righteous fury. "I—I—will be the one who controls my destiny." The last vestige of his control slipped from his grasp as he swiped a hand across the d'jaryek controls.

Everything blurred in a sea of rage.

He had no place here. No place anywhere.

His entire family had seen to that.

If Rhone had been born a girl—if his sister had never been born— then he would be the one destined for the sovereignty.

And he wouldn't be subjected to the haughty musings of Altais Imuriv. His little sister. In that instant, Rhone wished more than anything that Altais would disappear. That she'd never existed to torment him. To take his place. That she could fade into the ether, just like a lost d'jaryek piece.

Without warning, Rhone's hand smashed into the center of the d'jaryek board. In his periphery, he saw his sister fly from her chair with a yelp.

"Rhone!"

Her scream was muffled.

Followed by a thwack.

Then silence.

His rage still consumed him. It was an effort for him to clear his vision and open his eyes to take in the truth. When Rhone's vision cleared, he saw the body of his sister, slumped against the wall of the game room.

Her head had smashed into it, trailing a smear of dark blood down the flickering walls.

"Altais?" Rhone said.

His voice trembled.

She did not respond.

Rhone fell to his knees, the guilt rocketing to his core.

The relief washing across his skin.

CHRISTINE RICCIO'S VILLAIN CHALLENGE TO RENÉE AHDIEH:

The Grandson of an Evil, Matriarchal Dictator Who Tried to Rule over the Universe Wants to Follow in Her Footsteps and Accidentally Loses His Temper, Killing His Sibling in a Game of Chess

THE EVIL VACCINE: KEEP THE DARKNESS AT BAY

GET VACCINATED TODAY!

BY CHRISTINE RICCIO

Evil is a plague upon our society. We must work together to snuff it out with the help of my vaccine. Do you need it? Refer to the serious symptomatic flags I've listed below. Paying attention to these early signs and actively following preventative measures will drive away encroaching darkness. Prevention is key! And the key to prevention is constant vigilance! My name's Christine Riccio, actual, professional, almost life coach, and I'm here to vaccinate your life.

Below are the telltale signs that darkness is poisoning your soul. If you're consistently experiencing one or more of these symptoms, please seek guidance and a vaccine from myself or your nearest Dumbledore figure as soon as possible.

- **YOU SEE RED WHEN YOU'RE ANGRY.**

You should never actually be seeing red unless you're standing in a room that's covered in red paint, or blood, or looking at an apple. If you're just seeing red, something's wrong. Don't panic, but you might be evil.

Home remedy to try (prevaccine-level symptoms): Go see an eye doctor.

- **YOU FIND YOURSELF HARPING ON INSIGNIFICANT GRUDGES.**

If someone blows out your birthday candles, you shouldn't be mad at them for more than ten minutes. If someone punches you, you're allowed ten days. If your grandson murders your only granddaughter because she beat him in chess, the acceptable anger period is ten years, but after that maybe schedule an appointment to meet and see if you two can work things out.

Home remedy to try: Watch the film *Frozen*: laugh, enjoy, and listen to Elsa's advice.

- **YOU ENJOY STROKING CATS WHILE YOU THINK.**

Cats are evil and stroking them encourages their evil thoughts to climb up into your brain. Be wary of combining cat-stroking and thinking, for the result can be catastrophic.

Home remedy to try: If animal-stroking is essential to your thinking process, switch to puppies. If you're allergic, try rubbing the head of a friend who cares about your health.

- **YOU LIE COMPULSIVELY.**

Tiny lies are generally okay: *No, I didn't accidentally break your super-cool Anthropology mug. Yes, I did watch that documentary about snails you recommended.* But it's a slippery slope and lying can quickly get out of hand: *No, I didn't accidentally destroy your original copy of* Deathly Hallows. *No, I didn't secretly murder your cousin. Yes, I floss every day.* Too far.

Home remedy to try: Never speak.

- **YOUR LAUGH IS SCARILY LOUD.**

Loud laughter is a clear sign of treachery.

Home remedy to try: Laugh silently or seek help from a life coach.

- **YOU'VE ADDED LORD TO YOUR NAME.**

The fact of the matter is you're not allowed to make yourself a lord unless you're the queen of England. And I don't know why you would do that because you're already the queen. Know that if you make yourself a lord, I will be suspicious and I will call a life coach to save you.

Home remedy to try: Community service.

- **YOU HAVE URGES TO KILL PEOPLE.**

You're never supposed to kill people. Maybe you're unaware, but it's actually against the law. Don't do it. Instead, get a life coach. Do not kill said life coach.

Home remedy to try: Channel these urges into something productive, like basket-weaving. Why get jail time when you can get a basket!

- **YOU USE PENNIES TO PAY FOR THINGS.**

Pennies are irrelevant and they should die. Smother this habit now before you become a threat to humanity.

Home remedy to try: Hot tea with honey.

- **YOU'D REALLY LIKE TO ATTAIN TOTAL WORLD DOMINATION.**

Really, what are you going to do with that? Why? Whatever you said in response is wrong.

Home remedy to try: Work toward acquiring total leadership over your local zumba classes, a real challenge for your mind and body, without all the hassle of war and politics.

- **YOU DON'T LIKE THE BEATLES.**

Why don't you like the Beatles? You're wrong. Try listening again. Listen until you like them.

Home remedy to try: Why don't you like them? You like them. If you still disagree, refer to bullet four.

໑ຌ

Happy not being evil! You're welcome! Be vigilant and get vaccinated! Please note the evil vaccine is 53 percent effective and may cause loss of your nose and/or the ability to frown.

Love,
Real, Almost Life Coach Christine Riccio,
aka PolandbananasBOOKS

JACK

BY AMERIIE

The thing is getting them to trust you. The animals.

Dad swears they taste different when they die fearful. Sharp, acidic. He insists that the butcher soothe them before bringing down the ax, though I'm not sure it makes a difference—to Dad's taste buds or to the animals. But then, my motto is "I don't eat anything with a face." I don't care that it's cliché—and it is, just as much up here as it is down there—because after hearing enough bleats and squawks and screams and last words, it's easy to stick to the vegetarian side of things.

I think about where these animals come from, the world far beneath the clouds, and how I'll never see it. How if the magick holding this stretch of cloud winked out and I fell into the vastness below, I'd explode into nothing—all nineteen feet four inches of me—and since I probably won't ever do anything great, it'd be like I was never here, was never even born.

I think about stuff like this all the time when I'm in the basement of our castle and I'm staining and stamping leather, doing everything I can to memorialize a life that ended on my parents' plates. Mom thinks I'm being dramatic and that it's the animations, westerns, and romances I watch on our flat-screen (magicked for size and reception, of course), and Dad thinks I'm fighting my nature and going through some teenaged rebellious phase, but I can't help thinking about the animals' last moments. My theory is, at the end, they smell their own blood before it's spilled no matter how you try to lull them. And I'm talking loads of animals. Do you know how much livestock have to die to feed even one family of giants? Seems to me there's something sacrilegious about taking a life and leaving nothing behind except for what comes out of your . . . well, behind.

There was a time, ages ago, when humans looked to the sky and just knew there was something powerful up here. Dad likes to talk about the glory days—how our royal line was up to our ears in gold and how things were When Giants Roamed the Earth—not that he's ever going to do anything about it. And this isn't a judgment; when he dies about a hundred years from now and I'm Empress of the Northern Hemisphere, I won't do anything about it, either.

I know humans like to think they're special, but it's galling that they've forgotten about us. There are rumors, but all are chalked up to fairy tales, myths, and fables. Still, people are curious, which I was counting on when I dropped the beans.

I hurled two tiny satchels of magicked beans over the edge of our cloud (careful to stand far enough away from the cloudline, of course) and knew they'd find their way to the right people, because magickal things have a way of being found when they want to be. Turns out one satchel ended up burrowing itself in the beach before it was picked up and the other tossed itself into the undercarriage of a delivery truck, eventually dropping onto someone's feet. (I know this because I see the sense in paying extra for the little tracking slip that magickally appears upon delivery, otherwise who knows where your packages end up?)

Yes, the beans were expensive, and yes, my parents would probably blow two gaskets if they knew, but what else could I do? Take another walk around the castle and observe the practically nonexistent change of season? Visit the market and maybe catch a urine-soaked whiff of a new shipment of humans rolling by? Perhaps watch a jetliner roar past in the distance?

Safe. Boring. And no one around to complain to.

Not much came of the first bag of beans, so I admit I had high expectations for the second. Those beans were supposed to bring up a friend, an ear, a confidante. Someone to tell me about the world below, since I was too scared to see it for myself. You know how people in those old movies share their lives with one another? I guess I was expecting that. I was not expecting a beanstalk-riding thief. Especially one who thought it was a cool idea to shoot up the magick beanstalk and steal the Golden Goose Dad had won in the PowerGlobe raffle, which we sorely needed because even if you're royalty, do you know how much it costs to magick a five-mile cloud in place?

And taking the Golden Goose *and* a bag of gold? That was just plain greedy. For folks like that, nothing's ever enough.

Which is why, as I run sandpaper for the hundredth time across this bare wood frame that I'm going to transform into a child-sized leather chair and I hear the window latch, I know that it's Jack.

He's come back.

ලෙ

The basement windows near the ceiling have old latches, which I'm assuming is how he slipped in last time. I hear his tiny feet hit the stone floor, and he takes a few steps but then freezes.

I turn. This is only the second time I've been this close to a human before—I mean, one who is here of his own free will and not dirty and scared and confused.

In my best grim voice (because that works on TV), I say, "Jack."

I don't even know if that's his name. Probably it isn't. I just call him Jack because after he stole the bag of gold and the Golden Goose, all week long Dad couldn't stop yammering about *that little Jack shit* who broke in. Mom actually ran after Jack during his getaway and saw him climb down the beanstalk and rub it three times, after which it shrank down to the earth below and out of reach.

"Don't tell me the goose has stopped laying those twenty-four-karat eggs."

"She's gone," Jack says. "I swear it."

Jack has a BBC accent. British news, not *Oliver Twist*. Don't know what he's doing on the coast of Massachusetts.

"You took a big risk coming back up here. My mom said she'd skin you alive if you showed up again. You get caught and you'll end up on someone's plate by morning."

"So—so it's true, the stories. That you . . ."

"Eat people? I'm a vegetarian. Never ate a face and never will."

"But the other giants . . . do they really eat babies?"

"Yeah, baby chickens, baby sheep, baby cows, baby whales—"

"You know what I mean," he says. His gaze darts all over the basement, over the wicker baskets and the stone floors and damp walls, like I've got a bag of babies tucked away somewhere like a bunch of onions.

The thing is, giants do have a thing for babies, including baby humans. It's something about the meat. Succulence.

Not that I want to kill the guy. First off, I've never actually killed anything before. Secondly, killing him seems wrong, not so much because he's an animal, human or whatever, but because we're the same age and so, somehow, we should be on the same team. Thirdly, he knows stuff and I can ask him questions, which was the whole point of me tossing down the magick beans in the first place.

But I do need to set precedence. "You're addressing the Princess of the Northern Hemisphere. Don't deign to think you know what I know . . . about . . . what you are meaning." Lines like this sound so perfect on TV, but Jack looks more doubtful than respectful, confirming my suspicion that I flubbed it. I move on. "Are you sure the Golden Goose is gone?"

Jack hesitates. I bet he's wondering if his walking out alive is contingent on telling me what I want to hear. "I know how to get it back, if that's what you want."

"You bring her back," I say, "and I'll give you something else in return."

Jack's eyebrows furrow; he's gotten suspicious. Give folks easy and they think you've just slipped something by them. This happened to our cook last week, when Sally Groper brought over a fresh arrival of oldies but goodies from below, about thirty or so senior citizens who got nabbed from Atlantic City or somewhere. The cook haggled with Sally, who was fine with it because everyone knows humans get tougher and less tasty the older they get—I don't know firsthand but I've attended enough barbecues to hear the talk—but then the cook made the mistake of smiling too soon. Next thing you know, old Sally raises the price by 50 percent.

I can see how being so close to a giantess whose parents eat humans for lunch and dinner and brunch on occasion would, you know, unsettle Jack a little. So I put on my best earnest look and I say, "Just turn around and climb back up those little boxes and crawl out that window and get down your magick beanstalk and bring me back the goose, and I promise I'll give you something really good."

He takes a few steps backward. "For instance? And how do I know you won't kill me when I bring it back?"

And eat me, I know he wants to add. It's a good question, I admit.

I say, "There's no guarantee you'll find the goose and come back with it, if you even plan on coming back at all. If I wanted to kill you, I could've done it already. You're here, I'm here, fire's blazing." I shrug.

He keeps walking backward until his heel hits one of the boxes. "You said you were a vegetarian."

"I am. Mom's another story, and she's an early riser."

That does it. Jack whirls around and pushes himself up the first box and scrabbles up the second and the third and all the rest and he's out the window, and I imagine he's running through the fog to the beanstalk.

I turn back to my wood chair and run my hands over it, checking for splinters, because nobody likes a pain in the ass.

ⓔⓧⓢ

Jack doesn't come back for another two weeks. It's around midnight and I'm sitting in the basement, sanding the seat of the wood chair even though I'm going to put a cushion and leather over it anyway.

The window's latch clicks, and there's a rustle of feathers and a low honk. Goldie the Golden Goose ruffles her feathers and finds a corner to hunker down in, glaring at Jack and shaking herself as if to get off all of his human stink.

Not that Jack stinks one bit. In fact, he smells a little different than he did the first time. I can't quite place it . . . water, sharp mint maybe . . . He smells the way I imagine a glacier waterfall might. Jack sits at the roaring hearth with his muscular arms propped on his knees. The fire-place is so large he could do a few cartwheels in there without grazing its stone walls, but he doesn't look scared at all. I mean, one nudge of my foot and he'd be in, headfirst. His dark hair is thick and would fill every nook and cranny of this basement with that gross burnt hair smell. The fire's big and Jack's brave.

"So," he says, "what do you have for me?"

"First, tell me about life down there. But you have to answer honestly, Jack."

He's yet to correct me when I call him *Jack*, and I'm starting to wonder if maybe it's his name. Or maybe he thinks he's safer with an alias.

"Be descriptive," I say. "Let me see it in my mind's eye."

Jack smiles.

It really is a nice smile.

"How about you answer a question for me?" he says. "I passed a fenced-off area and there were thousands of sheep grazing on something that looked like clouds, but that can't be right. Is it some kind of grass?"

"Something like that."

"But they're real sheep from below, aren't they?"

"Just because something isn't from down there doesn't make it any less real."

"Agreed," Jack says. He looks away from the fire and gazes around the room. His slack expression says Nonchalance but his eyes scream Greed.

I say, "We don't keep treasure in the basement."

Jack turns to me. "What did I do?"

"It's more the gleam in your eye."

"I'm too small for you to catch any gleam."

"You have a dog?"

"My uncle has a cat."

"You ever catch it slinking around, looking suspicious?"

Jack doesn't answer.

"Exactly. And it's smaller to you than you are to me. But still you see." I lean back, satisfied. "So don't think I don't see you, Jack."

Jack stares back at me for a few moments. "You don't sound like a princess." He starts to glance around the basement again but catches himself. "This castle is a bit . . . empty, isn't it? I thought royals had staff everywhere."

I don't dignify any of this with an answer. It's not like it was in the old days, when there were plenty of gold bars and jeweled treasures to hoard. There are banks now and high-tech security, and all the valuable stuff isn't tangible, just information and 1s and 0s. What did he expect?

"I, uh . . . I passed . . . a pen . . . There were . . . people inside. Human beings."

"So?"

"I don't mean to sound judgmental—"

"Then don't."

I sigh. Wood and leather don't talk back. People, on the other hand, are exasperating.

I sit in silence, questioning the efficacy of the magical beans' law of attraction, and Jack says, "So how do giants get below the clouds? Do you climb down beanstalks? What if you run out of beans?"

"We go down with the rain, and when it gets really hot, we rise back up with the vapor."

He looks at me like he doesn't know whether to believe me. "And if it's too cold . . . if there isn't enough water going up?"

"We're screwed."

Jack shakes his head but at least he stops with the questions. I hope he isn't one of those astute people, you know, the kind you can never be comfortable around because it's like they see through everything you do? Dad says people like that have only two stations in life: at your right hand or on the sharp end of a pike.

The thing about giants dropping in on the world below is this: only a few ever go—from this cloud, only ten or fifteen, and I hear it's the same elsewhere. I think that's partly because it's depressing, seeing how the world has moved on and thrived without us. That's probably why the ones who go down terrorize small towns and villages and farms while they get our meat and produce and flat-screen TVs. It's why they leave the occasional crop circle even though you aren't supposed to do that anymore, just to let the world know WE ARE HERE.

As for me, I'll never leave this cloud. I know there's more to life than golden eggs and leather crafts. I know I'll never surf a great wave or hike the Grand Canyon. Because as much as I want to, it's too scary to think New, to think Different.

Jack says, "Would you mind showing me your castle? I don't mean to be rude, but you can't blame me for being fascinated."

Don't mean to be rude, says the thief. Jack wants to see what else he can steal, more like.

But I haven't had anyone over in ages, and last time, well, let's just say things didn't go as planned.

So I tell Jack it'd be best if I rub the edge of my cardigan over his body so that the human scent of him can be covered by lint and ozone.

The last thing we need is Dad *fee-fi-fo-fum*-ing it down the stairs. (The battle cry *fee fi fo fum* translates roughly from the old giant tongue to "fight destroy conquer expand," but it's suffered an unfortunate downgrade and now just means "I'm really pissed.")

I look down at Jack, who at full height reaches the top of my knee, and there's this awkward moment when he lifts his arms and extends them toward me and he looks so helpless and trusting . . . so human. I'm endeared to him and repelled at the same time. I wrap my fingers around him, and it could be my imagination, but I think I feel his heart thudding against one of my fingertips. I grip his warm body tighter. His ribs feel fragile against the bones of my pinkie; his butt is soft against the meat of my palm. Muscle and bone and blood and water . . .

"Ow!"

His voice is so sharp I nearly drop him. "What?"

"You were squeezing me to death."

Squeezing me to death. A dare, a challenge. It's only a split second, but in this moment I feel electric.

I don't apologize, because it wouldn't be right, a giant—and a royal one at that—apologizing to a human, but I loosen my grip and place him on my right shoulder.

Upstairs, the moonlight reflects off heavy copper pots hanging in the kitchen, shimmers off great stone walls. I walk straight through and head for the receiving room to show Jack the paintings, sculptures, and artifacts (all crafted by humans) that our family has collected for generations. I hurry past the recessed, oversized nook just outside the kitchen. In the nook's center stands a bigger-than-life-sized bronze bull. The silver light of the moon glints off its horns. I hate the oily, charred smell in there; it clings to the walls.

"What's that?" he says, pointing to the bull. "It's huge. I've never seen an iron bull in a house."

"It's bronze."

"I was expecting, I don't know, stuffed men on the walls—human heads, maybe."

"Don't be ridiculous."

"Come on, bring me closer!"

I know he isn't going to shut up until I do, so I pad over to the bull.

"This is amazing. Can I sit on it?"

The last thing I need is Jack falling off. "Absolutely not. It's not a toy."

"All the wood bits and ash on the floor—nice touch."

I pause.

"Come on, just for a second."

I sigh and lift him off my shoulder and I get that feeling again, the urge to squeeze and squeeze. Power over life and death, here in my hand, a gift. But I just place Jack on top of the bull and watch him sidle up to the bronze animal's neck.

"I summered in Texas once," he says. "There was a restaurant that served peanuts by the bowl. You crack them open and toss them onto the floor. The entire floor, covered in shells." Jack does this gymnast thing as he talks, placing his arms straight down in front of him, his palms flat against the bull's back as he stretches out his legs. "It's brilliant. At least, it was. There was a lawsuit."

Next thing you know, Jack's hand slips, and he cries out and nearly crashes to the floor. And then I hear her big mouth. I forgot all about that damned thing.

"'Tis late, 'tis late!

And who is this young man?

A human boy, a wicked thief!

Blood payment we demand!"

I rush to the ornate wood cabinet against the wall that holds some of the more magickal pieces Mom and Dad and my great-great-great-great-great-I-may-as-well-stop-now-because-you-get-the-idea-grand-parents have collected from humans over the last two thousand years or so. I already know it's unlocked because no one would dare burgle Dad, even though Mom locks the cabinet when we're hosting feasts because you don't maintain a monarchy by being stupid.

I throw open the left door and reach for the topmost shelf and close my hand over the stupid harp. I know she won't shut up now that she's awake, so I do my best to smother her. She's really a bust of a pearl-draped woman sculpted onto the front of a harp, but don't let the serene face fool you—she isn't afraid to throw you in front of a jetliner, especially when she's screeching about you sneaking out when you're just going to the kitchen for a snack. I press my fingers against her strings so she can't vibrate them, and I swipe Jack up from the bull.

A boom of thunder sounds from upstairs and I know it's Dad. I sprint for the basement and head straight to the window.

"Time to go," I say as I shove Jack through and drop the harp after him. She's a lot smaller than the average-sized harp so she won't be impossible for him to lug on his own.

"Is it gold-plated?"

The harp gasps. "I am not an *it*, and I most certainly am not gold-*plated*."

"She's gold-plated," I hiss. "Now get going!"

Jack hesitates. He looks up at me with this lopsided expression and I think this might be like one of those moments in a story where the guy says this awkward thing, and the girl says this sarcastic thing, and there's a moment of silence and they just stand there until he lunges and kisses her anyway . . . You know the story?

Well, that doesn't happen, because first of all Jack's, like, a fourth of my size, so not only would the logistics be off, I'm just not that into him; second of all, my dad's thundering down the basement stairs, and I can already imagine him bellowing *I'm going to kill you* once he gets a look at Jack. Unlike in that aforementioned made-for-TV story, Dad will mean it.

And he'll probably eat Jack on top of everything.

So, yeah, forget about the kiss.

⚉

Jack ends up in the clouds every couple of weeks or so, but I never know exactly when he's going to make his appearance because he doesn't know, either; it's something to do with the magick beans and the phases of the moon. It takes three beans to grow the stalk, and he has less than half a bag left because he wasted a bunch before realizing all moons don't cultivate good beanstalks. Once he jumped on a stalk just as it started to grow, and as usual, it shot him upward. But it stopped about halfway. *I was just hanging there at twenty thousand feet. It took me ages to climb down and I won't go on about how many times I nearly slipped. I could've died.*

Jack has lots of Almost Dying stories. He's explored underwater forests with faulty air tanks, still taking time to skim his fingers over swaying treetops. He's spent two nights in the Gobi Desert with a half-filled canteen. He's scrambled out of ancient tombs just as their tunnels are collapsing. He's eaten python in a Beninese rain forest to consume the snake's powers. He's spent one full night alone in a haunted Japanese forest without a light source, his back against a tree trunk.

Jack just isn't afraid of anything, not even castle-dwelling giants in the sky.

We're sitting near the cloudline, near Lookout South, and I stare up at the constellations, feeling small despite my bigness. There are an infinite number of galaxies up there, but I've never given serious thought to leaving this five-mile stretch of cloud. I've always known my world to be practically microscopic, but since getting to know Jack, it's managed to shrink even more. Part of me wonders if he's telling the truth about all the things he's done, when he's *summering* here and there, tagging along with his antiquarian, wanderlustful uncle and his beloved tabby cat. Even though my only requirement was that he be honest, I realize it doesn't really matter. Because Jack isn't afraid to dream, isn't afraid to try new things, and this has come to mean more to me than anything else.

"What have you never done," Jack says, "that you've always wanted to do?"

I've been so caught up in his stories and the inability to offer any interesting ones of my own that I just blurt it out: "Everything."

Jack looks up at me with his fine-boned, deceivingly good face. "Okay."

"Okay?"

"Okay. You just need to start small."

I know plenty about *small*. If we are only as big as our dreams, Jack is the giant, here. "You know I haven't even looked over the edge of the clouds before? Not even at the lookout points."

"Isn't this your kingdom? The seat of your empire?" Jack picks at bits of cloud and rubs them between his fingers until they evaporate. "You can do whatever you like."

I shake my head. "I'll never look over. It's too dangerous."

"Never say never. And anyway, you don't have to set out to climb Mount Everest from the start."

We've got distant relatives there. They hate it. Used to be they could host vacations for giant folk, since anyone who witnessed them whooshing down the sides of the mountain never lived to tell the tale; but now humans have smartphones and the internet and it's too risky, being seen, even if the giants stay up in the clouds. I tell Jack this and he asks me what's so different about Mount Everest, why giants there might be seen even in the sky when giants aren't seen everywhere else, like here.

"Because," I say, "when humans visit places like Mount Everest, they're already prepared to see something they haven't. They *want* to be blown away. So they see giants and villages in the sky and a bunch of stuff that isn't even there. They want to believe."

Humans didn't have a choice before, believing in us or not. They were forced to see us, reckon with us. But their numbers grew faster than ours, and they created guns and bombs and lasers, and magick doesn't have the same kind of exponential growth as technology. Magick is an ancient thing; it's always been here and always will be, and so it takes its time. It isn't concerned that its wielder might need it to step up from anticannonball defense.

I look at Jack sitting there and think back to the way I'd unknowingly put the squeeze on him in the basement. Is it bad that I want to do it again, to squeeze harder, to discover firsthand the limits to . . . ? To what, I don't know. I just know I want to push.

"Want to know a secret?" Jack says. "I used to be scared of everything until I was fourteen. I couldn't cross the street without nearly having a heart attack."

I don't believe it.

"But then I went with my uncle to that rain forest and we ate that python, and lo and behold. New man."

The python story is one of Jack's more believable ones, but I'm not sure about the instant transformation.

Jack points to his head. "I think a lot of it is in here. It's human nature. How we're built."

But I'm not human. And anyway, giants don't push, don't test the limits, don't strive to conquer—at least, not anymore. Somewhere along the line, we recognized when things got hopeless.

"I'm summering on Martha's Vineyard," Jack says, "and a boy I know tattooed a toad's head onto his chest."

I start.

Jack goes on. "And this is a boy who never in a million years would consider getting a tattoo. It was his breakout moment, when he got outside himself. But it wasn't some horrible tattoo that did it." Jack points to his temple again.

A toad's head tattoo. Even the best artist can't save that one. "Maybe the tattoo was just a bad life choice."

Jack shakes his head. "No, I saw him out more, at the theater, different restaurants, beach bonfires." Jack leans in and grins. "Then one day he disappeared. He finally broke out. He hated living there, on the Vineyard. So I think it did the trick."

"I need a breakout moment," I whisper. High above the earth, all of us giants do.

Jack hops to his feet and strides toward the lookout platform at the cloudline. "Come on!"

Just the notion of going all the way out to the platform adds tons to my feet, but I stand and slowly walk after him. Still, when I get to the farthest point I've ever ventured, which is where I was when I flung the bags of beans to the earth below, I stop. Jack, however, is there, jumping up and down.

"You're almost here," he calls from the platform. "If I can do it . . ."

I want to, but I just . . . I can't. The thought of standing at the cloud-line, staring down at that vast unknown . . . It's almost physical, this inability to move.

Jack rushes over, his eyes determined as a TV general's. "Your legs will feel shaky, but don't let your mind trick you into not trusting your body, not trusting yourself. Even climbing Mount Everest starts with a single step. You can do this."

I can do this.

Can't I?

I take a step, then another. Jack hoots and backs away, looking like one of those ridiculous parents in those diaper commercials, watching their kids toddle for the first time.

It's breezier at the platform. I take a step up and wobble even when my feet are rooted to the stone.

"It's all in your head," Jack says. "Just a little closer to the railing."

I can do this.

I raise a shaky hand and grab the railing.

"Just a peek," Jack says.

I lower my head, but before I can see anything, I squeeze my eyes shut. I'm gripping the railing so hard I swear I might break it.

Jack says, "Look down." But when I throw my eyes open, I look straight ahead.

Jack whoops and I jerk my head down to see him jumping onto the railing. He throws his arms above his head. His eyes are hard and wild and it's enough to send me stumbling back off the platform.

Unlike Jack, I'm not interested in plunging to my death. Jack doesn't understand because Jack isn't a safe boy.

Another part of me doesn't want to always be safe, either. If my people are going to be great again, we can't hide behind *safe* anymore. My body's buzzing and my fingers twitch and my eyes burn. We deserve so much more. But I'm not brave enough to lead my people anywhere.

I take a step back. Another. Another.

Jack jogs over. "Next time, then." He looks at me with steely eyes gone soft. "Next time you'll look down. There's plenty to see. You'll love it, I promise."

I nod, defeated and trying not to look it. "It's just . . . kind of cold, that's all."

"Definitely. I was getting cold, too," Jack says. "Fireplace? You could work on your chair." He rubs his arms vigorously, even though we both know it's pretty warm up here, the magicked atmosphere and all.

He's a kind liar.

We head back to the castle, and all I can think about is how badly I want to be like Jack, how badly I want an all-cares-to-the-wind risk-taker inside of me, too.

But there isn't.

☙❧

"You're already here. You've done the hard part." Beside me, Jack laughs. "All you have to do now is open your eyes."

It's the first time Jack has been back in a month, and the first thing he did when he got here was ask me to take him back to Lookout South. I only gave in because he wouldn't shut up about it.

"There's a special desert I'd like to visit," Jack says breezily. "Rocks are said to slide across the baked earth on their own."

I've got a tight grip around the railing and my eyes are shut, just like they've been the entire five minutes we've been standing here. It was easier making it out to the platform this second time, but now that I'm here, my body betrays me. My hands shake and my legs feel like they're about to float off with the wind, and the only thing keeping me from keeling over is my royal pride.

"Are you familiar with the place?" Jack says.

It's a lot windier than last time, and my palms are slippery. "What?" I say, still refusing to see anything but the backs of my eyelids.

"The desert. Mysterious forces . . . ?"

"Let's talk about it back at the castle." I'm embarrassed at how breathless I sound but too scared to sound any different.

"I'd love to see a rock pushing itself across the ground," Jack says, as if he can't tell I'm this close to breakdown mode. "I'm going to see it one day. It's all in the mind, you know. Be clear about your desires and you'll achieve them."

"I can't concentrate on anything you're saying. Can we please—"

"Take a peek. Then we go back and we don't come here again unless you suggest it."

"Jack—"

"A peek. Otherwise I will haunt your dreams with my bucket list."

The guy's persistent enough to figure out a way to do just that. I want to kick and applaud him at the same time. How can so much bravery fit into such a tiny body? How beautiful the human world must be, to create creatures as fearless as Jack. And it used to be ours. I'm the future Empress of the freaking Northern Hemisphere. I should at least be able to see it beneath my feet and be unafraid.

I can be like Jack.

No. I grip the railing even tighter.

I can be more.

Inhale.

Exhale.

I crack open my eyelids.

Pinpricks of light shine against the dark curtain spread before me as far as I can see. And then I see past it, to everything I've only experienced on television: salt-spraying waves; rustling trees; red canyons; rolling knolls; sweltering jungles . . . The potential of it all is enough to make this cloud feel more claustrophobic than ever.

I can be more. My own voice sounds so much stronger in my

mind than it ever has in real life, and for one second I really believe it. *I can be—*

A gust of wind rushes in, and my knees buckle, and just like that, my eyes are shut again.

But I don't step back. I take a deep breath and dare one more glance at the world below. A second later I feel like I'm going to fall over and I know I'm done. "I'm ready to go, Jack."

"As you wish, Your Highness."

I back away, and when the firm stone beneath my feet turns to soft cloud, I remember the way I felt just moments ago and I promise myself this won't be the last time.

We head back to the castle and Jack chuckles. "Your breakout moment," he says, nudging my calf. "And you didn't even need a tattoo."

෨෨

"Spend a night in an ice hotel."

"Traverse the piranha-infested waters of the Amazon on a log raft. No paddle."

"Ride the back of a blue whale."

"Swim through space. Naked."

"Jack, you can't swim through space naked."

"I don't care. I want to do it anyway."

Jack and I are standing at the cloudline, leaning over the railing of Lookout South to stare at the land far below, lights winking through the darkness like stars in the midnight sky. We're rattling off a bunch of things we've never done but want to. I've gotten better at this game, at being specific as I stare down the world.

"Swim in the turquoise waters of Oahu," I say.

"Not too ambitious," Jack says. "That will be one you check off first."

I hold up my hand and position it so that a cluster of lights fits in the space between my thumb and forefinger. "Maybe," I murmur.

Sure, I could swim off the coast of Hawaii, but right under my feet are all those lights, all that life. There's a swath of black over to the left, where the ocean stretches into the horizon and a lonely light from some yacht reaches out. We're like the ocean, us giants—always here, still a mystery. Humans have forgotten they don't know everything.

The wind lifts my long hair off my shoulders and I close my eyes, and for a second, I imagine this is what it must be like to ride a beanstalk as it shrinks back down to earth . . .

"Gold coin for your thoughts?" Jack says.

I smile. He's comfortable enough to make these kinds of jokes now that we both know he isn't out to steal anything. But I don't answer. Mom always says I'll make a great ruler. *You think but don't talk too much, and you don't wear your emotions on your face.* I used to take offense to that because she might as well have been saying *You'll make a great robot.* Sometimes it takes time to see the value in something.

"May I ask you a question?" Jack asks.

"Shoot."

"You're always sanding that chair, etching another flourish. But it could've been done ages ago, right?"

The wood chair is the best thing I've made so far. Sturdy, smooth, beautiful. It looks like the work of someone who knew what they were doing. I keep going over and over what I've already done, and if something has been holding me back from finishing the seat, I don't know what it is, exactly. I shrug.

Jack says, "Do you want to hear something funny? Well, I suppose it's more a question." He laughs nervously. "This is going to sound ridiculous, but . . . when I first started coming here, I thought you were planning to skin me alive or whatever. You know, use me as upholstery or something."

I laugh so hard I have to wipe my eyes.

"Were you?"

"Are you kidding me?" I say between giggles.

"Were you?"

I stop laughing. Jack looks more serious than I've ever seen him.

He looks up at me, his eyes moving side to side as if he's trying to see deep into my soul, one eyeball at a time.

I turn my gaze back to the gold-dotted darkness below and lean farther over the railing, letting the cool breeze whip my hair against my face.

"Jack, it never crossed my mind."

ೞ

Jack doesn't return for a long time, so long that I begin to think he isn't ever coming back. Summer slides into autumn, and my parents head to a cluster of clouds over Germany on royal Northern Hemisphere business.

And then, one midnight, Jack returns.

We're in the basement and Jack is leaning back onto his hands while staring into the fire. Goldie, basking in the warmth of the hearth, ruffles her feathers and raises her head for a second. She looks at Jack's hand like she wants to stab it with her beak. She's still miffed about his absence; I think he grew on her.

Jack speaks for the first time tonight. "I considered staying away."

"Maybe you shouldn't have come back."

"It's not like you were going to come down."

I don't answer.

"And anyway, my uncle and I are back home to Cambridge this week." He sighs. "So you don't want to be friends anymore?"

"Jack, you like your uncle's cat, right? But can you really say you're friends?"

"Yes."

I shake my head, and Dad's words fill my brain and then my mouth. "It's not my nature."

"It doesn't have to be your nature to not have friends."

But Jack doesn't know what I mean, and it's best that way, anyhow.

I say, "Remember that cabinet? My parents just got something I know you'd like to see." For days, Mom couldn't stop talking about that missing harpy of a harp, but then she found something more interesting to put in its place. The moment I saw it, Jack popped into my mind, because I knew he'd love it. "Just didn't know if you were coming back."

Jack looks sheepish, as expected. I don't wait for a reply, just scoop him up and take him upstairs, and he only squirms a little.

We get to the bull room, and I set Jack down on one of the cabinet shelves, next to a tiny black velvet pig that trots around and hiccups silver marbles. Jack *oohs* and *aahs*, and the pig nuzzles his hand.

"Does it bite? What does it eat?" he asks. "Doesn't it get lonely locked up in here?"

"No and nothing and I don't think so."

There are so many wondrous things in this cabinet, things that have made me proud ever since I really stopped to look: human-sized helmets and swords from antiquity; enormous goblets that were stolen from giants who lived in the depths of Mount Ararat but reclaimed; a golden egg that is said to be one of the first ever laid; a human-sized, jewel-encrusted crown that was given to one of my ancestors for mercy shown; a fortified slab of wood said to have been part of the hull of Noah's ark, which a crew of giants helped build.

What does Jack see when he looks at these things? Money? Fame?

I see a proud history, buried and overlooked.

Jack runs a fingertip along the dulled edge of a saber. "My uncle would love this."

"I'm sure." I set Jack on the floor and secure the cabinet.

Jack walks over to the bronze bull, presses his palms against its breast, and looks up expectantly. I lift him onto the bull's neck and he lies back, but as soon as he puts his hands behind his head, he starts. He twists around to see what poked him in the head.

"Is this a latch?" he says.

"Stop squirming—you'll fall."

"It is. Am I lying on a door?" Jack pushes himself to his feet and shuffles backward so he can see the hinged door, which runs like a spine down the bull's back. "Brilliant! It's some kind of trunk, isn't it?" If I let him continue his attempts to pull the thing open, he's going to slide off the bull and break something.

"Relax," I say.

Jack straddles the bull's haunches, watching wide-eyed as I undo the latch. As soon as the door is opened, he launches forward and lowers himself into the empty space.

"It's so slick inside . . . Wow . . ."

"Do you smell blood?" I ask because I'm curious.

"What's that?"

"Never mind, nothing." I'm sticking to my original theory.

"So uh . . ." His voice slides funny, an attempt to smooth the sharp edges of caution. "I'm guessing this isn't your father's bullion box." A forced laugh echoes upward.

Am I sad? I knew in my gut it would come to this, even before I really knew. But yes, I do feel a pang of regret; just because you know something's coming doesn't make you feel any less bad for it.

I close the lid and latch it so that no matter how hard Jack pushes, it won't open.

The thing is getting them to trust you, the animals. He's got fear permeating every bit of his body, but it's not like I care about *sharpness* or *acidity*. That's not what this is about.

I walk to the cabinet and pull open a drawer. I bet this is what a person feels like when they have to slaughter one of the chickens they've been feeding all year. But Jack isn't a chicken and I'm not just any person. I'm the future Empress of the Northern Hemisphere, and just as Jack ingested the python, just as he ingested fierce, unflinching power incarnate, I have to ingest Jack so that I can take my people into our next era. There's a lot to learn, and I can't do it scared.

Jack wouldn't want that.

I grab a box of matches and turn to face the bull. In one of those TV stories, this would be where I change my mind, where I think about all our conversations and how Jack has helped me open up, find myself. I'd overcome my natural instinct to see us as two different species and I'd let him out and we'd be friends or maybe even romantic interests while everyone pretends not to notice a relationship between a giantess and a normal-sized human boy would never work in the end because logistics, and that's just for starters. But this isn't TV—it's real life.

So I swipe the match against the side of the matchbox and ignite the wood beneath the bronze bull. I consider staying here, because perhaps I owe Jack this much, but I'm not a masochist and punishing myself won't change anything so I decide to do some work on that chair, maybe finally pick a leather piece for the seat. That'll clear my head.

I open the door to the basement and hear the first of Jack's shouting. I've seen Dad use the bull plenty while hosting feasts and barbecues, enough to know that about forty minutes from now, the echoed cries from inside the bull's bowels will have long gone silent, and the smoke pouring from its nostrils (which were engineered with pipes to make human cries sound like a bull's bellows) will have thinned to wisps, and all will be done. I shut the door behind me and walk down into the basement.

I shiver a little—maybe because it's chilly, maybe because I feel bad about what I'm about to do tonight (you know, breaking my "I don't eat anything with a face" motto), maybe because I feel the importance of this moment—and I tell myself, *Even climbing Mount Everest starts with a single step.* Considering everything to come, eating meat is a small sacrifice I'm willing to make for the greater good. And there's a certain beauty in this, really, because it's because of Jack's belief in me that even this tiny step is possible.

I sit at the hearth and pick out a leather piece I saved from a while back, a skin I had tanned after one of Dad's meals. Though I'll probably need a few more, this piece is smooth and supple, which makes up for the stupid toad's head marring its surface. Like I said, bad life choice.

The boy and I never even got a chance to exchange more than five words before Dad snatched him up. But that's okay. It's cool, as they say below. Because I was smart enough to toss down two bags of beans instead of one, and in forty minutes, the fearless powers of the python will course through my veins.

The world was ours, once. *Fee fi fo fum.* Perhaps it can be ours again.

Thanks, Jack. This chair's for you.

TINA BURKE'S VILLAIN CHALLENGE TO AMERIIE:

"Jack and the Beanstalk" Meets Phalaris of Agrigento

GIANTS AND TYRANTS

BY TINA BURKE

Surely you know "Jack and the Beanstalk," but are you scratching your head over who Phalaris was? Be glad that you never met him! Phalaris of Agrigento was a Sicilian tyrant from the sixth century BC, who is included on many Most Horrifying Historical Figures lists. He might have been the epitome of villains, renowned for eating babies and roasting his enemies to death in a giant bronze bull.

Mashing "Jack and the Beanstalk" with Phalaris allows for a contrast between new and old villains in Ameriie's story, "Jack." To understand my point, let's look more closely at giants and tyrants.

THE COMMON DENOMINATOR FOR BOTH IS HORROR.

Told in first person, Ameriie's story subverts many tropes. The empress's perspective allows the reader to explore the mind of a giant and the heart of her culture. The reader identifies with her and is lured in line by line, downgrading the horror happening around her—and ultimately the horror that befalls Jack.

GIANTS ACT AS A METAPHOR FOR GROWING UP.

"Jack" offers a new outlook through its focus on a giant at the cusp of adulthood. When we're children, we can't wait to grow up. We want to be adult- or giant-sized, yet somewhere along the way, we no longer admire and idolize the difference that we sense; we become afraid of the unknown. Ameriie's giant feels the same way. She wants to see the world far below her cloud, but she's afraid and can't even peek over the rail. Ironically, Jack persuades her to do it, to be brave, to claim her future. He didn't realize what that meant for him.

WE CAN OFFER NEW PERSPECTIVES THROUGH FAIRY-TALE RETELLINGS.

One common exploration of the struggle between good and evil, heroes and villains, is the fairy tale. Fairy tales speak to our love of happy endings, and fairy-tale retellings in particular speak to our moral codes while affording the opportunity for marvelous adventures. Although giants are normally considered mythical monsters, they become more in retellings; finally, they have been granted a chance for validation. Ameriie's story provides a tipping point in favor of the giant. The reader likes Ameriie's giant and roots for her. She's more complex and layered than the giants in the original story.

"JACK" SUBVERTS THESE REPRESENTATIONS AND PLAYS WITH OUR EXPECTATIONS.

"Jack" challenges age boundaries in character and culture. Love of her people and family drives the adultlike protagonist even while she frets about her still-forming identity, enjoys trivial pursuits (e.g., watching magicked television), and performs chores and daily duties (e.g., staining and stamping leather). The blurred age boundaries create a universal feel to the story and highlight the similarities between our life and that of Ameriie's giants. Are we so different from Jack? Or from Ameriie's giant? Would we have made the same choice to betray a friend when faced with the demands of custom and family pressure?

ॐ

"Jack" forces the reader to reconsider expectations of both giants and tyrants. After all, we can discuss the meaning of giant representations in literature or realize our own complicity in cultural stereotyping not just the giants in our lives.

GWEN AND ART AND LANCE

BY SOMAN CHAINANI

Wednesday

FROM: GWEN
TO: ELAINE

Lance du Lac just asked me to Prom. On the *phone*.

FROM: ELAINE
TO: GWEN

Is that the Goth kid with greasy hair who smokes under the
bleachers during football games, because I smell it when we
cheer on the sidelines
Do you even know him
What did you say

FROM: GWEN
TO: ELAINE

Yes
No

You think I answered his *call*? He left a VM. So creepy. Texted back I'm going with someone else

FROM: ELAINE
TO: GWEN

???

FROM: GWEN
TO: ELAINE

!

FROM: ELAINE
TO: GWEN

ARTHUR PENDRAGON ASKED YOU TO PROM?

FROM: GWEN
TO: ELAINE

:)

FROM: ELAINE
TO: GWEN

OMG. Dying. Dead. Those abs. Those blues. What a stallion. They should replace that David statue with his. And put it in my house.

FROM: GWEN
TO: ELAINE

Rather have the real thing. Art and I belong together.

FROM: ELAINE
TO: GWEN

Good luck. No girl has pulled the sword from that stone. #Excalibur

FROM: GWEN
TO: ELAINE

Takes a queen to pull #Excalibur

FROM: ELAINE
TO: GWEN

OMG. YOU'RE GONNA HOOK UP WITH
ART PENDRAGON.

FROM: GWEN
TO: ELAINE

Don't tell anyone. Will post on Insta when we're official.

FROM: ELAINE
TO: GWEN

Secret's safe with me.
Btw just booked our hair and mani-pedis for Saturday

FROM: GWEN
TO: ELAINE

Perf, picking up my dress from the tailor's! It's straight off the
runway from Milan . . .

ROUND TABLE BANK
ALERT—Dear Guinevere, Your account balance has been
overdrawn. Please log in . . .

FROM: MORGAN
TO: GWEN

Hi girlie! Got the other cheerleaders' $$ for Prom limo—did you
send yours?

FROM: DAD
TO: GWEN

Guinevere, the bank just e-mailed me an overdraft warning
for your account. What don't you understand? Our assets
are frozen until the SEC investigation is complete. There is
no money for you to spend. I had the bank block charges
for your Prom limo and Prom dress so you wouldn't incur
further fees.

FROM: GWEN
TO: MORGAN

Ugh, I wired the $$ but my phone has been glitchy. Would never
miss the limo with you girls. Especially when you see who my date
is . . . :) Will give you a check tomorrow!

FROM: GWEN
TO: ART

Hi! Amaaaazing job at the game yesterday!! KNIGHTS RULE!
I cheered super loud to distract the other team during that field
goal—pretty sure they missed because of me!

With all your hard work on the field you probably forgot Prom's on
Saturday! Better ask that special someone before it's too late . . .
:)

FROM: ART
TO: GWEN

Gwen! What's up?
You ladies did great yesterday
And yeah. Prom. Ugh.
Btw Lance said he asked you but you're locked. Who's the lucky
guy?

GWEN AND ART AND LANCE

FROM: GWEN
TO: ART

You're friends with Lance?

FROM: ART
TO: GWEN

Yeah, we go back
Don't hang at school much
Complicated

FROM: GWEN
TO: ART

What else did Lance say about me?

FROM: ART
TO: GWEN

I know he likes you. Told him he shoulda asked you sooner.
You really don't want to tell me who you're going with huh
:P

FROM: GWEN
TO: ART

You don't know him.

FROM: GWEN
TO: ELAINE

CALL ME NOW.

FROM: ELAINE
TO: GWEN

Sorry I hung up on you.
You told me Art Pendragon asked you to Prom and now you're
telling me he didn't.
I can't believe you lied to me.

FROM: GWEN
TO: ELAINE

And I can't believe there's a $2000 BET POOL about whether I'll hook up with Art Pendragon at Prom! I told you not to tell anyone!

FROM: ELAINE
TO: GWEN

I didn't! I only told the squad.
How was I supposed to know you were MAKING IT UP

FROM: GWEN
TO: ELAINE

Suppose Art finds out!

FROM: ELAINE
TO: GWEN

Knight Cheerleaders = Circle of Trust

FROM: ART
TO: GWEN

Hey. You seen the #Excalibur tag on Joust?

FROM: GWEN
TO: ELAINE

THE WHOLE SCHOOL IS ON JOUST BETTING IF I CAN PULL #EXCALIBUR. ART WANTS TO KNOW IF I'VE SEEN IT.

FROM: ELAINE
TO: GWEN

Can't talk. French tutor.

FROM: GWEN
TO: ART

I hadn't seen it! Not really a fan of those shady apps.
You must be flattered. Guess people want us to go to Prom
together :)

FROM: ART
TO: GWEN

Flattered? Not sure about that
All the Knights want us to go together too.

FROM: GWEN
TO: ART

So why don't we?

FROM: ART
TO: GWEN

1. You're going with another dude
2. I told Lance you were hot and he said you and I look
alike, which means I'm a narcissist and want to hook up
with myself

FROM: GWEN
TO: ART

1. Another Dude's appendix burst and he's in the ER and can't go
to Prom so now I can go with you!
2. Lance is just jealous. You and me belong together. Prom King
and Queen in gold crowns. Rulers of Camelot Prep. Don't you want
me as your queen?

FROM: ART
TO: GWEN

2. Couldn't do that to Lance.

FROM: GWEN
TO: LANCE

Hi Lance! So nice out tonight. Too bad we have that English test tomorrow. Mr. Merlin said the essay is on whether "Hades and Persephone" has a happy ending. We could study together if you want. Btw, you wouldn't care if Art goes to Prom with me, right?

FROM: LANCE
TO: GWEN

I'd rather talk on the phone.

FROM: GWEN
TO: LANCE

Reception is bad in my house.

FROM: LANCE
TO: GWEN

Well to answer your questions, yes, I'd care if you went to Prom with Art seeing that you lied to me about going with someone else. And no, I don't want to study together, because the last time we studied together, we had sex and now you're asking me if you can go to Prom with my best friend.

FROM: GWEN
TO: LANCE

Calling you.

Thursday

FROM: ART
TO: GWEN

Lance said you studied together last night for Merlin's. You should have told me.

I was up till 2 a.m. googling whether "Hades and Persephone" has a happy ending.

(I say no. Girl gets kidnapped, ping-pongs between two God brothers, and goes to hell.)

Studied together? More like Lance gave me some ideas for the essay question. (There was no ping-ponging btw, and she does get to leave hell for a few months at a time. I'd say the ending is happy. Girl gets to be a *queen*.)

Lance said he was going to your house
Texted him for like 3 hours after and he didn't answer

Forgot my book at school, Sherlock. He came over to let me borrow his. Since when is Lance your best buddy

Next time invite me.

I SAID IF YOU TOLD ANYONE WE HANG OUT I'D HURT YOU.

I didn't tell him we hooked up. I told him we studied.

FROM: GWEN
TO: LANCE

STUDIED = HOOKED UP YOU IDIOT

FROM: GWEN
TO: ART

Hey :) Why don't we blow off first two periods and study for Merlin's at my house?

FROM: ART
TO: GWEN

Lance and I are at the gym.
Trying to get him swole but he keeps texting during sets ha ha.
Says it's the girl he's taking to Prom but won't tell me who

FROM: GWEN
TO: LANCE

I'M NOT GOING TO PROM WITH YOU.

FROM: LANCE
TO: GWEN

You said you'd think about it when we were cuddling.

FROM: GWEN
TO: LANCE

You know how Merlin talked about "Persephone's Crisis"? i.e.
Persephone could never exist as a person outside of her mother until
Hades took her to hell? Well, maybe she needed Hades to take her to
hell for her to find out what she really wanted.

FROM: LANCE
TO: GWEN

So you're Persephone. I'm Hades. And hell is Prom?

GWEN AND ART AND LANCE

FROM: GWEN
TO: LANCE

I should have never let you come over last night.
Or any night.

FROM: LANCE
TO: GWEN

Then why did you?

FROM: GWEN
TO: LANCE

Because when I'm with you I don't feel lonely.

FROM: LANCE
TO: GWEN

I'm the only guy you feel safe with. You're the only girl I trust. Art will never see you the way I do. Art will only see what you want him to see. You and him have that in common. Why do you think you both keep me a secret? Ha.
I'm the only one who knows the real Art and the real Gwen.

FROM: GWEN
TO: LANCE

Just because we hooked up doesn't mean you know the real me.

FROM: LANCE
TO: GWEN

The real Gwen can't take four steps without knocking into something and peeking around for someone to blame it on. The real Gwen puts concealer on the tiny birthmark on her cheek because she can't stand a flaw and yet is drawn to me, whose face is a mess.
The real Gwen has a room full of well-thumbed books and yet acts barely literate in class so boys won't think she's a nerd. The real

Gwen is complex and weird and cool and yet pretends to be shallow and simple and empty. I see through all of it. Real Gwen is the one I love.

FROM: LANCE
TO: GWEN

It says you read my last text.
Take me to Prom, Gwen. Who cares what people say?

FROM: LANCE
TO: GWEN

Say something.

FROM: GWEN
TO: LANCE

You can't understand. Camelot is the only place where people still *believe* in me.
Please, Lance. Art is who I'm meant to be with.
Let me and him go to Prom.

FROM: LANCE
TO: GWEN

You got it. See ya

FROM: GWEN
TO: LANCE

Thank you, Lance. It means a lot.

FROM: GWEN
TO: ART

Hey Art, looks like Lance is fine with it!! Says he'd be happy for you and me to go together. So . . . what time are you picking me up? :) We can just go in your car instead of some cheesy limo

FROM: DAD
TO: GWEN

Guinevere, please give Cara the keys to the storage unit when she comes for them. They're doing the appraisal of your mother's clothes and jewelry today.

FROM: MORGAN
TO: GWEN

Hiiiii lovely, still no sign of your limo $??

FROM: GWEN
TO: MORGAN

Omg meant to write you—my date wants me to go in his car. Ugh :(
Btw, if my first payment somehow goes through, mind sending it back to me?

FROM: ASSISTANT GIRL
TO: GWEN

Hello, Guinevere, it's Cara Dos Santos. Your father said you'd be expecting me.
I'm outside Lioncelle Storage with the appraiser. Do you have the keys?

FROM: GWEN
TO: ASSISTANT GIRL

No.

FROM: ASSISTANT GIRL
TO: GWEN

He didn't leave them with you?

FROM: GWEN
TO: ASSISTANT GIRL

Nope.

FROM: GWEN
TO: ART

You're being quiet :)
Wait till you see my brand-new Prom dress
Would be fun if we could get you a tie to match!

** LIONCELLE STORAGE **
SECURITY ALERT—Dear Guinevere, Our records indicate the removal of one vintage gown from your storage unit early this morning. Please confirm . . .

FROM: GWEN
TO: MORGAN

Hey . . . you seen Art around?

FROM: MORGAN
TO: GWEN

He's probably with Lance.
Lance lives near me and Art's always there

FROM: GWEN
TO: MORGAN

Since when??

FROM: MORGAN
TO: GWEN

Since forever. Why do you think the Knights leave Lance alone even tho he's a loser
He's Art's BFF

FROM: GWEN
TO: ELAINE

911 Are Lance and Art still in the gym? Art isn't answering my texts.

FROM: ELAINE
TO: GWEN

Been in the gym all morning. Haven't seen either of them.

FROM: DAD
TO: GWEN

Guinevere, Cara says you just told her you don't have the key! And yet the storage unit informed me you stopped by to take one of your mother's gowns early this morning—a gown that was to be appraised and sold TODAY. Call me IMMEDIATELY.

FROM: GWEN
TO: DAD

Let's have this conversation when we're on the same continent.

FROM: GWEN
TO: ART

Didn't you say you were at the gym with Lance?

FROM: ART
TO: GWEN

Hey! What's up?
Lance and I blew off first couple periods so we could study

FROM: GWEN
TO: ART

Um. Okay. You said you were at the gym. But we're all cool for Prom, right?

FROM: ART
TO: GWEN

Actually Lance thinks it'd be funny if he and I just went together
We hate Prom and we want everyone in that bet pool to lose
Ha ha

FROM: GWEN
TO: ART

Ha ha

FROM: GWEN
TO: LANCE

You just unleashed the fires of hell.

FROM: LANCE
TO: GWEN

Not even sweating.

Friday

FROM: ELAINE
TO: GWEN

TELL ME YOU'VE SEEN IT.

FROM: GWEN
TO: ELAINE

? Went for a run when I got up. Haven't been near phone.

FROM: ELAINE
TO: GWEN

Someone started a Joust account for @Excalibur and posted a bunch of pics of Art side by side with limp noodles. Everyone's saying Art has "issues." That's why he's never been with a girl. That's why he's never asked you out!

FROM: GWEN
TO: ELAINE

Oh how rude! Poor Art.

FROM: LANCE
TO: GWEN

Pick up your phone. NOW.

GWEN AND ART AND LANCE

FROM: GWEN
TO: LANCE

Getting warm, isn't it?

FROM: ART
TO: GWEN

Lance is saying you started @Excalibur.

FROM: GWEN
TO: ART

ME? I'm the one trying to take it down! Lance is just mad
I wouldn't go to Prom with him—that's why he's being cruel.
Art, whoever did this to you is a real cockroach. My cousin
works at Joust. I'm texting her to see if she can delete the
account. Ask Nadia Croes. She's on the cheer team and in your
homeroom and will tell you how hard I've been working to
fix this.

FROM: GWEN
TO: NADIA

Listen—whatever Art Pendragon asks you about me in
homeroom, say yes, otherwise I'll tell the girls you were in
the bathroom with Boris Polanski at halftime instead of helping
us sell Popsicles

FROM: ART
TO: GWEN

Ok I asked Nadia and she backed you up.
Sorry I doubted you. Thanks for your help.
It's just weird coming to school where I used to have fun and now I'm
being bullied by someone I don't even know.
Lance still swears it's you.

FROM: GWEN
TO: ART

Lance and I have very different definitions of what it means to be your friend.

FROM: ART
TO: GWEN

All the Knights are on my case.
Saying I'm a virgin and all that.

FROM: GWEN
TO: ART

They're pissed that I like you instead of them. Besides, I think it's romantic if you're saving yourself.

FROM: ART
TO: GWEN

Who I hook up with isn't anyone's business.
But I don't hook up to get off or to tell people or to feel better about myself or because I feel lonely on a Friday night.
I want real love.

FROM: GWEN
TO: ART

That's . . . amazing.

FROM: ART
TO: GWEN

People are sticking wet noodles to my backpack
Wtf

FROM: GWEN
TO: ART

Mmm, probably isn't the best time for you to be going to Prom with Lance, is it

FROM: ART
TO: GWEN

Ha

FROM: GWEN
TO: ART

For all we know, he's the one who started @Excalibur

FROM: ART
TO: GWEN

Don't be stupid

FROM: GWEN
TO: ART

I'm serious.

FROM: ART
TO: GWEN

Lance du Lac is my boy.
He'd take a bullet for me.

FROM: GWEN
TO: ART

Maybe he's in love with you. Maybe he thinks if he can't have you no
one else will. Or that humiliating you in front of the whole school means
he can be there to comfort you. Or all of the above.

FROM: ART
TO: GWEN

And here I thought you two were hooking up ha ha

FROM: GWEN
TO: ART

WHAT??? DID HE SAY THAT????

FROM: ART
TO: GWEN

No ha ha chill out
It's just you two avoid each other at school but then hang out
secretly
Usually means you're hooking up

FROM: GWEN
TO: ART

One could say the same thing about you and Lance.

FROM: ART
TO: GWEN

That's low

FROM: GWEN
TO: ART

Like you said, who you hook up with is none of my business :)

FROM: ART
TO: GWEN

I'm just not gonna show up to Prom at all

FROM: GWEN
TO: ART

That won't solve anything. Look, think of it like the story from Merlin's:
I'm Persephone, you're Persephone's mother, and Lance is Hades.
You need to *fight* for me.

FROM: ART
TO: GWEN

Huh? Doesn't Persephone end up being Hades's queen?

FROM: GWEN
TO: ART

OK, fine. Then you're Hades. Whatever. Look, you need to show up with a girl who will shut everyone up. The girl every boy at Camelot Prep wants to be with.
Taking me to Prom will fix everything.

FROM: ART
TO: GWEN

But why would Lance hurt me
I don't get it

FROM: GWEN
TO: ART

Why do you keep asking me about Lance?

FROM: GWEN
TO: ART

Art, you there?

FROM: ART
TO: GWEN

You really think Lance started the Joust

FROM: GWEN
TO: ART

I think it's time the King of Camelot had a queen.

FROM: ART
TO: GWEN

No one will mess with me ever again.

FROM: GWEN
TO: ART

Exactly :) See you at lunch

FROM: GWEN
TO: ART

Hey . . . can't find you at your usual table. Everything okay?

FROM: LANCE
TO: GWEN

You seen Art?

FROM: GWEN
TO: LANCE

No. You?

FROM: ELAINE
TO: GWEN

You need to get to the park by school

FROM: GWEN
TO: ELAINE

Can't. Merlin's rambling about how much he liked my essay on the test and that I need to participate more in class. Won't stop talking. Literally texting behind my back right now.

FROM: ELAINE
TO: GWEN

Art just beat the crap outta Lance

FROM: GWEN
TO: ELAINE

WHAT

FROM: ELAINE
TO: GWEN

Art said Lance started the Joust. Left Lance curled up in the dirt. Think he's crying.

FROM: GWEN
TO: ELAINE

COMING

FROM: GWEN
TO: LANCE

Lance you okay? Lance text me you're okay

FROM: ART
TO: GWEN

Hi. What time should I pick you up tomorrow night?

Saturday

FROM: LANCE
TO: GWEN

Remind me to get beat up more often.

FROM: GWEN
TO: LANCE

All it took was some Chinese take-out and a Game of Thrones marathon.

FROM: LANCE
TO: GWEN

And you there with me.

FROM: GWEN
TO: LANCE

Please don't tell anyone about the stuff I said about my dad and our family. I shouldn't have talked about it. No one knows.

FROM: LANCE
TO: GWEN

I would rather be drawn and quartered than betray a secret
from you.

FROM: GWEN
TO: LANCE

How romantic.

FROM: LANCE
TO: GWEN

Every second I spend with you is romantic.
Except the you leaving super early this morning part.

FROM: GWEN
TO: LANCE

Stuff to do

FROM: LANCE
TO: GWEN

What stuff?

FROM: ART
TO: GWEN

Hey. Lance definitely started the Joust cuz it got taken down
last night.
Sucks being lied to.
Trusted that kid with my life.

FROM: GWEN
TO: ART

Exactly how long have you two known each other?

FROM: ART
TO: GWEN

A long time
Told him it was better if kids at school didn't know
This way we could do our own thing

FROM: GWEN
TO: ART

Maybe it wasn't healthy for you two to be that close.

FROM: ART
TO: GWEN

Yeah.

FROM: GWEN
TO: ART

Is that why you never asked me out? Because Lance liked me?

FROM: ART
TO: GWEN

Lance would really freak out if you were my girlfriend, wouldn't he

FROM: GWEN
TO: ART

Well, forget Lance for a minute. Do *you* want me as your girlfriend?

FROM: ART
TO: GWEN

I'm taking you to Prom, aren't I?

FROM: LANCE
TO: GWEN

Ugh fell back asleep. Haven't eaten all day but too sore to get out of bed. Need to brush my teeth. Art hasn't called or texted. Think me and him aren't going to Prom haaaa

FROM: GWEN
TO: LANCE

Maybe it wasn't healthy for you two to be that close.

FROM: LANCE
TO: GWEN

Yeah.
It's tough to drop someone you've known that long.

FROM: GWEN
TO: LANCE

People leave and enter your life for a reason.

FROM: LANCE
TO: GWEN

Yeah. They do. :)
Well at least there's one silver lining to all this . . .

FROM: GWEN
TO: LANCE

What's that

FROM: LANCE
TO: GWEN

You and I can go to Prom now

FROM: GWEN
TO: LANCE

Um. You're not going to Prom. You need to stay in bed and rest up.
Dr. Gwen's orders.

FROM: LANCE
TO: GWEN

Will you rest up with me?

FROM: GWEN
TO: LANCE

What was that about still needing to brush your teeth

FROM: LANCE
TO: GWEN

That got me outta bed ha ha. Wanna come over around 6? Craving pancakes. Gonna hit Griddle Cafe.

FROM: GWEN
TO: LANCE

The one on Benwick Ave?

FROM: LANCE
TO: GWEN

Nah. Corbin St.

FROM: GWEN
TO: LANCE

OK. Wait until later. Line is probably long.

FROM: LANCE
TO: GWEN

Too late. Pulling up, ha. No line at Griddle, but it's a mess at the salon next door. All the girls getting their hair done for Prom. One looks just like you lol

FROM: GWEN
TO: LANCE

Lance? I'm sorry—please pick up

FROM: LANCE
TO: GWEN

YOU'RE GOING TO PROM? WITH *ART*? AFTER HE BEAT ME UP FOR A JOUST THAT *YOU* STARTED?

FROM: GWEN
TO: LANCE

Look, he asked me to go and I couldn't say no. It's just a dance, okay?

FROM: LANCE
TO: GWEN

All this time I didn't think I was worthy of you. But now I see you're not worthy of me. You and Art will make a perfect pair.

FROM: GWEN
TO: LANCE

Lance, I'm sorry.

FROM: LANCE
TO: GWEN

We're done. Don't ever text me again.

GWEN AND ART AND LANCE

FROM: GWEN
TO: ART

Hey . . . I think you should make up with Lance. You two were best friends. Don't let it fall apart over something stupid.

FROM: ART
TO: GWEN

Something stupid? He humiliated me. Let him rot in hell.
But I'll thank him for one thing.
He brought you and me together.

FROM: GWEN
TO: ART

He's your real friend, Art. Not me.

FROM: ART
TO: GWEN

You and Lance have very different definitions of what it means to be my friend :)
Pick you up at 6

FROM: GWEN
TO: LANCE

I can't do this anymore. I want to tell Art I started the Joust. But if I tell him, he won't go to Prom with me. And he needs everyone to *see* him at Prom with me. What do I do?

FROM: GWEN
TO: LANCE

Lance? Please talk to me.

FROM: ART
TO: GWEN

Almost at your house

FROM: ELAINE
TO: GWEN

EVERYONE is talking about how hot you two look. People are like stepping out of the way for you guys and when you danced, everyone stopped dancing and just watched. Like you're royalty or something. You killed it, Gwen. Every girl here wants to be you.

FROM: GWEN
TO: ELAINE

Thanks

FROM: ELAINE
TO: GWEN

Where are you? Don't see you

FROM: GWEN
TO: ELAINE

Bathroom. Needed a minute.

FROM: ELAINE
TO: GWEN

Hurry. Announcing Prom King and Queen soon. Art's standing here alone. Other girls chatting him up.

FROM: GWEN
TO: ELAINE

Yeah. Coming.

FROM: ART
TO: GWEN

Where are you? They're bringing out the crowns.

GWEN AND ART AND LANCE

FROM: GWEN
TO: ART

Do you love me, Art?

FROM: ART
TO: GWEN

Uhhh did you pregame too hard lol
Get over here

FROM: GWEN
TO: ART

You don't even know me.

FROM: ART
TO: GWEN

Of course I do. Why do you think you're my date
I really like you.

FROM: GWEN
TO: ART

Tell me things you like about me.

FROM: ART
TO: GWEN

I like your blond hair
I like your blue eyes
All of it

FROM: GWEN
TO: ART

You have blond hair
You have blue eyes

You could be talking about yourself
What do you like about *me*

FROM: ART
TO: GWEN

You're a badass.
Girls are scared of you and do whatever you say.
Guys have the hots for you.
You have power over people.
You're not Persephone.
You're Hades.

FROM: GWEN
TO: ART

That's what you like about me?

FROM: ART
TO: GWEN

No one would have messed with you the way Lance messed with me
You're not weak like me
I want to be more like you
Hurry. People asking where you are.

FROM: GWEN
TO: ART

You don't know me. I'm not strong. I'm not strong at all.

FROM: ART
TO: GWEN

Uhh definitely too much bubbly

FROM: GWEN
TO: LANCE

I made a mistake

FROM: ART
TO: GWEN

Elaine says you're in the bathroom

Do I need to come get you

FROM: GWEN
TO: ART

Just need a minute

FROM: GWEN
TO: LANCE

I love you, Lance

I want to be with you

But I don't know how to be with you and still be me

FROM: ART
TO: GWEN

You locked the bathroom

Open the door

FROM: ELAINE
TO: GWEN

WTF???

Got them to delay crowning 5 mins

HURRY

FROM: ART
TO: GWEN

I'm yelling through the door

Can you hear me?

FROM: GWEN
TO: LANCE

Lance . . . please . . .

FROM: LANCE
TO: GWEN

I'm here

FROM: GWEN
TO: LANCE

What?

FROM: LANCE
TO: GWEN

Outside Camelot. Calling you but line keeps dropping
Which tower are you in

FROM: ART
TO: GWEN

You okay in there?
Janitor's getting me the key.
Please answer me.

FROM: GWEN
TO: LANCE

Tower A. 2nd floor bathroom.

FROM: LANCE
TO: GWEN

Open the window. I'll climb up and get you.

FROM: ART
TO: GWEN

Got the key.

FROM: LANCE
TO: GWEN

Hear me? I'm calling your name

FROM: GWEN
TO: LANCE

Can't hear or see you
Glass is thick and frosted on the inside
Where are you

FROM: LANCE
TO: GWEN

Don't worry, I'm climbing up
Try opening it

FROM: GWEN
TO: LANCE

I can't. It's jammed.

FROM: LANCE
TO: GWEN

Push harder.

FROM: ART
TO: GWEN

You dead-bolted the door! WTF.
Gwen, open it!

FROM: GWEN
TO: LANCE

Art's ramming against the door

FROM: LANCE
TO: GWEN

Gwen. You have to push harder.

FROM: GWEN
TO: LANCE

I can't do it.
I can't just . . . leave.

FROM: LANCE
TO: GWEN

Why?

FROM: GWEN
TO: LANCE

What about Art?

FROM: LANCE
TO: GWEN

Art has the whole world to love him. He always will.

FROM: GWEN
TO: LANCE

What do we have?

FROM: LANCE
TO: GWEN

Our own screwed-up little kingdom with a broke-down palace where
nothing can stop us from being together. And I will stay up here on this
ledge, outside the window that you won't open, while I text with one
hand and hold on with the other until you get it through your thick skull.
I love you, Gwen. Rich or poor; ugly or fair; young or old; inside and out.

I love you.
I love you.
I love you.

FROM: GWEN
TO: LANCE

Catch me if I fall

FROM: ART
TO: GWEN

They pushed me onstage.
I'm onstage, Gwen! In my crown!

FROM: GWEN
TO: ART

My beautiful Art
You're right. I am Hades.
Kidnapping your Persephone.
But one day you'll look back and see that only someone as pure as
you could bring together two broken souls

FROM: ART
TO: GWEN

What? Gwen, please
They're announcing you
I need a queen!

FROM: GWEN
TO: ART

Long live Arthur
All Hail the King

FROM: ART
TO: GWEN

Gwen?

FROM: ART
TO: GWEN

Gwen!

Samantha Lane's Villain Challenge to Soman Chainani:

A Modern-Day Mash-Up of the King Arthur Legend and Persephone-Hades Myth

THE BAD GIRL HALL OF FAME

BY SAMANTHA LANE

Q Search

samanthalane

dreadpersephone

bornwicked

killersingers

camelotgwen

Which BAD GIRLS are the baddest?

▶ WATCH
Videos You Might Like

dreadpersephone

377 posts   **100.8b** followers   **12** following

Persephone • lover of pomegranates and winter

The choice was simple. I'd either be a maiden all my life, controlled by my overbearing mother, or I'd take an opportunity to escape to another world. Just didn't expect to transform myself into a formidable queen, more feared than my husband! #sorrynotsorry

Comments

Samanthalane commented on your post:

Coming-of-age tales and villain origins have a lot in common. Teens are fighting for their independence and against familial pressures. Villains are frequently fighting against societal and moral expectations in their origins. One of the reasons I love the Persephone myth is that she combines both. Though I do not view her as a villain, many do, as she is associated with death.

Villains' backstories are all about opportunities and choices. Throughout, we are shown the various crossroads where they could have turned back and continued to live a life of good. We, the audience, are torn between wanting them to cross over to the dark side and hoping that maybe this time they won't. Characters with agency are more complex, which is why I love them so much. Villains do horrible things, and we still root for them in spite of that. We are drawn to people who make mistakes, like us. Very few of us are stalwart and true 100 percent of the time. Villains represent what we cannot and will not do in real life.

As I see it, Persephone made a series of choices that led to her becoming one of the most feared goddesses in the pantheon, instead of continuing to live a simple life with her mother. In "Gwen and Art and Lance," Gwen made the choice to be with someone who her high school society viewed as the wrong choice. Villainy is liberating.

bornwicked

788 posts   **500k** followers   **3k** following

The Wicked Witch of the West • it's not easy being green

Am I really so wicked? Or did the world paint me that way simply because I am different? And if I am wicked, was I born that way or made wicked by the world's reaction to me?

Comments

 Samanthalane commented on your post:

The other route for villains is the view that they are simply victims of circumstance—that they have been tricked into becoming villains, by fate or by those around them. This question has been explored by modern retellings time and time again. Are some people just destined to become villains, and they don't have a choice in the matter at all? Historically, fairy tales and myths took this route, depicting people as either good or evil for no reason. But modern society has turned away from the view of passive characters and wants characters to be active participants in their destiny.

In "Gwen and Art and Lance," Gwen takes an active role in what unfolds. She manipulates the situation around her to suit her needs and doesn't apologize for it. She isn't simply along for the ride, but is in charge of the entire operation.

killersingers

186 posts   **300k** followers   **0** following

The Sirens • follow me into the sea

ONCE HANDMAIDENS, WE HAVE BEEN REBORN. NOW WE SERENADE YOU, TEMPTING YOU TO JOIN US.

Comments

 Samanthalane commented on your post:

Origin stories are all about transformations. In stories of the past, we saw characters being physically transformed into villains or monsters. Medusa was once a beautiful woman. Anakin Skywalker had to be burnt to a crisp and don a mask in order to complete his transformation into Darth Vader. But physical transformations aren't the only way villains are made. In "Gwen and Art and Lance," Gwen has transformed herself into the "It Girl" at her school. She has skillfully climbed the social hierarchy of high school and manipulated those around her to get what she wants. Villains' monstrousness, either physically or through their personalities, provides an excellent mirror for the hero. The better and more complete the transformation into a villain is, the better the hero has to be in order to defeat them.

camelotgwen

203 posts   **31k** followers   **1k** following

Guinevere • queen bee

CAN A BELOVED HERO BECOME A VILLAIN? CAN A VILLAIN TURN OUT TO BE THE HERO?

Comments

Samanthalane commented on your post:

We like our villains powerful, and one manifestation of power is narrative control. Who decides who the villain is and who the hero is? In "Gwen and Art and Lance," Gwen takes power by being in control of information and withholding information to fit the narrative she wants. Over the years, our society has become fascinated with characters who are not fully evil or fully good, but instead lie somewhere in the middle. Our obsession with antiheroes and antivillains is a result of social ideals being rewritten. We are unmaking the concept of wickedness. As the popularity of the "heroes" in *Batman*, *The Punisher*, and *Suicide Squad* shows, the lines between heroes and villains have become blurred. There is no clear distinction between hero and villain anymore, which is the theme that modern stories and retellings are exploring.

SHIRLEY & JIM

BY SUSAN DENNARD

TO: Jean Watson
FROM: Shirley Holmes

This story begins with a kiss.

From my family's pool boy. His name was Antonio. He was cute, and I liked the way a dimple formed in his right cheek whenever he smiled.

I was also super curious about kissing, so even though he was almost eighteen and I was only fourteen, I thought, *What the hey?* Opportunity was knocking, and you know me: once I've set my mind to something . . .

Well, the kiss was too sloppy, and for the record: tongues are gross. So that one exchange of saliva was more than enough to turn me off from kissing and from boys forever. Or at least for a while.

Not that it mattered to my dad. He caught me, see? And holy whatsit! William Holmes was on the phone with Headmistress Hudson an hour later, and the next morning, I was on my way to Baker Street Preparatory School. (Where young minds grow into brilliance! That's what the brochure says. Have you ever looked at it, Jean? I think that's the back of your head on the last page.)

No exaggeration, though. The very next morning, I was out of my family's estate and moving into that dormitory with you.

Meaning (as you've no doubt deduced by now) that the story I told you about pissing off a "Mr. Antonio" at my last school was a total lie. The first one I ever told you, Jean, and the *only* one until our senior year.

The truth is, I was embarrassed about that kiss with Pool Boy Antonio. Plus I wasn't very popular at my first high school, my personality being—what is it Headmistress Hudson always says? Abrasive. So Baker Street Prep seemed like the perfect chance to reinvent myself.

A Rebel with a capital *R*. That was what I wanted to be. Someone who didn't do what the establishment expected. Someone who didn't do what her daddy expected. And I know, I know. I never convinced anyone of that image, least of all myself.

Fall semester, senior year. That was when a True Rebel showed up, and a pecking order established in the ninth grade was suddenly obliterated by a mysterious newcomer.

It was lunch when he arrived. We were in the cafeteria, remember? I was lecturing you about why you were never going to pass AP bio if you kept mixing up pneumatocysts and nematocysts. (I'm sorry about that, Jean. Looking back, I was such a condescending a-hole. Aka my dad.)

First came Headmistress Hudson, bustling into the drab dining hall with her usual animation. She pushed through the pizza line (boys) and then the salad line (girls) like Moses at the Red Sea.

Then a collective gasp crossed the cafeteria. All the way over to our shadowy table, remember? Right as I was getting to the best part on cnidarian morphology, you twisted around to look.

"Holy crap," you said. "I hope he's a senior." I followed your gaze . . .

And my lungs hitched. Until that moment, Jim had been blocked by Headmistress Hudson's bouffant. *Holy crap*, I thought. *I hope he's a senior.*

I don't know how to explain it. Nothing about Jim Moriarty looked that good. Fitted jeans and a flannel button-up? Totally hipster. Thick-framed glasses? Not in style anymore. Dark hair, all sideswept and dramatic? Definitely not achieved without product.

Yet the instant the school turned its gaze upon Jim Moriarty, everyone sat a little taller. Then, in a bolt of lightning, rumors raced through the hall. Whispers of *I heard he got expelled from his last school for hacking into the computers and changing his grades* and *He got arrested for erasing all of a bank's digital debt records* and (the only one that actually sounded plausible) *His parents died in a car crash and his uncle raised him.*

Even his name—Jim Moriarty—just oozed bad boy. Or Gothic hero along the lines of Mr. Rochester and Heathcliff. Or maybe even one of those vampires who girls are always falling for on the CW.

I was hooked. Immediately. Like everyone else at Baker Street Prep, I wanted Jim's swagger. I wanted Jim's boredom. I wanted his lazy smile and complete uninterest in the school, the students, the world.

He was everything I could never be, don't you see?

Like, do you remember how he waltzed into AP bio the next day, took the exam (the one we'd crammed for all night), and then waltzed right back out with fifteen minutes to spare?

Ms. Adler didn't stop him. She just watched him saunter away, hands in his new uniform pockets. She didn't stop him the next day, either, or any of the days Jim abruptly vanished.

None of us did! We all just watched him go, thoroughly jealous that he could live by some internal clock only he heard. We guessed he went off to smoke cigarettes or snort Adderall, but we were wrong.

Jim Moriarty went to the library.

I know, Jean, because I went there with him.

಄

It was October. First week, third period. Jim had been at Baker Street Prep for almost a month. I had study hall that period, but rather than go to our dorm to practice the violin (as I should've done), I'd gone to the library. I used to go all the time, alone, when the procrastination bug hit or I was keyed up about an upcoming chess match.

Now, I bet you didn't know this, Jean, but there's a chess table in the farthest corner of the library. Like, if you go past the main space with the cathedral ceilings, then circle around that lounge area with the armchairs that have more holes than leather, and you finally duck through those really tall bookcases on the right—the ones that are so close together your shoulders almost touch either side—you'll find the board.

It's beside a dusty window (seriously, I don't think it's been washed in a decade). There's an almost-as-dusty chessboard with two armchairs on either side of the table (mostly still leather since no one ever uses them), lit by a sad little wall sconce flickering overhead.

I'm, like, 99 percent positive that until Jim Moriarty came along, I was the only person who knew that chessboard was there. I mean, the narrow shelves hold books in French and Spanish and German—and let's be honest: don't no one read in French or Spanish or German unless it's for class.

So there I sat, staring at the board in a makeshift Boden's Mate pattern. The chess match against Scot's Yard High was still a few months away, but I'd been reliving last year's ass-kicking almost every night. Seriously, I would see pawns and bishops and Boden's Mate in my sleep.

The landscaping crew was outside, hazy figures with wide-brimmed hats and a lawn mower that needed a new carburetor. At least, that was my diagnosis based on the hum-hummmm-hum-hummmm sound it made.

The crew had just scared the house sparrows from their nest above the window, and I was watching those dark, winged shapes swoop and swirl when a voice said, "Black bishop to F-five."

I jumped. I might've screamed, too. It was actually really embarrassing, but in my defense, no one ever came back there. I mean, I was so accustomed to being alone I'd actually pick my nose sometimes.

I snapped my gaze to the shelves. Jim was standing there, with one of those little half smiles he does, where only the left corner of his mouth tows up. Elusive, that smile.

"Can I play?" he asked, motioning to the black side of the board.

I nodded dumbly, and Jim glided into the empty armchair. Leather squeaked, making him smile with *both* sides of that perfect mouth now.

He was amused. An emotion I wouldn't have known Jim Moriarty could feel, yet there he was. Grinning.

At me.

He set a book on the floor beside his chair. I hadn't noticed he was holding it since I'd been so focused on hiding the tremble in my hands. *Madame Bovary*, it read. Par Gustave Flaubert.

"Is it good?" My voice was shamefully tight, but can you blame me? There was a hot, mysterious guy who could read in French and who wanted to play chess with me. Things like that had never happened to Shirley Holmes.

"The story's okay" was Jim's vague reply. Neither a yes nor a no. His gaze had already settled on the board, his forehead knitting down the middle in a way I would soon come to recognize. To look forward to. Because that furrow meant he was playing chess.

With me.

"It's also a scary story," he said at last.

"How so?" I shifted my weight to move my hands beneath my thighs. They were still shaking—the bastards.

"It's about a woman who spends her whole life believing in fairy tales." His dark eyes flicked to mine. Then, in a move that would have set the whole school to sighing, he eased off his glasses.

He looks younger without them. Those thick black frames do a lot to hide his real face. Plus they leave two red marks on the bridge of his nose whenever he takes them off. Something about those marks made him seem . . . vulnerable. Exposed.

I swallowed. "What's wrong with believing in fairy tales?"

"Reality will never live up."

"Oh." This conversation had quickly moved out of my depth.

Yes, you did read that right, Jean. I'm admitting that there's something I don't know better than everyone else, and I'm admitting that I felt—gasp!—uncomfortable by it.

But then Jim made his move (knight to F3), and I was back in my element. He'd made a mistake, see? Not an amateur move—he clearly knew how to play—but definitely not an advanced move, either.

I wasn't about to go easy on him just because I thought he had nice eyes and was quite possibly the Coolest Person Who Had Ever Lived. Instead, I slid my bishop diagonally two squares before settling back to let him stare and frown and stare some more. The rest of the game unfolded in silence.

A short game because I slaughtered him. Like, I had his king in about ten moves.

"Checkmate," I declared, sitting higher. Puffing out my chest. Preening, as you always accuse me of doing.

He laughed then. A sound that would've slayed the school. It slayed me. Such surprise. Such deep delight. Then he was slipping his glasses back on and smiling full wattage. "Play again tomorrow?"

Deer in headlights. All I could do was muster a nod.

"Good." He pushed to his feet, swooped up his book, and headed for the tunnel of shelves. But at the edge, he glanced back. "See you tomorrow, Holmes."

It was such a light tone. Playful. Flirty. And leaving me with no clue how to reply. *See you tomorrow, Moriarty* was a mouthful. And *See you tomorrow, Jim* was what everyone else in the world would say.

So I offered up a smirk and said, "See you tomorrow, James."

As soon as the reply left my lips, I was cringing inside. No wonder no one ever invited me to the winter formal. I could not—and still cannot—flirt.

But Jim laughed. That same surprised burst of sound. Sure, it was now muffled by walls of foreign literature, but I, Shirley Holmes, had made him laugh.

Twice.

☙❧

Jim and I played every day after that.

He got better. So did I, though.

Especially during the third week of October. Halloween was coming up, and Jim had commented on the heat wave right as we sat down to play.

"It's weird," he said, squinting through the dirty glass at a sunny afternoon. "Halloween should be cold and rattling with leaves. Or, at the very least, kind of cool outside."

"Thanks, global climate change!" I moved my pawn to A4. "Seriously, though, James. Get used to it. It's never cold here, so if you're looking for a white Christmas, you'll have to head up north. The only Decembers I've ever lived through hotter than these were when my family lived in Johannesburg."

I was showing off a little. Hoping he'd ask about my South African mama.

He did (score!), so I relayed my go-to story about that time baboons broke into my grandmother's kitchen and crapped everywhere.

"Your family sounds cool," he offered at the end of the tale. His face, his tone . . . they were withdrawn. Sad, almost. And I hoped-hoped-hoped he would talk about his family. Or anything at all to do with his past or where he'd come from. I mean, had his parents died in a car crash? Had he been expelled for changing grades?

The latest rumor was that his uncle used to work for the CIA before leaking classified files and then vanishing off the grid, and while I did find a Gregory Moriarty who'd done all that (yeah, Jean, I Googled him), I couldn't confirm he was Jim's uncle.

And Jim certainly didn't reveal anything about it. Instead, his head tipped back to watch me from the bottoms of his eyes, a hard gaze that set my hands to shaking again.

Were I someone else, I'd have offered up some kind of "sexy move." I'd have flashed a coy smile or batted my lashes or . . . or giggled knowingly (that's a thing, right?). Basically, I'd have done anything other than what I actually did, which was to turn red-faced and plop my knight to a stupid spot on the board.

"You want to be a lawyer," he said eventually, attention still on me. It was his turn in the game, but he wouldn't break that stare. "Your friend Jean Watson mentioned it."

My lips puckered to one side. He had spoken to you about me. That had to be a good sign, right? Also, why did you never mention this to me, Jean?

"I mean," I said with a shrug, "I've always planned on being a lawyer. You know. Go to Harvard, like my dad."

"Why?" His eyes finally returned to the board. And I finally breathed again. "Are you just really passionate about heretofores and notwithstandings?"

"No." I huffed a chuckle, heat rising up my neck. "I want to help people, actually."

"You mean you want to help your wallet," he countered. "Or maybe it's your daddy's wallet."

"It's not like that," I insisted. Yet even as the argument flew out, I knew that it was like that. Still, I floundered on. "My dad uses the law to win justice. For victims. So I want to do the same."

"But you do know that at least ten thousand convictions are wrong each year. Sounds to me like the 'criminals'"—he air-quoted that—"are the bigger victims there."

"Come on, now." I leaned on my knees. "What about the convictions that are actually right? What about the people who really need help, and it's up to the lawyer to make it happen?"

"Please, Holmes." He made a face. A frowning, disappointed thing. "It's never that simple, is it?"

Were he my father making that expression, I'd have instantly shriveled. Were he Ms. Adler or the headmistress or basically anyone in the world, I'd have rolled right on my back with my tail between my legs.

And honestly, if you'd asked me a few minutes before this happened *How would you react to Jim Moriarty's disappointment?* I'd have expected to shrivel. I mean, I was crushing on him so hard. But instead, I found heat building in my belly. Found my fingers tightening around my bishop, my knuckles paling as I squeezed.

And as Jim continued: "Most people don't steal or kill or sell drugs because they want to, Holmes, or because they love being 'bad guys' so much. They do it because they're born to a life with no exits. No chances. Unlike you or me, they can't just walk through walls."

"Walk through walls?" Squeeze, squeeze, squeeze. "What does that even mean?"

"It means you're lucky to be where you are. Who you are." Abruptly, he shot to his feet, the chair groaning back across the floor. "Wait here." In three long steps, the towering bookcases swallowed him whole.

And I just sat there, inexplicably furious. I wanted to smack him. Or to break this bishop in two. I mean, no one—no one—had ever told me that the law was a stupid career path to follow.

And no one had ever accused me of doing it for the money, either.

Jim returned in under a minute. "Here." A book fell onto my lap. Worn hardcover, barely taller than my hand and no thicker.

Gabriel García Márquez's *Chronicle of a Death Foretold*. The English translation.

"Read it," Jim ordered, "and tell me who's guilty at the end. Tell me who you, as a lawyer, would lock away."

"And should I write a five-paragraph essay on it, too, Professor Moriarty?" I shoved a pawn to H3. "Or will there be a pop quiz tomorrow?"

He sighed and settled back into his seat. "You don't have to read it. I just think . . . it's a good book, okay?"

I didn't answer. It was childish of me—that sullen silence. Not to mention totally irrational. Yes, I can be abrasive, Jean. But you know me! I don't ever let my temper come out. I make mistakes when I'm mad, and mistakes are for people who are not the offspring of William Holmes.

I moved my pawn to E5—a move as foolish as they come. I mean, instantly, the whole game unraveled for me, and in about fifteen turns, Jim said, "Check."

A minute passed, during which I only managed to expose my king all the more, and when he finished with "Checkmate, Holmes," all I could do was glare.

☙

Remember that night I woke you up because I was crying?

I told you the book I was reading was sad, which was a lie. I mean, *Chronicle of a Death Foretold* wasn't meant to be sad. It was supposed to be a commentary on who's truly to blame: those who commit a murder or the village that does nothing to stop it?

Yet underneath, tangled between its sentences and its beats, there was a love story. A girl—Angela—whose life was controlled by the men around her. A girl whose worth was based on what she could give. A girl who finally found what she wanted in life . . .

But she was too late to claim it, leaving only one end for everyone: a senseless death foretold.

☙

I didn't tell Jim I had cried reading the book. I simply said, "The whole village was guilty" when I eased into my armchair the next day.

The landscapers were right outside our window, weed-hacking and hedge-trimming in a roar of engines and snapping branches. We were halfway into our game before they passed, and I was finally able to add,

"The townsfolk knew the brothers planned to kill Santiago, but no one intervened."

"So who gets punished?"

"The brothers."

"Even though everyone around them was just as guilty?"

"Well, the village didn't stab Santiago twenty times until his intestines fell all over the dirt! That was Angela's brothers."

A shake of Jim's head, but not with annoyance. His eyes were crinkling behind his glasses as he jumped his knight forward to take my pawn. "You're way too smart for the law, Holmes. Too smart to believe in things that aren't real."

I slid my rook to D4, claiming a black knight. "And how is justice not real, James?"

"None of it is." He waved to the board. "Not the rules. Not the game." He jerked his head toward the window, hair flopping with that gut-wrenching perfection. "Not the pruned trees or keeping up with the Joneses. Least of all that legal system you plan to get a 'degree' studying. They're just myths. Giant lies that we all agree to believe in. And the only reason they hold power over us is because we let them."

I'll admit that my jaw fell open a little. Then, in a move of ultimate poise and eloquence, I said, "Huh?"

And Jim laughed. Maybe it was the tenth laugh or maybe the hundredth that I'd conjured from him, yet it was *this* laugh that sent me tumbling head over heels.

Yet even though I was falling—so fast and with so much blood roaring in my ears—the idiocy of Jim's next move (black queen to E6) allowed my brain to operate, my mouth to articulate, "All those things, James. Those . . . myths. They give us order. A framework to live in."

"They also give us war, Holmes. And genocide and poverty and"— a wave around the library—"an upper class. Don't you see it? Shared mythology is what creates us versus them."

"Soooo?" I dragged out the word to emphasize my complete and total confusion. "Do you want chaos, then? No school or government or games? Are you an anarchist, James?"

"Hardly, Holmes." A snort. "More like . . . Let's just say that I want to find what's real. I want to feel it—whatever it might be. And then, while the rest of the world sits cozy and oblivious inside their glass houses, I will be walking through walls."

"Oh?" I said with fake interest. "And how do you plan to do that, sir?"

"Same way I always do." And there it was again, Jean. That sad, broken smile—though it vanished two heartbeats later as he rested his elbows on the table. Steepled his fingers over the board.

"Want to know something about me, Holmes?"

"Yes," I breathed with far too much enthusiasm.

He didn't notice. His eyes drifted down to the board. "I came to Baker Street Prep for something, and once I find it, I don't plan on sticking around."

Everything inside me went cold. "What is it you're looking for?"

"A key," he said calmly. "To a door that people don't want opened."

It was then that I saw the reality: he was the nephew of Gregory Moriarty, and just like his uncle, he wanted to whistle-blow and declassify and expose people he thought had done wrong.

But before I could dwell on what that might mean or what key he might be looking for, he said, "Oh, and checkmate."

I blinked, lost for a moment. I'd completely forgotten that a game still waged between us. But wait—hadn't Jim lost his queen to me a few turns back?

I honed in on the black and white squares . . . and then groaned. Because dammit, he'd used the same move that gets me every time.

Boden's Mate.

Boden's freakin' Mate.

⚬✕⚬

Another month passed. The same routine unfolded each day. Me versus Jim. White versus black.

Jim won more often, and I didn't even care. But now the walls were shrinking in.

Then one day we had our first stalemate. It was early December—the day I skipped fourth-period orchestra, remember? I told you I had cramps, but the truth was that the chess game had run long.

Dad had told my older brother, Mike, and me the night before that if we didn't close out our semesters with the highest GPAs, then we were officially uninvited from the family trip to Aruba. What a jerk, right?

On top of that, Jim kept asking me questions about you, Jean. What's it like for her being a senator's daughter? Has she ever been to the Capitol? Does she ever talk about her mom's policies?

I was jealous, and I was pissed. It was the basic recipe for Shirley Losing at Chess, which was why I ended up whittled down to just my king.

In my defense, though, Jim wasn't much better off: he had only his king and a rook left.

We were seriously stuck, and I was tired of running my piece back and forth across the board.

"Stop chasing my king," I snarled.

"If I saw a way to do that," he clipped back, "then obviously I would. How about, instead, you stop running away from my rook?"

"Let's just draw, James. This game is never going to end otherwise."

A pause. Then his eyebrows perked up with mischief. "And what would happen if it never ended, Holmes?"

"I'd miss orchestra, which would be bad."

"Why? Will it trigger the apocalypse? Fire! Pestilence! Famine!"

"Ha-ha." I snapped my king over a square. The same move I'd been making for a full ten minutes.

And he scooted his rook after . . . only to pause, fingers twirling across the jagged top. Then his lips curled up. He moved his rook diagonally. Yeah, not sideways, but *diagonally*.

I blinked. Then wagged my head like a cartoon who'd just been slapped. "You can't do that."

"Says who?"

"The rules!"

"Which we know don't matter, Holmes. Not if we both agree to stop believing in them." His grin spread wider and wider, and I knew from the hair prickling on the back of my neck that I had stepped right into his trap.

But I didn't care. Because my pulse was picking up speed. My stomach was spinning in a good way. This wasn't like that time I had salmonella. This was like that roller coaster at Universal Studios.

And I wanted more of it.

So when Jim next declared, "From now on, rooks go diagonally, and kings can move like queens," I didn't argue. I simply settled into the new rhythm until at last I won. An hour later, right before the bell rang for the end of fourth period.

And guess what? The apocalypse didn't come, and Mike told me Aruba sucked anyway.

ᥲᦆ

In January, Scot's Yard won the chess match. Of course. Dad was irate (do you remember that phone call? You said you could hear his shouts from the girls' bathroom), but I didn't care.

Oh, the chess team thought I cared. You should've seen how they hung their heads on the bus ride back to Baker Street. All of them bracing for my shouts . . .

But I didn't shout. I was scarcely thinking about Scot's Yard or how, yet again, I had fallen for effing Boden's Mate—my eternal curse, that move.

No, instead, I was wrapped up in a new book from Jim. *Pedro Páramo*. A tale swirling with ghosts and purgatory and the lives that could have been.

I loved the book. Devoured it in a night. Even in all its magical realism and intangible betweens, it felt real to me. Familiar.

Yet the next day, I said, "I hated it. It never felt grounded."

A crooked smile. Jim knew I was kidding, but he didn't push me for a real reaction. He just eased his pawn to D6.

A bad start for him, but I was feeling charitable that day. Plus I didn't want the game to end. Not yet. Not after reading that book and putting the puzzle pieces together.

Oh, don't you see? Jim is a ghost. Forever just passing through. That day in the library, he was trapped in purgatory until he found whatever mysterious key he needed to move on. Meanwhile I was just beginning to realize that one day I would blink a heartbeat too long and find that when my lashes had lifted, Jim was gone.

I wasn't ready for that. Those stolen moments with him in the library had become precious to me. I'm sorry, Jean, and so ashamed to admit it. But it's true. We had built an entire world trapped in time, perfect in all its layers. In its dust motes and sunshine. In its broken carburetor to rattle above the sparrows' cries. In the stink of bio-lab hand sanitizer to burn over the must of old French pages.

I knew our glass walls wouldn't last, and that had left my humor foul. "What else do you have for me, Professor? Maybe something with a happy ending this time? Is that too much to ask?"

His eyes squinted. Thoughtful and perhaps a bit pleased. "So no winter formal for you tonight, then?"

"Oh," I said with a flippant shrug. "Is that tonight?" Obviously, I knew when it was. But no one had invited me, and I knew for a fact that no one had invited him, either.

I won't lie: I was afraid he might ask you to the dance, Jean. Ever since he'd plied me with those questions about the Watson family, I thought maybe he was into you.

But now I see the truth.

And I also see what an idiot I was.

"I'm not going," I added, just in case Jim wasn't aware of my solo status.

"All right, then, Holmes." He nodded slowly. "I have a book in mind for you. Where's your dorm? I'll bring it."

"Boys aren't allowed in the girls' wing."

"Come, now." A smug bounce of those eyebrows. "As much as I love when you talk rules and regulations, I'm interested to see a different side of you." He eased his queen to D7, dragging his thumb across the top. A caress I couldn't tear my eyes from.

The movement set off the roller coaster inside me. My throat closed up. My stomach ached with need, loop after loop. And it wasn't Jim's words, as flirty as they'd been, that did it. It was the movement— the offer implied in his fingers against the queen: *Why be what you're expected to be? You could be like me, Shirley Holmes, if you just tried.*

The thing was, as much as I wanted it and as much as I hungered for Rebellion with a capital *R*, I wasn't ready to be a ghost. Not yet.

But I also wasn't ready to lose my world trapped between. So I smiled, cheeks on fire. "Room fifty-four, James. On the corner. But wait until after the winter formal starts, okay?"

"Your wish is my command, Holmes."

If only that had been true, Jean. If only that had been true.

☙

He came to the window. Not to the door, as I had anticipated. You were (of course) at the winter formal with Marty, and I was sitting at my desk, pretending to do calculus homework. But I'd been staring at the same problem for an hour without getting anything solved.

I put on makeup with you—do you remember that? While you were getting gussied up for the dance, I made you show me how to create the illusion of cheekbones. Contouring, you called it. But as soon as you left, I wiped it all off. I was afraid Jim would notice and then make some comment on the "myths of beauty."

A tap at the window sent me jumping from my chair. The window was right above my desk, but I had the blinds down. I hadn't seen him approach over the sliver of roof right outside.

I lifted the blinds, his face coalescing in the darkness. Hazy and terrifying through the glass. I turned off the light before finagling open the window, and then he said only one thing: "Join me."

I didn't think twice about it. I didn't think about the rules or the sharp angle of the roof or the forty-foot drop beyond. I didn't even think about how awkward I looked, clambering onto my desk and squeezing through the window.

But here's the thing I see now: we all want that vampire from the CW so badly that sometimes we forget sunlight kills.

ⓔⓐ

The roof is beautiful at night. The asphalt shingles glitter more than you'd expect. A fairy path that Jim followed while I followed Jim. First we crossed the newer roof above the dormitories until that gave way to the moss-covered, wood shingles of the original school.

Jim was so comfortable and easy in his angled lope across the roof. Meanwhile, I moved as best I could, out of my element but wishing this height, these shadows, and this magical guide could be mine.

When at last Jim came to a stop, I recognized from the nest in the gutter and the dark shape of the hedges below that we were directly above our library nook.

Jim turned to me, glowing in the starlight. "Let's sit on the edge." A command in his tone, yet a question in the way he extended his hand—one I answered by giving him my own hand. His fingers were frozen to ice, but strong all the same.

Jim crouched at the roof's lip. He helped me sit so my feet dangled over the hedges. Our hedges, always growing despite the landscapers' best attempts to stop them.

In hindsight, it was crazy foolish of us to be up there. I mean, a drop that could break my bones plus a cocktail of hormones and neurotransmitters were booming through my blood. My brain. My heart.

It was exactly the sort of thing I never did, yet all thought and reason and basic Darwinian good sense had shut down in favor of an electric light show in my chest.

I thought . . . I hoped Jim would ease down beside me. Close. Touching.

He didn't. A chasm of two feet spanned between us.

Clasping his arms to his chest, he lay back. Legs swinging. Shingles creaking. The wind swept over us, damp with the closest thing to seasons we ever get here. Fragrant with earth and yesterday's rain. With leaves decomposing under the live oaks.

No winter here. Just one life giving way to another.

"Your hands are warm, Holmes," Jim said eventually, and I realized he had curled his own fingers into fists. Holding in my heat, I wanted to believe.

"Yours are cold. Have you considered gloves?"

No laugh. He was too wrapped up in his thoughts that night.

To cover the embarrassment charging up my cheeks, I mimicked his pose and lay back. Then I hugged my arms to my chest and fixed my eyes on the sky.

The heat fled my face as fast as it had come, and in an instant I understood why Jim had put this space between us.

When you have eliminated the impossible, whatever remains must be the truth. It must be what's real, and I needed that gap between us to feel it.

I'm sorry, Jean. I know this all sounds so completely unlike me. But that's why I have to tell you—don't you see? I'd never felt anything like it. Not then and not now. No drug has come close to it. No adventure. No dreamscape.

Air beneath my feet.

Darkness to hug me tight.

All with the universe spread above me, speckled and humming and so damned alive that there could only be one outcome from it all: a death foretold and my intestines on the dusty earth below.

☙❧

Jim's phone buzzed at nine thirty. I jolted. Lost. Almost asleep.

He eased it from his pocket. "An alarm," he explained lazily. "It goes off every night, so I don't miss curfew-call at ten."

I swallowed—my mouth was dry; would he notice?—and eased up onto my elbows. "You come here every night, then?"

A grunt of acknowledgment as he pushed to his feet, dusted off his hands, and then helped me to rise.

"Your fingers are still cold," I said with a smile.

"And yours are still warm," he murmured back, offering a grin of his own. But it wasn't a real one. It wasn't the one I wanted.

As before, he guided me across the roof. Transitioning from the thwack and creak of ancient wood to the muffled glitter of asphalt, and finally back to my window.

Our room was dark, Jean. You were still away, and although I could have asked Jim to join me inside—the formal wouldn't end until eleven—I knew he would refuse.

Or maybe . . . maybe I simply knew he wouldn't fit inside my cage. He was too big for those walls.

Instead, we sat on the windowsill. He faced outward, feet resting on the roof. I faced in, feet atop my desk. Atop my calc homework.

Music thumped through the windowsill. A beat that suggested "YMCA" was playing in the gym, accompanied by that torturous dance I know you think is fun.

Neither Jim nor I spoke. But unlike the silence before, where the entire universe had cradled me and called me friend, this silence was strained. I could feel the tick of Jim's internal clock, and there was no denying that the bomb attached was about to go off.

The breeze kicked at his hair while he picked his thumbnail. A half-hearted movement I didn't have the guts to interrupt. I just watched. I just waited.

At last, he shifted toward me, and in that instance, the scrape of his jeans was too loud. Too real. Too inescapable, and made all the more so by his eyes, rooting on my face. Dark behind his glasses.

My heart picked up speed. Not because I thought he might kiss me—though god knows I wanted him to—but because there was something wrong. Something off.

"What, James?" I said, harsher than I'd intended. Breaking the spell that had fallen over us.

His forehead tightened. That stare was killing me. That pause was killing me. Until finally: "I saw you got into Harvard, Holmes."

Nothing could have surprised me more, Jean. I hadn't told anyone about my acceptance e-mail. Not you, not my parents. "How do you know?"

"I was poking through the school's server." He said it so nonchalantly—as if it were perfectly normal. As if I shouldn't care.

But I did. "Why were you on the school server? And why were you looking at my e-mails?"

His hands lifted defensively. "It wasn't on purpose, Holmes. I told you, I came here to find something."

"A key," I said, my tone mocking and harsh. "So you can walk through walls and whatever other nonsense it is you like to do."

That hurt him. I saw it in the way his face fell. "Someone has to step outside the rules," he said eventually. "How else can I help the people enslaved by them?"

"And why do you have to help them at all? Hacking into the school's system will get you expelled."

"So? So what if that happens? Why do you care?"

"Because . . ." I stopped. I had to swallow. Had to gather my thoughts and tamp down this heat that strained against my stomach.

"Because what?"

"Nothing." I looked down at my shadowed calculus homework. A slow rhythm was thumping through the walls now, completely at odds with the frustration building in my lungs. It was the same fury I'd felt when Jim had grilled me on becoming a lawyer.

Irrational. Childish. And bubbling over too fast. I mean, why should I be the one to confess how I felt? Wasn't it obvious?

Jim didn't push me, though. Not yet. Instead, he asked, "Will you go? To Harvard, I mean."

"Of course."

"Then why haven't you told anyone about the acceptance? It came in two weeks ago, Shirley. What are you waiting for?"

My breath caught. He had said my name. For the first time ever, Jim had said my name, and it was all too much.

I angled my body toward him, one shoulder inside the dorm, one shoulder out. "What do you want from me, Jim?"

He shook his head. "Don't make me say it. Not if you can't." His voice was softer now. His body, his face moving ever so slightly toward me. "Or can you?"

"You're going to leave, aren't you?" Our faces were mere inches apart now. "Once you find what you've come for, you'll leave. But I won't."

"You could, though," he murmured. Closer. Closer. "Come with me, Shirley."

"Where?"

"Outside."

"I need more than that, Jim." My forehead scrunched up. "I'm not like you—I like walls and rules and structure."

"I see." He gave a tiny nod, and the bomb finally went off. Detonating in my rib cage, it kicked out a single, booming heartbeat straight against my ribs.

Then it happened. Finally, and so gently.

That's the only word I can find to describe what we shared. The way Jim pulled me to him. The way he leaned in. The way his gaze flicked from my lips to my eyes, making sure I wanted this.

I did. So badly I thought I would drown from wanting.

He closed the space between us. Our mouths touched. Just a brush of skin—his upper lip grazing my lower. That was all it was, but I couldn't breathe. Or move. Or think.

For the ten seconds or ten minutes or however long our lips hovered together, I tasted the outside. The real. The free fall of Jim and me, together for one perfect moment.

His hands, warmer now, tangled in my hair. My hands, a bit colder, cupped his face. Deep. Long. Starving. Jim kissed me like we were dying.

Because time was up, and this was good-bye.

 මෙ

This story ends with a kiss.

I mean, sure: while I watched Jim disappear across the rooftop, the night folding over him, I prayed that I would see him again. That our time was up *for now*, but not forever.

Yet I knew. People don't kiss like it's their last, unless it is.

The next day, a Saturday, I went to the library. I had no other way of finding Jim. No phone number, no e-mail. And though I didn't think he'd actually be there, I went to check anyway.

You probably don't remember, but it was a gorgeous January day. So bright that sunshine cut right through those foggy windows, and the sparrows sent shadows flying across the floorboards.

On my chair lay a tattered red book with gold letters stamped onto the cover. *Grimm's Fairy Tales*, it read, and a chuckle bubbled in my chest at the sight of it . . . until my eyes hit the chessboard, atop which two pieces glowed in the sunbeams.

A white queen and a black king, tipped sideways.

Checkmate.

I didn't cry. I thought I would, but as I sat there staring at those pieces, no tears pricked behind my eyes. No sobs gathered in my lungs. Instead, something warm shimmered through me. From my toes, it gusted and raced and grew until all I could do was clutch my arms to my chest and smile.

I smiled so big it actually hurt my cheeks. It hurt my ribs and my lungs, too.

Eventually, I scooped up the book of fairy tales. There was no message or anything inside—I hadn't thought there would be since the book and the chessboard were message enough.

Then I sauntered languidly away from the table, away from the sunshine and the sparrows and the landscaping. Away from that stolen world trapped between. And as I walked—with a very Rebellious angle to my strut, if I do say so myself—I thought everything was going to be okay.

I thought, like an idiot, that we would be together one day. That I was in love with him, and he, despite everything, was in love with me back.

But I was still just Madame Bovary, clinging to fairy tales that could never be. Which is what had set us apart from the very beginning, though I didn't see it until too late. It's what will set us apart forever: what we believe in. Or rather, the fact that I, Shirley Holmes, believe in something at all . . .

And he, Jim Moriarty, does not.

ᘔᖇ

Now here we are, and nothing's okay.

I need to apologize for what happened to your family. For what Jim did to them and so many people when he released those files.

Scandal in Bohemia, they're calling it on the news, and then there's a picture of your mom with the headline Senator Rita Watson's private e-mails hacked; Evidence of bribes in the Senate.

I think I helped him, Jean—I think I helped Jim get access to those files that have left your mom facing expulsion. But I swear I didn't mean to. I swear I didn't know what I was doing. All I can guess is that Jim somehow used your e-mails to gain access to your mom's server, which in turn gave him access to all her files.

I also know that this Scandal in Bohemia has everyone freaking out and blaming your mom. But while the media and the masses are so focused on the pawns getting crushed by kings, they're forgetting that not all kings are bad.

Jim's certainly forgotten it, if he ever knew it at all. That's why I have to stop him before any more files get leaked. Before any more innocents get hurt.

I know, I know. We're supposed to start our first semester together at Harvard in a month, but I can't do that anymore. Don't you see? Not while your family is hurting. Not while Jim Moriarty is still out there somewhere, walking free.

But I'll find him, Jean. I'm taking a class on computer forensics now, and everything I learn I'll use to make this better. Being a lawyer was never for me—at least Jim was right about that—but helping people and getting justice for the victims . . . that *is* me. Starting now and on my own terms.

Sometimes the only way to fix a broken wall is to patch it up from within. I'm not a ghost trapped in purgatory, nor a girl waiting for men to decide her fate.

White queen to E6. I'm coming for you, Jim Moriarty.

Checkmate.

—Your BFF,
Shirley Holmes

Sasha Alsberg's Villain Challenge to Susan Dennard:

A Young Moriarty

Dear Sasha, the 411 for Villains

BY SASHA ALSBERG

The thing that unnerves me about James Moriarty is that he doesn't have any unrealistic powers or live in a made-up world. Quite the contrary, actually. He lives in the United Kingdom. He is a professor, mathematician, son, and brother. Without adding the criminal-mastermind factor to him, he seems like a pretty ordinary guy.

So why does this bother me? Well, it creeps me out because this guy—this crazy, intelligent, psycho man—could very realistically live in this world. Our reality. Which means he could also be online, stalking villain forums, giving advice on how to dance on the ashes of your enemies.

And so could I . . .

DEAR SASHA, THE 411 FOR VILLAINS

ABOUT ME:

Some of you may think you know me, but maybe that's just what I *want* you to think. Have you ever thought of that? It only took a few sweet nothings and words of a white lie to structure my ultimate façade. It was good fun for a while, but now I am ready to share my advice with some sorry souls who need a little help in the criminal-mastermind world.

Being a criminal mastermind isn't a job; it's a lifestyle.

Love,
Sasha

One Fed-Up Failure ⇄ Sasha

Dear Sasha,

I have been struggling with the criminal-mastermind lifestyle. Not because I don't want to become one, but because whenever I try to do something evil, well, I get caught. I've had to move ten times in the past year just to avoid the cops. Do I just suck at being a villain? All I want is to weasel my way into people's lives and take all their money. Is that too much to ask? That being said, how can I avoid getting caught? I need your help.

Sincerely,
One Fed-Up Failure

Sasha ⇄ One Fed-Up Failure

Dear Fed-Up Failure,

Wow, you got yourself in a pickle, haven't you? It sure is a bummer when you can't do what your heart desires. Something you need to remember is we all have to start somewhere and learn from our past actions.

You seem to be trying a bit too hard to stay inconspicuous. Try becoming close friends with some trust fund babies and earning their respect. Get close to them. It may take a while, a few months to a few years, but once you have them in your grasp, clamp shut and take everything you can grab and get the heck out of there.

Don't run and hide; get ahead of the game and work your way up to the top.

You got this!

Best,

Sasha

Undermined Underlord ⇄ Sasha

Dear Sasha,

I have been trying to blackmail my arch nemesis, Fredrick, for two weeks now. I need him to respect me and the power I have over him, but I'm having a serious problem . . . He thinks I'm a joke. Whenever I threaten to expose his secret life as a cosplayer, he seems to not care. I'll insert a section of our text messages:

Me: Fredrick Monstepi, you need to deliver $100,000 to the corner of Sher Drive and Lock Street by Wednesday, July 5, or else I will expose your secret life of cosplay to the world . . .

Fredrick: Hello again, Nigel. Might as well get some promotion from this, so make sure when you "expose" me to tag my cosplay page: @FredCosALot. Thanks, buddy.

Do you see the disrespect he has for me? I am sick of this. Please, Sasha, tell me what to do. I need your supreme guidance.

Sincerely,

Undermined Underlord

Sasha ⇄ Undermined Underlord

Dear Underlord,

The problem is simple. Your leverage against him is so utterly weak that it's not even a threat. Cosplay? Really? Cosplay is so cool! Nerd culture is nothing to be ashamed of, and neither is cosplaying. So what you need to do is find something juicy to use against him, like a dirty hobby, a secret dungeon, a hidden child, or a missing ex-lover. It needs to be something police-worthy, and if he has nothing, make *something* up.

Also, Fredrick knew who you were, so that broke one of the major rules of thievery: never expose yourself until the time is right.

Good luck on your quest, Underlord.

Best,

Sasha

Professor James Moriarty ⇄ Sasha

Dear Sasha Marie Alsberg,

I know a lot about you. I have been studying you for a while through this forum of yours, and let me say, I'm impressed. But I now have some tips for you.

When you are submerged in this criminal underworld, everyone is your enemy. You help these sorry excuses for masterminds become who they strive to be, but in the meantime, you are helping them gain an upper hand. You are breeding criminals, making them your equals, when really you should be degrading them, tricking them, and making them no more than an ant under your shoe. With your hand feeding these men and women, they will one day come back to bite you. And who is to blame? That's correct: you.

With the internet at our fingertips today, it just seems too easy to get what you want. I learned the hard way. It all started with manipulating a few peers as a young lad. They were the puppets on my strings, and it has escalated since then into my now empire of deception.

Don't get me wrong, girl. I do appreciate your efforts, but in my world, you are the ant and I am the shoe. This is no threat—just advice from one mastermind to another who has been playing this game far longer than you've been alive.

Best regards,

Professor James Moriarty

Sasha Alsberg has signed off.

The Blessing of Little Wants

By Sarah Enni

Sigrid Balfour hated having to use magic to balance an enormous pile of paper while unlocking her dorm room door. In her extracurricular studies, she was just getting the hang of bending time. Using powers to prevent a clumsy disaster felt mildly humiliating.

Then, adding insult to injury, a voice from within startled her so badly that she shrieked and threw the papers into the air. Sigrid raised her hands, sheets scattering around her like a paper cut blizzard. A whispered breath and the source of the voice was flung onto the bed and pinned there.

Breathing hard, Sigrid examined her intruder. "God bleeding dammit, Thomas," she said. He blinked, and Sigrid realized she was still holding his paralysis. She lowered her hands.

"All I said was hello!" Thomas said, stretching his arms and legs to shake off the lingering sting of magical binding. "Bit jumpy?"

Glowering, Sigrid flicked her wrist. Thomas started, clutching at his chest. He gasped an inhale. "What was that?"

"Made your heart skip a beat," Sigrid said. "Who's jumpy now?"

"No need to get all kinetic on me," Thomas sniffed. He sat up and ran a hand through his helter-skelter hair, dark brown and tinged with the occasional grey. It never obeyed—Thomas looked flushed and wind-blown even on the clearest London day. He relaxed against the wall, as comfortable as if it were his own dorm room, which, based on the amount of time he spent here, it might as well have been.

"If you can't stand the wrath, don't set fire to the kitchen," Sigrid said, bending to pick up loose sheets. She placed a stack on the desk and drew back a curtain to let in the dying sunlight. Had Thomas been sitting here in the dark?

"Did you hear that the proclamation on limiting magic passed?" he asked. "They didn't even amend the language on practical use. Pendle Hill has the right to keep us from using the most basic spells—"

"Thomas."

"It's bad enough magic is stretched thin as the queen's mustache, now—"

"Thomas!" Sigrid raised rigid half fists, threatening imminent stran-gulation. Thomas quieted. She pressed her hands together. "Not today. Please."

She'd listened to some version of this rant for years. That Chancellor Duhamel and his government were conspiring with Pendle Hill lead-ers to scout and recruit witches born with acute natural abilities, then teach the weaker ones as little as possible to thwart their magical capac-ity. There was only so much magic in the world, and it ebbed and flowed as witches were born and died, learned and forgot how to be powerful. Duhamel and his cronies aimed to keep as much as possible for them-selves. Three years ago it sounded like a conspiracy theory, but it wasn't just fringe observers wondering about it anymore.

Sigrid and Thomas both curbed their substantial powers to avoid Pendle Hill's merit award system, which involved long visits to the chan-cellor's office, from which students returned quieter, more cautious. Diminished, somehow.

Thomas reached down and grabbed one of the loose sheets. He began reading in a fake British accent he knew Sigrid couldn't stand:

"'In my time at Pendle Hill, I've learned that cooperation between witches is paramount to solving the problems facing our kind, particularly the crisis of distribution of the world's finite supply of magic.'" He paused, pretending to adjust a monocle. "'Diminishing magic in the United Kingdom cannot be tolerated, but only through robust negotiation can the International Chamber of Spellcraft hope to balance the needs of the many—'"

Sigrid groaned. "Stop, please. Filling out applications is like meeting the tax accountant you never knew lived inside you. It's horrid."

"I don't know why you even bother," Thomas said. "Any position available will be beneath your abilities." He crumpled up the paper and tossed it to her.

She caught the wadded-up ball with a sigh. "What choice do we have?" Sigrid asked, weary. "We can't risk letting anyone know how powerful we are. We have to do the same as everyone else—get a position, live a normal life."

Thomas shook his head, face full of pity. He chewed the ever-present cud of khat leaf he kept tucked in his cheek. "A cubicle gig doing busywork until you retire or die? I wouldn't call that a life."

"The minutiae of a normal existence: Dating. Seeing friends. Yelling at said friends about what's on telly," Sigrid said, uncrumpling the application. She had one particular friend in mind but didn't dare say the name: Annabel Bates. Thomas and Annabel never quite got on. As in, on speaking terms. But if Sigrid had to brave a future filled with as many trifles and as little magic as possible, the thought of meeting Annabel at the pub every night was a silver lining. She tapped the mostly empty pages. "There's something to be said for little wants."

"I've seen what you can do," Thomas said quietly. "What we're both capable of. I don't think we could have 'little wants' if we tried. We need to *do* something—something big. We need to make a change."

"You sound like my father."

"Your father was a great man." Thomas shrugged.

Sigrid looked away. "Not to me."

Annabel appeared in the doorway and knocked gently. "Sorry—is this a bad time?" Sigrid sat up straight. Annabel's lips were pink and puckered as a petal, her hair a shining sheet of golden brown.

"It's a fine time," Sigrid said, flashing a bright smile.

"Have you had a minute to look over my CV?"

Sigrid slapped her forehead. "Ugh. I forgot, Bel. I'm sorry."

Annabel glanced at Thomas's satchel by the bed, spilling books onto the floor. "Too busy at the library?"

"Something like that," Sigrid said, rolling her eyes at Thomas.

"Well, listen, the application for the position at Chancellor Duhamel's office is due next Friday. I don't want to be a pain, but it's a position in his office, like his *actual office*, and—"

As Annabel went on about the potential of collating the chancellor's personal memos, lights began to dance at the corner of Sigrid's vision, amorphous shining shapes that spun across Annabel's face. They broke apart into tiny pinpoint stars, rotating in foreign constellations. Thomas's magic worked this way sometimes, when he wanted to show Sigrid something beautiful, or when he couldn't rein it in. The lights formed a halo around Annabel's face, then broke apart to ring her neck.

Altering another witch's sight or mind was reserved for sorcerer-level graduate students, spellcraft neither condoned nor achievable for almost anyone at university level. But Thomas had been showing Sigrid private magic since first year. She'd never told Annabel or anyone else; both she and Thomas had worked so hard to hide the extent of their powers. At times, Sigrid worried Thomas had hidden it *too* well. He was nearly invisible to their classmates and, besides her, hadn't made any real friends. She wished it was possible to praise the beauty of his spell-craft and show him off to the world. But ultimately she did as she always had: kept the special parts of Thomas close, and secret, and safe.

The stars dissolved as Thomas rubbed at his eyes, yawning.

"Sig? Hello?" Annabel raised an eyebrow.

Sigrid blinked, clearing her mind. "Sorry."

Annabel shook her head, smiling. "I think you hung with me there for about ten seconds. A record!" She nodded to the stack of papers behind Sigrid. "How're your applications coming?"

"Oh, you know . . ." Sigrid held up the partially crumpled sheet. "Swimmingly."

"Right," Annabel said drily. "I'll remember this moment when you get every position you apply for, per usual." She backed away from the door. "Well, let me know when you get to it." Annabel sauntered down the hall. Sigrid stood in the doorway, watching her.

"If you want evidence that magic is shrinking, look no further than Annabel Bates," Thomas said. "She couldn't conjure a sense of direction."

Sigrid threw a pen at his head. "Cork it, you elitist hag."

Thomas swatted the pen, sending it flying. It snagged a hanging mobile of tarot cards, sending the hand-painted figures spinning: empress, page of wands, fool, death. Sigrid moved to the bed, displacing pillows to sit beside Thomas, forcing their limbs together into a comfortable jumble. Magic had a particular warmth, a kind of glow that lingered after a series of spells had been cast. Thomas seemed to radiate that heat all the time. The khat leaf made him smell ever so slightly of licorice. Together those elements felt like home. Thomas was the only one who knew—really knew—what Sigrid was. At his side was the only place she could relax.

"The way you look at Annabel . . ." Thomas shook his head. "She's the one making you think you want a boring normal life. But you're Sigrid, the Viking queen." He put an arm around Sigrid's shoulders and pulled her in. "You're destined for something more. You could be a legend."

She knew Thomas meant to be reassuring, but Sigrid wasn't sure whether a destiny like that was a blessing or a curse. She watched the tarot mobile slow. The last shaft of sunlight illuminated the tower card, a portent of change, on which two medieval figures plummeted to their deaths.

ᥑᛡᤄ

The tea in the Pendle Hill fourth-year clubroom was always weak and a little too cold, its scattered couches so worn they felt like sacks stuffed with hay. But its makeshift library was a sanctuary, with books packed two-deep on gently sagging shelves and stacked in leather-bound stalagmites. Thomas had read them all so Sigrid felt she had, too. He'd begun reorganizing the collection using a mix of the Dewey decimal system, alphabetical order, and unknowable whimsy.

Thomas was stretched over the room's sole table, piles of open books before him. At his elbow was a legal pad jammed with frenetic scribbling. His feet were tucked under the chair, half fallen out of cheap loafers that had begun to fray, clinging desperately to peeling soles. Sigrid wanted badly to reach down and tuck his ankles back in.

At the click of her approaching heels, Thomas looked up. He gave her outfit a once-over. "Looking positively witchy."

Sigrid wore huge sunglasses and a ratty tweed overcoat purchased at the estate sale of a rich, eccentric crone. "*Cadaverous* was how one man on the street described it."

His smile was luminescent. "Yes. That's it exactly."

Sigrid tripped on one of the books piled at Thomas's feet and stopped in her tracks. Gingerly, as though handling an ancient artifact, she picked up the navy hardcover. She held a gasp in her throat.

The book was so familiar to Sigrid, she could have drawn its cover from memory: a gold foil outline of Scotland's northern coast, with a giant *X* floating in the far northeastern sea, just past the last island.

"Where did you get this?" Sigrid asked.

"Which?" Thomas looked up. "Ah. Rummage sale. Felt old in all the right ways. Why? What is it?"

"It's *Unnatural Troubles*," Sigrid said. "A biography of Alice Gray. I had this exact book as a kid—read it so many times I about had it memorized . . ."

"Alice Gray?"

She raised an eyebrow at Thomas's confused look. "Of the Hether Blether expedition?"

He shook his head.

"Seriously?" Sigrid removed a stack of volumes from the other chair and sat on the edge, clutching the book in her lap. "Oh, but you'll *love* this story," she said. "I can't believe you haven't heard of it. That's what you get for being born a Yank." She cleared her throat, relishing the moment.

"It was about twenty years ago, right after McClatchkey introduced his theory of magical scarcity," Sigrid began. "Alice was attending Pendle Hill at the time. She was an incredible witch, top of her class, had a position with the International Chamber lined up—the works. When the McClatchkey study proved that magic was a static resource being stretched disproportionately over a bloating population, everything was chaos. It was the end times—countries were hoarding magic, charlatans claimed they could create more."

"This part I know," Thomas said.

"Oh, you've decided to start listening in modern magical history?" Sigrid said drily. "Bully for you. Anyway, Alice started researching a legend from Orkney, near the northernmost bit of Scotland, about an all-knowing and reclusive sorcerer. Supposedly he lives on a mystical island called Hether Blether, which disappears most of the year. If any witch sets foot on the island, they can claim it, along with all the sorcerer's wisdom.

"Omnipotence might come with some answers to the magical scarcity problem, or at least that's what Alice thought. And she wasn't alone. She got a group of eight other witches together, and they formed an expedition to go north in search of Hether Blether and its sorcerer. But something happened."

Thomas leaned forward, listening. Sigrid's cheeks flushed with the thrill of telling the story that had entranced her as a child.

"They ferried to Eynhallow, an abandoned island off the Orkney coast. According to legend, if you want to find Hether Blether, you launch from there. That was the last time anyone saw them alive." She paused. "Weeks later, investigators found Alice and two others among monastic ruins on Eynhallow, laid out in an occult formation and covered in black markings. They hadn't been killed; they died of exposure."

Thomas's eyes widened.

"Another three were found on the shore. They had internal wounds, but no soft tissue damage. It was almost like they'd been taken under the sea, crushed"—Sigrid pressed her hands together in the air—"and washed up on the sand."

Thomas's smile was gone, but his eyes glistened. Sigrid had his full attention. As she went on with the story, her vision darkened at the corners. A mist clouded her eyes. Thomas was so focused on her story he was imagining it in his—and now her—mind.

"The final three weren't found for ages," Sigrid continued. "Investigators thought maybe their boat had been taken up by tides, or that they'd gotten lost in the Orkney fog and were dashed on the rocks of another island."

Thomas envisioned a steely grey haze over choppy whitecapped waves. Sigrid had read every account of Alice Gray and the Hether Blether expedition in her father's expansive library, and she'd pictured Eynhallow's shore much as Thomas did now: dreary with mist, a dark shadow hinting at a rowboat through the menacing fog.

She went on: "Eventually, they found the wreckage, at the bottom of the North Atlantic."

Thomas's vision shifted, dreamlike, under the waves into a murky netherworld. Sigrid's skin bristled with goose bumps as Thomas imagined the brackish dim. His ocean floor held dark dunes of sand interrupted by crags thrusting upward like carnivore teeth. The boat lay on its side, nestled between two bloody-knuckled outcrops.

"A hole had been drilled into it," Sigrid said, her voice eerily distant. "From beneath."

Thomas imagined a hole on the boat's damaged bottom, pristine and circular.

"The final three witches were found nearby."

They appeared, vivid as Thomas's smile had been to Sigrid just moments ago: skin grey and bloated, wispy hair floating up from lifeless heads. Their feet were buried in the ocean bed's ashy sand, bodies twisting in the current like tangled seaweed.

"So much worse." Sigrid pushed back against the pull of Thomas's vision. "They'd been there for ages."

Under her influence, the witches' skin lifted away, peeling off their necks and arms. Their faces came into sharper focus, eyes open to reveal milky-white irises. Vaguely, Sigrid registered Thomas grabbing her hand.

"They'd been branded, too," Sigrid said, pressing into Thomas's perspective and projecting pentagrams of warped scar tissue on the witches' chests. "Before they died."

Thomas squeezed tighter and tighter, folding the bones of her hand in his fist like a bundle of sticks. "Sigrid," he said, voice strained.

Just as quickly as it had appeared, the vision was gone, replaced by the dim light of the clubroom. What remained was a splitting headache.

"What was *that*?" Thomas said, releasing her hand. "You were changing images in my head . . ." He exhaled like he'd been holding a breath for days. "Have you always been able to do that?"

"I'm not sure." Sigrid clutched her throbbing head. She thought of all the times Thomas had foisted visions on her in the last three years. "Doesn't feel quite right, does it?"

Thomas adjusted his shoulders as though shaking something off. "Do you think Alice found him? The sorcerer?" Thomas asked.

"If she didn't," she said, "then what the bloody hell killed her?"

Thomas looked away. "So what happened to the next team?"

"What?"

"The ones who tried it next. What came of them?"

"Thomas, everyone in the Hether Blether expedition *died*. Horribly. People weren't exactly lining up to repeat their mistake."

"Mistake?" Thomas said, stunned. "They knew exactly what they were doing—trying to save magic. Being brave is a risk, not a mistake.

They wanted to be extraordinary. To embrace all that they were capable of. To be legend."

Descriptions of Alice Gray's body filled Sigrid's mind. Her skin sucked tight around her bones, scarred with symbols no expert had been able to interpret. "Why be extraordinary if that's the cost?"

Thomas grabbed her wrist. "Because of the cost of doing nothing." He met her gaze with a challenge. "People die either way. If you act, at least their blood isn't on your hands."

Sigrid shook off his grip and stood. "Alice might have owed the world some magic. I don't think she owed us her life."

"*Sigrid!*" Annabel swept into the room. "Time to get your head out of those books, Sig, ol' girl."

"You've no idea," Sigrid agreed. She grabbed her bag and turned her back on Thomas. "I need a break from him."

"Who?" Annabel threw an arm around Sigrid and steered her toward the billiards table in the other corner. A group of scraggly boys were getting ready to start a game. They twisted chalk on their cues and watched the girls approach. "Here's what we're going to do," Annabel said. "We're going to watch these wankers play pool, bet on the one with the cutest arse, and by the end of the night we won't care about who's won, or applications, or London, or any damn thing."

Sigrid looked back and saw Thomas stuffing his satchel with books. She could see the disappointment in his eyes.

Sigrid was easily seduced into Annabel's world of casual fun. When Annabel was around, it seemed so simple to knock off and *enjoy* things. To ignore the part of her brain that buzzed with anxious thoughts, focusing instead on a drink, a flirt, the possibility of comfort and peace. In time she could learn to mimic the easy cadence of Annabel's crowd, Sigrid told herself. She could be happy.

The billiards table was crowded with Pendle Hill's finest. They stood close, jostling and throwing insults, alive with laughter. Sigrid wondered when, exactly, they'd all grown so comfortable with one another. Annabel leaned against the wall, talking to a student whose name Sigrid couldn't recall. Blake, maybe, or Blair, or Blaine. They were talking about positions, of course.

"I'm after one with Manchester United," BlakeBlairBlaine said.

"Wow!" Annabel said. "That's on."

"Wait—what?" Sigrid said, sharp. "You're a witch. You know that, right?"

"Right?" he said. "What of it?"

"You can do magic. And you want to work for a football club?"

"Not just any club, is it?"

Sigrid shook her head, incredulous. "Who cares? You'd never be able to use your abilities. You'd be forever hiding what you are."

BlakeBlairBlaine shrugged. "It's not like I'm saving the world, levitating small objects or hexing stains out of my loafers. Parlor tricks."

"Exactly," Annabel laughed. She tossed her gleaming hair. She was *flirting*, Sigrid realized, and with that unevolved cretin.

Sigrid longed to retaliate somehow, to decelerate the billiard balls until they retraced their trajectories. Maybe send the whole room back to a few minutes before the game had even started. Show Annabel and all the rest a fraction of the power they so casually dismissed. But she'd been so careful to keep the extent of her powers under wraps; just because she wanted to prove a point didn't mean she suddenly trusted her classmates.

In that moment, Sigrid understood that being extraordinary wasn't something she could curb forever. There was no opting out.

Parlor tricks.

"Right." Sigrid turned to Annabel. "Want to get out of here?"

Annabel hesitated. Sigrid's stomach dropped. Her face flared red at the sight of Annabel's pitying expression.

"Well," Sigrid said. "It's been a gas."

Annabel twisted her mouth up. "Oh, come on, Sig. Don't go." Her fingers grazed Sigrid's, lightly.

Sigrid drew back her arm. "'Don't go' is not the same as 'stay.'" She pulled the satchel strap over her shoulder. "Have a good life," Sigrid said, stepping away. "You deserve it."

ைை

That Sunday morning, like every other, Sigrid waited for Thomas at the kebab stand by the river, across the Thames from Parliament. Thomas's approaching form was unmistakable: shoulders curled under a wool camel coat and a short-legged gait slightly off for his limber frame.

"Kebab?" His eyes brightened at the food cart's rotating slab of lamb. Thomas always offered, and Sigrid always refused. They fell into an easy stride, pacing side by side. They'd been taking these walks since the first term. It was here that Thomas had admitted no one in the States knew he was a witch. He hadn't been back to visit in three years, so far as Sigrid could recall. And it was where she first admitted out loud that she'd been holding back in lessons, afraid to show anyone all that she was capable of. It felt like whispering secrets into a forgetful wind.

They sat on a bench just off the walkway, under a dogwood tree. The sun peered from behind clouds, falling on the river's choppy surface like flashing diamonds.

"So—Alice Gray," Thomas said. "I've been researching her and Hether Blether. Her diary was in the school library. Hadn't been checked out in a dozen years. She was top of her class, brains beyond reason. Awash in banality, striving to be great."

"I know." Sigrid knew the diary. She knew all the books Thomas must have devoured in the last few days. The story of Hether Blether had consumed her for years. Now it was all coming back again.

Thomas ran a hand through his hair, leaving spikes in its wake. "She's you," he said.

"What are you on about?"

"She's you, Sig, I swear it. She was extraordinary, and looking for a mission worthy of her talents. Saving magic."

"Fat lot of good it did her, or any of her friends."

Thomas shook his head. "That isn't the point. They were willing to try." He paused. "And anyway—there are theories." Sigrid squinted at him. Thomas continued: "Things they could have done differently. There are legends from Iceland and Norway about what travelers can do to ward off the sorcerer's influence, or to stay mentally agile in his presence. He poses riddles, apparently, some kind of clever ultimatum, and those who answer are magically bound by the outcome." He nudged her gently with his elbow. "There's also the fact that we're far more powerful than Alice was."

"We can't know that."

"If Alice or any of the witches in the expedition were as powerful as we are, she would have noted it."

"What are you saying?"

"We could do it, Sig. You and me. By claiming the island and gaining all the sorcerer's knowledge, we could save magic." Thomas turned to her, his face cast in mottled shadow under the flowering tree.

Thomas leaned back against the bench, eyes shut. "The day I learned that the word for what I am was 'magic'—that was the best day of my life." As he spoke, the velvety white petals of the dogwood tree's flowers began to unfurl. "You can't tell me this is all life is. Just another way to wear a suit and work till we expire." The petals began to shimmer, filling with blues and reds and purples. "Alice wanted the world to open for her, to show her something incredible and new. She saw the chance to be a legend and she took it."

Sigrid felt a shiver as the idea bloomed in her mind, wild and absurd and—somehow—inevitable. Sigrid's heart kicked into overdrive. For the first time, she let herself envision the future that would unfurl from going north to face a great unknown.

Gently, she placed a hand on Thomas's shoulder. He opened his eyes. Sigrid nodded up at the tree. The dogwood's flowers had blossomed in fluorescent hues, gleaming like gently folded rainbows. Thomas blinked and every petal released, fluttering down around them like natural confetti. Flecks of lavender and fuchsia and goldenrod settled in his hair and on his shoulders, brushing his lapel like a telltale kiss.

"Alice Gray never found that new, incredible thing," Sigrid said.

"She died trying," Thomas said. "That's more than most of us will die doing." He searched her face. "You're more than Alice Gray could have ever hoped to be."

Sigrid thought of Annabel's wide eyes and easy smile. She imagined leaving a mind-numbing position in the city to catch drinks with Annabel at a pub, hoping half-witted hooligans would pay their tab, waking up with fuzzy heads the next morning, the greatest hope being a repeat of the previous day.

The thought that she could learn that rhythm was a lie she could no longer stomach.

"For all the witches hiding their power. For magic." Thomas's hand grazed her cheek, thumb wiping away the single tear that fell there. "For Alice."

Sigrid rested her hand on his arm. He gave a surprised shout as she pinched him, hard.

"For ourselves."

∽

They wasted little time. Monday morning, they were at the train station. Thomas was a wreck. He couldn't figure out the ticket machine or navigate the station. He became so overwhelmed that Sigrid eventually told him to shut up and follow her lead. The moment she deposited him in the train cabin, he folded a new leaf of khat in his mouth, sank low with his head against the windowpane, and began to snore. Sigrid sat on the bench across from him and bit her nails, watching London recede in their wake.

Her pack sagged at her feet, stuffed with survival equipment and magical tools. She'd brought an iron stake—according to legend, a must for any traveler hoping to come upon the hidden island—and a carnelian stone to help point the way. Several small cloth bags were filled with various gemstones and crystals: healing and amplifying, heart-opening and evil-warding. These items, and matches, and their wits.

Hours later, Thomas woke.

"Hello," he said, groggily righting himself.

Sigrid stared at him. "What are we doing?" she asked. "Alice and the others were prepared. They planned extensively. They'd been circling together for weeks before they left—knew each other's magic, inside and out."

"You know my magic," Thomas said. "You know everything." He reached for Sigrid's feet, propped on the bench beside him.

Sigrid drew them back.

He sighed. "You've been preparing for this your whole life."

As they chugged farther into the Highlands, the world became over-saturated in the eerie blue-green of a dense forest, or of leagues under the sea. A curve in the tracks revealed a wide, churning river outside the window. The train soared over it on a bridge so thin Sigrid felt like they were flying.

He was right, of course. Every kilometer they traveled felt like it was bringing Sigrid closer to where she was meant to be—or, perhaps, where she could not have avoided ending up.

⚬✕⚬

Ferrying a boat to Eynhallow was difficult. It was the off season, and local fishermen were superstitious about the tides. Finally, they found an ancient mariner swathed in a cloak, eating canned fish beside a rusted trawler. They had to repeat their request three times while the man gummed sardines with golden teeth, but eventually he'd nodded. Neither Thomas nor Sigrid dared ask any questions when he immediately ushered them onto his boat and untied it from the dock, its sputtering engine jettisoning them away from shore.

The wind was icy and merciless. Sigrid inched nearer to Thomas, aglow as ever with warmth. His eyes, clear and sharp as glass, darted across the water as the boat sliced through the sound. The fisherman killed the engine and the trawler glided toward a dilapidated dock. Sigrid leaped from the boat's deck to the dock, grasping Thomas's hand in terror. Luckily, the dock held, though its wooden slats were soft under her tread.

"Best be careful, miss. Fog's rolling in," the mariner said, his Orkney accent nearly unintelligible. "Don't seem right, a young woman traveling the islands alone."

Sigrid narrowed her eyes in confusion. Within moments the trawler receded into the mist.

"Crazy old dodger," Thomas muttered, shouldering his pack.

Eynhallow was tiny and flat, tipped like a dish in a sink. The tall end, buttressed by craggy cliffs, rolled down to a shallow shoreline on the other side. The edges of the island were hidden by a creeping mist. Like many places empty of people, Eynhallow brimmed with all manner of the inhuman. Sigrid felt a lingering dread, and the buzz of unfamiliar magic just under the skin.

The island's undulating green was littered with moss-covered boulders and anonymous cairns. The whipping wind sent a chill right to the bone. It was not hard to believe, navigating the pockmarked landscape, that this was about as close as one could get to the edge of the world.

Thomas set off north and slightly west, across the heart of the island, directly through the monastery remains where Alice Gray and her two fellows had been found. He moved among the ruins with an odd ease, as though returning to a place he once knew. The rubble was crawling with latent hexes. The wind seemed to whistle around the crumbling ruins—or was it a whisper?

Sigrid crouched in the grass near Alice's final resting place. What force could possibly have made someone so smart and accomplished willingly lie down to die? Sigrid shut her eyes and tried to call forth any residual magic, anything Alice might have left behind. There was something . . . a wisp of feeling. Sigrid opened herself to it, allowing her heart to be touched by what remained of Alice's soul.

Fear.

Fathomless, unhinged fear. And, tangled in the dread and anger, a warning:

DON'T TRUST THE CHOICE.

Sigrid recoiled, pulling her wool coat tight around herself.

Thomas led them to the shore. Their footsteps in the short, wiry grass made no sound and left no mark. The fog bank had farther advanced, and there was nothing now to differentiate the steel-grey ocean from its ruff of murk. They stood at the water's edge, squinting.

Sigrid tried not to think of the other explorers, found on the sand, grasping. The image of their half-rotted bodies crept over her sight in that now-familiar way. In the cold, surrounded by such powerful and foreign energy, she lacked the will to fight off Thomas's visions. Sigrid saw what he saw: the gruesome spectacle of death. Just beyond the bodies, one of the rowboats was beached, nodding in the lapping waves.

"Thomas," Sigrid warned. As quickly as the vision crept in, it washed away. But Sigrid blinked, once, twice, and still the boat remained.

Thomas grasped it by the bow. He'd conjured the boat whole cloth from his own mind.

"Are you ready?" he asked, planting one foot inside the vessel. He reached a hand out to her.

Alice's warning echoed in Sigrid's mind. But she and Thomas had come this far. There was no turning back.

Sigrid took Thomas's hand and crawled into the boat, gasping as it teetered in the shallows. They shoved off from shore, and within minutes Eynhallow disappeared.

Sigrid held fast to the iron stake. With her other hand, she worried the carnelian stone hanging around her neck, which seemed to pulse and warm as Thomas rowed.

"What's it saying?" Thomas asked. "Are we on the right track?"

Sigrid shut her eyes and held the stone tight in her palm. She called forth the memory of Alice's ghost and its desperate cry. As the stone throbbed, Alice's warning grew louder, stronger, and more urgent.

"We're getting closer," Sigrid said. "Keep rowing."

The mist around them, dark as pitch when they left the shore, began to warm and brighten. It was a contrast to the growing burden of Alice's screams, pressing in on Sigrid's mind.

"Closer," she said, breathing shallow. "Very close."

Not a minute later, the boat scraped rocky land. Thomas leaped over the bow and dragged it farther ashore. Steep cliffs loomed over the shore. They walked cautiously, looking for any path, any sign of life.

"Don't lose grip of the stake," Thomas called over his shoulder.

Sigrid held it to her chest with a white-knuckle grip. If she let go, Hether Blether could disappear entirely. The stone in Sigrid's hand began to throb with heat. "The sorcerer. He's near," she whispered.

A sharp crackling was the only warning before rocks rained down on them. Thomas grabbed Sigrid and shoved her against the cliff, flattening them both. When the storm of debris slowed, they saw a shape atop the crag, a darker shadow in dark fog.

Sigrid examined the cliff side. She tucked the iron stake into her bra. Its rough edges cut the gentle skin of her chest. Using slim footholds and crevasses in the cliff's sheer sides, she climbed closer to the top, until finally her aching fingers grasped a flat edge with grass and stubborn-rooted plants. Sigrid looked up and saw Thomas peering over the side.

"How did you—"

Before Sigrid could finish her question she felt her toe slipping. "Help," she gasped.

Thomas just stared.

Sigrid's grip on the shrubs and barbed plants started to give way, shallow roots peeling back from the crag. With a final desperate heave, Sigrid dragged her elbows over the top. Using the last of her strength, she hauled one leg, then another, over the edge.

On her knees, she took gasping breaths. From the corner of her eye, she saw the filthy toes of Thomas's trainers. "You rutting bastard," she rasped, lifting her head.

But past Thomas, through the dawn-like glow of mist pressing in on them, a dusky shape moved . . .

Walking. Toward them.

Thomas turned. Sigrid stood. The figure moved through a halo of golden light. It took the shape of a broad-chested man wearing an elegantly draped tunic with a wide braided belt, and a heavy cloak lined with fur.

"It's you," Sigrid breathed.

He had olive skin and a mass of dark curls. His trimmed beard held two prongs of grey. He seemed to hold light, to exude an aura of calm.

"I don't know your name," she said.

The man shook his head. "You've brought much with you." He waved a hand and the earth beside him cratered, forming a pit of loamy dirt. With a snap of his fingers, a fire appeared there, absent kindling to stoke the flame. It burned green and sulfurous. "It must all be sacrificed to get what you seek."

Sigrid shook her head. "How do you know what I'm after?" she asked.

The man held his arms wide. "You seek everything," he said simply. "Like all the rest. But first you must choose."

"Choose?"

The man shifted his dark eyes to Thomas. "The others. Or yourself."

Sigrid shook her head. "I don't understand."

"Only one of you can continue. If you seek to know all, to apprentice the heavens, to shape the universe—you must make a decision."

Sigrid looked down and gasped. The iron stake was in her hand, biting the thin skin of her fingers.

Thomas stepped back. He stared at her with an eerie calm, the look that had returned fire for so many all-night arguments. The same expression that had gawked, unfeeling, at her as she teetered on the edge of the cliff.

"This was the choice you gave Alice Gray," Sigrid said, meeting the sorcerer's black eyes.

He raised an eyebrow. "After a fashion."

In the end, the expedition had been asked to sacrifice one another so one among them could gain everything. And they'd all said no. Alice had said no.

Extraordinary, Thomas had called them. *Brilliant.*

Selfless. Stupid. Brave.

Thomas had no weapons, but his hands twitched at his sides, itching to gesture magic into being. Sigrid's vision began to darken. He was calling magic to him, and pulling her into his sight—he never did learn to control it.

"What happened to saving the world?" Sigrid whispered.

"One of us would," Thomas said, shaking his head. "And one of us can die trying. A legend. Just like Alice."

The blackness overwhelmed her vision. Then Sigrid saw herself through Thomas's eyes, staring back with a look that could cut diamond. Her white-blond hair, loose from its braid, whipped around her head in the chaotic ocean wind. She stood just a few yards from the cliff's edge, legs spread wide, arms tight at her sides: a warrior's stance. Her grip on the stake was so tight, blood seeped between her fingers.

Thomas was waiting for Sigrid to follow in Alice Gray's footsteps. To take the selfless path—to be brave. When Thomas said Sigrid could have it all, he meant until it cost him something. He wanted her to sacrifice herself, leaving Thomas to save magic and take all the glory.

But Thomas had said it himself: if Alice had been half as powerful as they were, things would have been different. *Don't trust the choice.* In her final moments, Alice had been filled with terror and regret for her sacrifice.

All Sigrid felt was calm.

Sigrid watched herself advance on Thomas, arm raised. She witnessed the cold glaze in her own eyes as her hand arced down, burying the iron stake in his stomach. Sigrid grabbed Thomas and shoved him back, pushing the stake farther into his soft belly, dragging him to the cliff's edge. Her hand was warm with his gushing blood. His body twitched, fighting the lightning-fast march to death.

"I didn't come here to save magic," she said, her ice-blue eyes calm and clear. "I came here to prove that I could."

And when she blinked—release. Thomas's head rolled up to the honeyed sky as his body fell backward to the shore.

In the next blink, Sigrid returned to herself, looking over the cliff's edge into nothingness. There was no sound of body meeting rock. The fog was too thick to see where Thomas found his final rest. All was silent besides the persistent waves and the steady *clunk-clunk* of the dingy battering the rocky shore.

She turned back to the man, breathing hard, hair in her eyes.

"Is it resolved?" His dark stare was relentless.

Sigrid began to walk toward him when pain exploded in her belly. She passed a hand over her stomach. It came away wet with blood. In her shock, a partially chewed khat leaf fell from her mouth.

Sigrid blinked and saw the bright arc of sky. She blinked and saw her hand coated in gore. She shut her eyes, mind spinning.

"Is it resolved?" the man repeated. "Have you chosen?"

Daring to open her eyes, Sigrid saw one thing clearly: the magical flame dancing at the sorcerer's feet. It cast no shadow, nor emitted any heat. It was nothing more than a trick—a figment of something real, created to give meaning to something abstract, subconscious. And on it would flicker, until the sorcerer had no more need of it.

Thomas's body had made no sound, as insubstantial in death as it had been in life. Just a figment of Sigrid's whim.

She drew up, the pain in her stomach melting away. The iron stake still lay in the crabgrass, but Sigrid splayed her fingers: no blood or markings remained. She stretched her neck and took a breath, feeling full, buoyed, whole.

"It is done."

"Good," the man said. He turned, beckoning her to follow. "Then we can begin."

Sophia Lee's Villain Challenge to Sarah Enni:

A Dark Sorcerer's Motives for Seeking Immortality or Omnipotence

WILL THE REAL VILLAIN PLEASE STAND UP?

BY SOPHIA LEE

I don't like villains.

Not because they're evil or because they're universally unpopular, but because they're weak—and I don't mean weak in terms of physical strength or magical power, but that they're weak in their characterization. So I asked Sarah to create something—or someone—different.

MY VILLAIN GOALS FOR SARAH:

1) A villain so compelling, I would question rooting for the protagonist
2) A villain with comprehensive backstory
3) A villain with incredible power and a desire to use it
4) A villain whose moral code was debatable
5) A villain who would make me reconsider what it means to be a villain

And so Sarah created Sigrid. Sigrid was a character that left me feeling both satisfied and conflicted.

HOW SIGRID DOES "VILLAIN" RIGHT:

1) She wanted to know the limits of her strength
2) She was focused and determined
3) She didn't want to waste her potential
4) She discouraged complacence
5) She was talented and powerful

WAYS SIGRID SETS OFF ALL THE WRONG ALARMS:

1) Her interests were only for herself, not for the greater good
2) She was tempted by (and succumbed to her thirst for) power
3) She believed she murdered her best friend
4) And felt no remorse about it
5) And considered no other options

Sigrid's character resonated with me so much that I wondered what it revealed about my own character. (Yikes.) Although I could see telltale signs of evil in Sigrid's actions, I could also easily see myself making similar decisions. It made me realize how much the line between hero and villain could be blurred.

I've always been the protagonist of my own story, but it's interesting to think I could be a villain in somebody else's. Somebody out there has tried to attain or achieve something, and I have stood in their way. To an extent, we're each an encapsulation of both protagonist and antagonist, hero and villain. Sarah highlights the flexibility of these roles with Sigrid alone.

Sigrid was ambitious, yes, and the immensity of her power was virtually inarguable. But she was also intelligent and relatable and, most importantly, comprehensible in her motivation. She stood in a grey field of ambiguity, and upon finishing the story, I discovered with welcome surprise that I wasn't entirely convinced that Sigrid was our villain.

I easily adopted the perception that she was solely a determined girl whose only crime—if even that—was that she wanted to see just how far she could push herself. That's not necessarily a bad thing. I mean,

I do it every day at school. Of course, she also mercilessly murdered someone who turned out to be unreal, and I, for one, don't do that at school. At least, not every day. But even though Sigrid was cold and ruthless, she also felt reasonable to a degree that leaves me wondering. Who is the real villain in this story?

Not only did Sarah leave me with questions about the ethical boundaries that restrict our fictional characters' categorizations of good and evil, but she also left me pondering the fictional setting of her story—a world that deals with magic in a unique and refreshing way.

THINGS I STILL WANTED TO KNOW AFTER FINISHING:

1) Who is the Harry Potter to Sigrid's Voldemort? Whose antagonist is she?
2) What will she do with her power?
3) What will magical politics be like afterward?
4) Can she decide who's allowed to use the magic reservoir?
5) What did Thomas represent?

Perhaps the answers to all my questions don't really matter. What I read was enough to make me genuinely think about *what* makes a villain, and that's what I wanted from the beginning.

THE SEA WITCH

BY MARISSA MEYER

The razor-sharp barnacles clawed at my fingertips as I strained to wrench them free of the rotting wood. I cursed them repeatedly as I worked, not having known the depths of my hatred for barnacles until this moment. Vicious, stubborn little parasites. Vile, thankless cadgers.

It wasn't long before I was also cursing my own feeble muscles and long, ink-black hair that wouldn't stop swimming in front of my face and obscuring my vision. Another barnacle sliced into my palm and I let out a scream of frustration. Grabbing the whale-bone knife from my sack, I lifted the blade over my shoulder with every intention of hacking the nasty creatures to pieces, but I resisted the temptation long enough for the fury to pass. My heart was still thumping, but reason began to return. I needed the barnacles intact or this wouldn't work. I needed them whole.

I drew in a mouthful of salt water, swished it angrily around my cheeks, then forced it out through my teeth. My tail flicked against the side of the long-drowned ship, making a hollow drumming sound that matched my pulse. Eyeing the barnacles, I resolved that I would not be deterred. They were the last ingredient I needed, and I would have them, no matter if they left my fingertips shredded and scarred. After all, what was this temporary pain to a lifetime of bliss?

Shoving my drifting hair out of my face, I returned to my work, digging the point of the dagger around the barnacles' edges. I leveraged it against the wood, prying and grunting. The wood began to crumble and I grasped the edge of a waterlogged plank and pulled hard, bracing my tail against the ship's side. It creaked and groaned and finally released, just as a particularly cruel barnacle sliced through the pad of my thumb. I yanked my hand away with a snarl. Blood blossomed like pearls on my skin before dispersing in the dark water.

"That's it," I growled, stabbing at the traitorous barnacle. With a *pop*, it dislodged and sank down toward the ocean floor. It wasn't as satisfying a death as I would have hoped, but no matter. I had what I'd come for.

Opening the sack that bobbed on my shoulder, I stashed the splintered plank of barnacle-infested wood inside. *Twenty live barnacles*, the spell demanded. I had twice that, but I wanted to be sure I had plenty, in case something went wrong and I had to start over. I'd never tried such a complicated spell before, nor had I ever so badly wanted one to work. *Needed* one to work.

That left only one more ingredient to gather: three silver scales taken from the tail of the merman I wished to fall in love with me.

I still wasn't sure how I would get close enough to Prince Lorindel to cut three scales from his tail, but the royal concert was tonight and he was sure to be there. Surrounded by his horrid entourage, no doubt, but they couldn't spend the entire evening at his side. And I only had to get close enough for a moment.

Three scales. Three insignificant little scales, and by this time tomorrow, Lorindel would be mine.

I shut my eyes, clutching my bag to my chest. Brave Lorindel, who had slain an elusive frilled shark and brought its body back for the entire kingdom to feast on. Kind Lorindel, who had labored beside the working merfolk to build shelters for creatures who had lost their homes in the aftermath of a devastating surface storm. Fair Lorindel, with his cunning, boyish smile. Good Lorindel, who was destined for greatness, who would be king, who would need a queen.

I opened my eyes, buoyed by the longing that pulsated beneath my skin.

I would be that queen.

My tail twisted in the wet sand as I turned away from the ship, shifted the bag on my shoulder, and pushed myself upward. I kept hold of my knife, ever wary of predators, but my thoughts still drifted toward my spell and my prince.

I ducked beneath the mast of the ship, which had fallen ages ago, its massive sails long eroded by the water, and was gliding over the ship's bow when a form rose up before me. I cried out and tried to stop, but my momentum carried me straight into the merman's chest.

A chuckle vibrated in the water around us. Hands gripped my shoulders, easing me away from him. My heart skittered as I recognized the face—that perfect, beautiful face. Lorindel's mouth was wide and amused, his black eyes locked onto mine, his blond hair swirling in the current.

"This is a surprise, Nerit," he said. And *oh*, my name, in that voice. A shudder cascaded from my neck to the tip of my tail. "What are you doing so close to the shallows?"

"I—nothing," I stammered before amending it to, "Just looking."

I swallowed hard. His hands were still on my shoulders.

He was *so close.* Never once had he been so close to me, other than perhaps a brief passing in the coral halls of the Sea King's castle. There had never been a reason for him to be so close to me. I was no one.

"Looking for what?" There was mirth in his expression. His eyes held me in place, as resolute as a barnacle clinging to the body of a ship.

I thought of the barnacles in the bag that even now bounced against my side. I thought of the spell book lying in my cave, the ingredients scrawled out by some ancient hand. I debated if I had any reason to lie—but then, what would I say if not the truth?

"Barnacles," I whispered.

"Barnacles?" His voice had a laugh in it. "Those mean little suckers? Whatever would you want with them?"

Before I could formulate a logical response, his hands were tracing down my arms, past my elbows to my wrists and, finally, my fingers. Every gliding touch sent a flurry of tingles across my skin.

"You're hurt," he said, his brow dipping with sympathy as he lifted my hand. The pad of his thumb traced mine. The tip of his tail brushed against my fin.

His tail. He was so close, and I was still holding the knife.

But how could I take three scales now without him noticing?

"Is this from the barnacles?" he asked, indicating the wound that had stopped bleeding.

I nodded.

A sly glint entering his eyes, Lorindel took my thumb into his mouth.

I squeaked. His tongue rolled over the tip of my thumb and a current of desire rocked into me. I dropped the dagger. The bag slipped from my shoulder, sinking toward the deck of the ship.

I swayed toward the prince, swooning, yearning . . .

"I've got it!"

Lorindel jerked back, fast as a skittish triggerfish. Turning his head to one side, he spat, his face blanching. "Took long enough."

I spun around.

Lorindel's three closest confidantes surrounded us—the twins, Merryl and Murdoch, eagerly flapping their gold-tipped fins, and beautiful, silver-tailed Beldine, the girl who had long been rumored to be Lorindel's future bride. She was holding my sack, already clawing through it while the others watched, smirking.

My brain was still fogged from Lorindel's touch, and it was a long, muddied moment before I could grasp the reality. This—all of it—had been a trick. A diversion to get my pack.

Mortification burned across my skin.

"Barnacles, just like she said." Beldine pulled a strip of wood from the pack. "Along with some fish bones, snail shells, and—" She gasped and recoiled.

I knew what she had seen before she reached in and pulled out the single octopus tentacle, holding it between her fingertips as if afraid it would bite her. She threw the tentacle onto the ship's deck and turned a repulsed scowl toward me. "No, you didn't. You *witch*."

I cringed. "Witch" was not an insult lightly used. Our elders told tales of sea witches long dead. They were said to be sickly, slimy creatures who fed on fish spines and used their cruel magic to bring misery upon innocent merfolk who stumbled unwittingly into their path.

"Nerit," said Lorindel, his previously tender voice now as rough as coral, "tell me the creature wasn't alive when you took this."

I glanced at him, my jaw unhinged. He looked angry, but also . . . ashamed.

Of *me*?

I tried to back away, but the twins were there to stop me, and I had nowhere to go.

The truth was that the octopus *had* been alive when I had taken my blade to one of its eight legs, holding the beast down with the flat of my palm while I sawed it off. This wasn't my choice, though. It had to be taken alive, for the spell to work.

My bottom lip began to tremble. I looked from the prince to Beldine to Merryl to Murdoch. All of them stared at me with the disgust I'd almost—*almost*—grown used to.

Merryl cursed beneath her breath, an odd tinge to her pallor as she looked down at the tentacle. "It's just like the sea horses all over again."

Of course she would bring up those damned sea horses, hateful girl. It should have been long forgotten, but they refused to forget. It was one of my earliest attempts to perform a spell from the old books, and I had required a ring of sea horses strung together in a protective circle. I had hunted down fifty of the tiny creatures, and ever-so-carefully pushed a needle through each of their spiraled tails, pulling the string through their flesh, one by one.

It was only a small wound. It wouldn't have *killed* them. And the spell would have given me the ability to command schools of fish. For weeks, I had dreamed of my own personal entourage of butterfly fish that would follow me everywhere I went. There were days when I still dreamed of it.

It would have worked, too, if Beldine hadn't found me, thirty sea horses in, and started shrieking as though she'd just seen a murder. Lorindel and the twins had not been far behind, and Lorindel had forced me to release the creatures. And the looks they had given me . . . the look *he* had given me . . .

That was the moment I realized I was different from them, some-how, and Lorindel's sneer spoke plainly that my differences were not endearing. In fact, my interest in long-forgotten magic was barely above tolerable.

I feigned indifference, and over time that indifference became a well-crafted shell. For years, I pitied those around me, those who were not enlightened to the possibilities of enchantment. Those who would live their trivial lives and die without knowing what it was like to undo a piece of the world and weave it into something new. I mocked the insignificant worries of my peers. I judged their silly gossip and believed myself above them all.

But I was a fool. For all the time I'd spent with my condescension, I could yet find no fault with Prince Lorindel. Years had passed. I was more alone than ever, and now I was desperately, agonizingly in love.

"You're *sick*," said the boy twin, Murdoch, lowering his face toward mine. I backed away, but he persisted. "You should be cast out with the bottom-feeders before your foul blood poisons the rest of us."

"N-no," I stammered. "I didn't do anything. That tentacle wasn't . . . It was . . . I just found it . . ."

"You're lying." Lorindel rounded on me, drawing closer until he was all I could see, as close as he'd been before, but this time I found myself shrinking back, searching for a way to escape the gaze that burrowed into my skin. "That was a beast of my father's kingdom, of *my* kingdom—and you mutilated it. And for what? A silly spell in some book?"

My heartbeat quickened, racing now. All my nerves teemed with the desire to flee, but I couldn't move, not even to escape Lorindel's wrath.

Even now I found myself hoping that I could make him see that I had no other choice. He must know that I had to do it, that I had loved him for so very long, that anyone would have gone to such lengths . . .

But my thoughts stumbled and finally halted—*he knew*.

He knew about the spell. They all knew.

"How?" I whispered. "How do you know?"

"We saw you leaving your cave this morning," said Murdoch, "and thought we'd take a look around."

Merryl folded her arms over her chest. "Always been curious to know what you do in that creepy place, all alone every day. We found your morbid collection, all those macabre little trinkets . . ."

"And then we found the book," said Beldine, gliding closer to me. "Conveniently left open to a spell meant to force someone into falling in love." She clicked her tongue. "You shouldn't have written Lorindel's name on the pages, sweet Nerit. It made it all a bit too easy to figure out."

I turned to the prince, pleading. "I meant no harm. I only thought . . . I'd hoped that if . . . if I could . . ." My chest felt as if it would cave in as I appealed to Lorindel, reaching for his hands, but he pulled away before I could touch him. "Please, Your Highness, you don't understand. I . . . I *love* you. I always have. I would do *anything* . . ."

"Then you will hold your tongue, and you will never speak to me again. You disgust me." His eyes narrowed, lacking any hint of pity. "I order you to leave my sight before I'm sick to my stomach."

As a sob quaked through my body, I turned and fled.

I swam as hard as I could, my cries swallowed up by the sea. I had only one place to go. Only one place that had ever felt like solace in a kingdom where everyone hated me, had always hated me, where no one even tried to see beneath my shell and understand how I wanted to be one of them, I wanted to belong . . .

But when I arrived at the entrance to my cave, I drew up short.

They had destroyed it. Clay pots were shattered on the floor. Squid ink had been smeared over my artwork and notes. Skulls and bones and fossils were left broken and scattered in the sand.

No longer a sanctuary, this felt more like a tomb.

With a wail of agony, I turned and swam upward instead.

☙

I lay sprawled on the sandy shore, staring at a dark sky that swirled with gems. I had been shivering for hours, my teeth chattering with every gust of wind, but I liked the cold. It was numbing, and the breeze had dried my skin, leaving rough trails of salt over my body.

Lorindel hated me.

For years, I had imagined myself invisible to him, and I had hoped the spell would change that. I had dreamed so many times of the day, that moment, when his eyes would pass over the crowd and find *me*, more brilliant and deserving than any other mermaid in the kingdom. I had known we were meant to be together. I had believed it down to my bones.

But I could no longer deny the truth. I was not invisible to him. I was *contemptible.*

I decided then, staring at the stars, that I would never again return to the sea. I would die here on this shore, cold and alone. Perhaps I deserved it. Surely I didn't deserve to be loved, for, otherwise, wouldn't I have found someone to love me by now?

Yes. This would be the fate of poor, pathetic Nerit. Perhaps a human fisherman would someday find my bones whitened in the sun, and I would become a legend. It was a better fate than any that awaited me beneath the waves.

"Hello? Miss?"

I gasped and jerked upward, spinning my body around to see a human male picking his way over the driftwood and scattered stones.

My hair prickled.

The man paused when he took in my expression. "I'm sorry. I didn't mean to startle you. To be honest, I wasn't sure if you were a girl or a seal. You were lying so still—I thought maybe you were hurt." He moved closer, stepping over a large piece of driftwood. "Are you . . ." His question trailed off as his eyes swept down my body. I didn't know if he noticed my nakedness first or my long tail, but either way, he froze. His eyes widened.

I turned and began to scurry down the beach toward the waves. The tide had gone out while I'd lain there, and the ocean was much farther away than I'd thought, but my arms and tail were strong as they propelled me across the sand.

"No—wait!"

I paused.

I didn't know why. I knew that I shouldn't. Every story I'd ever heard of man told me to escape into the water and never look back.

Perhaps I was not so keen to die on this beach as I'd thought.

Maybe it was my broken heart, or some part of me that was enchanted by the idea of this being, this man, calling for me. Wanting me to stay.

This man who didn't know me and therefore could not yet despise me.

I licked my lips and looked back over my shoulder.

He hadn't moved. His hands were held out, perhaps in an effort to keep from frightening me any more than could be helped. In the faint moonlight, I could tell he was not beautiful, but neither was he unfortunate to look on. He was of slight build, with dark hair cut short and a rather pointy nose, almost beak-like. When he smiled, though, he had a pronounced dimple in his left cheek that was very nearly charming.

He was smiling now.

I swallowed.

"Hello," he said, barely above a whisper, as if to be louder would startle me away. And perhaps it would. My fingers were still burrowing into the sand. My tail was a twitch away from pushing me the last length into the water.

"My name is Samuel," he said, taking one step closer. When I did not move, he dared to take another. "And you are a dream sprang to life."

His gaze slipped down to my tail again, one curious, rapturous look. "And you're *beautiful.*"

The compliment struck my heart as fast and sharp as a hunter's harpoon.

His stunned gaze found mine again, and he seemed to grow bashful. His attention dipped to the sand, then to me. Out to the ocean, and back to me.

"I'm sorry," he said. "You probably have no idea what I'm saying. Can you speak? Do . . . do your kind have . . . a language? I wonder if maybe . . ."

"I understand you."

His eyes widened again.

"My name is Nerit."

He stared at me for such a long time that I thought maybe he had forgotten there were ocean and stars and sand at all. Maybe he had forgotten all the world but for me. It was the first time anyone had looked at me like that.

Samuel eased himself down into the sand and smiled his warm, dimpled smile. Then he asked me to tell him all about the world beneath the sea.

☯

I came to the same beach every night after that, and always Samuel was waiting for me. We were both shy at first, nervous and bumbling. But soon talking to Samuel became as natural as swimming through the salt-heavy waters. We would stretch out beside each other and I would be hypnotized by the cadences of his voice. I loved to listen to him. I loved how he hardened his consonants and drawled his vowels. I loved the stories he told. Tales of sailors lost at sea who came back telling of merfolk and Sirens.

He told me of the townspeople who laughed at them and those who believed.

He told me of wars fought in distant lands, and gods who were loved and gods who were feared, and how his favorite sound was church bells on Sunday afternoons and how his favorite food was something called bread coated with sweet butter and sticky marmalade. My mouth watered when he tried to describe them, though I couldn't begin to imagine these foreign flavors.

He told me how he had once had a sweetheart, but she had married a man who wasn't poor like he was, and how he had spent the last three years of his life trying to be happy for her.

Weeks passed before Samuel dared to touch me. A brush of fingers through the tips of my drying hair. Then a knuckle against my shoulder. He never touched my tail, though he often stared at it with mystified awe.

"You must be beloved," he said one night, a month after our first meeting. "You must be admired and doted upon by all your brethren in the sea."

A laugh escaped me before I could stop it. Samuel cocked his head and furrowed his brow in a way that was adorably human.

I considered lying. I was pleased by the idea that Samuel saw me that way—*beloved*—and I didn't want to destroy such a perception. But I couldn't lie to him, not after he had told me so many truths.

"No, Samuel. I am . . . not well liked by my kind."

Samuel frowned. "How can that be?"

"They think I'm strange. My whole life I've been shunned, mocked for my talents, and pushed away . . ." I swallowed hard and forced my tongue to still, worried I'd said too much. Would Samuel begin searching for the reason now? Would he, too, begin to see whatever horrible traits the others saw in me?

A hand pressed into my lower back, just above where skin met scales. I sucked in a surprised breath and dared to raise my eyes. Samuel was closer now, his eyes full of sympathy and kindness. It was baffling to me that I had ever looked at him and not thought him handsome. Now I was certain he was the most beautiful creature in this world.

"They are jealous," he whispered. "They are blind fools who cannot see the treasure before them."

He kissed me. His lips were gentle, but the kiss was roughened by the salt on my mouth.

He pulled away with a sigh. "You are the sea," he murmured.

"I love you," I murmured back.

Fear quickly tightened around my chest and I wished that I could pull the words back into my mouth, but Samuel's grin widened.

He took my hands into his. "My lovely Nerit, I must go away."

The dread that struck me at these words was immediate and painful. I had been too rash. I had ruined everything.

But he continued, "But I will return on the night of the next full moon. I want to find a way for you and me to be together. Some means that will allow you to be by my side forever, so we may never again be parted. I . . . I hope this is what you want also?"

Weak, tenuous joy trembled in my chest. "Yes," I said. "I want this also."

"Then I will find a way, my darling. Will you promise to be here when I return?"

My heart was pounding, my pulse running as hot as if I had his human blood in my veins. I nodded and did not shy away when he kissed me again.

☙☙

I returned to my cave for the first time in weeks. It was just as I had left it, all destruction and mayhem, but no longer did the sight fill me with agony. No—now there was only willful determination.

Two weeks.

I had two weeks before I saw Samuel again, and I knew what I would do.

I loved him for his optimism, for his belief that he might be able to find a way for us to be together, but I knew he would never find such a way, not unless his human witches had magic like we had beneath the sea. No—if we were to be together, it would be my doing.

I began to search for the book. Digging through the scattered bones and skulls. Shoving aside piles of lobster claws and abalone shells. Pulling curtains of kelp and seaweed away from the dark basins where hot air erupted up from the earth below.

I found the book beneath a crush of broken bottles and sea glass, half sunken in sand. As I wiped the mud off the giant clamshell pages, it became clear that some of the spells were missing. I flipped through them hurriedly.

Ah—the love potion. Of course.

No matter. I no longer wanted the love of Prince Lorindel. I no longer needed to trick anyone into loving me at all.

My heart raced as I searched for the spell that I *did* need. The shells clacked as I turned through them again, skimming through the book once, then twice—

There. A spell carved into the pearlescent pages by some sorceress of ages ago. The spell that would turn my fish's tail into a pair of human legs.

I read through the ingredients. The skins and organs of water snakes. The spinal cord of a sea otter. Fish eyes and squid tentacles and a single black pearl. Blood given willingly from a merfolk's chest.

All ingredients that could be harvested easily enough.

Then I began to read through the warnings—for where there was magic, there was danger.

Upon drinking the elixir, it will be as if a sword were cutting through the merfolk's stomach. Once transformed, the merfolk will maintain all manner of grace, though each step taken upon these legs will be as an abomination walks, and it will be as though daggers were being thrust into the soles of these human feet.

Let it forthwith also be known that if a merfolk sacrifices their natural life in pursuit of a land-dweller's love, then only through marriage may they obtain an immortal soul and a share of man's happiness. If that human should rather choose to marry another, then at the sun's first light following the marital vows, the merfolk will perish and become naught but foam on the crest of the ocean's waves.

This fate can be eluded if the merfolk chooses, instead, to take the human's life before sun's first light. This shall be done by plunging a dagger of carved bone into the heart of the human who once was loved. By this act, the merfolk will once more become a creature of the sea and nevermore will they be permitted to venture to the world of man.

I read the warnings with interest, if not fear. Surely Samuel would marry me and we would be joyful together for eternity, but I did not relish the thought of feeling as though a sword were cutting through my stomach or daggers were being thrust into the soles of my human feet. Imagining it made me feel faint, but I thought of Samuel and his kiss, and resolved myself.

After all, what was a lifetime of pain when coupled with a lifetime of bliss?

I set aside the book of spells and began to gather my ingredients. Two weeks was a long time to wait. An eternity to wait.

But when Samuel returned for me, I would forever leave this miserable ocean behind.

ᥱᢙ

The elixir was black as squid ink, though when it caught the light, it shone as if a sky full of stars were captured inside. I used my dagger—recovered from the ship's wreckage—to scoop the pasty liquid into an empty snail shell and tried not to imagine it sticking to my throat as I drank. Trying not to imagine anything beyond Samuel's arms around me.

Clutching the shell in one fist and my knife in the other, I took one last turn around my cave. I had done little to clean it up. There was no point. I would never see it again, and even now I felt no sadness at its loss. There was nothing to miss. No one to say good-bye to.

I flicked my tail, pushing myself toward the surface.

The moon was drooping near the horizon when I burst out of the waves. It was as bright and round as the gem on the Sea King's scepter, and the water around me was alive with green glowing algae. It was a perfect evening to be ashore. I swam to the beach, my stomach feeling as if I had swallowed an entire school of herring.

Samuel wasn't there yet, which was for the best. I didn't want him to witness my pain as the spell undid my body and wove it back together.

Setting the knife on a rock, I cradled the shell in both hands. I looked into the swirling, inky liquid, then down at the tail that was not as strong or graceful as some of the other merfolk's, but that I had always thought a fine sort of tail.

Fine or not, it was keeping me from being with Samuel.

I tilted the shell against my lips and drank.

No sooner had the elixir slipped down my throat than I felt a stab of pain cutting through my belly. I gasped and reached for my stomach, certain that I would find a blade buried in my flesh, but there was nothing there.

The pain continued, searing through my guts until I was sure I was being turned inside out.

I screamed in agony and collapsed.

ᥱⲭᦞ

It was with much effort that I opened my eyes again. The world was bleary. Dried salt had tangled my lashes together. My heart was throbbing. My blood a chaotic rush through my ears. I gasped for air. It tasted different. Colder. Crisper.

It was still night, but the moon had trekked halfway across the sky. Storm clouds were on the horizon, threatening to reach land within the hour. There would be no sun tomorrow, my first day as human.

I bolted upright.

Human.

My jaw fell as I took in my body. Somehow, the absence of my tail was more shocking than the addition of human legs. I traced my shaking hands down my pale thighs, over the hard shins, to the toes that curled on my command, as obedient as my fins had once been.

A cry of elation escaped me.

I was human.

I rolled onto my side and moved to stand, but as I put my weight onto my feet for the first time, I yelped and my legs buckled, hurtling me back to the sand.

The pain was furious—not as horrible as when I had first tasted the elixir, but enough to leave me whimpering when I thought of standing again.

I had to, though. For Samuel. For our future together.

Gritting my teeth, I tried again, and this time I succeeded, locking my knees to hold my body upright. It was as if I stood on needles. I hissed, my face scrunched against tears.

It was tolerable, I told myself.

I would tolerate it.

I took a step. Flinched. Stepped again.

The pain did not lessen, but through strength of will I kept myself moving forward. I was walking. It was painful, but it would not kill me. I could go on, and so I would.

Soon Samuel would be here. He would embrace me and give me his arm, and what would pain be then? Nothing but an annoyance buried beneath my elation.

With this thought, I heard him.

I turned toward the footsteps coming down the beach. I spotted him before he spotted me and my body lightened, my heart soaring on the feathers of a white-winged tern. He was just as I remembered him, moving among the driftwood with an eager gait, picking his way among the broken shells and stringy kelp.

He looked up, beaming. "Nerit, you're here. I—"

He halted, his smile deadening as he realized that I was not lying on the sand, waiting for him. His expression slackened as he took in my body, all bare skin and uncertain legs.

I had never been embarrassed by my nakedness before, but suddenly I felt vulnerable standing before him. I swallowed, believing it must be the newness of my strange body, but I could not keep from wrapping my arms around myself.

"Samuel," I breathed. I wanted him to grin again. I wanted him to scoop me into his arms and laugh with glee at my unexpected transformation.

He did none of those things. He seemed stunned and, after a long moment, horrified.

"What did you do?" he asked—nay, demanded.

My smile became strained. "I . . . I've made it possible," I said, daring a painful step forward. "I've made it so we can be together, like we wanted. After this night, we will never have to be parted, just like you said."

"No. This can't be." He stepped back even as I came nearer. His hands went to his head, burying his fingers in his hair until it stuck out at all angles. "No, no, *no*."

"Samuel, what—"

A shrill whistle sent a cascade of ice down my spine, followed by a male voice that I didn't recognize.

"She is a beauty, I'll afford you that."

I looked up and spotted a pair of men standing on the nearest dune. They held an assortment of chains between them.

The man who had spoken shook his head. "But I don't see any fish's tail. Where is the mermaid, Sam?"

"She . . . this is . . . she *was* a mermaid, I swear." Samuel gestured toward my body with dismay. "I don't understand. This is some dark magic. She . . . she must be a witch! Take her as a witch!"

I stumbled backward. "Samuel, what's going on? Who are these men?"

"We have a witch already," said the second stranger. "Vladlena with the All-Seeing Third Eye."

"But if this girl needs a job, I think we can come up with something for her to do," the first man said with a hideous smirk. "Fisker and Holt's Traveling Circus is always looking for *off*stage talent. Will save us from having to build that saltwater tank, too."

He took a step closer to the edge of the dune and I noticed something that had been hidden from my sight before. A harpoon.

I whimpered, beginning to understand that Samuel had brought these men. That he had told them about me. That he had . . . what? What had he done? "Samuel?"

His eyes flashed. "You," he said, snarling, "were going to make me *rich*. A thousand guilders they would have paid me. And now you're . . . you're *worthless*." He threw an angry gesture toward my legs.

"Naw," said one of the men. "I wouldn't say that. We'll find a use for her. Don't you worry."

I heard the telltale sounds of sand and rocks slipping down the embankment, but before the men could reach me, I snatched my forgotten knife from the ground and fled into the sea.

I swam as hard as I could until my limbs burned and I was cursing my pathetic human legs. I swam until I could no longer see the shore. I didn't know if Samuel or either of the men chased after me. If they did, they must have given up once the storm arrived. I was soon caught up in thrashing water and torrential rain, and I became sure that I was dying. I welcomed death, even, sure it would be less painful than the heart that was ripped to pieces in my chest.

I didn't know how long I stayed bobbing among the waves, so much colder now than they had felt before. My teeth were chattering and the current battered my body. By the time it dragged me ashore, bedraggled and famished, the shreds of my heart had already begun to stitch themselves into something angry and vengeful.

ⓔⓧⓞ

I remember little about those first days. I stole what clothes I could from the lines in a small fishing village and scavenged for mussels and urchins on the beach like nothing more dignified than a common gull.

Days turned into weeks, and I grew braver, sometimes leaving my cold beach coves to wander the village alleyways. When the humans did not chase me away with sharp sticks and stones, I grew bolder still. I drifted through their markets and slipped away with carrots and cucumbers when I could.

Weeks gave way to months.

I learned of money and took to begging for the hard, round coins that could buy sustenance. I learned what bread was, though butter and marmalade never crossed my palate. I watched the other women and took to combing my hair and styling it off my neck as they did.

Months gave way to years.

I watched. I listened. I moved from village to town to city, though could never stand to be too far from the sea, for listening to the lulling hush of the waves at night was the only way I could capture any sleep.

I took a job at a shop that sold dried herbs and medicines. I was a natural alchemist, the owner told me once, watching me grind tarragon leaves into a paste. I did everything with anger.

I waited. I waited for my death, because I knew that someday even abhorrent Samuel would find a woman to be his wife, and on the morning after their wedding, my life would be stolen from me. I had no fear of dying, but neither did I long for it. My life was fueled by hatred, and I waited for a chance, any chance I might have to seek vengeance on the man who had betrayed my heart, who had stolen my eternity.

Then, one afternoon, as I stood outside the shop smashing blue juniper berries with my knife handle, I saw him.

He was with a girl—a lady with perfect yellow curls. I watched them from across the street, elbows linked, lovers' smiles.

Samuel turned and looked at me, directly at me, and there was not even a hint of recognition.

My heart stilled, encrusted with every moment of agony I had endured since our last meeting.

I set down the berries and followed them.

I found his house. I asked questions. I learned that they were engaged and that the wedding was mere days away.

I watched. I waited.

I did everything with anger.

ⓧ

I did not attend Samuel's wedding, though I could envision his carefree, dimpled smile as he said the vows that should have been mine. I could envision his pretty, innocent bride. I had learned that she came from a family with some affluence, and no doubt Samuel was pleased that his charm had won him the wealth he'd longed for.

No—I did not go to the wedding.

Instead, I went to the home he would soon share with his wife and waited there with the reassuring weight of my dagger in my fist, the spell book's warnings echoing in my head.

It was late when the bride and bridegroom finally retired to the bedchamber, full of boisterous laughter from too much wine. It was not long before their cheer died down into even, drowsy breathing.

I emerged from my hiding space and went to stand over the bed.

The girl was pretty enough, captured in the light that filtered through their lace curtains, but I had eyes only for her groom.

Samuel. How had I ever thought him beautiful?

My grip tightened on the dagger's handle. The bone seemed warm, almost alive in my hand.

I considered waking Samuel so he might know my face one last time. So he might understand it was I who was robbing him of his joy, as he had once robbed me of mine. I wanted him to see my eyes and to know it was his own heartless betrayal that had murdered him. But I worried that he might overpower me if he was awake, even in his drunken stupor, and I would not let anything keep me from taking his life this night.

I had waited far too long.

I anchored one leg against the mattress and raised the knife. I watched Samuel's chest rise with a breath and sink again. Rise and sink. Rise and—

I plunged the blade into his heart.

His eyes snapped open. His mouth parted in a silent scream.

The girl, too, awoke, but her scream was not silent. Blood was already on the sheets and on my hands, and I was smiling. No—I had started to laugh, though the sound was drowned out by the hysterical bride.

I laughed because Samuel was looking at me. And this time I knew that he remembered.

I abandoned my blade in his chest and ran.

The streets were empty. I had long grown accustomed to the pain in my feet and it didn't hinder my speed as I ran. I knew the moment Samuel died, because I collapsed there on the cobbled street and felt the pain of a sword once more cutting through my gut. This time, I refused to swoon. I swallowed my screams and kept pushing forward, crawling on my elbows, dragging my useless legs behind me until they had stitched together and melded once more into a fish's tail. It no longer felt agile and strong, but rather like a clumsy weight tied to my body, which had to be dragged across the ground. Rocks and glass tore into my flesh. My muscles burned.

I crawled all the way back to the ocean. The water called to me, giving me strength, and when I finally reached the surf, it welcomed me, engulfed me, beckoned me to come back home.

Home.

I had thought I would never return, but there was no sorrow in my heart as I started swimming toward the castle of the Sea King. I was once again a creature of the ocean, and I was going home. A smile rose on my face and I looked adoringly down at my body, re-formed.

My eyes widened. I froze and cried out, but the sound was lost in a flurry of bubbles that raced back to the surface.

Twice, magic had undone my body and woven my flesh back

together, leaving me forever changed. I was no longer looking at the sleek, graceful tail of the merfolk, but rather the dark, oily body of a serpent.

☙◈❧

"You are no longer one of us," Lorindel said, one lip curled with disgust as he inspected my serpentine body. "You do not belong here, Nerit."

All around the crystal throne room, merfolk tittered at Lorindel's spite and my chastisement. In my absence, the old king had died and Lorindel had ascended to his throne. Predictably, he had taken Beldine for his wife. She sat beside him nursing a newborn child—their sixth daughter, I was told.

I tightened my hands into angry fists. I yearned to scream at him, to tell him that this was the only place I could possibly belong. But then, no, maybe I had never belonged here at all, and maybe this was his fault, and those like him. Those whose minds were too small to appreciate my talents. Those who had treated me as an outcast long before they had cause to.

"Where would you have me go, Your Majesty?" I asked with no effort to mask my derision. "For you say I do not belong in your kingdom beneath the sea, yet I do not belong to the world above, either."

Lorindel snarled. "Where you go is not my concern. You are an abomination and a disgrace. I will not have you sullying my kingdom with your presence. If my people choose to seek you out for your dark talents, I cannot stop them, but I will take no part of it. From henceforth, you are not welcome here."

Not welcome here.

Fury burned in my chest, clawing its way to the surface of my skin. Who was this man to decide where I was or was not welcome? Who was he to belittle what I had gone through, the suffering I had endured, when he could have prevented all of it with nothing more than a smile and a word of kindness?

Not just Lorindel. All of them. Samuel and Beldine and the entire kingdom and the entire world. They had all shunned me, belittled my work, mocked my dreams, betrayed my heart.

There was no kindness to be found here. Not for poor, pathetic Nerit.

I narrowed my eyes and my gaze drifted back to the newborn child. She was wrapped in a seal pelt blanket. A shining tail swished drowsily, prettily from the swaddling.

I turned my attention back to the Sea King, a smile sharpening over my teeth.

"Cast me out, then, if that is your wish. For you are right, oh, my wise king. Once they know what I can do, your people *will* seek me out for my dark talents. The innocent ones and the desperate ones. And help they shall receive, though great misery will come to all who do not heed the warnings of my terrible magic. My own misery is proof enough of that."

I turned away. The gathered merfolk parted to let me pass, their eyes following me with wary distrust. This time, for the first time, they had every reason to be frightened of me. I was the stuff of their childhood nightmares, after all. Those sickly, slimy creatures that lurked in the depths, drunk on their own wickedness.

Never mind their fear. They would still come, those innocent, desperate fools. They would come to me for gifts and blessings and curses. They would come for poisons and cures, and I would fulfill their wishes and deliver to them their miserable fates, as my fate had been delivered to me.

I was an abomination, undone and rewoven back together. I was the sea witch.

Zoë Herdt's Villain Challenge to Marissa Meyer:

What If the Sea Witch Had Previously Been in the Little Mermaid's Shoes but Decided to Kill the Love Interest and Turn Back into a Mermaid Instead?

Villain or Hero? You Decide!

BY ZOË HERDT

I've been thinking about our villain, Nerit. She faced life-altering decisions every step of the way—when her love potion plot was outed, when she fell in love with Samuel, and when she left her kingdom for the very last time. She chose to take her life in her own hands rather than blindly follow the norms of her society out of fear. Even though it cannot be said that Nerit made the kindest choices—I mean, she did *murder* someone—she always stuck to her own beliefs, and that is admirable.

We all dream about doing something larger than life. The difference between the hero and the villain is that the villain always takes that dream and forcibly tries to make it into a reality, no matter the obstacles in the way. Nerit dreamed about being loved by someone who was as equally unashamed of her as she was of herself. When the opportunity arose twice, with both Lorindel and Samuel, she went against moral and social conventions to try to make it come true, performing powerful and illegal magic that could—and did—result in morally questionable consequences. Nerit didn't focus on the cons, however, as she had faith in her own talents and was willing to go to the ends of the earth to get what she wanted. Say what you want about her, but Nerit is fearless.

Now, I think I'm a relatively good person. I brake for squirrels that run into the street, and I'm proud to say I've never cheated on any of my school tests, though that's not to say I've never given the latter much thought. While staring down at a blank Scantron sheet during an AP calculus test that I was totally unprepared for, you bet I was dreaming how great it would be to sneak a little peek at the test of the student next to me. She was flying through those questions with ease, and the right answers were there for the plucking.

The problem is, I am a coward. Despite how desperately I needed those answers, I could not and would not dare try that sneaky maneuver. I just knew in every fiber of my being that the moment I turned my eyes even a fraction of an inch to the left, my teacher would pounce on me and that would be it. I would be thrown out of school and forced to live a wandering life on the streets, out of work, because who in their right minds would hire a seventeen-year-old who can't solve a simple derivative? Oh, and on top of that, it was wrong, against the rules, and did I say wrong?

Okay, that might be a tad dramatic, but honestly, that's what passes through my mind every time I toy around with the idea of doing something bad. My focus always jumps immediately to the consequences, usually overdramatizing them to the point that I believe this one decision, no matter how small, will dictate how the rest of my life plays out. I then decide that it's better to play it safe and do the right thing rather than follow that inner voice that tempts me to take the other path.

Are you like Nerit? Find out if you are a hero or a villain with this quiz.

WHAT WOULD YOU DO?

1) You are traveling on a path when you pass an old woman begging for food. She looks hungry, but you have only a small loaf of bread and need something to eat for the next day of your journey. You . . .

    a. Keep it for yourself. You need the food for energy, and you're sure someone else will come by with food for her.

    b. Give the old woman your food. You don't know how long she's been without food, and you can find something when you get to your destination.

2) After your teacher leaves the room, you notice that the answer sheet for the next test is sitting on the edge of her desk. You . . .
    a. Take a look. If your teacher didn't want you to see it, why did she leave it in plain sight?
    b. Close your eyes and flip it over. You and your classmates will pass or fail on your own.

3) You are offered the opportunity of a lifetime! Unfortunately, if you take it, you will hurt your friend's feelings. You . . .
    a. Take it. These opportunities don't come around every day, and your friend will understand. If they don't, were you ever really friends?
    b. Turn it down. Friendship is more important than any opportunity. What's success without someone to share it with, right?

4) While you are walking, you stumble upon an ancient spell book that teaches powerful dark magic. You . . .
    a. Read it. You might not use it, but it's good to know— just in case.
    b. Give it to the proper authorities so they can destroy it. No one should have access to something this dangerous.

5) Like Nerit, your true love—or so you thought—betrayed you after you risked your entire life to be with him or her. You . . .
    a. Return the favor. As they will soon know, you are not to be messed with.
    b. Move on. Creating more pain won't solve any problems.

ANSWER KEY:

Mostly A's: Villain

Though you might not feel the urge to go on a crime spree, you possess all the tools you need to become a serious villain. Some may call you selfish—but you think you're really just looking out for yourself. Just bear in mind that stories are fiction—the villains in real life face real consequences.

Mostly B's: Hero

Welcome to the club. True, you might not always get the recognition you want or deserve as you're busy looking out for others, but people can rest easy knowing you're always there to help.

BEAUTIFUL VENOM

BY CINDY PON

What did it feel like to have your body slowly turn into stone?

Mei Du slithered between the dust-coated statues of gods and goddesses and knocked them over, one by one, with a swipe of her powerful serpent body. They were large figures and crashed with thunderous noise. She avoided the tumbling stone fragments with finesse, smooth and graceful as a dancer, sliding between their ruins. Dust obscured her vision, rising high toward the pitched temple roof.

She paused in front of the lone statue that remained, and as the air cleared, the Goddess of Purity's impassive face emerged, perfect lips pressed together in an enigmatic smile, the orbs of her marble eyes blank and unyielding. She stood tall and majestic, the folds of her white robe carved to drape elegantly over her frame. One hand was pressed over her heart, and the other arm was extended, palm lifted heavenward, as if in benevolence or forgiveness.

But Mei Du knew the truth.

From the time she was just a girl, Mei Du had prayed to the Goddess of Purity, believing her to be just and the protector of women. But no longer. The goddess's betrayal still stung. Mei Du had thought that her heart had grown as cold and hard as all the mortals she had turned into stone, but the Goddess of Purity's image pained her like a fresh-cut wound. She fought the urge to cower and sob, remembering the humiliation and hurt like it'd happened yesterday—and she was once again a helpless girl with some other name.

The snakes on her head hissed, thrashing until her scalp burned. Mei Du raked her yellowed nails over her face, crusted with warts and pustules, eyes roving to the dark corners of the derelict temple. She listened, the rough green scales of her arms prickling.

A man was approaching.

She had been on the run for centuries, but her legend and infamy had only grown, as had the number of those who were determined to slay her. Always men—she knew they pursued her with murder on their minds, for there was no capturing the evil Mei Du alive. Death was the only solution, the only ending to her story.

Yet she had eluded them this long—had suffered their taunts and curses, the burning and cutting, the stones hurled at her head. After years of abuse, she had turned on her persecutors, wanting vengeance and enjoying grim satisfaction in their deaths. She refused to remain a victim.

Morning light filtered through the broken lattice windows above, penetrated the eroded wood of the massive door panels. The temple door scraped open, and she flexed her hands. There had been rumors. Rumors whispered enough that they had even reached *her* ears during her solitary travels through the provinces. The mortals spoke of a great warrior, trained by the masters, said to be faster and more agile than any man, inhumanly strong with his bare hands and lethal with a weapon— a true hero. A hero who had been blessed by the gods. He would be the one to end Mei Du's reign of terror.

Is this him? Has he finally come?

The rotten door slammed closed again, and dust swirled, glittering in the sunlight. The shape of a man emerged in the gloom, and she was reminded of Hai Xin, his powerful presence blotting out the light.

Mei Du lifted high on her coil, and the snakes on her head writhed with anticipation.

She was ready to meet her match.

∽

Jia Mei Feng sat very still in the deep, curve-backed chair as the royal portraitist used brush and ink to capture her likeness. The artist had thoughtfully adjusted where she would sit in her family's opulent main hall, pulling the carved chair away from the others. The Jia manor was the most extravagant in their town of Qin He, but despite the family's high status as rich merchants, it was not every day that they received a visitor from the palace. Her mother had made certain of securing this one opportunity to present Mei Feng's portrait to the emperor, for a young woman could not climb higher than becoming an imperial consort, one of over a thousand brides the emperor kept at the palace.

The artist had slid a door panel open, seeking the right amount of light, before he began. She saw him glance at the scrolled paintings adorning their walls—prized originals by masters long dead. Her mother, Lady Jia, flitted behind the man, her silk sleeves billowing with her nervous movements. Mei Feng wished her mother would stand still—she was making her anxious.

Lady Jia's pacing was accompanied by a string of dialogue she seemed incapable of stopping. "You must paint so many beautiful women for the emperor, Master Yang," she said. "It is such an important and honored task, to travel these provinces to find new brides for him. I mean, we rely on your skill to convey our daughter's beauty. How can a man, even an emperor, not fall in love with such a perfect face?" Her mother swept a graceful arm toward Mei Feng, her dark brown eyes bright with pride.

Mei Feng winced inwardly. But she had been schooled too long in the art of being a proper young mistress to let it show in her features. Instead, she kept the same faint curve of a smile on her lips, letting her eyes gaze dreamily into an unseen distance.

"My daughter's beauty is known throughout the province," her mother prattled on. "But beyond that, she has been well taught in all the arts that will please our emperor: embroidering, singing, dancing, and playing the zither. Mei Feng can recite and write poetry, has been instructed on how to properly serve tea should the emperor desire it, and knows all the ways of pleasing him in the bedchamber."

Mei Feng almost closed her eyes—but she had better control than that. Yet she couldn't prevent the warm blush that spread from her face to her neck, until the tips of her ears felt on fire. Oh, how she wanted to leap from the chair and run back to her quarters, tear all the pins from her hair, carefully arranged in artful coils and plaits, laden with rubies and jade.

Horrifyingly, her mother did not stop. She did not even pause for breath.

"I personally taught her everything from *The Book of Making* myself." Lady Jia dipped her chin coquettishly. "Mei Feng knows what she needs to do to quickly become with child—make healthy sons for the emperor."

Mei Feng's hands were folded in her lap, resting against her skirt, gorgeously paneled in pale green and pink silks, embroidered with delicate butterflies. Her fingers tightened, lacquered nails digging into the backs of her hands. *How much longer?*

"I am sure she is as fertile as a sow with nine pairs of teats—" Master Yang said.

Her mother drew a sharp intake of breath, covering her mouth with one sleeve.

Mei Feng blinked twice; she did not let the shock touch her composed face.

"But I do not choose the emperor's imperial consorts for him," the artist went on in a gruff voice. "What I do is try to paint the best representation that I can of the young women brought before me." He flicked the ink from his brush with an annoyed turn of his wrist into a cerulean bowl filled with water. It rested on an enameled tea table that depicted pink peonies nestled within verdant leaves, one of Mei Feng's favorite pieces in their grand main hall. "You are ruining my concentration, Lady Jia," Master Yang went on. "If I make a mistake and blot the painting by accident, I will not be there to explain to His Majesty that the mark is not a giant wart or mole with a hair growing from it like a cat's whisker."

Lady Jia snapped her fan open, flapping it to give herself some air. She appeared ready to faint.

Mei Feng's serene smile might have lifted a small fraction at the corners.

She loved her mother. She truly did. But Lady Jia could be a little willful and pushy when it came to arranging a betrothal for her youngest daughter.

"Well, then," Lady Jia said. "You've made yourself clear, Master Yang. I'll leave you in peace." She turned in a flourish of silks and gardenia perfume and retreated down the wide steps into the courtyard below.

The artist dipped his brush into the inkwell, gathering the ink he needed on the brush head, before giving Mei Feng a playful wink.

"Shall we start over, then?" he asked.

⚭

Mei Feng wandered the lush grounds of the Jia manor trailed by her two handmaids, Ripple and Orchid, meandering through the estate's magnificent courtyards. The royal portraitist had taken all morning to paint two likenesses of her. Lady Jia had exclaimed in pleasure when she saw the final pieces, praising the artist. But when the man offered to show Mei Feng, she had declined to see them. Her mother had tilted her chin in disapproval. Mei Feng knew she risked being rude, but she didn't have the heart. Her fate now rested upon a stranger's ink strokes on rice paper, and whether or not another stranger found her features pleasing. She wanted to marry well and make her parents proud, but a part of her hoped that the emperor would not like the look of her—for she was not yet ready to leave her family forever.

Spring was in full splendor, and the gardens were a riot of fragrance and color. She passed peach trees, their branches laden with deep pink blossoms, stopping in front of a clear pond; water trickled from the rockwork built above. The two handmaids chatted behind her as Mei Feng fed the orange and silver-speckled fish. A large toad she had named Grouch because of his wide, frowning mouth plopped loudly into the water, in hopes of finding something he could eat, too.

She laughed at the sight of him kicking his fat legs and continued on to her favorite spot among all the courtyards—the Pavilion of Quiet Contemplation. Lifting her emerald skirt, she climbed the stone steps and settled onto a bench, one that offered her a view of the crabapple trees. Wisteria wound their way up the columns of the pavilion in bursts of lavender and periwinkle, dousing the air with its sweet, peppery scent.

Grouch the toad croaked from the pond, deep and satisfied, the noise carrying to her on a soft breeze. Birds hidden overhead twittered and argued. Mei Feng leaned back, releasing a long breath, letting her arms rest heavy at her sides. She was never alone, but at least she was not being presented or observed for a small time—she treasured these rare moments of peace.

A hush blanketed the garden, so subtle that she didn't notice at first. But suddenly, the sounds of the courtyard had fallen away until even the rustling of leaves had disappeared. Mei Feng froze, the flesh on her arms pimpling. Where had her handmaids gone? Searching the tranquil surroundings with a sweeping glance revealed nothing. The two girls were nowhere to be seen. Ripple was prone to playing jokes, and Mei Feng almost rose, determined to find the errant handmaids, when the appearance of a figure farther down a stone-paved path stopped her.

A young man approached—a stranger—and her pulse quickened. Mei Feng clutched her skirt between damp fingers, not knowing what to do. The Jia estate was immense, and she resided within the inner quarters, where men were not allowed. As an unwed girl, she was meant to be safe here, sequestered, hidden away from prying eyes.

"Ripple?" Mei Feng called out, hoping the handmaid would appear from behind a tree trunk, or from where she had been crouched behind the rocks. "Orchid?"

"They are dozing for a while," the stranger said. He climbed the steps of the pavilion, stopping at the entrance.

"Dozing?" she whispered.

He smiled at her and bowed formally, elegant and assured. "Do not worry for them."

"Who are you?" she asked.

The young man looked to be eighteen or nineteen years, dressed in a long deep blue robe, his black hair pulled back in a topknot. At seventeen years old, Mei Feng had only ever met a handful of young men, all family—cousins or uncles. She had not seen many of them, but she knew that this young man was very handsome, with a glow about him that seemed as if he were lit from within.

Without so much as asking, he settled beside her on the stone bench. Shocked, she sidled away from him, filled with both fear and fascination. Inexplicably, the air seemed to waver around them, and for a brief moment, Mei Feng thought she heard the distant roar of the sea, tasted the tang of ocean mist on her lips.

"You can call me Hai Xin," he said. His voice was warm and pleasant, filling the unseen recesses of her mind and her heart.

"Hai Xin," she repeated, somehow finding the words, enveloped in his charm. "'Hai' for the sea, but which character for 'Xin'? Does it stand for 'star' or 'heart'?"

Smiling, he brushed the back of her knuckles with his fingertips, sending a pleasant shock through her body. It had been unexpected and unacceptable. No man had ever touched her before, much less so intimately. But when he carefully drew her fingers open, one by one, then covered her palm with his own, she didn't resist. "You are as intelligent and curious," he said, "as you are beautiful, I see."

Mei Feng's breath hitched in her chest. She knew she should leave, but she felt entranced—seduced by the warmth of his hand against her skin. "What are you doing here?"

He didn't answer for a long moment, concentrating on her hand, sweeping his thumb in slow circles over her open palm, then tracing an index finger across her inner wrist until she shivered, flustered by the tangle of unfamiliar sensations assailing her. "I come," he said, "because I heard that you are the most beautiful maiden in An Ning Province." His fingertips trailed up her inner forearm. "The rumors were not exaggerated."

She should have snatched her arm away, screamed for help, but she felt curiously docile; all her attention—her entire being—was focused on where Hai Xin's skin touched hers. "Oh . . ." She swallowed, staring at his hand caressing her arm. It was a beautiful hand, strangely perfect, well manicured and strong. The hand of a noble? Or a well-known scholar?

Hai Xin gave a small tug, and she shifted, facing him on the bench. He cupped her face briefly. Then his fingers were stroking the nape of her neck. Mei Feng's head tilted back; her eyes closed. Her mind had been bled blank, as if someone had carried all her thoughts away. Nothing existed in this world except for Hai Xin's touch. His lips brushed against her earlobe, his breath warm and sweet, and she trembled with pleasure.

Suddenly, the atmosphere changed, and he pulled away, breaking their embrace. She felt robbed of his touch, aching, as the sounds of the world came crashing through.

"Mei Feng," her mother called. "Where are you?" Lady Jia's wooden heels clacked against the cobbled path.

"Interrupted," Hai Xin said. "Regrettably." He lifted her hand and brushed his lips over her knuckles; everything felt right again—his supple mouth against her flesh. "Next time, then," he said, and rose. Hai Xin glided down the pavilion steps just as her mother rounded the corner.

Mei Feng's mouth had gone dry, her heart battering an unsteady beat against her chest. Her breaths came fast: erratic and shallow. Her mother would scream now, call for the sentries who guarded their home. Instead, she said nothing as Hai Xin strolled past Lady Jia down the same garden path. Mei Feng swore she saw his blue robe sleeve brush against her mother's bare arm, but Lady Jia acted as if she did not see him—acted as if Hai Xin did not exist at all.

Squeezing her eyes shut, Mei Feng didn't know if she was frightened or relieved.

"Daughter," her mother exclaimed. "Why are you hiding here? It's time for the midday meal."

☯

Only three days passed before Hai Xin appeared again, this time in Mei Feng's bedchamber.

She had lived those days in between in a daze, wondering if she had hallucinated the episode, wondering if she was somehow going mad. Her thoughts had dulled, heavy and sluggish, but her flesh had come alive, sensitive, tender. Mei Feng went about the rituals of each day, having her hair brushed and arranged by Ripple, drawing on her cool underclothing and silk skirt as if she were in a trance. Her body tingled, pinpricks of anticipation dancing across her skin, longing to be touched again.

Fear and caution lurked in some dark corner of her mind, caged and muted. She knew Hai Xin—this strange, seductive man—was dangerous. But it was a distant concern, a problem she knew she could not solve. Better not to dwell upon it.

She was lying in bed, her hair spread like a fan over her brocaded cushion, when Mei Feng felt his presence. Hai Xin's silhouette appeared behind the finespun gauze of her bed curtains. He exuded power . . . and desire. His hunger for her was tangible. It gripped her heart like a vise, tightening her throat. She tried to lurch away from him but lay like stone upon the platform bed, unable to move. Hai Xin had used his sorcery, immobilizing her. There was no escape, nowhere to hide.

He slipped beneath the silk sheet like a whisper, hot hands twined in her loose hair within a breath. Only a husband was allowed to see a woman's hair unbound; only a husband had the privilege to touch it. He pressed himself against her, whispering into her ear, promising wedded bliss and beautiful children, promising paradise. His lips and finger-tips roamed across her throat, over her abdomen, brushed against her breasts. She gasped with pleasure, even as the fear in the deep recesses of her mind expanded, screamed in warning.

"You taste as sweet as you look, beautiful girl," Hai Xin murmured against her hair.

"One of your greatest assets is your beauty, daughter," her mother had told her, over and over again.

"Our brood will be stunning," he said, then kissed her so deep and long she couldn't breathe.

Mei Feng felt his excitement. She remembered all those line draw-ings she had pored over endlessly in *The Book of Making*, tutored by her mother. She willed her arms to move, to shove him off, but her body betrayed her.

A door panel slid aside, and Orchid's voice broke the oppressive silence that had wrapped the bedchamber. There had been no other sounds except for Hai Xin's beguiling words between his kisses and the roar of her heartbeat within her ears.

"Mistress?" Orchid called out in her lilting voice. "I've come to douse your lanterns."

Light, slippered feet crossed the reception hall toward the bedchamber.

In an instant, Hai Xin vanished, as if he had never been there at all.

The only indications of his presence were the lingering heat of his touch against her feverish skin and the tang of salt in the air—a whiff of the sea.

"Your virginity is the one virtue more valuable than your beauty," her mother had also repeated time and again. "The emperor expects his brides to be presented to him untouched, pure. Don't ruin it by dabbling with some stupid boy."

Thank the goddess for Orchid's arrival, Mei Feng thought as she feigned sleep. *It had not gone that far.*

She clutched the crumpled sheet over her chest with shaking arms, finally able to move her limbs again, and did not let the tears slide down her face until the handmaid had retreated from the bedchamber, leaving her in darkness.

ೞ

Nowhere was safe.

Mei Feng knew that if she kept her handmaids close at all times, they could be magically lured away. She knew that if she locked herself in her bedchamber, or even the stone cellar beneath the manor's large kitchen, Hai Xin would still find her. She had no inkling who she was up against, except that he was no ordinary man.

Lighting incense each morning, she prayed to the Goddess of Purity for strength and safety. The goddess was known as the virgin and sym-bolized wisdom and peace. Girls often sought her guidance in matters of the heart and marriage, and prayed to her for protection. Mei Feng beseeched to be shown some way to escape or defeat Hai Xin. She was certain he was some monster or demon disguised as a handsome young man. She spoke to no one about her troubles.

Four days after Hai Xin had come to her in the bedchamber, an excited Orchid dashed into the main hall, where Mei Feng was taking tea with her mother. Ripple ran right at the other handmaid's heels.

"Lady Jia, Lady Jia!" Orchid exclaimed, out of breath. "A message! A royal message sent from the imperial palace!" She proffered the gold tube, ornately etched with a deep green dragon bearing five claws on each foot, a symbol only the emperor could use. Her mother sprang up, snatching the tube from the handmaid.

The two girls shuffled backward but did not leave the hall.

Her mother opened the tube and retrieved the rolled message. Mei Feng could see the dark sweep of calligraphy across the rice paper and the deep red ink of the imperial seal in several places on the page. Lady Jia read with care, then read again. She lifted her glowing eyes and said, "Dear daughter, you are to be wed to the emperor. You will be an imperial consort. The gods and goddesses have smiled down on our family."

Her mother swept across the stone floor and clasped Mei Feng to her as the two handmaids thrust their faces into their palms and wept for joy. Mei Feng would need to take servants with her to the palace, so the two girls' fates had been altered drastically, too, with one royal decree.

Lady Jia released her and touched Mei Feng's cheek. She winced, remembering Hai Xin's uninvited touch, stoking desire on her body while instilling fear in her soul. But her mother didn't notice that she had recoiled. "A royal envoy will arrive in three days to escort you to the palace." Lady Jia turned to the handmaids, waving them off with her elegant hands. "Don't just stand there, mewling. We must get ready!"

The two girls dashed off, chattering, their words tumbling over each other. Her mother glided down the main hall steps, likely with a hundred tasks to delegate before Mei Feng's leave-taking.

She was left alone standing in the middle of the empty main hall, clutching her arms around herself.

☙❧

The Jia manor was caught in a chaos of activity in the days following, before the royal envoy's arrival. Mei Feng was thrust along by the frenetic activity, like a blossom dropped into a river and propelled on a strong current. She was led from one place to the next and nodded in acquiescence often, as her mother arranged for everything to be ready before she left home.

Things were so rushed and hectic Mei Feng never had a quiet moment to herself, or with her parents, to say a private farewell. Instead, when the royal envoy arrived with a grand carriage drawn by six magnificent black horses, followed by a procession of imperial guards carrying the emperor's crimson banner, she only had time to clasp her mother's and father's hands briefly, holding back the sting of tears.

She didn't want to go.

"We are so proud of you, daughter," her father said, his smile broad and plain, despite his thick beard.

Her mother squeezed her fingers. "Your fortune shines on the entire family, Mei Feng. Write us. Visit when you can."

She could return to see her family once a year—if the emperor allowed it.

"Yes, Father," she whispered. "Yes, Mother. I will."

Then the envoy guided her into the royal carriage, and Ripple and Orchid were helped into a plainer one right behind that was filled with the chests they had packed for Mei Feng. After an official decree was recited by the envoy and a trumpet sounded, heavy curtains fell across the windows of the carriage, and it rumbled off. She couldn't even peer under the heavy brocaded cloth to see her parents or her home one last time as they sped away from everything she had ever known.

ᙅᗄ

They traveled swiftly toward the imperial city, stopping at inns that were soon cleared for the royal procession. Mei Feng was treated well, given the most delectable food at every meal—but she had little appetite. She missed the company of Orchid and Ripple, but was kept in solitude within the royal carriage, like something special and precious, a rare and caged bird.

They were rolling through the countryside, surrounded by silver birch and colorful wildflowers (Mei Feng had cut a small hole in the carriage's thick curtain), when they lurched to a sudden stop, thrusting her forward on the plush, cushioned bench. She grabbed the edge of it to prevent herself from falling off. Men in her procession shouted at one another from without, their voices muffled. Scrambling over to the carriage door, she peered through the cut in the curtain. Mei Feng could see nothing but fields of golden grass nestled beneath gentle, sloping hills.

The gruff voices of her imperial guards argued outside. Something blocked their path, and they were deciding what was the best course of action. Then, in a sudden whoosh, their voices were gone. Disappeared, as with the gentle rustle of the swaying grass and the distant birdsong. Mei Feng was left in a complete and dreadful silence.

She knew what this meant.

The thick brocaded curtains were stripped from her carriage, and sunshine pierced through, stinging her eyes. She turned her head from the brightness as the door crashed open, torn from its hinges. A dark shadow filled the doorway, blotting out the sunlight. Mei Feng's chest seized in terror.

Without a word, Hai Xin yanked her into his powerful arms. They felt like flesh, but his hold was as strong as stone, immovable like a mountain. He glided low across the wild grasses into the fields, flying, and she was carried like a rag doll against his chest.

She could hear no heartbeat there.

"The emperor will have to find some other girl," Hai Xin said. "I have my own plans for you."

He set her down on her feet in the field, but she clung to him, too weak from shock and fear to stand. Hai Xin took this as an invitation and bent over to kiss her, capturing her lips and her breath. She knew for certain now what he wanted. He had whispered cajolingly about children and wedded bliss, but it was clear what Hai Xin was truly after—what his aim had been from the start.

Mei Feng shoved away from him and stumbled back. "No," she said.

"No?" His black eyebrows lifted, and an amused smile curved his mouth.

She turned from him and ran. But the golden grasses were tall here, growing above her knees, and she was disoriented and frightened; a strange stupor like spilled ink spread across her mind. Mei Feng tripped and crashed to her knees. Hai Xin pinned her to the ground before she could blink.

"No!" she shouted at him, the declaration reverberating powerfully, ricocheting through the empty countryside.

"I am Hai Xin," he said, and the words filled her whole being so her body tremored with them. "God of the Sea."

Mei Feng forced herself to look into his face, stared into his eyes. Light spilled forth from his gaze, but darkness, too, swirled within. It was like falling into the sun—like drowning in a star-filled sky. Then she was tossed on tumultuous waves, tasting brine in her mouth, her vision blinded by rough sands and the swirl of the sea.

"You cannot say no to me," Hai Xin said, and his voice swelled, thunderous as an ocean storm. "I take what I want."

☙❦

After it was over, Hai Xin disappeared.

His weight was heavy upon her, and then it was gone.

Mei Feng lay on the ground for some time, unable to move. The tall grasses swayed beside her, whispering—a consolation. Finally, she forced herself onto her feet and somehow managed to stand. Her legs shook, knocking against each other, as she tried to straighten her silk skirt. A sleeve had been ripped at the shoulder, and several peach panels torn from the tunic. She attempted to re-tie the embroidered belt around her waist, but her fingers trembled too much. Instead, she smoothed her hair, tucking loose strands behind her ears, and picked a few rough stalks of grass from her locks.

Her heart felt constricted, and she could not take a full breath.

Suddenly the air before her shimmered, and her body went rigid, terrified it was Hai Xin again.

But it was a woman instead, tall and regal, clad in a flowing white dress. Her black hair was arranged in high, elaborate loops, woven with emeralds, and a silver crown rested against her brow. She was more beautiful than any woman Mei Feng had ever seen, with perfect features, reminding her of the statues hewn of gods. She realized then who this woman was and fell to her knees.

"Goddess of Purity," she said, barely above a whisper.

Mei Feng had prayed to her for guidance, and the goddess had come to comfort her. She had witnessed this cruel act, this terrible misdeed by another god; the goddess had come to make things right.

"How dare you utter my name?" The Goddess of Purity spoke in a clear voice, as cold and cutting as glass.

Mei Feng's head jerked up, confused.

"I pulled the strings of fate, chose you myself to be delivered to the emperor as a new bride," the goddess said. "And you let yourself be defiled instead. Who will want you now?"

Mei Feng leaped to her feet, arms thrust forward, palms open in supplication. "Goddess, no. I didn't want this. I tried to fight—"

"Did you say no?"

"I did," Mei Feng replied with vehemence. "I tried to push him off." The tears finally came, hot against her cheeks, and a sob tore through her sore, battered body. "But I didn't have enough strength."

"Did you refuse him during his first visit?" The goddess arched one black brow. "Did you say no during his second?"

Mei Feng stared at the Goddess of Purity, suddenly understanding. "It is not my fault." She dashed her tears away in an angry gesture. "You cannot blame *me* for this."

"Oh?" The goddess raised her arms in a graceful arc, expanding, growing to twice her size. She towered over Mei Feng. "How dare you, pathetic mortal girl, presume to look upon a god, much less consort with one? You were blessed with beauty and used it to lure an immortal's attention."

Mei Feng shook her head, unable to speak. Unable to believe what she was hearing.

"You will be punished for reaching so high, girl—for letting a god spill his seed in you." She pointed a finger at Mei Feng.

Her body stiffened, and pain arced through it; agony racked her mind and her soul, her flesh. Mei Feng's blood boiled, and she fell facedown into the dirt, burning pain radiating from her legs. She cried out, but no sound came. Pushing herself onto her hands, she tried to rise. She watched in horror as the flesh of her arms turned green, the color of mold, and her skin blistered with pockmarks and warts. "What is happening?" she growled. Her voice had turned thick and gravelly, monstrous.

"Fitting punishment," the goddess replied.

Something hissed beside her ears, tugging at her scalp. Mei Feng swatted at her hair, but it had disappeared. She grasped the thick body of a snake instead, and it writhed in her palm, sinking its fangs into her wrist. "No," she said, and heard hundreds of serpents hiss in unison, felt them wrench against her head. She tried to go to the goddess, to plead again for her innocence, and slithered toward the immortal, only realizing then she no longer had legs.

The Goddess of Purity smiled a serene smile. "Fitting punishment indeed." She conjured a large, bronzed mirror and held it toward Mei Feng. "You are now as ugly and horrifying as you were once beautiful and alluring."

Mei Feng gaped at the image reflected back at her. Her face had turned a putrid green, lumpy with warts. Her eyes had become sunken holes, the orbs pure black. They stared back at her without any trace of humanity, of feeling. Black snakes writhed where her long raven hair had been, undulating, fangs bared. She reared back from the goddess, dropping the mirror; it thudded to the ground.

"Beautiful Phoenix doesn't seem such an appropriate name any longer," the goddess said. "You will go by Mei Du from now on—Beautiful Venom. Although there is nothing pretty about you, is there? I do enjoy the irony." The goddess turned her wrist in a flourish, and the mirror disappeared. "I thought I would let you gaze upon your own face this once, understand what you have become. But as a word of caution, I would avoid your own reflection from now on."

Mei Feng slid forward, throwing herself at the hem of the goddess's dress. "Please, lady!" she rasped. "Have mercy. I have done nothing wrong."

But when she looked up, the goddess was already gone, and the snakes hissing against her ear was her only reply.

☙❧

Mei Du fled in grief and terror after the Goddess of Purity inflicted her punishment. Not knowing where to go, where she could hide, she slithered through farms and terraced fields, passing small villages or finding herself lost in large towns. Disoriented and confused, she left destruction in her wake.

Stone statues of her victims marked a macabre trail of her travels. They were young and old and from every class—their only similarity the horror forever etched into their grey features. One peasant woman had dropped to her knees, hands ripping at her own hair. A young scholar had been turned to stone with his arms thrust out, hands splayed, hoping to ward off an unspeakable evil. A small boy of seven years had collapsed onto his side, legs drawn into his chest in a fetal position, mouth agape and eyes shut tight.

But it had been too late.

What was seen could not be unseen, Mei Du learned, when it came to the power of her gaze.

It didn't take long for her infamy to spread. Soon, mobs were chasing her, wielding spears and axes, the farmers carrying heavy spades or pitchforks. Their legs were no match for the power and speed of her serpentine coil, but sometimes they managed to corner her, and she had no choice but to look in their eyes to survive. It never took more than three people turned to stone before the crowds would retreat, screaming curses and obscenities, or moaning in sorrow and fear.

They cast flaming torches at her, burning the green scales of her serpent body and blistering the thick, pocked skin of her torso and arms. Expert archers shot at her from afar, puncturing her abdomen and back. She wrenched those arrows out and threw them aside. Her wounds healed almost instantly. Mei Du's curse had been to *live* in this mortal realm, not to die. Her punishment was to suffer in her monstrosity and solitude, to cause death and wreck havoc, inflict tragedy and terror.

Months slid into years, and the years slid into oblivion. In the beginning, she missed her home, her family, wondered if they grieved for her, grateful that they would never know her terrible fate. But then her loved ones' faces began to blur and fade, as did the details of her mortal life. Sometimes a small memory would emerge, like desert winds revealing a long-forgotten treasure in the sand—the fragrant scent of jasmine tea, a lone lotus perched on a deep green leaf in a tranquil pond, or the sound of laughter drifting over a high manor wall—stirred something wistful within Mei Du's chest. These shining, scattered moments from another life always left her feeling bereft.

As time wore on, those remembrances disappeared. And as people continued to hunt her with sticks and knives and axes, as they continued to taunt her with curses and slurs, she began to look each and every one of them in the eyes instead of averting her gaze. She took pleasure in turning their contempt into stone.

Mei Du knew that she would live long, reviled and hated.

It was as the goddess had wished it.

ⲟⲭⲟ

Then, that fateful day, the one prophesied to slay her finally found her. Mei Du crouched motionless behind a thick pillar; there were ten in the abandoned temple, rising to the tall roof like sentinels. The red and gold paint on them had long since flaked off. She wanted a glimpse of this glorified hero who the mortals were convinced could end her. The dust dissipated to reveal a young man not yet twenty years, holding a sword in one hand and a shield in the other with a majestic eagle etched upon it. Both the sword and shield gleamed, polished to a mirrored shine.

But it wasn't this that caught Mei Du's attention, not the young man's height nor the taut muscles of his bare arms—it was the faint glow that limned his frame. There was no mistaking it. The God of the Sea had held the same inner light. This young man was no mere mortal; he was divine, or touched by a god somehow.

Blood roared in her ears, and she slid back, her long serpent coil whispering against the stone floor. Fear gripped her as those encounters with the god disguised as Hai Xin erupted again, memories she had buried long ago—had forced herself to forget. She trembled, a tremor that vibrated to the tip of her tail. The young man turned his head in her direction, his hand gripping the sword tighter. His black hair was pulled back in a topknot, revealing strong cheekbones and the masculine cut of his jawline. He smelled of metal and sweat, and the bloodlust that had become so familiar to Mei Du over the centuries, emanating from the men who hungered to kill her.

The first time one had found Mei Du in an abandoned dwelling, she had hoped for help, understanding, some sort of salvation. She had hoped he had come to free her from this unfair curse cast by a vengeful goddess. But Mei Du's hope dwindled with each man who appeared, on purpose or accidental misfortune. It had dwindled with each encounter suffused with their fear and loathing, always screaming, sometimes fumbling for a sharp weapon, until she ended it by meeting their gaze.

A few were so overcome with terror they shut their eyes. Those she sank her fangs into, tasting the bitter venom that filled her mouth. Wild animals would come later to eat the corpse.

She never had to wait very long.

But this would-be hero *was* different, as the rumors had declared. She could feel it in her bones just as she could taste the bright scent of him in the air. He was god-touched somehow. Perhaps the Goddess of Purity had sent him as a test, or the God of the Sea as an envoy to reclaim what he never should have taken so brutally in the first place. Mei Du didn't know, but she saw again in her mind's eye the innocent girl struggling to her feet, legs shaking as she tried to rearrange her torn skirt. Mei Du felt again that girl's pain and confusion, horror and heartache.

Rage filled her, as hot as the torches that have been thrown over the years, blistering her skin and scorching her scales. She waited for the intruder's gaze to turn in another direction, and in that instant, slithered across the temple behind another pillar, faster than he could blink. Hissing deep, the sound reverberated through the vast space, and the man stiffened.

Sweat gathered at his brow, and she at last tasted his fear in the air, sharp and sour. She felt a spike of pleasure from the scent. Perhaps she'd take her time, tease him as a snake would her prey. God-touched or not, this man would die like all the others—screaming in agony and regret.

The intruder edged farther into the temple, sword raised, his silver shield lifted at chest height. His movements were assured, powerful, yet he kept his head lowered and his gaze averted.

Mei Du grinned, the act so unnatural it felt as if her face had split, cracking the pustules and thick scales of her cheeks. The man slipped behind a pillar, and she slithered to the lone statue that still stood: the Goddess of Purity. She hissed again and circled the sculpture, taunting the intruder.

She caught a brief glimpse of the angry serpents on her head reflected on his shield.

The man had skulked closer, hiding behind another pillar.

Mei Du screamed, a guttural and primal sound, then thrust her shoulder against the goddess statue. It teetered, groaning as it swayed. She shoved it with both hands, and it crashed uproariously. *Good riddance*, she thought as dust rose. Knowing the man's vision would be obscured, she seized the opportunity and slid to where he hid, her heightened sense of smell revealing to her exactly where he cowered.

She slid toward him within a breath but was surprised to see the intruder disappear as swift as the wind behind another pillar, the thick air shrouding him. Mei Du lunged forward, anger and hurt coiled heavy in her chest. She scrabbled on her hands low to the ground, before rising high on her serpent coil to meet her enemy—to look him in the eyes.

The slightest breeze stirred behind her.

She whirled, fangs bared.

A flash of silver, too late, and a thin whistle as the blade fell.

Then darkness veiled her.

∾

Benjamin Alderson's Villain Challenge to Cindy Pon:

Medusa. Go!

∾

WITHOUT THE EVIL IN THE WORLD, HOW DO WE SEE THE GOOD?

BY BENJAMIN ALDERSON

For me, villains are extremely important factors in young adult literary fiction. Without them, how do we see the good in a novel? But there are some villains who aren't all evil, or at least didn't start out that way.

My yiayia used to read Greek mythology to me as a child. Even when I was that young, Medusa interested me. Her story was different from the others. I never could understand why she was a villain. I bombarded my yiayia with questions, wondering why the goddess Athena blamed Medusa for the actions of Poseidon, the God of the Sea. Was Medusa a villain or a victim?

Cindy Pon puts her own spin on Medusa in "Beautiful Venom." An advocate for diverse fiction, she completely changed the Medusa character from the one we know from ancient Greek mythology and brought her into the twentieth-first century in a new and unique way.

FAVORITE PART AND LINE:

Okay, Ben, deep breath. This story just loved messing with my emotions, especially the conversation between Master Yang and Lady Jia while Mei Feng is having her portrait painted. The exchange is filled with humor and jests, and it left me clutching my stomach in laughter. That leads to my favorite line from the story. "I am sure she is as fertile as a sow with nine pairs of teats" is laced with sass and sarcasm and is intended to shock Lady Mei. And it worked perfectly. I had a completely laugh-out-loud moment. Hilarious.

FAVORITE CHARACTER:

Mei Feng, aka Mei Du. Throughout the whole story, my heart really went out to Mei Feng. First she is being practically sold off to the emperor by her family. Mum and dad, get it together! Then she stumbles across this "evil" presence that is almost stalking her. *Then* the evil presence steals her innocence, and *she is blamed for his actions*. I mean, come on. I couldn't help but feel that this story is a reflection of modern views of rape: blaming the victim instead of prosecuting the villain. Hmmmm, a very raw and honest representation, something I am really glad has been brought up in this young adult story, as it is we young adults who must take on this situation and talk about it.

MOST MEMORABLE MOMENT:

The conversation between Mei Feng and the Goddess of Purity. You would expect a goddess to be good and trustworthy. But Cindy completely flipped this. The way the Goddess of Purity deals with what Mei Feng had just been through is shocking. It really goes to show that although you are in a position of authority and are looked at as a "good person," actions speak louder than words. And trust me, the Goddess of Purity has a lot to say. She is filled with bitterness and jealousy and portrays herself in the most perfect way, as the *evil* b . . . eing she is.

HERO TWIST:

At first, when we meet Hai Xin, I thought he was going to be the hero of the story. He came in, pulsing with power, and took Mei's breath away. I was like, "Oh yeah, hot love interest—you go, Mei." Then I carried on reading! And boy, I did *not* see him being the God of the Sea. To be honest with you all, he was more than a god—he was a *jerk*! I mean, *hello*! It makes perfect sense! This take on Medusa with an Asian twist was just perfect.

ISSUES THAT ARE LEFT OPEN-ENDED AND HOW I FEEL ABOUT THAT:

The important issue that Cindy has highlighted so brilliantly is the way victims of rape are treated. In the story, Mei Feng is blamed and scolded for "catching the eye" of Hai Xin. The Goddess of Purity blames Mei Feng for Hai Xin's actions, but she is the victim. It is sad to say, but even in today's world, people have the same views as the Goddess of Purity when it comes to rape. Questions such as "What were you wearing?" and "Did you say no?" and "What did you do to provoke it?" are asked to the victims of rape, instead of focusing on the criminal behind the act. Cindy deals with this in a sensitive yet *honest* and *raw* way. Her story highlights the issue perfectly, presenting it to young readers. I hope you, as a reader, interpret this story in your own way, but still come together and *talk* about this issue. We must not ignore it.

IN CONCLUSION:

As a reader, I was able to fall into this story . . . if only it were a hundred thousand words longer! I am a huge lover of twists in stories, and the ending of Mei Feng's story defiantly quenched my thirst for twists.

I almost wish I could speak to Mei Feng, or write her a letter. I would start off by saying, "You're not alone." I would tell her she was not in the wrong and that there are people who would listen and believe her. It is important that victims of such events know they are not alone and they are not to blame.

Mei Feng taught me that villains have stories, too. Seeing their perspective gives me a better understanding of the characters, which helps me understand their actions. It takes the dark to see the light and the bad to see the good.

But what drives both is a whole other story.

DEATH KNELL

BY VICTORIA SCHWAB

I.

Death is a boy with brown eyes.

A boy with bare feet and worn knees and a shirt missing a button.

A boy with copper hair and lashes that part like clouds.

It is raining when he wakes at the bottom of the well.

He is curled on his side, tucked in like a withered rose, and his body rustles in a papery way as he unfolds, back coming to rest against the mossy stone side of the well. He inhales, the air stale in his waking lungs, his pulse a low *tap-tap* beneath the storm as he holds out his hands to catch the drops of rain. Death has lovely hands—one smooth, the other skeletal—and water beads against his fingers; it drips between his bones.

He looks up with those eyes the color of wet earth.

He has seen them reflected—not in the well, for the well is empty—but in the places where water gathers after rain. They do not seem to belong to him, those eyes, though of course they do, set into his face like knots in an old tree.

Young face.

Old eyes.

Overhead, the rain slows, stops, turns to mist as he gets to his feet.

He does not know how long he's been asleep—hours? days? weeks?—but now he is awake, and he is cold, and he is hungry.

Not a stew-and-potatoes kind of hunger—that is a thing he knows but doesn't know—but a purposeful hunger, a marrow-missing-from-your-bones, no-blood-in-your-veins, heart-dragging-itself-along kind of need.

Death is awake, and so he is hungry.

He is hungry, and so he is awake.

He climbs slowly, steadily, out of the deep hole, fingers finding the holds. He swings a thin leg over the side of the well, sits for a drowsy moment on the stone lip.

It is nice to be awake.

Beyond the well, the world has changed again.

It is always changing. One day he climbs out of the well to find the leaves green, and the next they are beginning to turn. He wakes more often in winter, sees bare trees, bare trees, bare trees for days on end. The summers are long and sleepy.

Today the air is cool and damp, with the fair palette peculiar to spring.

He swings his legs absently, knocking bare heels against the mossy rocks. He knows he cannot be the only death, but he is the death of this place, with its rolling hills and its rocky cliffs, its wind like music, and its old stone well. The hills spill away around him, one side leading to the sea and the other to a forest, and there, through the mist, beyond the woods, the subtle shadow of a town. On and on, the world spills, waiting.

Something clenches in his chest. A hungry heart.

His feet hit the grass, and it begins to wither. The ground has gone to green again, the barren places where he'd stepped before now filled. Weeks, then. Maybe months.

He tries to step on stones as he begins to walk.

His strides are long, his steps are slow, but the distance falls away beneath him. He steps one foot down the hill, and the next in the field, one foot in the field, and the next in the forest, one foot in the forest, and the next at the edge of the town. He takes another step, but his bare feet move forward a single stride, solid, ordinary.

That is how Death knows he is close.

The town—Fallow, that is the name on the wooden sign—is waking around him, men and women spilling from their homes, moving in a stream of bodies toward the church.

He stops in the middle of the square and looks around, humming softly, the tune familiar, though he doesn't remember how, the words, if he'd ever known them, now lost.

He is a stone in the river. It courses around him.

Death slips into the crowd, tucking his hands—one flesh, one bone—into the worn pockets of his worn trousers. As he strolls down the lane, he plays a game with himself, trying to guess who it will be. The old man with his basket of bread. The young mother clutching her little boy's hand. The girl bobbing on her father's shoulders.

Last time, it was winter, and the life belonged to a man sound asleep.

Before that, a pair of children too close to the cliffs.

Before that, he cannot remember. He has lost track of the order, the faces, the names. They are spots of light in his mind, flashes of warmth.

Up ahead, the church bells begin to ring.

The girl squeals as her father tosses her.

The boy begins to cry.

The old man coughs.

Death follows them all.

His bone hand aches.

II.

The girl is sitting on a flat stone grave.

The whole world's still wet from the storm, and the damp leaches into her skirts and chills her legs, but she's never known a person to melt from rain. Catch a chill, maybe, but her blood's always been hot as the rocks in summer.

"Isn't that right?" she asks, tracing her fingers over the grave. She does that more often than not, carrying on half in her head and half out loud, dancing between them the way one does from stone to stone in the low tide, and it drives her father mad, but the way she sees it, the dead don't know the difference. They hear it all the same, whether it's on her tongue or in her head.

The girl's got her hands busy, braiding a crown out of weedy flowers—it's the day of the spring festival, when all the girls become May Queens and all the boys go as Green Men, and summer's waiting at the edge of the woods, peering through the trees. The tall grass starts whistling around her, and she imagines it's her mum, asking her to sing. She listens a moment, picking the tune, then kicks off, humming until she finds her mark.

"*I met a lad with wide brown eyes,*" she sings, her fingers weaving stem to leaf. "*He came to me in a dream. He was the fairest boy I'd never met, the loveliest I'd ever seen. I knew him by his smile, I knew him by his steps, I should have known to run—*"

"Grace," calls her father from the house, and she trails off, letting go of the song. She can picture him standing there, scanning the garden, squinting into the field, casting a look at the cliffs, as if she's fool enough to go near them when the rocks are wet.

And for a breath, she thinks of ducking lower. Of pressing her whole self to her mother's grave, and letting him look till he gives up and goes to the church without her. She thinks of it, but doesn't do it. Instead, she sets the flower crown on the grave (it was for her mum anyway) and rises, sprouting like a weed.

The church bells start ringing in the distance. Up close, they clatter and clang, but from this far out, the song is sweet and even.

"We're going to be late!" bellows her father.

She jogs back to the house, barefoot, and he lets out a short, exasperated sound at the sight of her, white dress smudged with dirt.

Grace doesn't think God will care about a little mud.

III.

They do not notice his bare feet.

They do not notice his damp clothes.

They do not notice the cold breeze that curls around him—or if they do, it does not last. Gazes flit past. Minds slip by. People are peculiar. They have a way of seeing only what they want, of *not* seeing anything they don't.

Death walks behind them through the town, searching their faces for the light.

A burning aura, like the last air escaping a log on the fire, sending up a plume of sparks and heat and orange flame. That's how he knows whose hand to take. His bone fingers flex.

He longs for the heat, for the lovely moment after they die when he holds their life—all they were, all they are, all they will ever be—in his hand, cupped like a wounded bird, before he sets it free.

The white church is a quaint little building.

Death doesn't go in.

He stands by the door, across from the priest, watching the congregation file past. Face after face. Life after life. None of them ready to end. He sighs when the stream of people trickles to a stop.

A funny thing happens then.

The priest turns, noticing him there. "You coming, son?"

Death smiles warmly. "Not today."

IV.

The service has already started.

Her father mutters as he slides into the pew.

Grace laces her fingers but doesn't really pray.

She thinks it's funny, to spend the morning in a church and the night at a bonfire, saying prayers, then casting flower crowns into the blaze.

"Got to have room," her mum used to say, "for the old gods and the new. One's tradition, and the other's faith."

But when she died, Grace didn't go to the church, didn't stay by the grave.

She went to the well.

Climbed the hill to the ring of stones and the pitted spot like a grave dug straight down, so deep no one has ever seen the bottom.

So deep that maybe it can touch the world below.

When her father's not drinking, he says that's blasphemy, that there's only heaven and hell and God with a capital *G*, but Grace doesn't care, because she saw the bare patches outside her mother's window, like footsteps in the grass, saw the same ones at the well, and felt the cold drifting up from below, and heard the whistle from the stones, like a song she couldn't quite remember.

"Give her back," she called, and the words echoed down, down, down into the well, and when they came up again, they were all broken.

The priest talks on, and Grace lets her gaze slip to the stained glass window.

It's a beautiful day, and when the service ends, she's the first one out, bursting through the doors as if she's been holding her breath, and now she fills her lungs with air, smiles at the taste of summer on her tongue.

Her father will go to the tavern and stay until it kicks him out.

The rest of the day belongs to her.

There's a giant oak tree past the church, tall as a house, and all around the base are red blossoms, a blanket of flowers they call farewells because they only come right when a season is ending.

They are the color of sunsets. Of strawberries.

Perfect, she thinks, for a crown.

Grace makes her way to the big old tree. She winds between the roots that sprawl across the ground and steps into the shade.

And stops.

The air beneath the tree is cold.

The blanket of flowers is threadbare, patches of red missing from the cloth.

Grace feels a prickle along the back of her neck, like someone's watching, and turns around to see a boy with brown eyes.

V.

Her name is Grace, and she is on fire.

Her life licks the air around her skin and sends up waves of heat, and his cold bone hand curls in his worn pocket, aching for the warmth.

Beneath the flames, she is a girl in a white dress speckled by mud, a heart-shaped face dotted with freckles, a braid of blond hair escaping in wisps, blue eyes so bright they burn.

He cannot shake the feeling he's seen her before, or, at least, seen pieces of her—those eyes, that hair—but he cannot remember where.

When he takes a step toward her, she takes a step back, glancing down at his bare feet, at the place where his toes dig into the ground, where the tiny red flowers wither and curl beneath his heels.

Her blue eyes narrow.

Knowing.

He thinks they always know, the way a body knows when the sun is up, the way a heart knows when it's in love, the way *he* knows to find the light, to take it in his hand, to snuff it out.

He wonders if she will run.

They try sometimes, the younger ones, and every now and then the old, but Death has that slow step and that long stride, and he can always catch them.

Only she doesn't run.

She holds her ground, and the fire in her eyes is stronger than a dying life.

"Go away," she says, her voice heady, the words rich with command, but he is no fae thing to be wished on.

"No," he says, his throat brittle from disuse.

Young mouth.

Old voice.

He draws his bone hand from his pocket, but she turns her back on him and crouches in the flowers, plucking the ones with the longest stems.

"For the festival," she says, as if the words mean anything to him.

"The festival," he echoes.

"It's the first of May," she goes on, piling flowers in her lap. "That makes today Beltane, with the May Queen and the Green Man, and the great bonfire . . ."

Something tickles the back of his mind, like remembering, but the memory itself is missing. Instead, there is a dark hole where memory should be, where it's been worn away by time, or dug out like the well.

The edges smooth, the drop steep.

"I'm not here for the festival," says Death.

The girl keeps threading her flower crown. "I know."

VI.

Grace forces her fingers to finish the crown while the boy and the tree lean over her.

She knows who he is, of course.

Knows even before she sees the dead farewells at his feet, even before she catches a glimpse of those bone fingers, even before he says her name.

She knows, the way a mouse knows the twitch of a cat's tail, the way feet know bad earth, the way children know fire.

She knows because she's seen him once before, out of the corner of her eye, standing beside her mother's bed.

She knows, and she is scared.

A horrible, heart-slamming-in-her-chest, run-run-run kind of scared. But her mother said there's no outrunning Death or the devil, so she holds her ground and tells herself there's more than one kind of quick in the world.

"I'm not ready," she says, hating the quiver in her words.

Death shakes his head. "It doesn't matter."

"Why me?" she says.

"I do not choose."

"How long do I have?"

Death doesn't answer.

"I want to say good-bye."

"No," says Death.

"I want to see the sun rise."

"No," says Death.

"I want to see the stars come out. I want to dance at the edge of the woods and throw my crown into the fire and taste the first summer fruit and—"

Death sighs, rolls those brown eyes, and says, "You're stalling."

"Wouldn't you?" she snaps.

The wind picks up, and overhead an old branch creaks, weakened by so many seasons and storms. She can hear the cracks spreading through the wood.

Not like this.

"Grace," says Death, holding out his hand, and it is nothing but bare bone, and the sight of it should give her shivers, but she can only stare with fascination, smothering the sudden, mad urge to slip her hand in his, to feel the cool, smooth surface.

The branch begins to snap.

And then, mercifully, a girl is calling her name, and she sees Alice Laurie standing in the road.

"Coming!" Grace calls, ducking out from under the tree a moment before the branch breaks and crashes down into the bed of red blossoms.

She doesn't look back.

VII.

Death frowns down at the fallen limb, at his empty hand.

The girl is halfway across the field, not running, exactly, but moving briskly toward the other girl, the one in the road, the one that doesn't burn.

He sighs, a sound like winter air through ice, and sets off after her with those long legs, leaving a trail of bare earth in his wake.

By the time he reaches Grace, she's alone again, and he walks right up and curls that bone hand around her shoulder. The heat licks his fingers.

"Caught you," he whispers, and she stiffens, perhaps waiting for the world to end, but that isn't how death works.

Hand in hand with life, that's how it goes.

"You could let me go," she says, keeping those blue eyes on the road.

"I can't," says Death.

The girl pulls free and turns on him, still gripping her red flower crown. "Why not?"

The question scratches at his mind. He tries to remember what will happen. He can't. But the knowing is there, solid as the hunger, that he cannot wait too long. He has to take her hand. Has to take her life. The knowing doesn't have words, but it's there all the same.

"I *can't*," he says again, willing her to understand.

She crosses her arms, and Death can hear a carriage coming up the road. The faint rattle of a wheel coming loose.

Again, he holds out his hand. "Grace."

"A life's got to be worth something," she says. "What will you give me for it?"

The carriage is rounding the bend behind her.

"What is it you want?" he asks, knowing the answer.

"A day, a week, a year—"

He shakes his head. "It's your time."

"Then let me have it. You're taking a whole life. The least you can give me is a day."

Death stares at the girl.

The girl stares at Death.

He could hold her down, grip her hands in his, lace their fingers against the road.

"Please," she says. "You owe me this."

Death frowns. "I do not owe you anything."

"Yes, you do!" she snarls as a gust of wind cuts through, tousling her hair, and he remembers.

Why she looks familiar.

Where he's seen those eyes before. Glazed with sickness, but just as bright, staring up from hollowed cheeks in a heart-shaped face. A woman's frail fingers reaching for his own. A small girl beyond the window, hair white in the moonlight.

"Yes, you do."

This time the words are a whisper, but he hears them all the same.

"Do you know what it's like?" she asks. "To lose so much? Can you even feel sadness, grief?"

He tries to trace his mind around its edges, feeling for the shape, but it is like everything besides his hunger, flat and dull and heavy.

"No," she mutters. "Of course you can't."

Death stares at the girl. He does not know what to say. What to do.

"Dusk," he says at last. "You can have until dusk."

Tears spill down her cheeks, even as she sets the crown triumphantly in her hair.

"Shake on it?" he asks, offering his bone hand.

At that, the girl makes a sound as sudden and high as birdsong, shakes her head, and turns away.

It was worth a shot, thinks Death, stepping out of the road as the carriage rattles past.

The wheel stays on.

VIII.

"Why?" he asks when she hands him the boots she nicked from Bobby Cray's porch.

"Some people track mud," she says. "You track death."

He sits on a low wall and tugs the old boots on, and they're just a bit of leather and cloth, but when he gets to his feet again and takes a few slow steps through the grass, it doesn't wither. He marvels at this, like a child first learning about tricks of light.

She holds out a leather glove, and he stares at it a moment before slipping it over his bone fingers.

"Last thing," she says, taking up the crown of green. He bows his head and lets her set the wreath in his red hair, but the moment it touches, the leaves go brown and brittle, and even though he cannot see the change, he seems to know what's happened, the good humor sliding from his face.

"This isn't a good idea," says Death, but this is Grace's day, bought and paid for with a life, and she will not surrender.

"It's all right," she says. "You'll just have to be a fall sprite instead."

In the distance, a fiddle begins to play.

A drum sounds steady as rain.

She takes Death by the arm. "Come on. We don't want to be late."

IX.

The festival sits with its back to the woods.

It is a circle of tents in shades of yellow and red, white and green; a platform of fiddlers and a pair telling stories and a dozen men and women with tables of food and drink.

The whole town is here.

Death has seen most of them already, making their way to the church that morning. That procession had been quiet, but now they whoop and cheer, their heads ringed with crowns, their lips brimming with laughter.

Death has never seen so much color, so much life.

The sun is high overhead, but men are already dragging dry logs from the forest and into the field, stacking them into a pyramid within a ring of stone.

A ring of stone just like the well, only there's no drop into darkness, only matted grass and piled sticks ready to be set on fire.

And all the girls have flowers in their hair.

And all the boys have crowns of leaves.

And everyone is happy.

"Here," says Grace.

She is holding out a piece of ripened fruit, the color of sunrise, and when he bites down, he remembers—laughter, an arm around his waist, lips against his skin. By the time he swallows, the memory is gone, fleeting as blue between storm clouds, but the warmth settles in his stomach, beautiful and sweet.

Someone starts to sing, and he knows that song.

He doesn't know it.

He can't remember.

But he can feel the place where it should be inside him, and when she sings the words, he feels them rising in his own throat.

The woman's voice carries as she sings old songs, of sailors and seasides and runaway girls, the kind of songs that sound like the wind bent into shape and thrum through Death's bones. An echo of an echo of something he knows. Knew. A flicker in his mind of another time, another name, a girl holding out her hand, and then he's blinking back the stars of memory, the flares of light made by the light of Grace's life throwing off embers beside him.

Grace holds out her hand.

"Dance with me," she says.

And Death hesitates, but the music is stirring something in him, every chord plucking at a string inside his mind, and when she takes him by the arm, he takes her, too, and they are spinning, first in slow circles and then faster, faster, and in between the strings and the turns, he remembers—lifting a girl into the air, a crown of yellow in her hair, a fiddle and a far-off song—but then it is gone, and he is here, in his body, in his bones, in his life without a life, a mind without a memory, and he wants to find his way back, wants to see the girl's face again, wants to feel more, more, more.

He laughs.

It is a strange sound, like a catching breath, a stranger feeling, like light in his chest, and he holds it close.

X.

They dance until dusk.

Until night falls and the music stops, and sweat darkens Death's red hair and shines in the hollow of Grace's throat. Her face is flushed and his is bright, and in that moment it is so easy to forget that he is Death and not just a boy with copper lashes and warm brown eyes.

She has seen him smile.

She has heard him laugh.

But the moment they stop dancing, she remembers.

He remembers, too. She can see it in his face. The flex of his fingers beneath the glove.

Just a little longer, she thinks. *I want to see the fire. I need to throw in my crown. It's bad luck, you know, if you don't say good-bye to the spring.*

"Grace," he starts, but then the crack and hiss of catching wood sound out their own music, and everyone is moving toward the waiting logs, and they are caught up in the current.

It catches slowly, the crackle of kindling at its center, the tendrils of smoke.

And then it roars to life.

Death stands, wide-eyed, beside her, fire dancing in his eyes, and she reaches out and takes his hand, careful to choose the one with a glove.

XI.

Death closes his eyes and basks in the heat.

He can feel himself smiling.

"Does it make you happy?" asks Grace.

And he is not sure he remembers what happiness is, but then she brushes her lips against his jaw, a warmth as sudden and bright as sunlight darting between clouds. There and gone, but not gone the way it was before, not *missing*.

He wants her to kiss him again, wants to kiss her back, but she is already moving, reaching up for the crown of red flowers in her hair.

When she takes it off, a pinkish stain lingers on her skin, and Death reaches up with his ungloved hand and brushes his thumb along her brow. And she is rimmed with light, throwing up sparks like embers, and when she smiles, he can see the light behind her teeth, can almost feel its heat.

She snatches the crown of dead leaves from his hair and tosses them both into the flames.

"Come with me," she says, and then she is pulling him away, away from the fire and the festival, away from the field, and into the woods.

They stumble through the trees, Grace in front and Death a step behind, and there's a lightness in his chest, and between strides, when the breeze is cool and her voice is sweet, he forgets.

Forgets that he is Death and she is burning, forgets that there is only one way for this to end.

"Grace," he calls after her, "slow down."

He wonders if, after all this, she's trying to run, but then she reaches a break in the trees and stumbles to a stop, catching her breath at the sudden swatch of sky.

And by the time he reaches her, she's sinking to the ground, lying back against the mossy earth to watch the stars.

Death lies beside her, the moss going brittle beneath him.

"Listen," she whispers.

As loud as the festival was, the forest is quiet.

"Thank you," he says softly.

"For what?" asks Grace.

For the spring dance, he wants to say, and the taste of summer fruit, for the bonfire and the starlit woods, and the memory of a life before. He is holding fast to each, cupping them in his hands, but they are already falling through his fingers.

He is getting cold again, the heat of the day dying down to embers in his chest. And he is hungry, and he is tired, and it has gone on too long.

He draws the glove from his hand. Lets it fall to the ground, silent as a leaf.

It is time, he thinks, his bone fingers drifting toward her hand. He wishes he could cup her life in his hands without letting it go. Keep it warm between them.

But that is not how death works.

But then she turns her head, those blue eyes shining in the dark.

"I want to go to the well," she says, and the words are so jarring that he pulls away, sits up. He thinks he's misheard, but she continues on beside him. "They say it's the place where the dead meet the living, where the living meet the dead. I want to call down to my mother."

And Death doesn't have the heart to tell her that's not how it works, that there's nothing at the bottom but cold earth and tired bones.

This is what she wants.

He has given her so many things.

He will give her one more.

XII.

It's been seven years since Grace went to the well.

None of the lads were brave enough to even climb the hill, but grief is louder than fear, and up she went to call her mother back.

But her mother never answered.

Now she stands there, side by side with Death, looking down at the ring of stone, the hole carved deep into the earth like an open grave, a place caught between the living and the dead.

"It's time," says Death.

"I know," says Grace.

"I'm sorry," says Death.

"I know," says Grace.

The boy leans down and unties the laces of his borrowed shoes, and Grace kicks off her own.

"What are you doing?" he asks.

"I want to go down."

Death shakes his head. "It is too steep."

"I'm not afraid of falling," she says. "I want to reach the bottom and press my lips to the cold earth and whisper to my mother. Will you show me how?"

Death looks between her and the well and then swings his leg over the side.

He turns, holding out his hand, and she looks into those wide brown eyes one last time before she pushes him in.

She half expects him to catch himself, to hover in the air, but he doesn't.

He falls.

Down, down, down, like all those words she hurled into the well, the ones that came up wrong, and then she hears the sound of bones crashing against the moss-slicked side, a body hitting stone.

Then nothing.

Grace stumbles back from the well, from Death, and runs.

Her chest heaves, heart trilling like a bird as she races down the hill.

Through the woods.

Past the dying fire as the distant sound of midnight bells ring in the end of spring.

She has done it.

The day is over, her time has come and gone, and she is running home, sprinting through the tall grass, when her foot catches something hard and flat laid into the earth.

She falls, cracking her head against the tombstone.

Her vision splinters into shards of light.

There is something warm against her face, like a hand brushing her brow.

Just out of reach is a crown of pale flowers, and her fingers drift toward it as the bells end, and the stars go out.

XIII.

Death is a girl with blue eyes.

A girl with bare feet and a white dress stained by red farewells and spring storms.

A girl with blond hair escaping its braid and a streak of ash on one sharp cheek.

It is a cloudless fall day when she wakes at the bottom of the well, uncurling like a leaf in spring.

One hand is smooth fair flesh; the other, crisp white bone.

Slowly, she gets to her feet, smoothing her skirts from habit, though habit is a thing that comes from memory, and she cannot remember anything.

She tips her head to the sky far, far above, one simple truth beating behind her ribs.

She is awake, and so she is hungry.

She is hungry, and so she is awake.

Jesse George's Villain Challenge to Victoria Schwab:

Hades Wakes Up after Being Unconscious at the Bottom of a Well in Ireland

DEAR DEATH

BY JESSE GEORGE

Dear Death,

You scare me. You're something that has taken me a long time to accept. I struggle coming to terms with what you're capable of. Sometimes you're expected; other times unexpected. You've taken people from me when I needed them the most. I have a few questions that I hope you can answer. Though I know deep down you'll never be able to.

What is it like to wake up with a hunger that can only be cured by someone's life? I can't blame you for doing what you have to do, but I find it difficult to understand you. When you see the burning aura, do you ever question fate? Do you ever attempt to resist? Or is the raging hunger inside you too difficult to contain? You give in to your cravings. You'd think you'd be able to let your prey live a little longer, but at the end of the day you can't show them grace, because you're on a set track. Hand in hand, you walk them down the aisle to their destiny.

It must be difficult to perform your act when you begin to know the life you're taking, though you make it seem effortless. You watch them before you cling to them. You observe who they are and what they're all about. As you drink them away, do you see a slide show of their life? I can't imagine that being an easy thing to partake in, yet you perform your act often.

Do you ever question yourself when they tell you "I'm not ready"? Does it ever slow down the process? They resist lacing their fingers with your bare-boned hand. They run from you, because in a way they feed on life, too. They're fueled by moments, memories, experiences, and people.

They don't want their time to end, so they resist you.

They resist their last dance with death.

Do you ever regret it? Do you ever look back and think you've made a mistake? That maybe they had a little bit more to give, a little more life to live? I often wonder if they stain your dreams. When you look up at the stars from the depths of your well, do you ever look at it as a display of the lives you've collected? After the sacrifice they've made for you, they still find a way to shine for you.

Do you ever stick around to see the aftermath? You climb out of the well and stroll out of the woods. The aura burns for you, and you feed. You feed on hopes, dreams, and memories. You feed on life. Do you linger in the shadows?

I'll never forget the time I received the news, when you decided to make a strike on someone so close to me. I was taken aback. I fell to the ground breathing in the question "why?" Were you watching then? As tears streamed down my face and my heart shattered? The bond that once was, beginning to fade? I wish there were some way I could go back in time and intervene. To get on my hands and knees and beg and plead for another way. Any other way. Take me instead, let her live. Would you have even heard me? Or is the call of death too strong?

You inhale life but exhale chaos. You set off a ticking bomb of emotions. Loved ones of the taken receive the call of hard-hitting news. They're taken aback as they attempt to come to term with the news. Reactions vary from cries of shock to overwhelming sadness.

When the church bells ring, do you ever wonder if it's the start of the funeral of the life you fed on? Do you ever consider attending? I always wondered if you attended the funerals of my loved ones. If you snuck in and found a seat in the back. To pay your respects to the lives you took.

Even though you wreck hearts, you have a way of bringing people together. How do you do it? Do you even realize you're doing it? People who've spent years apart come together to unite over the loss of a beautiful soul. I'm not sure I could ever grant you the title *hero*, but there are positive side effects to your madness.

Have you ever realized how many people fear you? Because I know, truly, that I am not the only one.

I hope this letter finds you well. I'm sure we'll meet eventually, but hopefully not anytime soon.

— Jesse

MARIGOLD

BY SAMANTHA SHANNON

Wilt go, then, dear infant, wilt go with me there?
My daughters shall tend thee with sisterly care;
My daughters by night their glad festival keep,
They'll dance thee, and rock thee, and sing thee to sleep.
— JOHANN WOLFGANG VON GOETHE, THE ERL-KING,
TRANSLATED BY EDGAR ALFRED BOWRING

This is a tale of a prince and a princess, two men on a quest, two queens, and a maid named Marigold.

You might reasonably assume that these are the perfect ingredients for a fairy tale.

It begins in 1850, when the Erl-folk were in England. (History holds that they originally came from Scandinavia, but they have a habit of turning up in all sorts of places, at all sorts of times. Their royal family, like any, moves its court between seasons, and seasons, for erls, can last for generations in our world.) Some people said they were faeries. Some said they were men and women who had stretched their natural lives with alchemy, or by making pacts with the devil that had left them twisted beyond recognition. Some said they were the offspring of demons, while others declared them to be the vengeful spirits of the dead.

What was agreed by everyone in England was that the Erl-folk were wicked. For when their pride is insulted or their territory trespassed upon, erls take something in return.

They take children.

☙☙

Princess Alice, second daughter of Queen Victoria and Prince Albert, disappeared on September the third of 1850, when she was seven years old. When she scampered into the woods that morning, saying she had seen a perfectly lovely fox, her governess had pleaded with her to come back. The woods belonged to the Erl-queen. It was common knowledge. An unwritten law.

But Alice had always been too curious about people who were nothing like her, and Erl-folk had intrigued her since she was old enough to know that they existed. Later, people would doubt that she had seen a fox at all, but the red hair of the Erl-queen's sprites.

The governess had called in vain. She had been certain, for an hour, that she could hear Alice singing; she had chased the voice until she was exhausted. A manservant found her lying beside a stream, cold as death and murmuring nonsense.

A search party was mustered, but the dreadful truth was soon apparent: Alice was gone. She was the latest in a long line of girls to be taken in a year.

The princess had been missing for a week when the Erl-queen's son arrived at Windsor to broker a deal on his mother's behalf. Queen Victoria had pleaded for Alice's safe return and offered a trade to the creatures of the forest. The Erl-queen was welcome to any person in England in exchange for Princess Alice. Anyone at all.

It was assumed that a person of some importance would be required in exchange for the life of a princess, and that the matter would need lengthy consideration, but the Erl-queen's son had made his decision at once. He had called her by name: Marigold Beath. No title. A servant in the household of the Sinnett family. Her employment had been an act of charity from the housekeeper, who had taken pity on a pretty orphan. Yet she, of all people, was known to the elves.

Eight girls missing, and now, by royal decree, the Erl-queen had Marigold.

Marigold was the ninth.

London, September 1850

Isaac Fairfax opened his eyes and beheld his moonlit image in the glass. How like his father he looked tonight; he could almost be his ghost. Grey eyes, a square jaw, and a hint of mustache. Marigold had always said how much she liked it.

Marigold. Sweat sealed his hair to his brow. His flesh ached for her touch. Her absence tore at his soul, leaving a wound where his heart had been.

Short breaths cut between his lips. His fingers were stiff on the buttons of his waistcoat, but he didn't call for a servant. No one was to know that he had left the house.

His head was throbbing. Why, *why* did it have to be her? How had Marigold caught the eye of the Erl-queen? She was quiet as a doll, and delicate, too, more of a household spirit than a living girl. Even he would never have noticed her had George, her elder half brother, not shown her to him. He had been hers from that first moment, when he had seen her through the window of the Sinnetts' house. She had been kneeling beside the stove in the kitchen, scrubbing the floor with care, never rushing in her work. Her hair had been tumbling from its cap, obscuring most of her face, and her hands had been raw.

That *hiddenness* about her, the sense that she could never be known, was what made her such a desirable maid. Employers did not like to know their servants as people—it was an uncomfortable thing, to imagine them as more than silent pairs of hands—but *he* had known her. He had known her more times than he could count. And every time had been a risk. Forbidden in the eyes of proper society.

His gaze had cast a light on her, elevated her from obscure to divine, and, oh, he had worshipped her. Her skin had been his altar; her lips, his confession.

Yet there had been other eyes on her, too, watching from the deep forests of Britain.

Isaac walked to the chest at the end of his bed. Inside was his sword, polished to a star-bright gleam. He would have Marigold back, and he would have her tonight—even if it meant taking her from the Erl-queen by force. Even if it meant facing whatever lay in the Forest of Erl, which swallowed all who entered it.

There was no enchantment on the weapon. There was no need for that. The Erl-queen feared steel. And iron, and clockwork. It was why she abhorred industry and, by extension, the industrious men with whom she shared her land.

His fingers skimmed the blade; he caught his own eye in it. Why *had* the foul creature wanted her, of all people? Why his Marigold? She was sixteen, far older than the girls the Erl-queen usually took, but they did say that her son had an eye for human women. Rumor had it that he frequented London's brothels, disguised as a man—but Marigold was no common whore. She would never have been unfaithful to him, never. She loved him—she had said so. No virtuous woman would allow an erl to court her, in any case, knowing their insatiable lust for mortal captives of the fairer sex. The Erl-queen's son might have known who she was, but she could not have known him.

His heart was all aquiver. In the coffeehouses and supper rooms of London, it was whispered that the Erl-queen's son was taller than any natural man. Instead of teeth, there were thorns in his mouth, hidden behind petal lips. His ears were gently pointed, like the tips of willow leaves. The moon was always in his hair. He moved like water, and his eyes were black through, without so much as a glimpse of white. They glistened in a face as ancient as Stonehenge.

They said Marigold had wept when Queen Victoria agreed to the exchange. That she had begged for mercy. Heartsick, Isaac closed his eyes. She must be terrified. She was terrified of almost everything in the world. And he, the man she loved, the man she trusted, had let that Erl-prince steal her away.

"Good evening, Isaac."

Sharply, he turned. When he saw the familiar smile, so like hers, he let out his breath.

"George," he said, and smiled back. "My friend."

George Beath stood in the doorway. Tall and fine of feature, with a head of golden curls he must have purloined from an angel, he might have been the most eligible bachelor in London if not for his name—*Beath*, a name that reeked of scandal. Everyone with ears knew about his late father's affair and the child he had brought back from India. His wife had chosen to take poison rather than live with the shame of his infidelity, and the man himself had soon followed her to the grave. George had been six years old at the time.

Now he was nineteen, and although he shared blood with Marigold, he was nothing like her physically. Marigold took very much after her mother; he took after his. Where she was dark and brittle, George was broad-shouldered and fair as a snowdrop. His clothes were always a little behind the fashion, and he often wore the same attire for several days at a time.

Isaac had long since forgotten to mind. Londoners had remarkable memories when it came to scandal, but George Beath was his dearest friend and had helped him countless times throughout their three-year acquaintance.

"The Erl-queen has had my sister for long enough." George showed him his pistol. "Let us teach her what we do to thieves in England."

Isaac nodded silently.

"You look pale." George clapped him on the back. "Better have a little brandy before we leave. Marigold won't want a milksop saving her from the Erl-queen, will she?"

"No. Yes, of course. But I shan't need brandy."

"Come, now, Ise. We all need a little brandy now and then."

"No. Thank you, but no. My head must be clear." He risked a glance at George and found a look of faint disappointment on his face. How he hated to turn down his counsel. "We are about to enter the Erl-queen's lands," he said with a nervous laugh. "And I doubt very much that her warriors drink brandy before battle."

"Oh, of course they do—or some preternatural cousin of it, in any case. Elves are hedonists." George took his hip flask from his coat. There were shadows under his eyes, mirrors of the ones beneath his own. "Come. Her Majesty will forget about the treaty once her nemesis is defeated. Put some fire in your belly."

The hip flask was presented a second time. Isaac looked at it weakly before gulping a little. It burned him to the navel.

He had never cared for brandy.

"How can you be so certain?" Already, he felt light-headed. "Even if Queen Victoria remains ignorant of our plan, the Erl-queen will know. They say she can feel every movement in every forest. She knew as soon as Princess Alice entered."

"Princess Alice was not armed with steel." George grasped his shoulder. "You are no child. You are no woman. You will be the one to slay the Erl-creature, Ise. For Marigold. You will be a hero of the empire, and to her, you will be king of it."

A handkerchief was presented. Isaac used it to smudge the perspiration from his temples.

"Yes," he breathed. "Yes. For Marigold."

George extinguished the oil lamp before he peeled apart the curtains and gazed at the street. Now the only light in the house was from the streetlamp outside.

"The cab is waiting for us at the end of Gower Street. Remember," George said, "when we arrive, we must resist the sounds of the forest. Everything there is a siren call." He faced Isaac with a weary smile, a smile that promised an end to their suffering. His eyes were forget-me-not unlike hers. "By dawn, Marigold will be back in your arms. Imagine how much more she'll love you."

George always filled him with such surety. Isaac glanced at the glass one more time, feeling a streamlet of warmth in his blood. His sword was at his side, and he wore a simple black coat over his clothing, the better to disguise himself in the shadows of the forest. He had turned eighteen in April, but for the first time in his life, it seemed to him that a man was looking back.

☙

Princess Alice had disappeared from a forest in Scotland, where the royal family had been staying at the time, but the Erl-queen's territory was in all forests. It was what had been agreed to when the first railway had been built, when the Erl-queen began to steal the girls in revenge for the destruction of the natural world, for the vapors and the blackened trees and the scars of industry. The elves preferred to dwell in savage ignorance than embrace the nineteenth century. It was said that their queen felt every footstep in every forest in the country, as closely as a man felt the heartbeat in his chest.

"Tell me," Isaac ventured, once they were safely ensconced in the hansom cab, "is it true what Princess Alice said when she returned?"

George sighed. "The child is a fool. The Erl-queen's feasts must have rotted her mind."

"But it is true."

His friend looked through the window. All was quiet on the streets of London.

"So a servant told me," he finally said. "The princess was weeping when she returned. She made it perfectly clear to her mother that she did not *want* to be back with her family. That she wanted to stay with 'the other queen of England.'"

Isaac shivered. "Why do you suppose the child would have wanted to stay with the elves?"

"Why, I just told you, Ise. The Erl-queen's feasts. She lures the children with crumbs of seedcake, and once they eat, they are bewitched. That's why she only takes girls, you see."

"I'm not sure I understand."

"A boy is far less likely to be tempted by cake. Boys think. Present a female child with something pretty or sweet, and she'll take it without question." He shook his head pityingly. "Did you notice that the Erl-queen always sends her son to make her bargains? She knows that sons can't be so easily tricked."

It must be true if George believed it, though Isaac had been fond of seedcake himself as a child and would probably have followed a trail of it anywhere. He had no sisters to measure himself against, but his mother adored purposeless knickknacks, and it was true that a boy had never been taken by the Erl-queen, and it *had* always been easy to soothe Marigold with little trinkets . . . When she had been most fretful, afraid that she would be ruined if he left her, a pendant or a comb would ease her mind. Girls, it seemed, were just like magpies.

Had the Erl-queen's son offered her more than a comb—some treasure of the forest?

No, he must not think of Marigold with that beast.

"Still," Isaac said, if only to divert his mind, "for the princess to say to her own *mother*—"

"Her Majesty was aghast, naturally, and has hardly looked at Alice since. Nobody dares speak of the Erl-queen in her presence, not even Prince Albert." George chuckled. "If she remains as ill-disposed toward the elves as she is now, you might emerge from this with a knighthood."

Other young men might have gloried in the thought, but for Isaac, it was painful. A knighthood would make it even more difficult for him to see Marigold. Every one of their trysts had been dangerous, both to his public dignity and to her reputation. George, who always kept watch outside, had protected them both.

"So might you," Isaac said, affecting a jocular tone. "You introduced me to Marigold. Neither of us would be in this cab if not for you, George Beath."

He allowed himself, briefly, to savor the memory of when George had brought her out from the Sinnetts' house. How she had looked at him with such awe and uncertainty, her eyes ignited by the moon. He had whispered her name and looked into those eyes—such eyes, all darkness, promising a thousand secrets. He still dreamed of that first night they had spent together.

"Oh, all I did was put you in touch," George said gently. "I would have been a poor brother if I had watched her waste away. All she wanted, from the moment she laid eyes on you, was to be your wife."

This made Isaac rather warm under the collar. The only thing he had never given Marigold was a proposal.

It was not to be. It never could be. She was too far below him: an orphaned scullery maid, born to an officer of the East India Company and his Indian mistress. George was all that was left of her English family, and he was so poor now that he could not support her. Only the compassion of people he had helped had kept him off the streets. All he could afford was some squalid garret on Earlham Street. How unjust that such a kind fellow should live in such a wretched state.

Isaac rested his brow against the window. His mother wanted him to marry Anne Crowley, who came with a large dowry and a respectable name, but even if he married her, he knew he would not be able to let go of Marigold. She was all gentleness and innocence, and she knew when to be silent. Anne was handsome, but too cold and too forthright.

If only the Erl-queen had taken her instead.

The cab stopped when the woods were in sight. George banged on the roof.

"Drive on, man. What's the matter?"

"I shan't go any farther, sir," the driver said. "The Erl-queen will see us."

"Oh, the devil take you." George clicked his tongue. "Come along, Ise. No time to lose."

They took leave of the cab. Isaac paid the driver a pound, over twice what he was owed. He could earn far more if he sold the story of the eligible Isaac Fairfax breaking the law, but they would have to hope that he was a half-wit.

The woods were clad in bonfire gold and red, yet the colors were somehow cold—hollow and illusory, like rich clothes left to rot on corpses. Isaac had the sense that looking at them was what it must be like to be lost in opium, seeing things that were not quite there.

"Isaac," George said, "remember what I told you. Don't follow the music. Ignore any peculiar lights or sounds." He placed a hand on the pistol at his side. "The Erl-queen steals little girls. She won't be ready for men, now, will she?"

Isaac nodded. "God be with us, George."

A wry smile curved George's mouth. "God does not walk in the Forest of Erl."

Together, the two men stepped toward the trees. As they crossed the boundary, a dark fog gathered around them and thickened in their throats. Isaac turned cold to his soul, but he pressed on. Marigold was waiting for them.

When a man entered any wooded place in England, he passed into one great Forest of Erl. So the tales claimed, in any case. Only Princess Alice had ever returned from the Erl-queen's realm, and she had said nothing about her imprisonment. This forest existed in a kind of spirit country of its own, and if he wandered too far into it, he would never find the way back out. If he *was* fortunate enough to emerge, he might find himself somewhere miles away from the place where he had entered. One could make the crossing in Hampshire and stumble out in Galloway.

When the fog cleared, Isaac shuddered. A bitter wind slashed at his face, unnerving him, before it stopped abruptly. As if the wind were the breath of the forest, and its mouth had locked closed.

They stood on fallen leaves in a silence so deep it was almost too much to bear. Their boots sank to their ankles. George hefted up the lantern he was carrying. Isaac hardly dared speak, but he forced himself.

"Did Princess Alice say where the Erl-queen hides?"

"No, but elves have an affinity with yews." George handed Isaac the lantern. "If we strike the bark from one, we will soon hear from the sprites. They will lead us to her."

The thought of damaging the forest chilled him—there was no greater insult to an elf—but George knew best. Being a man of varied interests, with an insatiable hunger to learn, he knew more about the Erl-queen than many scholars did.

They walked a little farther. Every footstep crackled, scraping at Isaac's nerves, and when he stepped on a hidden twig, it let out a sound like a gunshot that echoed through the forest. Sweat trickled from his hairline. He was certain he could see green eyes among the foliage.

"I see no yews," he murmured.

The trees, whatever sort they were, were impossibly tall; even their lowest branches were higher than Isaac could have reached, even if he had thrown a stone. At first glance, it was an ordinary forest, aside from the colossal trees, but when his vision sharpened, he found the imperfections. The trunks bled golden sap. The cracks in the bark glowed lambent red. He saw that the forest was only a mask, and the poison beneath, the poison of the Erl-queen, was oozing through the fractures. Everything was washed in a queasy greenish light, and it all seemed to curve—as if he were peering through a glass bottle, or all of it was a picture printed on a newspaper and he was pulling its edges toward him, warping it strangely. It made him giddy and breathless and frightened all at once.

He had only taken a few steps, and already he was disoriented. As if he had taken the whole bottle of brandy.

George wavered, too. His path had been straight at first, but now he veered to and fro, making the lantern sway. Watching it made Isaac feel as if he might be sick.

"She must know now," he whispered. "She must know of our coming, George."

She knows.

Isaac turned on his heel, drawing his sword. The voice had been so close to his ear that he had felt breath fluttering there, and it did not belong to George, but no one was behind him.

A shadow scuttled in the corner of his eye, and a titter, high and childlike, sent a cold draft down his nape. He spun to face it with a hoarse cry, just in time to see a ribbon of scarlet disappearing behind a tree.

"What is it?" George hissed. "Isaac?"

Sprites. They had come already. Their blood-red hair was famous—what Alice had followed into the woods. A lesser sort of Erl-folk, but no less dangerous. They would be carrying word of the strangers' presence to their queen.

"I heard—" His tongue was clumsy. "A voice."

The voice of a son, a servant, a sentinel.

This time, George also flinched. His eyes reflected the lantern.

All around them, dead leaves shifted and danced, resurrected from their grave. They reeled into a churning column; it moved the way a dancer would cross Pandemonium's ballroom, and it flickered with the vestige of the autumnal red. Dizzied by the sight of it and frightened half to death, Isaac tightened his hold on the sword. As he watched, the column gained sharp edges and corners, firmed and whirled itself into the shape of a man: pale, barefoot, and almost naked. All that protected his modesty were frayed breeches, palest silver-green and coated with fine hair. More flaxen hair poured over his shoulders in abundance and streamed to his waist, clinging to his skin as if he had risen from water. His entire body was knotted and gnarled with muscle.

"Men," this formidable creature observed. "Human men in the Forest of Erl."

The pointed ears marked him as an erl, but the black eyes were the true seal of his heritage. Maggot holes into oblivion. This could only be the Erl-queen's son.

Isaac thrust his sword forward, gripping it in a white-knuckled hand. He had seen the fanciful illustrations of elves in *Punch*, but he had never felt such terror as he did when he beheld their prince with his own eyes. No drawing could capture the way the creature bled the warmth from the air around them, the sense that he was more element than being, the certainty that he had no business taking the form of a man. He had been here since the world was new. All this Isaac knew from only a glance.

"We have come for Marigold Beath," Isaac said. His hand shook. "Tell us where you took her."

"Don't speak to it, Isaac." George's pistol was aimed between those ghastly eyes. "It has no power over metal."

"Is that so, man of flesh?" the Erl-queen's son purred. "People will believe almost anything if they hear it in a coffeehouse. If rumor has it, then it must be true. Do you believe *everything* you hear about Erl-folk, Isaac Fairfax?" He took a step toward them. "Do you believe everything you hear about me?"

The eyes were on him now, penetrating his soul. Isaac swallowed the sour taste that was rising in his gorge. When he looked into those eyes, he saw a world without order. He saw the chaos of prehistory. Despite what the gossips had whispered, he could not imagine this . . . *thing* in the brothels of Covent Garden.

"Tell us—" His mouth was so dry. "Tell us where you took Marigold, damn you."

"Marigold Beath is safe," was the calm rejoinder, "just as Princess Alice was. How cruel of you, it was, to take Alice away! She left without injury, but Marigold is older. She has tasted our food and sipped our honey. If she leaves the forest, she will die."

"Lies," George sneered. "You bewitched the princess, and you stole my sister. Take us to her at once, or I will help the Erl-queen understand how it feels to lose a member of one's family."

The Erl-queen's son tilted his head. "Oh my. Do you mean to break your own queen's law?"

"The laws of England have never helped me. Neither have they helped my sister." George locked gazes with the fiend. "Marigold needs her brother."

"Or does her brother need *her*, George Beath?"

Isaac stared. There was one thing the gossips had painted with some accuracy: the smile of thorns. It was as if the stem of a rose had been stripped and each thorn pressed into coal-black gum. A red tongue licked over them.

"She will not be pleased that you have come for her," the Erl-prince said. "She does not speak well of you, gentlemen. Not at all."

How did the Erl-queen know of them already? Surely even sprites weren't that quick on their feet. Isaac tried to find his voice—he was ready to plead for Marigold's life, to fall to his knees and beg—but George's patience snapped violently. Isaac cried "No" an instant too late; the bullet pierced the Erl-queen's son where a man's heart should be. He looked down at his chest with a sort of curiosity.

"Oh, England," he said. "When will you learn?"

He crumbled into nothing. Isaac threw himself upon the heap of leaves.

"George," he choked out, "he might have led us to Marigold. Why in God's name did you shoot him?"

"He would have lured us into a trap," George said curtly. "You saw his mouth. They speak of roses without thorns, but elves are roses without blooms."

"You killed her *son*. Their prince." He hunted desperately through the leaves. "If this forces open war—"

"Oh, for goodness' sake, we are *already* at war, Isaac. My poor sister is a prisoner of it." George kept his pistol close. "On your feet, now. Help me find a yew."

Isaac's hands fell limp. "Yes. A yew."

He had almost forgotten that they were looking for one. Yes, they must find a yew and tear the bark from it, and the sprites would return and lead them to the Erl-queen.

George extended his free hand. Isaac took it. Once he was upright, he used his cuff to smear away the sweat from his upper lip, tasting salt and fear. The leaves did not stir again.

He could not consider the repercussions now. If he could come out of this with Marigold in his arms, and her gratitude to him, even treason would be a small thing.

Yew. Yes, he knew what a yew tree looked like; he had seen them often enough as a boy in Surrey. He followed George farther into the gloom, staggering a little. When he looked over his shoulder, he could still make out the grass beyond the trees, and the light of the hansom cab beyond, but that light was ebbing.

"George," he said, "ought we to leave a trail?"

"No, no. Once the Erl-queen is dead, her hold on the forest will be released."

"You know this for certain?"

"Nothing is known for certain about the elves. This," George said, "is intuition, and I trust mine implicitly. I trusted that you would love Marigold as fervently as she loved you, and was that not true? I trusted that you would one day make her a good husband, and I know that you will prove me right." He stepped over a root. "You must ask her, after this, Isaac. You must marry her."

"This hardly seems the time for talk of marriage, George."

"You have delayed for too long. Marigold's reputation will be in jeopardy by now."

Isaac had no room for these thoughts. "Her reputation?" For some absurd reason, he chuckled. The forest was addling his wits. "She was sent by royal decree, George. Surely nobody could question—"

"Her honor was never in peril before, while I was there to protect you both, but she has been with the Erl-folk for three days," George said, shooting him a doleful look. "Unchaperoned. Unprotected. You saw that creature. How . . . bestial it was."

"Marigold would never—"

"Of course not, Ise, but London is a nest of gossips and busybodies. They will wonder how any woman's virtue could survive in the company of such wildness. No one else will have her."

It was as George was saying this, in his earnest tone, that Isaac heard the music. At first it was gentle, almost imperceptible, but it soon engulfed his hearing. "Do you hear that?" he asked, but George had already pressed ahead, taking the lantern with him. Isaac turned drunkenly.

"He called us cruel," he murmured to no one in particular, "for taking Princess Alice away."

☙

A light flared in the forest, blue and pulsing. He followed the song toward it without care, forgetting about George, about Marigold, about the Erl-queen's son. Every faery tale warned of the voices of the elves, of stone circles concealed in grass that ensnared whatever stepped inside them—but although Isaac knew this, the knowledge was distant, so it hardly seemed like it mattered at all. The forest was safe, and there was something miraculous waiting for him where the blue light shone, something that would put an end to his anguish. All he needed to do was go to it . . .

Soon he was following a stream, where iridescent fish were swimming. Their teeth were needles jutting out of their turned-down mouths. He waded in and cupped his hands, saw his own image in the water. The same face he had seen in the glass but happier, with bloodshot eyes.

He blinked, and he was standing before the mouth of a cave. Giddy, he lurched into it. His gloved hands rasped against stone. He breathed in an ambrosial scent.

Isaac, someone was calling. *Isaac.* The wind itself was whispering his name.

"Marigold," he said.

Isaac.

He forced his body through the cave, scrabbling at its walls, splashing through the stream. Blind and deaf, he dashed his head against a low rock, but the pain was washed away by the realization that Marigold was close. He would have her back. She would be his to love again.

When he emerged, he shielded his eyes. Light was streaming from above him, glorious sunlight, softened to amber where it fell through a canopy of ochre leaves. Birds were chirruping from low branches, which were laden with rainbows of fruit. Had it not been nighttime on the other side?

He was standing in a sheltered glade, an Elysium in the depths of the forest—and all around him there were women and girls. A child with golden ringlets was laughing on the grass, her cheeks and brow flecked by the sunlight. Older girls, no more than fourteen, were fishing with spears. Others were dancing or picking fruit or making chains of wildflowers. One woman had a prune for a face and silver hair, and she held a newborn baby in her arms.

They wore simple clothes. Many wore trousers, like men, or had their skirts bound up around their knees, while others were clad in dresses that looked for all the world like they were made of butterflies. He had never seen so many girls together without a chaperone. Was it a mirage? He was drunk on the cloying scent of flowers . . .

And at the end of the stream, where water pooled deep and clear beside a waterfall, was a woman with hair that shone like the finest lacquer. She wore a gown of emerald-green silk, hitched up to bare her slim brown calves. She poured water over her hair from a jug, renewing its luster. Her head was tilted into the sunlight, and her eyes were closed. He could have stared at her forever, so peaceful did she look.

"Marigold," he breathed, because he could not bear to be silent. Then, louder: "Marigold!"

Her head flicked to face him. Her eyes grew wide, and Isaac's face broke into a smile. She was alive. He should admonish her for dressing so improperly, but instead he ran toward his treasure, arms outstretched to grasp her.

She screamed.

Isaac stopped dead. Marigold scrambled away from him, slinking down the rock until she was knee-deep in the water. "No. *No*," she said. To the girls, she shouted, "Fetch the Erl-queen! Why on earth did none of you stop them?"

The children in the glade sprang to their feet. "Mother," they chorused. "Mother, help Marigold!"

The plea was taken up all around them, until it echoed like a cry into the mouth of a bell. Isaac hardly noticed. All he could do was gaze at Marigold, and it seemed all she could do was gaze back, but there was nothing familiar left in her eyes. He looked upon a changeling.

"Leave me, Isaac Fairfax," she said in a tremulous voice. Her skirts drifted on the surface of the water. "Let me go."

"Marigold, you are bewitched." He held out his hand. "The Erl-queen stole you. I can take you back."

"Back to what?" Marigold shook her head. "Back to a life as a scullery maid, rented for profit?" She sank deeper into the water. "She says he'll murder me. George. He's always longed to do it, you know. If I return to that world, I am not long for it. I pitied you once—you were deceived—but I cannot forgive you. I *cannot* forgive you for not seeing through George's lie . . ."

She had never spoken like this to him. The quake had left her voice. Now she sounded so *cold*, so hardened.

"Lie," he repeated. "Marigold, what on earth do you mean? Nobody rented you."

"Look to George. Look to your own heart. Did you never realize that when I wept, I wept because I was afraid—not happy?" She crossed her arms over herself, as if to shield her heart. It made her look so young, so fragile. So like *his* Marigold. "I know now. I know that I am whole, that I am strong, and I am free to make my life what I will. You will *not* take me, as Queen Victoria took Alice. As my father took me from my mother."

"Marigold, enough of this." She must be addled by the Erl-queen's feast, but he was beginning to feel angry. All this way he had come for her, and all she could do was call her own brother murderous and talk about the mother she had never known. "You are confused, my love. You are not yourself."

She raised her chin. "I believe I am best-placed to decide what I am. I am more myself than I ever was."

"You were perfect before." His throat was full. "You *are* perfect, Marigold."

"No. I was compliant," she said bitterly, "because that was what you wanted. He knew what you wanted, Isaac. My brother knows you like your women to be soft-spoken, to flatter you and simper for you!" Her hand struck through the water in frustration. Isaac flinched. "He blackmailed me. He saw me as his ruin, his mother's death—in my cradle, I was poison to his name—and he meant me to pay for it. To pay my debt by marrying you, even if I had to spend the rest of my days in misery. He cared nothing for my happiness. Only his *reputation*." Her face was contorted. "Oh, Isaac—do you still not see?"

Tears were in her eyes; her teeth were bared in anger. Leaves were shifting in the glade. The children emptied baskets of them, carpeting the grass.

This could not be Marigold.

"He was using both of us, Isaac," she spat. "He told me he would kill me, the first time, if I refused to do what you wanted . . . and after, he promised he would ruin me if I was not the perfect mistress. He would tell the Sinnetts we met, allow them to find us. He was the one who arranged our meetings, wasn't he? He always knew where we were." Marigold rose from the water. Rivulets streamed from her hair, soaking her sleeves. "He befriended you because he thought you were weak-willed. My brother has a silver tongue. If you married me—if you could be persuaded, in the end, to marry me—he believed the Beath family would be raised to its former glory. That he would no longer be in destitution." She shook her head. "I was never yours. I do *not* love you. I never did. If you care for me at all, leave me."

Isaac was close to choking. "I *cannot* leave you." He could not understand—*would* not understand. "George told me. He told me you loved me, that you wanted to see me—"

"A scullery maid in a household you had never visited. When did I become besotted with you?"

"You saw me through the window!"

Now she looked pitying. "Do you really suppose that one can fall in love with a person through a window?"

He could not stand this. He couldn't look at her, knowing she would flee from him if he tried to take her in his arms again.

"Marigold, come here."

Isaac was jolted from his memories. George had come into the glade. The children fled from him, crying for their mother.

"George," he said faintly.

"Marigold," George said, ignoring him, "you will stop making a fool of yourself and step out of the water. Come with us at once."

Marigold stumbled deeper into the pool, so the water came past her waist. "No, George," she said, eyes flashing. "I have had enough of your threats—your scheming—"

George clicked his tongue. "You see, Isaac. Bewitched, just as I said." He strode toward her. She looked half wild with fear. "Marigold, I don't want to have to hurt you."

"Leave me *be*."

Isaac cringed at her shrill tone. This was not her voice, not Marigold. George was right.

"You are becoming hysterical, sister." George was always so calm, so unruffled. He fixed her with an unblinking stare, the sort one would use on a deer before shooting it. "Marigold, Isaac has given me his word that he will marry you when you return to England. You see? You will be Marigold Fairfax, a respectable lady of London, with a husband who adores you. Your reputation will not be ruined. And our family name will be restored. You'll see."

But Isaac had never promised to marry her. George must know that it was impossible. He must always have known that Isaac was meant to court Anne, surely, yet he spoke of the possibility so often . . .

"Reputation." Marigold laughed. "Our father used my mother to slake his desire, stole her newborn child, and left her to rot—and she was not the only woman to suffer that fate." Tears glossed her eyes for a fleeting instant before they turned to flint again. "You used me to get what you wanted. So did Isaac. Yet it is *my* reputation in peril. Do you truly wonder why I want to stay here?"

George's pistol pointed at her heart. "George," Isaac cried. "How dare you threaten her?"

"Don't be a milksop. I will shoot her if it saves her life," his friend snapped. "A decent surgeon will take out the bullet. She'll only have a little scar."

"Shoot me, then," Marigold said before Isaac could protest. "Shoot me. Like an *honorable* man." She held out her hands. "He'll kill me either way, Isaac. The Erl-queen knows the future. If you let him take me back, he will strangle me before I turn seventeen. He will tell you that I ran away to find my mother, that I drowned at sea, anything to make you forget. No one will know the truth."

His heart was breaking. He was a statue struck too hard by a chisel, splintering all over. His eyes grew hot and damp. George claimed he had done it all for her, so she might have a chance of love with a man above her station. Could his dear friend really have been little more than a procurer, a parasite with designs upon the Fairfax fortune? Had George truly believed Isaac would make Marigold his bride, even if it meant lowering his own reputation? It was more than he could bear. And he could not believe it of George, his friend . . .

Wind murmured around them, carrying leaves with it. The light vanished from overhead, turning the mist the stern grey of pewter. Isaac felt a chill on his neck.

A woman had appeared in the center of the glade. Earth cracked from her shoulders as she rose to her full height. Her skin was the darkest bark, her hair was a wreath of ivy, and she wore nothing but a veil of gossamer. Inside her face, just visible through it, were the same black eyes she shared with the prince—for this could be none other than the Erl-queen, the other queen of England, the creature who had stolen all these girls from those who loved them. The creature who had terrorized a country.

"Leave," she said in a soughing voice.

Isaac unsheathed his sword again. It had been easy to kill the Erl-queen's son. Now he was not so afraid.

"Not without the girl," George said. "Release my sister from your bewitchment, or I will shoot you, as I shot your hell-spawned offspring."

"Victoria made a bargain. A life for a life." The forest rippled as she approached, half walking and half drifting, like a wraith from a nightmare. "Leave."

Marigold splashed through the water and ran toward the monster. George grabbed her and pulled her, writhing, against him. He pressed the pistol to his sister's jaw, and she began to cry out: a hoarse, enraged sound. Her breast heaved as the Erl-queen watched them, her face betraying nothing through the veil.

"Isaac," Marigold gasped, "Isaac, you must see what he is."

"Quiet." George only had eyes for the Erl-queen. "You will stand aside and let us leave."

"If she leaves," the Erl-queen whispered, "she dies young."

Isaac swallowed. "And Princess Alice?"

When the Erl-queen turned to look at him, the forest seemed to move with her. Leaves and petals clung to her veil. The birds warbled a frenzy of song. The wind sighed. He almost lost courage, but he said, "Will the princess also die young?"

"Her wedding will be held in the shadow of death. She will be melancholy all her life and will not outlive her mother. Two of her children will be slain," the Erl-queen said. "Two more will die before they truly lived. She was happy in the Forest of Erl."

"She *protects* us, Isaac," Marigold said, her voice low and strained. "The Erl-queen protects us from being hurt, being killed. She brings us here to save us from our fates, to give us a happy life. She is *kind* to us. She saw in the pool that George would—"

"Riddles and blasphemy." George gripped her arm. "Back to London we go, my dear. Isaac, with me." His face was almost bloodless. "We must get Marigold away from here. She needs protection from a man, not this monster."

Isaac hesitated.

He ought to listen to Marigold. He thought he had loved her . . . but he had loved a façade. Whatever might or might not be true of George, he was her blood, and a shrewd man—he knew what was best for her. And to leave her with this hellish thing that had worked such an enchantment on her mind was surely to leave her for dead.

"No, Marigold," he said thickly. "I want you too much."

She closed her eyes and turned her face away.

That was when the Erl-queen's son appeared beside his mother. As Isaac beheld the creature he was certain they had killed, he turned cold to his very soul.

"If we Erl-folk had any weaknesses, we would take care for humans not to know them." The mouth of thorns smiled at them both. "I did ask you, Isaac Fairfax," it said, "if you believed *everything* you heard about me. You believed that girls were easily distracted. You believed I could be slaughtered with metal."

Steel had never harmed them. It had been a lie, all of it—baseless gossip, London whispers.

They had no weapons. No means by which to guarantee their safe passage. As Isaac realized how grave a mistake they had made, George ran, hauling Marigold with him by the hair. She screamed at him in fury. In his wake, Isaac desperately swung his sword at the Erl-queen's son, shouting "Get back, villain," no longer knowing whether he was fighting to reach Marigold or to protect George, or simply to preserve his own life—but when he slashed open that glistening skin, all that came out were sap and flies. Thousands of flies. He screamed as they surrounded him, as they infested him. The last thing he saw were the rose-thorn teeth.

⚬⚬

It must have been hours later when he woke. George was nowhere to be seen. Isaac's sword lay dull and stained among the leaves, too far away to grasp.

The Erl-queen and her son stood over him. Bloodied mouths. Glinting black eyes.

Oh, those teeth, those terrible teeth, red with death.

"Do not weep, Isaac Fairfax," the Erl-queen said softly. "This story has a happy ending. Marigold is safe at last from the monsters who imprisoned her."

A whimper was the only sound that passed his lips. He could not move; he could not speak; he could not scream as the forest drank him into its embrace. Somewhere in the dancing shadows, Marigold was singing. And darkness was encroaching on the glade.

REGAN PERUSSE'S VILLAIN CHALLENGE TO SAMANTHA SHANNON:

Erl-Queen Retelling in Nineteenth-Century London

EVIL REVEALED

BY REGAN PERUSSE

Folklore is awesome because, historically, it is both a tool for entertainment and for warning against dangers—both natural and human-made. Societal expectations of behavior are woven into these fantastical stories, and they are used as guides to explain what is "right" and what is "wrong."

Within the realm of folklore, the Erl-queen fascinated me the most. Originating in Scandinavian folklore, she is a faerie queen who lives deep in the forest, where she lures young children and kidnaps them. She is a villain created to scare young children from straying too far from home and also a story to scare society about women who seek too much power, or any power at all. Because while the Erl-queen is "evil," she is also inherently a very formidable (badass) independent woman. Enter Samantha Shannon's "Marigold" . . .

MARIGOLD, AKA VICTORIAN ENGLAND'S MOST DESIRABLE BACHELORETTE:

Why, why *did it have to be her? How had Marigold caught the eye of the Erl-queen? She was quiet as a doll, and delicate, too, more of a household spirit than a living girl.*

Samantha turns this "maiden in a tower" trope on its head when it's revealed that the saviors are, in fact, Marigold's captors. Men, if they desired, had the power to not only control but also destroy every aspect of a woman's life in Victorian society. This twist also showed how easily a woman's desires are dismissed without a thought.

GEORGE BEING THE ABSOLUTE WORST PERSON ON THE PLANET:

"Riddles and blasphemy." George gripped her arm. "Back to London we go, my dear. Isaac, with me." His face was almost bloodless. "We must get Marigold away from here. She needs protection from a man, not this monster."

Marigold did not want to be saved. The Erl-queen's reign was not a prison but a sanctuary. For the first time in her existence, Marigold could make her own choices regarding her happiness, and she would do anything to not have to forfeit that to anyone.

MARIGOLD KILLIN' IT BOTH LITERALLY AND METAPHORICALLY:

A whimper was the only sound that passed his lips. He could not move; he could not speak; he could not scream as the forest drank him into its embrace. Somewhere in the dancing shadows, Marigold was singing.

Marigold and the Erl-queen show women taking power back in their own hands and ultimately shattering the notion of female fragility and meekness with a hammer.

Oh man, was it an interesting contrast to place this powerful woman in nineteenth-century England! Did you know that Victorian England was one of the most visibly conservative times for women in Western history? Women were not only oppressed politically and socially, but in many ways physically as well. They were confined to their "separate sphere," deemed only able to exist to rear children and to balance out the moral taint that their husbands produced in the outside world. They were the moral light to civilization, too weak for work and surely too weak for evil.

All this historical baggage came to a head wonderfully in Samantha's story, which makes the reader confront the ambiguity of evil head-on. Two men set out, determined to save this "poor girl" from the grasp of the evil Erl-queen, only to have the tables turned on them—and the reader. Evil in many cases is a matter of perspective, and society tends to villainize things they don't understand (such as female independence). Sometimes true evil isn't understood until it's too late, but sometimes, if we're lucky, it is immortalized as a lesson for others.

Folklore is funny that way.

YOU, YOU, IT'S ALL ABOUT YOU

BY ADAM SILVERA

You've made a name for yourself. And no one remembers the old one.

You threw away your birth name because an eighteen-year-old building a reputation as a respectable crime lord was difficult enough without being held back by the name Amanda. For the past four months, you've gone by Slate, the dealer of the finest memory drugs. You're worshipped for the way Daze can make the city forget. You're celebrated for the way Token can revive memories as far back as childhood. You're feared for the way Trance can implant false stories others forge. Your reputation is godly, but precautions such as your mask are still to be taken.

Hiding doesn't bother you. If believers never see God's face, why should they see yours?

These days, unfortunately, you're a god who has to get her hands dirty. You shouldn't be out here at the dock for this deal. Neither should Karl, who's parked a couple of blocks north to take you home once this transaction is done. But your last assistant, some clown who was twice your age, thought it would be funny to sell your drugs at half price and skip town. He certainly wasn't laughing when you tracked him down, brought him back, and force-fed him an entire bottle of Daze until he could only remember six select words. Now he spends his days and nights walking the streets and uttering your warning to anyone passing him: "Slate is not to be betrayed."

You let him live, but you took his life.

Fair trade.

You walk to the edge of the dock, the stink of floating trash overpowering the rotted flesh that makes up your mask. You stare at the decapitated Statue of Liberty beneath the moon, finding it oddly beautiful. You expected destruction like this after little gangbangers working for Pierce started spiking people's drinks with his new Brawn serum last month, but you didn't think the steroids were so charged that it'd make the users psychotic enough to scale up the statue and pound away at its face with their fists until it crumbled onto the island. Thankfully, Lady Liberty got the last laugh when she took those bastards down with her, crushing them.

Footsteps cautiously approach you.

You know your client is on time without checking your watch. No one gets a second chance at an appointment with you, the most wanted girl in the city. The cops want you and the junkies want you. You're more wanted than Pierce and his superstrength serum. You're more wanted than Local and his tracking bugs, which are so reliable that even cops are illegally using them. But no one wanted you dead or locked up in prison more than Franklin Ladeaux, the young scientist undoing all your work with his Retrieve vaccine; you took care of that. Now you're wanted most by Karl, thankfully. You need this one good connection in this life of masks that makes you want to be yourself.

"Are you her?"

You turn around and answer with your mask.

The client is supposed to be eighteen, but he looks to be in his early twenties instead; heartbreak can age a person. He's six feet, a little taller than you, but you knew to expect this. You stalked him online to see if there was actually a chance he had enough money to pay for your most illegal drug. Turns out his father launched a successful new app for college students looking to date. The irony of this meeting doesn't surprise you.

He avoids your face, backing away, the gym bag in his hand trailing along the ground.

It's not news to you that you look like you're attending the creepiest masquerade ever. What would be news to the world is how the rotted flesh pulled across your face once belonged to your father's hand. The bones of his fingers, entwined by rope, keep the mask tight across dozens of tiny scars he inflicted upon you. But that story isn't anyone's business but your own. Not even Karl knows about this.

"You're her," he says.

The certainty in his voice is rewarding considering how many posers are out there pretending they're you. You're as unmistakable as your product is unrivaled.

"I'm Mike," he says.

You know.

You know his name and you know why he's here.

You reach into your jacket pocket, and your fingers brush against the small pistol while grabbing the drugs. "It's eight thousand for Trance." You've never killed before, but if he tries haggling on this evening when you're desperate to get back home for some normalcy with Karl, this boy will have a third eye before he even realizes you've grabbed your only-for-absolute-emergencies gun.

He tries handing over his gym bag, but you hold up your hand and he halts. You point to the backpack leaning against a grimy crane that's missing a wheel. "Put the money in there," you say. The aluminum inside the backpack will interfere with any signals in the event Mike was recruited by Local to bug you. The price on your head for being the most wanted girl in the city is huge.

You should start increasing your rates for how risky this is becoming.

Mike kneels between the bags, shuffling cash from one to the next.

If there's even one dollar missing, you'll put him through a pain he won't be able to forget even with a strong dose of Daze.

"I need my girlfriend back," Mike says, looking up at you as if this is a surprise. Even if you hadn't stalked him online to see his recent relationship status switch from *IN A RELATIONSHIP* to *SINGLE*, you'd know what was up. Love is the reason Trance is such a top-seller. "She found out I was cheating on her. It was a mistake, seriously. I'll never do it again. We just need a fresh start."

You hate hearing the stories. You didn't care about the woman who needed Daze to forget the sins against her sister and start anew. You didn't care about the man who needed Token to remember his dead stepfather more vividly. You didn't care about the man who needed Trance to trick his boss into giving him a promotion he didn't deserve. You don't care about this kid needing Daze to get his girlfriend back. But you listen because a god is only a god when they know how to serve their worshippers.

"Daze will work, right?"

"Your doubts are not my problem. My reputation has gotten you this far."

This is why the cops and bounty hunters want you so badly. The authorities don't care as much about people forgetting their own drama or taking a stroll down memory lane. They care when Daze, Trance, and Token are used against others. The authorities are too caught up in locking you away to see the good of what you do. How some takers are better off. Some were nobodies off the streets. Others needed escapes from abusive situations, new identities. But they don't see that. They chase you down because they think what you're doing is unethical. Except you don't force this on anyone.

Not anyone who doesn't deserve it, at least.

Mike finishes depositing all the cash into your bag and looks up at you.

You toss him the drugs, which he catches with shaky hands. He stares at the small velvet pouch containing the four Daze seeds. "How should I—"

"Your move, not mine," you say.

You only supply the seeds. It's up to them to plant it.

You're betting on him bowing out of this completely. You doubt his desperation. You also care so little you're already thinking about putting his father's eight thousand dollars toward a yacht for you and Karl.

Mike stares at the pouch with a loser's smile. "Who said you can't buy happiness, eh?"

You roll your eyes.

He takes a couple of steps toward you, and the gun is out of your pocket so fast the smile is still on his face. But he doesn't beg for his life. "You're an angel," he says. Even as he looks upon your face, masked with flesh so rotten it's gone charcoal black, he calls you an angel. This is a first. You've been called a god for your power and you've been called the devil for your fierceness, but you've never been called an angel for your services.

Mike looks as if he wants to bow before you and kiss your feet, but instead he turns away from you and the gun you're pointing at him.

An angel. Interesting.

"Put the gun down!" This new voice rips you out of your reverie. A bald, muscular brute in a tacky denim vest and wielding a shotgun steps out from behind the crooked crane.

You hate being told what to do.

You almost shoot Mike while the gun is fixed on him, but you can see the pure terror and surprise on Mike's face—he didn't set you up. The accomplices in these ambushes are always so proud to have gotten you, but that doesn't last long. In the past, you've used Trance on your opponents, turning them all against one another. It's always amusing when you force the accomplice to strangle the mercenary who recruited him.

You nod at Mike, and he gets your signal, fleeing with the powerful seeds you've sold him. He was right. You are an angel.

But even an angel has to put her halo down from time to time.

You turn your attention to the tacky brute, and you wonder how you'll make him kill himself. A bullet to the head is too easy.

"You probably shouldn't let someone run off with the drugs you're hunting me down for," you say, eyeing the bag of cash from your transaction. You'll go home with the bag and whatever money is in this clown's pocket, if anything.

"We don't care about your drugs," the brute says.

Two more figures file in from your left, where Mike ran away. One is a woman, pretty if you're into faces with less personality than a mannequin's, and slender enough that breaking her arms should be easy. The other is a young man in a black lab coat with a face in desperate need of a mask—swollen nose, black eye, receding hairline.

"Let me guess. You work for Pierce." Only power-hungry junkies hopped up on Brawn would be bold enough to take you on weaponless.

"We know you kidnapped Franklin," the wannabe scientist says.

You cringe. You've always hated the name Franklin.

"Where is he?" the girl asks. She looks to be in her early twenties. She's likely the victim of many poor life choices, but stepping into the arena with you will be the one she loses her life over.

"He's gone forever," you happily report.

"You don't kill," the girl says.

"Oh, I kill. I just don't get blood on my hands."

This confuses them. You're sure they're picturing the manner in which you killed their boss. You take advantage by dashing left, hiding behind a collapsed dumpster piled high with stained planks. Four bullets sail past you. You wonder how long those bullets will fly before they drop and sink through the ocean.

You pop out for a moment, wasting another bullet from the brute, who's not only a tacky dresser but also a terrible shot, and you dive out from the other end of the dumpster, rolling onto your back and taking cover inside a high stack of construction beams. You crawl your way around the beams, a lot like the days of high school when you would flee underneath the bleachers to hide from your bullies. Except now those who are out to get you aren't teasing you for the scars on your face. The three of them are wondering if they stand a fighting chance against you.

You slide out the mini blowgun from your boot and insert two more Trance seeds.

This is your favorite part.

You take aim as they all group together.

You blow into the steel pipe three times, each seed finding its home in the neck of your enemies. You crawl out from underneath the beams, like a sniper bold enough for a fistfight, as the three of them wince in pain and realize what's about to happen to them. The brute points his gun at you, and you point your finger at him.

"You don't want to pull that trigger," you say, and he doesn't. "Go back to base or wherever the hell you came from and kill everyone in their sleep. When you're done, tie concrete blocks around your ankles and go for a swim in the ocean."

"Don't do it!" the girl shouts, holding the brute back. But he knocks her to the ground with a simple push, sending her rolling twice, and walks off.

The wannabe scientist stands there, helpless. He knows if he runs, you'll tell him to stop. Maybe the stories have trickled down to him, too, that you made others cut their legs off for challenging you to a fight and then running away.

Trying to run away, at least.

"Brute, wait!"

The brute stops.

"Give me your wallet."

The brute tosses you his wallet. There's nothing inside. You knew it.

"Carry on."

The brute walks off to go kill anyone looking for their poor leader who should've never gotten in your way.

"Please." The wannabe scientist cautiously approaches you. "I just wanted to find my friend. Have mercy."

Mercy.

The client called you an angel.

All these people after you, confusing you for the devil herself, and he saw the good in you. A little mercy can't hurt.

"Fine. You hate each other," you say, reprogramming any alliance they previously held. "You want to beat each other to death."

You watch the switch in their eyes—once fearful of you, now monsters to each other. You sit on a barrel, legs dangling, watching the fight. The girl finds a pipe, and, well, it turns out a little mercy *can* hurt. A lot. The wannabe scientist is dead within minutes. The girl looks at you, bloodied from the few punches her victim managed to land on her, and awaits instruction from you.

"Finish what he was too weak to do."

The girl loses the fight against her own pipe in less than a minute.

That was fun.

You finally collect your bag of money, which is unquestionably heavy, but it's nothing you can't handle considering you've thrown around heavier things—and people. You make your way to Karl, looking around to be certain you're not being followed, and you stop in your tracks when you see a familiar face—your old assistant. His shoes are untied, and he smells of piss and other nastiness.

"Slate is not to be betrayed, Slate is not to be betrayed," he chants, walking past you with dead eyes.

A dose of Retrieve could save him, could give him his life back.

But you don't carry that vaccine around, and you've already shown mercy once tonight.

You rush to Karl, putting the chants behind you as you cross empty streets, and tap on the passenger's window of the Ford truck he's in.

Karl unlocks the door, and you jump in, throwing the money in the backseat.

"I heard gunshots," Karl says, scanning your body up and down.

"I didn't shoot anyone," you say. You're not lying. "Or get shot."

"I'm happy you're okay." Karl smiles at you, and although your client's smile a few minutes ago was pathetic, that one felt more real. You know Karl doesn't approve of your business, but he continues to love you anyway. He's a treasure.

You lean in and kiss him. "The client called me an angel," you tell him.

Even though you rescued Karl, you know in his nods he's struggling to find a greater truth in this.

You'll prove him wrong.

You'll prove everyone wrong.

You grab the black handkerchief from the glove compartment and blindfold yourself, as is procedure. In the event someone ever captures you, the first thing they'll want to do is drug you with Trance so you'll reveal where you live. They'll get your supply and then kill you. Now that you have Karl, you've erased your address from your own memory and can relax knowing that someone can kill you, but they'll never find everything you've worked so hard to create.

Your home has to remain a secret. Even from yourself.

ೕ

You remove your blindfold after stepping through your front door. You let Karl deal with his bastard cat while you bullet straight to your Memory Bank. As you spin the dial of your vault—2-4-8, because you tortured your father for two hours and forty-eight minutes before killing him—you wish you could just throw that cat out the window and make Karl forget it ever existed. But there are only a few things that make Karl happy, so you let the cat live, even though it hates you.

See? You're good. You put others before you.

You open your vault and put away the extra Dazes and Tokens you had on you in case that kid wanted more than just Trance. You don't close it immediately. You nod in approval at all you've done. The client was right. You *are* an angel. You've come to the rescue for many who've gone through traumas. It's not as if painful memories shrink away as quickly as all your old childhood belongings melted the night you set your house on fire. Your services are needed.

You've come a long way.

The seeds here, particularly the grey Dazes and green Tokens, do good. The Tokens will grow in someone's mind like a garden, where someone can grab a memory off a tree as if it were an apple. The Dazes will blossom, too, except they'll hide whatever memory needs to be hidden in its trails of thorny vines.

You've come a long way, Slate, but there's still work to be done, and you know it. No matter how you or the others spin it, you know that what comes from the violet Trance seeds is less of a garden and more of an abyss. But you're not the one creating the abyss or pushing others into it; you just hand others the shovel to dig that hole themselves.

Except once.

You were called an angel today. Prove it to yourself.

In the colorful garden of green, grey, and violet seeds, there are a few pink ones. You pull out one pink seed and a pocketknife and close the vault.

You play some classical music and meet Karl in the living room, joining him on the floor while the cat scratches the couch's armrest. Your flute of chardonnay already awaits you on the diamond-shaped coffee table, as is routine in your household. You sit on the outrageously overpriced Oriental rug you bought simply because you could, kicking one boot off your foot on the spot where you tracked in mud last week and the other where you spat out Karl's favorite red wine. You're positive the seller would die of a heart attack if they saw the carpet today.

You fall flat on your back, staring at yourself in the ceiling mirror, and let the music calm your pounding heart.

Karl inches toward you with your chardonnay. "You okay? You seem a little on edge."

"Do you think I'm an angel?"

The mirror doesn't show you as an angel, but what the hell does a mirror know? Mirrors only know what you show them, not the other way around.

Karl hovers over you, blocking your reflection, and smiles down at you. "I would have to be a clown's ass to think the girl who saved me from a burning bridge is anything less than angelic."

"Would you love me if I didn't save you?" You're not sure you want the answer, but the question is out there.

But Karl's smile doesn't break. "No shit, Slate. I was just too busy thanking you after you saved me to fall in love with you."

"When did you fall in love with me?"

"You know the answer," he says.

"Maybe I forgot," you say.

"Been dipping into your supply of Daze lately?"

"Tell me why you love me or I'll make you forget your parents," you joke.

"Don't threaten me with a good time," Karl says. He laughs. He stops hovering over you and lies beside you, taking your hand in his.

You both look at the mirror above, the you-shaped constellations gazing back at you. The cat runs across the room like a shooting star, staring at its own reflection through the closed window.

"I love how hard you work at creating a better world," Karl says, massaging your palm. "I know everyone doesn't get it. I sometimes struggle with it, too. But the police and mercenaries will eventually wake up to your good one day. I can't wait until we don't have to sneak into masquerade-themed proms just so we can dance together in public. And I hate how our first kiss at that Korean restaurant was in the dark corner instead of under all those lit lanterns. I wish everyone could see you for who you really are. They will soon enough." He sits up, pulling you with him by your wrists. "Once you're done fixing the world."

He wants everyone to see you for who you really are.

But he should see you before everyone can.

You press one hand against his broad chest and gaze into his green eyes. Your other hand reaches for the pink seed in your pocket. He closes his eyes and leans in to kiss you, and you swiftly put the seed on the tip of your tongue.

The kiss lights you up with the same electricity that it always does— victory as charged as a lightning storm and high-voltage love. The pink seed rolls into his mouth, dissolving on his tongue before he has the chance to realize it's there. The kiss twists within moments. You open your eyes when he goes still, beaming when he opens his own. You find terror, as expected, from someone who's no longer under Trance and kissing someone he doesn't actually love.

He rips himself away from you as you laugh.

"*You.*"

"*Me.*" You tilt your head and blow him a kiss.

"Wh-wh-where am I?" Karl looks around, confused, and the only thing he recognizes is his cat. Well, there's you, of course. But that's obvious: you're unforgettable. You watch Karl's eyes as they scan the room. He spots the four-pronged candelabra, which would actually be a decent weapon in the hands of someone who wasn't scared of a fight or at least knew how to make a fist; that person is not Karl. Not before, not now.

You draw your pocketknife and flip it open, twirling it between your fingers.

"I wouldn't," you warn. You tap the flat of the blade against your cheek. "Unless you want a mask, too."

"You drugged me," he says.

"Ah, there's that astute scientist brain of yours, Karl."

"What? That's not my name," Karl says.

"Yeah, well, Franklin is an old man's name."

"It was passed down to me!"

"I didn't care for it." And you refuse to call Karl by that name.

"It's all about you."

"So what if it is?" You step toward him, the pocketknife dancing between your fingers, and corner him between two oversize prints of modern art. "You have a good thing going for you here, Karl. You and Retrieve kept getting in my way, but I'm merciful. I let you live and, more important, I gave you a new life. You haven't even said thank you."

"You're an egomaniac," Karl says.

"And you're unappreciative," you say. "You're alive, for starters. I also let you keep that damn cat." You thought the cat would grow on you, but it's hard to love something that tries to scar your face further, leaving scratches on your cheek like tally marks. You take another couple of steps toward Karl, closing the space between you two, and press him against the wall with the hilt of your pocketknife. You roll the knife around and drag the tip of the blade up his chest and stop at his neck. "Would you be happier dead?"

"You won't kill me," Karl says, avoiding your eyes.

You grab his arm and whisper in his ear, "I already have." He tenses with your breath against his face. "I resurrected you, but you will die again. I don't have to shove a knife in your throat to do so. The city will forget about you. Without Daze. All they need is time and they'll forget about you the same way they do when airplanes vanish without a trace, or when children go missing."

"My friends will find me," Karl says.

You shake your head. You're sure that tacky brute will have gunned down many of his friends by now. He's probably already on his way to drown himself. "Corpses aren't exactly known for their detective skills, I'm afraid. You're missing, Franklin Ladeaux, and there won't be anyone around to find you by the end of the night." You laugh in his face, which an angel wouldn't do; you know this, but you can't help yourself. You create hope for many, and you're stealing it from the person who tried to undo all your work. You're not one for poetry, but you can stomach it this time.

He tackles you—while you're laughing, like a true coward—and he actually manages to take you down. You clutch the pocketknife, ready to swing it across his throat in self-defense, but he pins your arm down with his knee and strikes you in the face with his elbow. He punches you—flesh on dead flesh on flesh. He goes for your mask, peeling it off your face.

Your face disarms him more than your mask ever has.

He's not disgusted by the scars on your face; he's surprised.

You strike him in the back with your knee, and he flies off you.

You roll backward onto him, twisting your body and locking your hand around his throat. You lean in as if you were going to kiss him, but Karl is at his worst, most repugnant self right now—Franklin. "You said you wanted the world to see me as I am," you say, ignoring the confusion on his face since he doesn't actually recall any of this—not what he said to you, not any of those romantic moments you shared together at proms or Korean restaurants, nothing. But you know all this, and you're all that matters. "Here I am."

He doesn't look away from your face, not even to see if the pocketknife in your other hand is inching closer to him. His life could be stolen at any moment now, if you choose to strangle him or snap his neck, but, with great concern and strain, he asks, "What happened to you?"

He hasn't even asked about himself. He has no idea that months ago you drugged him with Trance in the middle of the night, while he was asleep in his lab working on a pill that could prevent your seeds from ever taking hold, with no one but that bastard cat keeping him company. And yet he asks what happened to you, what your past is.

You help others, but you don't care for them. And aren't angels supposed to care?

"Bad parenting happened," you find yourself admitting, for the first time ever. "My father took his cruelty out on me and I finally gained control when I stole his life."

Saying all this out loud reminds you of childhood, when you wanted to hear fairy tales of princesses being saved from dragons by knights. Except growing up in your household taught you two important things: You have to be in charge of telling your own story. And sometimes the princess needs to get off her ass, pick up a sword, and slay the dragon herself.

Your happily-ever-after began when your father's life ended.

And now you wear the crown and wield the sword, at all times.

"I'm sorry," Franklin says. "I didn't know. But none of this makes you entitled to someone else's life. Let me go. Turn yourself in. We can get you the help you need. You'll never be innocent again, but you don't have to be so guilty."

"It's touching how much you care. Too bad you won't remember trying to be the hero."

Franklin shakes his head. "You will. Good luck living with yourself."

You slam the hilt of your pocketknife into his forehead, knocking him out. You climb off him, kicking his side to make sure he's actually laid out. No groans, no winces. You ignore his cat's meowing and walk over to your Memory Bank to grab another Trance seed.

You catch your reflection in the mirror. There's no mask hiding you at your purest.

"An angel." The word doesn't feel right, and it's not because of the scars on your face. You could've killed Franklin instead of taking his memories hostage and hiding them behind an identity of your making, but you continued to let him breathe. This is a fate his friends weren't offered—a *privilege* his friends weren't offered. Franklin is a trophy you parade around, not simply put away in a case to collect dust. He tried to beat you and you won, fair and square. Now he gets to serve you. And while angels serve the people, they above all bow before a single voice. "You're a god," you remind yourself.

You smile and return to Franklin's body.

Maybe he's not exactly a dragon. Maybe you're not the angel the client believed you to be. But this life is still one of your own design, and that's the way you like it. You roll the Trance seed around your fist, imagining what life you'll design for him next. Every name he's worn so far will remain good and buried, but he's in excellent hands with you. The world knows this.

You'll make a name for him. And no one will remember the old ones.

CATRIONA FEENEY'S VILLAIN CHALLENGE TO ADAM SILVERA:

A Female Teen Crime Lord Concealed by a Mask

❦❦

Behind the Villain's Mask

by Catriona Feeney

My original idea for Adam Silvera's villain prompt was inspired by a blend of the supervillains Harley Quinn and the Joker. The combination of their sociopathic tendencies, energy, agility, and intelligence left so much room for exciting evil-doing, and a big part of their characters is the masks of makeup they wear. I could only imagine the fun Adam had, playing around with the possibilities while exploring Slate's character.

The mask itself is one of the things I love most about Adam's story. The imagery and the history behind it drew me in, while simultaneously repelling me with its grotesqueness. Paired with the narrative, Slate's physical mask points toward the metaphorical masks that we ourselves wear. Everyone puts on façades at certain times for various reasons. Whether to exert a sense of professionalism when dealing with customers, or to display our very best side on a first date, we use different masks to present different sides of ourselves to those around us.

However, the way in which we are perceived isn't solely dependent on our own individual output. We can't always manipulate how others see us, as often there are also societal expectations and assumptions that come into play. But when you actively choose to put on a mask that has certain meanings, you can subvert or control how other people see you.

Slate undermines those expectations. Her scar-covered face does not fall within the prescribed ideas of "beauty" as defined by our present culture. Nor does the mask of rotted flesh she wears to cover those very scars. Slate's mask's purpose is not to fit in and conform to societal beauty standards and present an idealized image of the female face. The mask *is* Slate's face. It is the image people recognize as belonging to the crime lord. Rather than attract, it repels and disgusts people. Most importantly, it is a trophy that also embodies Slate's strength and control. Furthermore, Slate does not *act* like your typical eighteen-year-old girl. (I can't say that I know any teen crime lords, but then again they wouldn't reveal their identity to me.) She certainly acts in . . . questionable ways, which is what I find so fascinating. Slate is ruthless and unforgiving, having been hardened and shaped into a calculating and resourceful villain with really creative ways of obtaining what she desires without getting her hands dirty. But most of all, I love how she is her own knight in rusty armor. She doesn't want or need saving from anyone, and she wears a mask all her own.

SO WHAT DOES YOUR MASK SAY ABOUT YOU?
Hero or villain, you must hide your identity when you are saving the world or trying to destroy it. You look at the masks lined up side by side. Your fingers trace a smooth jawline as you decide which will be your new face. You hesitate for a second before ultimately going with your gut instinct. You fasten the mask to your face. Was it . . .

THE EYE MASK
Some say the eyes are the windows to the soul, and you like to let people in . . . but only a little. You allow others to learn a bit of your deepest self before they get to truly know the everyday you. Maybe it's a way to repel people from the start, to not get hurt down the track. Or maybe

you are too afraid to open up to people on your own, so you give them the opportunity to look and see for themselves.

THE ANIMAL MASK

There is something within you that you are desperate to hide. Unfortunately, it isn't so deep down that others can't see it, so you wear the face of an animal just in case. If you slip up or reveal too much, you can blame it all on the beast. You are just in character, you say, merely playing a part . . . that's all.

THE LACE/HALF-FACE MASK

You like to intrigue people and keep them on their toes. You maintain an air of mystery that only serves to entice people. They feel like they know you from the half-clear view they can see, but they don't quite realize that you're masking so much more beneath the thin veil covering your face.

THE ANONYMOUS MASK

You are a natural leader and like to control how others perceive you. More than that, you *know* how to influence how people see you, and this mask does the job just right. Perhaps it is the face of another, or perhaps it is a representation of one of your own many faces. Either way, you aren't hiding behind the mask, merely using it to force people's gaze.

THE PAINTED FACE

You are comfortable with who you are, and by manipulating the paint, you can highlight and accentuate the traits you want the world to see, front and center. No matter how vibrant or abstract that layer of color, it is entirely and completely you.

Julian Breaks Every Rule

BY ANDREW SMITH

THIS IS NOT SPERM DAY

Steven Kemple would not die.

Maybe Steven Kemple wouldn't die because I knew his real name. So every time I think of him, it's always *Steven Kemple, Steven Kemple, Steven Kemple*. All my other victims—Crazy Hat Lady, Camaro Douchebag, Unfriendly Bicycle Meth Head—I just kind of naturally made up their names. This was Iowa, after all, and anonymity here was as rare as an ocean breeze. I preferred not to know anything at all about the strangers who lived on the streets around my house, especially the ones I'd killed.

Everyone else knew everything about everyone. That's how small towns like Ealing are: we all go to the same church and the same school, shop at the same market, fire up the barbecues on the same days, shovel the same snow, step in the same dog shit.

And I hated Steven Kemple.

You probably already hate Steven Kemple, too, at least a little bit. You kind of hate the way his name sounds. And I haven't even told you anything about Steven Kemple yet—about the oatmeal thing, or how he'd handcuffed me in my underwear to a drinking fountain when we were in middle school, or the party I had.

Who knows? Maybe Steven Kemple will die at the end of this story—which may or may not be foreshadowing.

Don't skip ahead.

But the fucker would not die.

Last week—this was in biology class at Hoover High—my best friend, Denic, told me this: "You know what I hate most of all about you, Julian? You can break any rule and nobody gives a shit. You could fucking murder someone right here at school, and all the teachers would be like, 'So what if Julian killed someone? We all love Julian.'"

In many ways, Denic was right. Also, it's okay for guys to hate certain things about their best friends, like if you had a friend who was really, really good-looking and confident around girls, or if your friend, like me, could get away with anything.

I had always been like that—the getting-away-with-things part, not the confident and good-looking thing. I can't explain it. I'd hate it, too, if I weren't me. But you're not allowed to. Your job is to hate Steven Kemple.

I'll bet that just now, when I said "Steven Kemple," it was like someone poked a rusty knitting needle slowly through your eyeball and into the center of your brain. And you're probably, like, *Man! I sure hope Julian kills Steven Kemple soon.*

Because I'm like that. Denic didn't know how right he was when he said I could get away with murder.

Oh, one more thing about *saying* names: "Denic" is pronounced "Dennis." Don't ask me why, even though now you'll probably need to go back and reread the last page so you can erase the "De-Nick" or whatever your stabbed brain has been narrating to you. You'd have to ask Denic's parents why his name is spelled that way. After all, they named him.

So, that day in Mr. Kang's biology class when Denic griped about my talent for getting away with anything—and let's face it, it really is a kind of superpower—we were doing a lab involving looking at epithelial cells, which was extremely gross and awkward because our lab group included Kathryn Huxley and Amanda Flores, who were easily the most all-around-together tenth-grade girls at Hoover. I'd never had the guts to talk to either of them, being the skinny loser that I was, and now here we were, thrust together in a compulsory assignment where we would have to discuss tissue samples harvested from our own bodies.

Like I said, it was gross and awkward.

Talking about my own personal epithelial tissue in front of Kathryn Huxley and Amanda Flores was every bit as humiliating as being handcuffed to a public drinking fountain in my underwear in the middle of Bloomer Park, which is something I know about but, naturally, did not get in trouble for.

Nothing, on the other hand, could deflate Steven Kemple's self-image.

Steven Kemple, whom I hated immensely and who also would not die, was our fifth lab partner.

Kathryn Huxley was horrified. "He can't actually expect me to do *that!*"

The "he" was Mr. Kang, and the "that" was scraping the insides of our cheeks (the ones on our faces) with a toothpick to goop out some of our epithelial tissue, which we would then smear like butter onto a glass slide and examine under the microscope.

"I'll do it," Steven Kemple said. Then he hooked an index finger inside his cheek and began mowing his flesh with the toothpick as he drooled and spluttered something barely intelligible that included the words "volunteer" and "sperm day."

I was disgusted by two things: first, that Steven Kemple would openly talk about his own sperm in front of Kathryn Huxley and Amanda Flores—while he had his hands in his mouth, no less—and second, the size of the tissue sample Steven Kemple extracted from his face. It looked like a pale, miniature leg of lamb.

Amanda Flores's mouth curled down so tightly it was almost like she could turn her face inside out.

Denic leaned in to inspect the object at the end of Steven Kemple's toothpick and said, "Dude. Did you just give birth?" Then Denic added, "Hey! That's a piece of oatmeal."

Steven Kemple rotated his wrist like he was a jeweler holding a rare diamond. "Yeah. It *is* oatmeal. From yesterday. I had waffles today."

I could have vomited, but it would have been too embarrassing in front of Kathryn Huxley and Amanda Flores.

Then Steven Kemple pointed his mouthbaby at me and said, "We should use some of Powell's."

Here's another reason why I hated Steven Kemple: to Steven Kemple, all boys were last names. To Steven Kemple, life itself was a continuous gym class. But the thing Steven Kemple did next was why he should have died that day, because anyone else who did it would have.

Steven Kemple wiped his day-old mouthbaby oatmeal on my left shoulder.

But Steven Kemple didn't die.

He could have swigged a pint of antifreeze and the fucker would not die.

You hate him, don't you?

CRAZY HAT LADY

Let me explain.

Crazy Hat Lady was the first.

Crazy Hat Lady used to yell at me for running past her yard and making her dogs bark at me. Did you notice I referred to Crazy Hat Lady in past tense? Yeah, that's major foreshadowing, too.

Of course I did not know Crazy Hat Lady's real name. But she always wore hats, and I assumed she was crazy because there was never any reason for her to get mad and thrash her arms wildly and yell at me just because her stupid dogs barked at me whenever I ran by.

I like to run.

Present tense, so you know everything ends with running shoes and a pulse for me.

The incident with Crazy Hat Lady happened two years before Steven Kemple talked about "sperm day" in Mr. Kang's biology class at Hoover High. Denic and I, who've been friends since we were in kindergarten, were tough-guy eighth graders, about to be liberated from Henry A. Wallace Middle School.

Iowans like to name their schools after prominent politicians who came from Iowa, as if to assert to the rest of the world that Iowa exists, and people who are not actually invisible come from there. Don't Google Henry A. Wallace. He was a vice president.

A dirt path through vacant fields connects the street I live on with Onondaga Street, which runs straight down to the creek I like to run along. The path also goes right next to Crazy Hat Lady's (former) house. That day, as usual, Crazy Hat Lady's two dogs—a long-haired wiener dog and an overweight shepherd–chow mutt—were behind a low cedar fence, running around like crazed convicts in Crazy Hat Lady's front yard. And that day, as usual, Crazy Hat Lady's dogs launched themselves into a hysteria of agonized barking when I came running up through the field.

Crazy Hat Lady opened her front door, flailing her arms at me.

"Why do you have to run here? Look at what you do to my dogs! Leave us alone! How dare you do this to us!"

She wore a leopard-print pillbox hat with a black mesh net that looked like one of those sacks you buy tangerines in, and a black pheasant feather spearing out of its top.

I never answered her. I felt her line of interrogation was more rhetorical than inquisitive.

But that day, just as I cleared the field and came out onto Onondaga, two things happened: first, Crazy Hat Lady's mutt scaled the short wooden fence around her front yard; and second, our local state trooper, Clayton Axelrod, rounded the corner in his patrol vehicle. So he saw everything.

The dog ran at me.

Crazy Hat Lady ran for her dog.

"Leave my dogs alone!"

I caught a glimpse—but only a glimpse—of her arms flailing as though she were attempting to extinguish invisible flames bursting from the top of her leopard-print pillbox hat.

The dog clamped his yellow teeth on my left wrist.

I realized something at just that moment: when a dog is biting you, shaking its head frantically as though attempting to remove a mouthful of flesh, it makes you really want to live. So I was kind of grateful—but only momentarily—to the dog for making me aware of just how much I loved my life.

"Leave my dog alone, you little prick!" Crazy Hat Lady yelled.

I slid my free hand inside the dog's collar and twisted. The dog began choking.

I think at that moment, because of a lack of oxygen, Crazy Hat Lady's dog realized how much he loved his life, too. In fact, there was so much love of life going on there on that morning beside the creek it was almost as though the dog and I had gone on a weekend retreat to one of those motivational seminars for depressed businessmen.

Trooper Axelrod got out of his vehicle.

Crazy Hat Lady, who ran very slowly, flailed and yelled, "Get the fuck away from my dog, you piece of shit!"

Trooper Axelrod, who wore very nice, shiny leather gloves, managed to grab the dog by the scruff of his ample neck fur. The dog unclamped from my bloody wrist, and Trooper Axelrod said, "Okay. You can let go of him."

As soon as I untwisted my right hand from the dog's collar, the fucker bit me again.

Thanks, Trooper Axelrod.

That was when Crazy Hat Lady finally caught up to us, yelling at Trooper Axelrod and me to get the fuck away from her dogs and her house.

I ended up with my mom and dad in the emergency room. I got four stitches and a tetanus shot in the left cheek of my pale, skinny butt, which everyone in the room, including the doctor, a nurse, Trooper Axelrod, my mother, and my father, looked at. I hated Crazy Hat Lady and her stupid dogs so much. And right when the needle was going in, that was when it happened for the first time. I thought, *I wish Crazy Hat Lady would die.* Wishes, like the thought of death, are almost always foreshadowing, and I wanted her dead. You might think that's an intense overreaction to the situation. But not me. Death was called for, in my opinion.

My day was ruined, but probably not as much as Crazy Hat Lady's would be, which is major foreshadowing.

In Ealing, a town where nothing ever happens and anyone who doesn't live here is only passing through—either in one direction toward Waterloo or Cedar Falls, or in the other direction, toward Iowa City— there is a gas station/peanut-brittle-and-venison-jerky shop/petting zoo called Bill and Carol's. The peanut brittle and deer jerky are not made there, even though the owners pretend that they are, and the petting zoo is the dumbest thing I have ever seen in my life. All the animals except three have died. The three animals in the Bill and Carol's Peanut Brittle and Jerky Petting Zoo that are still alive are a desert tortoise, a Chihuahua with three legs, and a twenty-four-foot-long Malaysian reticulated python. The python would not eat the tortoise because of its shell, and the Chihuahua is very nimble, more so than the other animals that used to be part of the zoo's collection.

So that day, at approximately the same time that my naked thirteen-year-old butt was being stared at by my mom and dad and a bunch of strangers in the emergency room of Ealing's Angel of Mercy Lutheran Hospital, Bill and Carol's twenty-four-foot-long Malaysian reticulated python, which was named Eddie, escaped from their woeful petting zoo and made its way down Onondaga Street, into Crazy Hat Lady's front yard.

Naturally, Crazy Hat Lady's long-haired wiener dog barked, yapped, and flung glistening strands of saliva. The other dog—the one that had bitten me—had been carted off to the dog pound to think about what he'd done for forty-eight hours. But Crazy Hat Lady, on hearing the commotion in her yard, assumed that the annoying runt who liked to torment her poor dogs had come back, running on the path beside her yard, which is what the little fucker liked to do.

She was wearing a lavender cloche with what looked like a bow tie pinned to its band. Her big mistake, besides choosing a green frock, was making an attempt to wrestle her long-haired wiener dog away from Eddie, who coiled his elm tree of a body around and around and around Crazy Hat Lady.

When I read about what had happened on Onondaga Street, I felt a little bit guilty, but only a little. Had I caused it by sheer will? Yeah, pretty sure I had.

Over the next two years, after what happened to the others—Camaro Douchebag, Unfriendly Bicycle Meth Head, Perverted Angry Substitute Teacher, and a few others—I came to recognize the fact that I was Ealing Iowa's Little Angel of Death. It only took one little trespass on their part, and I would think, *You should die, Camaro Douchebag, or Unfriendly Bicycle Meth Head, or whoever*—and not just die, but die in the most strangely unpredictable manner imaginable, like death by space junk, for example, which is what hit Perverted Angry Substitute Teacher when he was driving in his convertible Fiat, which is a fleet vehicle for perverts.

Every last one of them died. I didn't ask why or how I controlled their fates.

I just did.

Which is why I couldn't for the life of me figure out why Steven Kemple would not die.

DON'T BE AN IDIOT, JULIAN

The Friday after Steven Kemple pulled something big enough to deserve a name and birth certificate from his mouth and smeared it on my

Herbert Hoover High School cross-country team polo shirt in Mr. Kang's biology class, Mom and Dad went to Minneapolis for three days.

"You know the rules, Julian," my dad told me before they both kissed me on the forehead and climbed into the Prius.

Of course, it didn't matter what the rules were. I could break every one of them, leave bloody corpses strewn throughout the living room, and Mom and Dad wouldn't even notice. This is probably foreshadowing.

Mom, who did not wear hats, slid her window down and waved. "And call us every night!"

They gave me permission to have a party. But let me be clear: "party" to a skinny, dorky fifteen-year-old from Ealing, Iowa, named Julian Powell meant my best friend, Denic, was allowed to come over and spend the night, and we'd stay up late eating pizza and playing the dorkiest, most violent video game that was our current obsession, which was called *Battle Quest: Take No Prisoners*.

Denic came over at five. The delivery guy from Stan's Pizza, a senior named Scott Neufeld, who was also on the Hoover High cross-country team, knocked on the door when Denic and I were about an hour into *Battle Quest: Take No Prisoners*.

I thought it was odd that Denic had ordered four pizzas from Stan's. We usually couldn't even finish one.

"Are you starving or something?" I said.

Denic carried the stack of pizza boxes into the living room.

"No. You'll never guess what I did," Denic said.

"Lost a bet that involved making an entire pair of pants out of four extra-large Stan's pizzas?" I guessed.

"No," Denic said. "I invited Kathryn and Amanda over. And they said *yes*."

"Did they tell you they eat a lot?"

"No. I just— Don't be an idiot, Julian."

I will admit that it was simultaneously thrilling and terrifying to think of being alone in my house on a Friday night with Kathryn Huxley and Amanda Flores.

"Why did you invite *them*?" I asked.

"Are you out of your mind?"

I was certain Denic's question was purely rhetorical.

"But I'm in pajama bottoms and a T-shirt," I pointed out to the fully dressed Denic. In fact, it was just at that moment that two things happened: first, the doorbell rang, which is not really foreshadowing because you already know who rang it, and it was someone named either Kathryn Huxley or possibly Amanda Flores; and second, I not only realized that Denic was fully dressed, but that he was dressed *nice*, like school-dance nice, which is something a fifteen-year-old guy would never notice about his best friend unless he found himself in a situation where he was embarrassingly underdressed in the impending presence of two very beautiful and smart, popular fifteen-year-old girls.

"You fucker," I said.

Denic waved his hand dismissively. "They'll think it's sexy."

"Then you should put on pajamas, too."

"Don't be an idiot. You know I sleep in my boxers."

"I'll lend you some of mine."

The doorbell rang again while Denic and I argued about fashion and sleepwear.

Denic repeated the mantra of the evening. "Don't be an idiot, Julian. Answer the door."

Amanda Flores laughed at me. "Don't tell me this is a pajama party. What are you? In fourth grade?"

I was pretty sure those were rhetorical questions.

And my pajama bottoms had 1953 Chevy pickups on them.

"No. I. Um. Always dress like this. Um. When I . . ."

Denic pushed past me and opened the door all the way so that Kathryn Huxley and Amanda Flores could see that he was dressed like a tenth grader, as opposed to a shoeless fourth grader with little red trucks on his pajamas.

He said, "Hi, Kathryn! Hi, Amanda! Are you hungry? We got Stan's. Come in!"

I kind of hated Denic at that exact moment, but not the kind of hate that would cause him to be crushed by a reticulated python, or end up strangled by a Windbreaker that got pinched in the rubber rail of an escalator, which is what happened last April to Camaro Douchebag the day he intentionally splashed me with mud when I was running. And, like I said, it's perfectly okay for best friends to hate each other from time to time.

It wasn't the kind of hate I had for Steven Kemple.

Kathryn and Amanda followed the very nicely dressed Denic into my living room.

Kathryn said, "Are your parents gone?"

She sounded so sexy and daring when she asked it. I nearly passed out, which would have been super embarrassing.

I managed to squeak out an answer. "Yes. They went to Minneapolis till Sunday."

"Nice socks," Amanda said. "Hey, aren't you the kid who got handcuffed to the drinking fountain in his underwear at Bloomer Park when we were in sixth grade?"

"It was seventh," Denic pointed out.

My socks didn't match. I hadn't noticed until Amanda Flores pointed it out. One was grey and one was white. This was turning out to be the worst night of my life, which, as you have probably guessed, is major foreshadowing.

Amanda and Denic got pizza and sat on the couch. I, the statue of an idiot kid in mismatched, saggy socks and pajamas with trucks on them, stood in the middle of the floor, uncertain I would ever move again.

Kathryn Huxley had her phone out. She was texting something, possibly begging for anyone she knew to rescue her from the hell of pizza and video games with that kid who had been handcuffed in his briefs for six hours to a drinking fountain in the park.

The Ealing newspaper ran photos of it.

And did Steven Kemple die?

No. No, he did not.

But what Kathryn Huxley was actually texting, I came to realize later, was the address of my house. She was texting it to pretty much the entire student body of Herbert Hoover High School.

Because *this* was where the party was.

STEVEN KEMPLE RUINS MY PARTY (WHICH IS MAJOR FORESHADOWING)

So that was how my dorky party, which was just supposed to be me (in my pajamas with trucks on them) and my best friend, Denic (who was dressed like a model in the "Teens of Style" section of the JCPenney catalog), blew up.

Once Kathryn Huxley sent out her text message, there was no stopping it.

I learned a lot of things I never really wanted to know about real teenager parties that night—like, for example, how once it's been confirmed there are no adults hiding out, random strangers between the ages of, like, twelve and eighteen simply let themselves inside your house from any available unlocked door or possibly window.

Denic, nicely dressed and eating pizza on the couch with Kathryn and Amanda, was teaching the girls how to play *Battle Quest: Take No Prisoners* while I, still standing like an idiot in the middle of the living room, was having an internal argument about whether I should excuse myself and change into some tenth grader clothes, or maybe at least get a robe.

Denic sat between the girls, who laughed and bounced, their legs pressed up against Denic like he was trapped in a place where you could die the most blissful death. I'll admit it: I was jealous.

I sat down beside Kathryn, but not close enough to touch her, since I was only wearing pajamas and that would have probably given me an aneurysm. I tried to will myself to relax and just have fun like the other kids were doing, but that was exactly when the first of what would turn out to be more than one hundred unexpected guests simply opened the front door without knocking and let himself in.

It was Steven Kemple.

It was Steven Kemple carrying a twelve-pack of beer.

"Where's the fridge?" Steven Kemple said.

"You can't bring that in my house," I said, but what I actually thought was, *Why won't you die, Steven Kemple?*

"Ha-ha," Steven Kemple laughed.

Then he tore open the top of the twelve-pack and handed cans of beer to the girls. He held one out for Denic, who looked at me. I could tell Denic wanted a beer, too, but I was relieved when he said "No, thanks."

"Hey! Stan's!" Steven Kemple swooped over to the pizza boxes.

I stood up, fully prepared to at least attempt to throw Steven Kemple out of my house. Kathryn Huxley and Amanda Flores were already drinking beer.

And Steven Kemple pointed the bottom of his beer can at me and said, "What are you? All ready for bedtime, Powell?"

I hated Steven Kemple so much.

Then the door opened again, and at least a dozen kids I recognized from Hoover High let themselves in. They were juniors or seniors, and I was instantly terrified. Two of the boys in front of the pack had wispy beards. They carried a beer keg between them.

"Hey, Pajama Boy!" one of the Beer Keg Dudes said. "Which way to the backyard?"

And I thought, *You can't call me Pajama Boy, Stupid Beard Beer Keg Dude.* (Ball return machine, Ealing 24-Hour Bowl-O-Rama.)

It was already too late to stop it, which is more foreshadowing than you need at this point.

It was all a blur. Within half an hour, my house was full of kids. Someone had commandeered my parents' entertainment system. Music blared. The living room became a dance club; the sofa, where I should have been playing video games alone with my best friend, some kind of no-limits hookup station. The entire house reeked of booze and cigarettes and vape mist.

I lost Denic when I went outside, which was even worse than inside. The backyard was jammed with kids. There was a funnel connected to a hose, and kids were using it to down entire cans of beer in single gulps. Everywhere kids were smoking pot, too. My yard smelled like the boys' locker room at Hoover. At least six boys were peeing on our back fence, which had turned into some massive public urinal.

A kid who had just disconnected from the funnel-hose beer contraption sprayed vomit toward a group of boys and girls who were smoking pot. They scattered frantically. It looked like the running of the bulls, except it was Iowa and not Spain, with barf instead of bulls.

I felt dizzy. Also, my socks were wet. I hoped it was only beer, but it probably wasn't.

"Hey. Kid. Your turn." Skinny Super-White Hairless Senior Dude Who Apparently Didn't Know How to Button His Fucking Dress Shirt So He Could Show Off His Actual Tattoo to Eighth-Grade Girls held the mouth end of the beer funnel-hose out for me. (Fell asleep inside the cardboard baler at the Hy-Vee.)

"No, thanks."

I decided I was going to call the cops on myself.

I waded through the sea of idiots and pushed my way back inside the house.

Seven kids were playing strip poker at the same dinner table where we have Christmas and Thanksgiving. I wanted to scream, but I was momentarily mesmerized by Amanda Flores's see-through bra. I had never seen an actual girl in an actual bra.

Then I realized Denic was playing, too. He was down to his boxers.

And everyone was laughing because Steven Kemple had just lost and was completely naked. In my house. Sitting on one of our dining chairs.

I decided then and there I would never eat again.

Denic looked at me apologetically and shrugged. "I don't know how this happened."

I mentally counted the layers of Denic's really nice outfit.

"Apparently you lost at least five hands is how it happened, Denic."

Then naked Steven Kemple stood up and grabbed my arm. "You can't watch if you don't play. Sit down, Powell."

I was being touched by naked Steven Kemple.

It was all too much.

I hated Steven Kemple so much. But Steven Kemple just would not die.

I tugged my arm free from the grasp of naked Steven Kemple, who made the wise decision to not chase me through the crowded living room dance floor and upstairs to my bedroom.

So, after being scolded not to cut ahead by the half-dozen girls waiting in line outside my bathroom, after walking in on Indistinguishable Grunting Couple having sex in *my bedroom*, where nobody had ever had sex as a couple (Hair dryer short-circuit, grain silo mishap), I managed to get to my parents' thankfully unoccupied room and call the state troopers to shut down the party.

I put my face in my hands.

There was a knock on the door.

Denic came in.

He sat next to me on my parents' bed.

"Dude. I am so sorry about all this."

"Why are you still in your boxers?"

"Two reasons. First, I didn't lose, and second, because Steven Kemple put everyone's clothes in the bonfire."

"There's a bonfire?"

"It's outside, at least," Denic said.

"That was thoughtful of them."

Denic nodded. "Yeah."

"Is Steven Kemple still naked?"

"Totally."

"I fucking hate Steven Kemple."

"Dude. Totally."

When the state troopers arrived at my front door, I answered it, still in my pajamas and soggy, mismatched socks. Unfortunately for me, the responding officer was Trooper Clayton Axelrod, who had kind of adopted me since the day he saved me from Crazy Hat Lady's dog and then stared at my ass while I got a tetanus shot.

He actually scruffed my hair and smiled when he saw me at the door. It was disgusting. Nobody is allowed to scruff my hair, no matter what size gun you're carrying.

"Hey, Julian! How are you? How's your arm doing?"

Every time Trooper Axelrod saw me, he'd ask about my arm, as though it had been miraculously surgically reattached or something.

"Oh. Fine, fine, Trooper Axelrod," I said.

Animalistic screams rose from the backyard, and the house seemed to be belching out the combined smells of urine, pot, beer, and cigarettes, carried on wave after wave of pulsing EDM, right into Trooper Axelrod's face.

Trooper Axelrod looked behind me at Denic, who was standing there in his boxers.

"Looks like you boys are having a slumber party!" Trooper Axelrod said.

"No, Trooper Axelrod. Kids are drinking. They're smoking pot. They're totally out of control and they need to go home," I said.

"Ha-ha!" Trooper Axelrod chuckled. "You never do anything wrong, Julian! Just have fun, and don't stay up too late! What a jokester!"

Then Trooper Axelrod spun around and walked back to his patrol vehicle. He called out over his shoulder as he got inside, "Just let me know if you want me to phone in an order to Stan's for you boys, Julian!"

Then he drove away.

"How do you *do* that?" Denic asked.

"I fucking hate myself."

☯

Sunrises are all about foreshadowing.

The party did not empty out until four in the morning, just when the sky in the east began to pale to a yellowish grey that reminded me of all the vomit in the backyard.

Well, the party didn't totally empty out. Disgusting Twelfth-Grade Back-Hair Guy in Tighty-Whities had passed out on the floor beneath the dining room table (Unattended open manhole cover). I had to actually touch him to wake him up, and then lie by saying everyone was waiting for him at the Pancake House over on Kimber Drive, and that walking there in his underwear was totally fine with all concerned parties.

He thanked me and said I was the best friend he'd ever had in the world.

Denic and I walked through a minefield of crushed beer cans on the floor of the living room. Outside, in the piss-swamp of my back-yard, it looked like we'd been struck by a meteor where the bonfire still smoldered.

Denic stood at the edge of the crater and shook his head. "Those were really nice clothes."

"They were so nice I wanted to punch you in the face," I pointed out.

"Well, admit it: you know you're not going to get in trouble for any of this when your parents come home tomorrow."

I said, "Yeah. Probably not."

Denic yawned. "You want to go in and play *BQTNP*?"

"Sure."

☙

I'm sorry if this disappoints you, but as much as you and I both may hate him, Steven Kemple did not die that day.

Neither did Kathryn Huxley, who probably deserved to die for blowing up a party that was only supposed to be me and Denic, and maybe those two girls, too—but that was it. Definitely *not* naked Steven Kemple, who would not die, and whose naked image is now perma-nently seared into the flesh of my tormented brain.

My parents came home on Sunday. Denic and I had managed to

clean everything up, and except for the smell of pee and the big burned circle in the backyard, things were pretty much just as they'd always been.

And Mom and Dad believed our story about the giant meteor that smelled like a urinal, but everyone knew they would. After all, Ealing Iowa's Little Angel of Death could break any rule he wanted—he could even try to turn himself in to the cops—and nobody would ever blame him for anything.

But Steven Kemple just would not die. And sometimes even Little Angels of Death need to resort to more worldly methods and take matters of the flesh and bone into their own hands. It's a dirty business, balancing the ledgers of the universe, but somebody's got to do it.

I know where Steven Kemple lives.

And this is major foreshadowing.

Raeleen Lemay's Villain Challenge to Andrew Smith:

A Psychopath in a Futuristic Setting

Julian Powell: Teen Psycho Extraordinaire

BY RAELEEN LEMAY

I love psychopaths.

Okay, that came out wrong. What I mean to say is, I love watching and reading about fictional psychopaths because they're so complex. What are their reasons for doing the things they do? Sometimes they have a moral code and actually feel what they're doing is right (such as Dexter Morgan killing murderers—what a good guy!), and other times they're just straight-up psycho.

Also, what makes psychopaths so terrifying is that they're *real*. Maybe there aren't actually dark wizards mass-murdering innocent Muggles in this world, but psychopaths are very much a reality, and they could be *anybody*. I bet Julian Powell's friends, teachers, schoolmates, and neighbors had no idea about the messed-up tornado swirling around in his head.

So maybe I should rephrase that first line. I love Julian Powell.

My favorite things about "Julian Breaks Every Rule":

- How straightforward Julian is. He never lies to you about what he's done or what he's thinking, which made him feel like a way more reliable narrator than you typically get with psychopaths. But it also begged the question of whether he *was* telling the truth, which caused me to have a bit of a crisis. WHAT IF HE WAS LYING THE WHOLE TIME? I got very into it, not gonna lie.

- The constant foreshadowing really helped build suspense in the story because no matter how much information it seems like Julian is giving away, you really don't know the ending until you get there. Upon reading the story a second, third, and fourth time, I learned a lot about what was *actually* going on.

- Julian is very much a typical psychopath, but he has some pretty clear differences as well. Normal psychopaths (obviously) don't have powers that allow them to kill people with their minds, but Julian does—or does he? Are those deaths just coincidences? Whatever the case, the intent behind his actions mirrors that of a regular psychopathic murderer. He believes somebody deserves to die, and it happens. As for Julian's ability to get away with anything: it's a pretty well-known fact that psychopaths are master manipulators and can essentially talk their way out of anything (seriously, have you seen *Dexter*?). So it shouldn't come as a surprise that Julian can get away with murder (literally or figuratively) and break any rule as well.

- To me, Julian felt like a normal teenager. Who hasn't in a fit of rage wished someone dead? But for average teens, it doesn't actually happen (at least, I hope not). And just like any other guy his age, he faces awkwardness around girls, jerks from school, and the stresses of hosting a party.

- Julian's inner voice remained very lighthearted throughout the story, which was a great contrast to his sinister thoughts and behavior. He also didn't stick to any moral code like Dexter does, which dehumanized Julian a bit and made him more frightening. Despite all this, I was completely on his side the entire time. This is a slightly terrifying thought when you're reading about a psychopathic killer (!!!), but I often find myself rooting for the villains.

- Speaking of Julian being a stone-cold killa, the ending of this story knocked my socks off. Here I was, thinking Julian would remain a quasi-telepathic murderer until the end of his days, but nay! This is the day when he plans to take control at last and kill the hated Steven Kemple with his own two hands. I didn't see that coming, and it had me itching to flip to the next page to find out what happened, but THERE WAS NO MORE. Touché, Mr. Smith. Touché.

Although this story left me with plenty of questions, it also provided me with a lot of ideas and theories. Does Julian actually go through with killing Steven? We'll never know! How far can he push his power of manipulation? To the moon, perhaps! The openness of the ending hurt my soul (just a little bit), but it was the perfect note on which to end the story. Strange, suspenseful, and definitely psychopathic, Julian Powell is a teen psycho extraordinaire.

INDIGO AND SHADE

BY APRIL GENEVIEVE TUCHOLKE

I didn't believe the Beast was back. Not at first. No one did.

The redheaded Bellerose twins claimed they saw it roaring in the moonlight at the edge of the Hush Woods. They said it was ten feet long with six-inch teeth and it seemed to "worship the night" . . . whatever the hell that meant. They said they took off running and barely escaped with their lives.

I just laughed in their faces.

I was sure they'd seen a bear or wolf or something else furry and large and got so scared, the cowards, that their reason and common sense shut down and their craven, sixteen-year-old brains conjured up a monster.

People in the Rocky Mountains had been trying to kill the Beast since the Colorado gold rush. It would appear, slaughter a few kids, and then vanish again. On and on and on for the last hundred and fifty years. It had all happened before, and it would all happen again. Unless I could stop it.

I'd been waiting for the Beast to return to our woods since I first learned how to use a bow. I practiced archery, hour after hour, while other kids did stupid, unheroic things like kick balls and fall off skateboards and take piano lessons.

I was ready. I was born for this. It would be stopped, right here, right now, by *me*.

Three nights after the Bellerose twins said they saw the creature, three nights after I laughed them off and called them cowards . . .

I saw the Beast for the first time.

I was night-hunting in the Hush Woods. I felt my skin prickle, instinct, basic and primal. I froze in my tracks and looked up . . . and there it was, crouching over a fresh kill, teeth ripping into a deer, bones crunching, blood spraying.

There isn't a cowardly bone in my body. I didn't run like the twins. I sucked in my breath, slipped lithely and shadowy behind a tall pine tree, and watched the creature that had killed so many people, the creature that had loomed so large in my imagination since I was a little kid.

The Beast was lupine in shape, broad nose, short ears, angular limbs, soft-looking fur. But there was something sentient about it, too. Sentient and savvy. It seemed . . .

Aware.

The animal tore off the deer's hind leg in one hard jerk, held it in its mouth, and sniffed the air. It turned and looked at me—straight at me.

I'd watched a lot of animals in the woods. Killed them, too. I knew them, knew their emotions. I'd stared into their eyes and seen surprise, and hunger, and fear, and indifference. But I'd never seen anything like the Beast's. Its eyes were sad, lonely, angry, proud. *Human.*

I should have nocked my arrow. I should have shot it, whoosh, slice, fur parting, skin tearing, muscles ripping.

This was my moment.

Instead, I called out, *"Who are you?"*

The Beast flinched at the sound of my voice, gaze still locked with mine. We both watched each other for one second, two, three . . .

And then it bolted through the trees, deer leg tucked between its jaws.

I didn't tell a soul. I was Brahm Valois, after all, heir to the Valois fortune and not some idiot redheaded twin. I couldn't tell people I'd seen the Beast bloodily eating a deer in a cursed patch of Colorado woods . . . and then had let it *go*.

People were counting on me.

They were expecting me to do what no one else had ever done.

Kill the Beast.

I dreamed about it, every night since then. But in my dreams the Beast didn't run away. It just tilted its head back and howled.

Someday I would put an arrow through its heart. I think it had known. I think it had seen this in my eyes. I held its fate in my hands, and it had run away.

☙

Valois is a rich ski resort town in Colorado. It's also my last name. That's right, my ancestor founded this town. My great-great-great-grandfather pissed off a French lord a hundred and fifty years ago—they hunted down Jean George Valois and threw him off a cliff. But he lived. The Valois men are survivors. He booked passage on a ship to America and then followed the gold rush up into the Rocky Mountains. My family has never lacked ambition—when Jean George's claim dried up, he paved roads and built hotels and saloons and churches. Then, when he was in his nineties, he built the first ski resort in the Rockies. The wealthy followed.

I have fourteen cousins and three brothers, and I'm the oldest male. And I could have ended up one of those spineless, sniveling, special-snowflake trust fund kids, but my dad is Brahm Valois the First and he didn't raise spoiled pansy boys. I've camped in freezing temps, in ten-foot snow. I killed my first buck when I was five and then helped skin it afterward. I spent my summers at hard-core wilderness survival camps, where I was dropped in the woods alone for a week with nothing but the clothes on my back and a hunting knife. I spend my days in five-star restaurants with pretentious one-word names, but I have also eaten squirrel, and possum, and jackrabbit, and swamp rat. I have nibbled on frog legs roasted over a spit in the wild . . . as well as fried in panko and served with lemon, grass-fed butter, and *frites* at the downtown Fourchette restaurant.

I saved our town from a forest fire two years ago. Me and my younger brothers—Jean George, Philippe, and Luc—were in the front lines, battling the flames day and night, no sleep. We turned the tide. We saved our town and Broken Bridge—the other rich ski resort twenty miles over. We rescued half the county from the burning inferno.

We were heroes.

Me and my brothers owned Valois, ran Valois, saved Valois . . . and my life could have gone on like this forever and forever for all I cared. Once I killed the Beast I'd have everything I wanted from life and could just coast on a wave of glory and self-fulfillment until the end.

That was how it was supposed to go, anyway. And then I met Indigo.

The first time I saw Indigo Beau she was sitting smack in the middle of the Hush Woods, not half a mile from where I saw the Beast a few weeks before.

I was half naked, stripped to my waist, wearing nothing but my muscled abs and my designer jeans and my recurve bow. I liked to slay creatures the way my French ancestors used to in their dark, black forests hundreds of years ago. Just me and sky and trees and arrows.

Indigo gasped when she saw me. Of course she did.

I have gorgeous blond hair, thick and glossy—it curls up at the ends like little twists of sunshine. I have sea-green eyes and healthy, glowing skin. I'd been running and hunting and fighting since I was a kid, and I looked like a god—tight waist, long legs, big pecs, boom, boom, boom.

Indigo was nestled into a pile of green ferns and a slanting stretch of sunshine. She had thick brown hair that draped halfway down her back, and she wore a yellow dress with a long blue scarf folded around her neck. She had a book in her lap, sky-blue cover with a red moon in the center.

I stared at her, rooted to the spot, hunter and prey.

There was something unnerving about her. I noticed it straight off. The way she sat in those ferns, pliant and nimble but also tense . . .

I thought maybe she was a dancer. I'd been to NYC and seen ballet—the Valois boys were cultured, even if we did live on a mountain. There was something of those sinewy ballerinas about her.

"*Bonjour, ma belle,*" I said finally, in my sexiest, French-iest voice.

Her gaze lingered over me, and I let it. I was used to this kind of attention. I rolled my neck and then my shoulders, like I was sore from hunting primevally with my bow in the savage wilderness. She stood up and raised her face to mine. Her eyes were a light, pearly blue, and they were sparkly and bright . . . but with something deep in them, too, deep and melancholic. She had a sweet, heart-shaped face and high-arched eyebrows and plump lips. She was gorgeous. I'd dated prettier, but not often.

I smiled at her, my thousand-watt Valois grin, but her body stayed tense and strained, as if I were an unpredictable wild creature that might attack at any moment, rather than a glorious specimen of refined mascu-linity. Her eyes kept shifting to my bow, like it made her uneasy, like she could see the ghosts of all the animals I'd slain, lining up behind me.

All right, then, time to get civilized.

"Hello there, stranger. I'm Brahm Valois the Second . . . *Valois*, like the town."

She stood up and put her palm in mine. She shook firm and quick, and then pulled her hand away and went back to clutching her book. She still hadn't said a word.

She looked at my bow again.

I narrowed my eyes. "I hope you aren't one of those tree-hugging vegan types. Because I'm a hunter and proud of it."

"I'm not."

"Not what?"

"A tree-hugging vegan."

"Good." I relaxed and flashed her another Valois smile. "Is that a romance?" I nodded my chin at her little novel.

She shook her head, and her long dark hair swished side to side.

"What, then? A book of spells? Are you reading about herbs and potions and boiling cauldrons? Because a girl would only hide in the woods to read a really dirty romance or some New Age Wiccan piece-of-trash spell book."

She laughed.

She had a nice laugh. A lot of girls don't. A lot of the girls I'd been with had laughs that were feeble or fake or forced. But hers . . . it was genuine. Genuine and fierce as a Rocky Mountain winter snowstorm that dumped three feet of snow in twenty-four hours.

"I'm Indigo Beau," she said, and her voice was genuine and fierce, too.

She sat back down in her patch of ferns, and I plopped to the ground next to her, dropping my bow and arrows off to the side. I held out my hand, and she gave me the book. It had a vague title—*The Lone Hunt.* I flipped through it, expecting to find a steamy sex scene or an illustration of smug-looking women standing on a hill in the middle of a thunderstorm, chanting a spell about sisterhood. But it was a nonfiction book about wolves—their habits, descriptions of their dens, pack dynamics.

I handed the book back to her. "Why are you reading about wolves?"

She shrugged, shoulders nestling into her blue scarf. "I'm interested."

"So . . . you in town for a while? Let me guess—your dad is a minor celebrity, like a professional golfer, and your family came here to rub elbows with the rich."

She just smiled, her chubby lips tilting up in a pretty way.

"I figured. That's why you don't know about these woods. Me and my brothers are the only people around here brave enough to walk through them." I pointed at a big, dead oak two dozen yards in front of us, its grey branches spreading out into the sky. "A hundred odd years ago they hanged three women from that tree, and now no one will go near this spot. They call it Hush Witch Glen."

This wasn't the whole story. People thought the woods were haunted, sure, but they didn't go in them because of the Beast. I didn't want to scare her, though. Not yet.

Indigo glanced around, as if searching for ghosts, blue eyes moving from shadow to shadow. The wind picked up suddenly and burst through the trees, shaking all the leaves at once. It was early October and the rustling was loud and crisp.

"I always get goose bumps when the wind does that," she said. "It swoops up out of nowhere, almost as if it's listening in on our conversation and wants us to know."

Indigo ran her hand down her arm. She did have goose bumps—I could see them.

"Yeah, the Hush Woods are an eerie place—people are right to stay away." The wind swooped in again as I said this.

Indigo pointed at my forearm, and now I had goose bumps, too. I never get goose bumps. When that coyote pack was hunting near my tent in Oregon and howling in my ears all night long? I was calm as the night sky. When I stumbled upon a baby grizzly outside Banff, Canada, and had to scrabble thirty feet up a tree to get away from its mother? My heart barely skipped a beat.

Indigo tilted her head, and her cheeks fell into a ray of dying sun. Her hair almost touched the ground, and it was straight and natural and soft-looking. I watched her for a second, kind of awed by her beauty.

She batted her eyes at the sunlight, shaded her face with her hand, and looked at me again. "Did they really hang three women here?"

"Yes. My great-great-great-grandfather Jean George hushed it up, which is why this part of the Rockies is called the Hush Woods. But it happened. Ask anyone."

"Why were they hanged?"

Indigo hadn't said much so far and I was doing all the talking, and that was fine by me. I really didn't want to ruin the nice, quiet moment by talking about the Beast, but dodging her questions was just going to make her more curious in the end. That's how girls work.

I hooked an elbow around one bent knee and ran a hand through my golden curls. "It was during the Colorado gold rush. A group of good-time gals from the saloons formed a league promoting the rights of women. They wanted to vote and own property and get equal treatment.

They held rallies and fund-raisers and tried to get laws passed, but behind their backs everyone called them the Valois Coven."

The sun was dipping down, and it was getting chilly. I didn't want to shiver in front of this new girl, but I was half naked and it was taking some concentration to appear indifferent to the cold every time an autumn Hush breeze blew down my spine.

"Go on," she said, blue eyes sparkling. "What happened next?"

She was really interested in what I was saying. Of course she was.

"Well, fighting for women's rights in a gold rush town made of ninety percent men is not going to end well. And it didn't. The good-time women in Broken Bridge joined the coven—I mean, the *league*—and their numbers grew. And then a boy went missing. He was only fourteen, son of the mayor. They found the kid's body in the woods a few days later, and it looked like it had been *chewed* on, and not by the usual critters like coyotes and wolves and cougars, but something else. Something more . . . delicate, and precise. Something had crushed his lungs and ripped out his damn heart."

Indigo flinched.

"Another boy went missing, and then a girl. Finally, Jean George Valois had the three leaders of the coven arrested. He called in a corrupt priest to officially declare them 'Night Witches.' The whole town came out. They threw rocks at the women until they fell to their knees. And then they strung them up and watched them hang for *sorcery and murder*. Mob mentality. It's a terrible thing."

Indigo nodded, eyes big, too moved by my gripping story to talk, no doubt. I am a natural-born storyteller—one of the many talents that run in my family.

"Of course, hanging the lead witches didn't stop the bodies from turning up in this forest. There were two more after the first batch. But J. G. Valois kept it out of the papers by shooting the only journalist in the Rockies reckless enough to investigate."

Indigo flinched again.

Did I feel a twinge then? A minuscule twinge of regret? Maybe. But I was proud of being a Valois. So what if my ancestor hanged some innocent women a long time ago to keep the peace? Who didn't have skeletons in the family closet?

Indigo was still just watching me with her big blue eyes.

"To this day, bodies are still found once in a while, chewed up and mangled." I sighed and rubbed my palm along my jaw. "A decade will pass, maybe two, and people start dying again."

Here it came . . .

"A Beast lives in these woods, Indigo. A Beast that hunts and kills humans. Whenever it rains too much, or too little, or whenever a bad flu sweeps through, or a wolf pack starts skulking too close to town, or when the moon shines too full or too bright, they say the Hush Woods Beast is back again and on the prowl. The Bellerose twins claimed to have seen it a few weeks ago, and I laughed it off, but then . . ."

Indigo screamed.

I jumped to my feet, grabbed my bow, spun around—

Nothing.

I nocked an arrow, slowed my breath . . .

Nothing.

Nothing but sky and trees and ferns and quiet.

Indigo slammed her hands over her ears and screamed again. The sound was sad and soft and chilling. I got goose bumps. Twice in one day.

I moved closer to her and kept my stance low, my bow ready. *"What's wrong? What did you see?"*

She just shook her head.

"Indigo, why are you screaming?"

She shook her head again. "The . . . the wind picked up, and suddenly I thought I could hear those women, crying out as the noose went around their necks. I heard them pleading their innocence while the crowd screamed for their blood. Then I heard a crack, and another, and another . . . and then silence."

She smashed her hands over her ears again. "Can't you hear it? It's faint, behind the wind and the leaves. It's like having a song stuck in your head. A haunting, terrible song."

I stared at her.

I certainly didn't hear anything, and I certainly didn't want to believe her. The Beast was real, yes, everyone effing knew that . . . but the Hush Witch ghosts?

Dead is dead.

Of course, I hadn't believed the twins about the Beast, and then I'd been proved wrong. But that didn't mean I'd be proved wrong again. It was really unlikely, actually.

I sat back down and put my arm around Indigo's waist. She lowered her hands from her ears. Her eyes were wet with tears. Girls cry so easily.

"Maybe I imagined it," she said.

I nodded. "Of course you did. But this *is* an eerie place, Indigo. You shouldn't come here again without someone like me to protect you. I mean it."

"Brahm?"

"Yeah?"

"I don't want to be hanged like those women. I don't want to die with a noose around my neck . . . snap, pain, feet twitching, *dark*."

I shivered when she said that. Probably from the cold.

"What a strange thing to worry about," I said. "People don't get hanged anymore. If you want to worry about something, worry about the Hush Woods Beast. You really shouldn't be out here on your own. Even in the daytime."

Indigo didn't answer. She slid the thick blue scarf from her neck and wrapped it around both our shoulders, like a shawl. It was warm from her skin and smelled like lavender and honey.

"Indigo, I'm going to take you to dinner tomorrow night. What do you like? Seafood? Italian? French? Thai?"

She shook her head.

"Are you a food cart type of girl? Want to get fish tacos and crepes?"

Chin, left to right.

"Well, what do you want, then?"

"I can't go to dinner with you."

"All right, we'll go to a movie."

"No."

"No?"

"No. I can't."

This was the first time a girl had ever told me no. I didn't know how to handle it, honestly.

"You can't go . . . or you *won't* go?" I sounded annoyed and kind of pissed.

Everything was really tense all of a sudden.

We both just stared at the sky for a bit, not talking. It was starting to turn pink and orange and purple.

Sunset.

I felt her jerk suddenly, her shoulder snapping against mine. She stood up.

"I have to leave."

"All right. I'll walk you home." It was a good three miles back to town, even with the shortcuts I'd honed through the years.

She shook her head again.

"Look, I'm not trying to hit on you, since I can see you're not interested, somehow. But the Hush Woods are dangerous at night. Let me walk you home."

"I *am* home," she said.

And just at that second, the setting sun blazed up, right in my face, and blinded me. I rubbed my eyes. When I opened them, she was gone.

ⓔⓕ

It was usually easy for me to forget about girls. Far too easy. I had a lot of distractions. But I couldn't stop thinking about Indigo Beau after I saw her in the woods. She'd crawled into my brain, and I couldn't get her out.

I expected to see her around town the next few days. Valois is small, small enough that eventually you run into people. I asked around about her at the coffee shops and some of the restaurants, to see if anyone knew where she lived, but that went nowhere. I even spent a few hours hanging out in the downtown library to see if she'd come in, looking for more books on wolves.

Nothing.

So I went back to the Hush Woods. I waited until evening, right before dusk . . . and—

I found her reading in the glen, sitting in the ferns, just like before.

She didn't look surprised to see me.

I sat down next to her, and we talked.

We talked about our siblings. She had four sisters to my three brothers. We talked about books and wolves and trees and places I'd been and places she wanted to see.

The sun dipped lower, and Indigo heard the witch screams again. I held her this time, and she let me.

I went back the next night. And the next. Night after night. Afterward, she never let me walk her home. She'd just disappear between one breath and the next. I'd close my eyes for a second, and when I'd open them, she'd be gone.

Someday she would trust me enough to let me in on all her secrets.

On the seventh night, I kissed her. Plump, warm lips sliding into mine. I lifted her hair with the back of my hand and kissed her neck. She opened the front of my shirt and kissed my collarbone. I groaned, and she grabbed my hair in her fists.

I tried to warn Indigo about the Beast again. I tried to get her to meet me in town instead of the Hush Woods. But she'd only shake her head and smile kind of sadly.

Autumn crept into winter. During the day, I hunted buck and antelope and mule deer with my younger brothers, arrows cutting through air, into flesh, bringing moans and blood. I spent a lot of nights roaring drunk at the Valois Watering Hole, beating up anyone stupid enough to challenge me. I even tried to fight some emaciated hipsters once, with their tight jeans and stupid beards and pretentious talk about small-batch microbrews, but they scuttled away before I could throw a punch.

Philippe was the first to call me out on it. He told Jean George and Luc I was meeting a girl in the woods—how he'd figured it out I never knew. He told them I was in *love*. They teased me and my temper sparked, and the four of us ended up breaking two mirrors, a glass table, and my mother's damn rococo cupid statue. Brahm Valois the First took away my credit cards and my black BMW.

And yet . . . I hardly cared.

I *was* in love. Philippe was right about that.

I was in love with Indigo Beau, and life could have gone on like this forever and ever . . .

And then they found the body.

A girl, fourteen. Soccer player, straight-A student, and daughter of Marie and Jon Jasper, owners of the best French bakery in town. Some tourist hikers stumbled upon the corpse at the edge of the Hush Woods. Her heart had been ripped out.

Indigo Beau lived in the Hush Woods, and the Beast was on the prowl.

I felt sick at the thought of her in that forest with it.

Sick.

It had been almost fifteen years since the Beast had killed some-one in the Hush Woods. No one had believed the Bellerose twins when they'd said it was back.

But they would have believed me.

I should have told someone.

The people of Valois had tried to kill the Beast in the past. Of course they had. But it was always too clever, too fast, too cunning. Generation after generation and still the Beast lived.

But now it would be different.

Now they had *me*.

I was the best tracker in Valois, next to my father. I wouldn't let the Beast go this time.

I would track it, hunt it down, put an arrow through its heart. I'd free my town from this curse.

I was born for this.

I'd become the town hero twice over. I'd march back into Valois, dragging the Beast's body behind me. I'd save Indigo Beau from the Hush Woods Beast, and we'd live happily ever after.

This is what will happen.

I could feel it in my bones.

໑๙

I went to Hush Witch Glen at sunset, but Indigo wasn't there. I waited over an hour, but she never came.

I was starting to get worried. Really, really worried.

The moon rose high and fat in the sky.

I went back to town and grabbed my cloak and my recurve bow. Yes, I own a black wool cloak. Philippe tried to make fun of me for it once, and I broke his arm.

I strode past the local Beast hunters gathering in the town square, mapping out their attack. They'd never find the monster.

It would come down to me, and me alone.

It had rained the night before, and I took it as a sign. The mud was going to help me fulfill my destiny.

I found the tracks near midnight. *Four toes, four claws.* Just like a wolf. I stretched out my fingers next to the print. It was the size of my hand.

The wind had a spooky feel to it, sharp and cold, bite and teeth. But it was more than that, too. I thought for a second I could hear voices. No . . . *screams.* Was this what Indigo kept hearing? Was this the cry of the hanged women?

If there *were* ghosts in these woods, then they'd have it in for a Valois, after what my ancestor had done.

The screams seemed to float around me like feathers falling from the sky. Goose bumps rippled down my arms and down my spine.

That was when the doubt set in.

Maybe I wouldn't kill the Beast.

Maybe it would kill me.

I'd never felt doubt before. The Valois men didn't feel doubt. We didn't even know what it was.

Lights.

The other hunters were moving through the trees, half a mile away, flashlights bouncing off the dark. Normally, they wouldn't dream of coming near the Hush Woods border, but now a fourteen-year-old girl was dead. That gave people courage. Vengeance is a brilliant motivator. Not that it would help them—they were too loud, too slow. The Beast would see them coming a mile away, just as I had.

The witch screams quieted down just as the wind picked up again. I sniffed the air. There was a new smell to it, metallic and pungent.

I spun around . . .

The Beast was tearing into a coyote, fur and paws and nose and gore. I'm not squeamish—that's for pansies—but the scene was harsh. Cannibalistic.

I looked away, up at the sky. The moon was bright red-orange now, like it was made of embers and glowing warm.

Everything smelled like blood.

I nocked my arrow. The brick-colored moon shone down, as if leading my hand.

I didn't make one effing sound. I was silent as the stars.

I took aim.

I rarely miss. When I shoot, it's to kill. But the Beast looked up as I pulled back the arrow. It looked right at me.

It tensed, as if to run.

But at the last second . . .

It stopped.

Stopped.

Something about its eyes, its expression . . . It was almost as if the monster was *begging* me to strike.

My arrow flew. It whistled through the air, nicked its shoulder, smacked into a tree.

I'd *missed.*

The Beast tilted its head back and howled.

And then it began to change.

Fur melted into white-blue moonlight skin. Paws pressed into the earth and dissolved into hands, fingers, feet, toes. Long spine twisted, curved, and softened into a back, a waist, hips.

Indigo sat naked on the muddy ground next to the mauled coyote. Her brown hair hung in her face, and her shoulder dripped blood.

I called out her name, but her eyes were already on mine. She looked fierce and proud and sad.

I took off my cloak and threw it around her body. She reached up and wiped blood from her mouth and teeth.

"So," I said. "It's you."

She just nodded.

"Tell me."

And she did. She sat there naked in the forest, smelling of night and earth and fur, and told me about her family, and its curse.

"One girl in every generation becomes a *Shade,*" she said. "That's what my family calls the Beast. The sun sets, and we shift. We hunt and kill, like an animal. The *Shade* picked me, the youngest, out of five sisters. I turned fourteen, and it began."

Indigo pressed her back into my chest. She was nestled into my arms, her head on my shoulder.

"My parents let me stay with them for as long as they could. We were careful. We lived outside town, on a farm in Minnesota. I quit school. No one knew. I thought I could control it. I thought . . . I thought a lot of things. My parents tried chaining me up, but I always broke free. I'm so strong, Brahm. So strong. And then one moonlit night I mauled a boy. They found his body six days later. His name was Ethan. He used to be in my class, in school. I'd known him since kindergarten."

Indigo started crying, her back trembling against my chest. I held her. I put my face in her hair and held her until the sobs slowed down and she was breathing normal again.

"My aunt was here in the Hush Woods before me," she whispered when she could talk. "And her cousin before that. The locals don't like to come to this forest, as you said. So it's safe. Safer. There's a cabin hidden deep in the trees where she lived. That's where I live now. My aunt took her own life. She was only twenty-two. She couldn't bear it. We all . . . we all find our way to death eventually."

Indigo's shoulder was still bleeding, but every time I moved to stanch the blood she just clutched me tighter.

"I will kill again," she said. "And I will keep killing until someone stops me."

☯

They found us an hour later.

We saw their flashlights first, white lights casting long shadows across the forest floor. She got to her feet, naked except for my cloak. I stood at her side.

They saw the blood and the coyote, and they knew. People aren't as dumb as you think. They aren't as dumb as you want them to be.

Jon Jasper stood at the head of the group. He looked at me and nodded, just once. "We're going to kill her. We're going to end this. Try to stop us and we'll kill you, too, Valois."

I saw the rope in his hand, the noose at the end. Indigo shrank from it. I felt her recoil against me.

My bow was ten feet away, right where I'd dropped it in the mud.

"*Change*," I whispered to her. "Change into the Beast and run. *Run*, Indigo."

"I can't." Her voice caught. She shook her head, cleared her throat. "It doesn't work that way."

My eyes met hers. She nodded. I nodded back.

They won't string her up like one of those three Valois women.

I could give her that much, at least.

The mob drew in, thick and tight.

They started with rocks.

I turned and threw myself in front of Indigo, long arms, broad shoulders, brawny back. The blows fell on me and me alone. I'm built like an ox. I didn't feel the stones, didn't feel the bruises.

She crouched beneath me in the dark. She matched her breath to mine, slow, steady, soft. I reached down and pulled the bowie knife from the straps around my left calf. She grabbed my shirt in her fist and squeezed tight.

"Do it," she said.

I cupped her tiny, pointed chin in my large hunter's hand, and tilted her head back.

I slit her throat.

She slipped to the ground.

I turned back to the crowd and dropped the knife.

The mob took a step back, waiting to see what I'd do next. But I just slid down beside Indigo Beau, slid into the blood and the mud.

The crowd left.

My brothers found me near dawn. They helped me up, arms supporting my weight.

"My bow," I said to Philippe.

He fetched it, handed it to me. I pulled the string back, muscles straining.

I nocked the arrow and shot Indigo Beau's limp body straight through the heart.

☙❧

I am the new Valois Beast. My hair is long and tangled, my beard thick, my clothes ragged. I sleep in dirt and old leaves. I hunt and I eat what I kill.

People scream when they see me in the woods.

That's as it should be.

I wait for her. I wait for the next Beast. I know she will come, five years, ten years . . . Sooner or later she will come.

But this time she won't be alone.

This time she will have me.

WHITNEY ATKINSON'S VILLAIN CHALLENGE TO APRIL GENEVIEVE TUCHOLKE:

Beauty and the Beast: Suitor's Revenge

Glamorized Recovery: Expectations vs. Reality

BY WHITNEY ATKINSON

Is Gaston cursed to be forever known as the villain? The answer is yes—not because of fate or luck, but because of his choices. The world seems pitted against villains. Whereas heroes get success, love interests, and unblemished reputations practically handed to them, villains are forced to put sweat and blood into each of their endeavors, a process that makes villains seem like they succumb to the pressures of life whereas heroes twist misadventures to benefit them.

If you were a villain, you would see firsthand how the gears of a hierarchical society work—rewarding the minor endeavors of heroes and punishing the slight advancement of villains. Perhaps your expectations, pure at heart, would be thwarted in a burst of smoke. So imagine yourself in Gaston's shoes. You might think the following . . .

Expectation:

You get the girl.

Reality:

Your heart swells the first time you see her. Darkness has reigned for so long that this new sensation overwhelming your chest feels like an unsolicited invasion, yet you feel compelled to talk to her. You do. Your heart quivers, then cracks, seeping into the once-hollow chasm of your chest. You are bleeding with emotion, fingertips tingling and vision dancing. But then she looks away. She can't be yours. She distances herself from you, and the once-quaking center of your chest crushes to an insatiable emptiness only ever slightly mollified by the urge for revenge.

Expectation:

You are accomplished at every skill you try.

Reality:

You spend meticulous hours perfecting your craft, honing your sense of purpose, and extinguishing any thoughts of imperfection. If only the girl could see *how much better* you are than her lover. A blade sheathed at your side feels like a loving hand there to grasp when you're feeling unsure. The wicked gleam grows in your eyes each time your knife finds the perfect mark, each time you add another tick to your body count. You notice how the townsmen cheer at the young man who has proven himself as the city's most revered and experienced hunter as you laugh, an isolated sound in a desolate wood, crouched in the puddle of blood surrounding your most recent kill. The irony is an iron fist in your gut.

Expectation:

You are loved by everyone.

Reality:

Eccentricity drives you to madness. Nights are spent, sleeves rolled up, elbow-deep in ink of nights toiling beneath shrouds of darkness, plotting. Darkness has become the only embrace you ever feel warmly enveloped in. All of your friendships have tapered to the single fact that when you are standing in a room full of other people, the atmosphere grows so thick it is almost as if you can feel those around you compartmentalizing in their minds all of the other places that they would rather be.

Expectation:

Every issue has a smooth, clear, and triumphant solution.

Reality:

Every failed attempt, every scornful gaze, every rejection, every shortcoming collects and settles in the gape that occupies your chest. You become heavy with hatred, lethargic, and dripping with disgust. Your blood and sweat stains the soles of your boots and leaves a trail of toiling everywhere you go, but you are still resented and alienated. Your status creates an impermeable shell around your existence, driving you further into exile, but this time, via a prison of your own making. Your brain has degenerated so completely that if any shred of the old, enthusiastic you remains, it must be smothered.

So if that's what's inside the mind of a villain, what do heroes deal with? Interestingly, the answer is, the same struggles. Except they overcome; they conquer.

Villains and heroes are chillingly more similar in that respect than a lot of people realize. The difference is that villains get stuck sometime during the battle. They succumb to the challenges they face, regardless of whether it is their own fault or due to the circumstances they are trapped in. There is something painfully relatable in the failure to overcome hardship, and to have that disappointment fester within you. In this way, heroes represent success, the acquisition of true love, and a prosperous future, whereas villains embrace the more realistic and less glamorized version of our reality—a world in which not every problem can be solved with a sweep of a magic wand or true love's kiss.

SERA

BY NICOLA YOON

PRESENT DAY

The detective pulls his eyes away from Kareena Thomas, the woman he's questioning. The lurid graphics and logos of *CNN Breaking News* demand his attention. Usually they don't have the television on in the interrogation room, but it's been an unusual day. He turns up the volume.

The news anchor's voice strives to be calm and dignified, but doesn't quite achieve it. He sounds somewhere between panicked and excited.

Panic is winning out.

In the upper right quadrant of the screen, a girl is marching slowly down the middle of Interstate 10, a major Los Angeles highway that runs east to west. All around the girl is fire. Every car in her vicinity is either in flames or a smoldering, burned-out husk. The quadrant expands to full screen and pushes the anchor's frightened face out of view.

The girl has become a familiar sight over the last twelve hours. The media has dubbed her Soldier Girl, because she's covered head to toe in camouflage. And because she doesn't simply walk—she marches like a general leading an army to war. Though she's being followed by a gang of men, they are not soldiers.

And they are killing one another.

The news helicopter above doesn't dare get too close. CNN has already lost two helicopters to inexplicable crashes. The other reason the helicopter doesn't get too close is the bodies. Decency says you can't show that kind of carnage on American television.

The drivers—the commuters, the beachgoers, the unlucky travelers who happen to be on the 10 that day—are not dying by fire. They are dying by fist. They are bludgeoning one another to death. They hit until their knuckles bleed, until white bone gleams, until teeth are loosened and spit out, until external injuries become internal ones. They beat one another until the world hemorrhages blood.

One more thing about the bodies: they are all men. Every single one.

The detective forces his eyes back to the woman in front of him. He'd met her once before, when she was a young mother. She and her daughters had narrowly escaped the clutches of a serial killer. It wasn't his case, but it was a strange one. Strange enough that he'd never forgotten it or her or her daughters, the younger one in particular.

Tonight when they brought Kareena Thomas in, she reminded him of their previous meeting. The mother said, "Then you already know. You already know about my daughter."

At the time, he didn't know what to think or believe. Her older daughter, Calliope, had just died. She had set herself on fire. Or she was set on fire. It was his job to figure out which.

But Kareena Thomas was sure. She said, "It was Sera. Sera killed her."

Of course he didn't believe her. Whoever heard of a fourteen-year-old girl killing her older sister by setting her on fire? No. He'd seen bad things over the years.

But mostly men did the bad things. Not little girls.

But that was twelve hours ago, before people started killing one another on a massive scale. No, not people—only men. First a street. Then a neighborhood. If it continued, all the men of this city would die at one another's hands.

And who was at the center of it all? Who was walking down the I-10? This woman's daughter.

Sera.

Eyewitnesses said any man who crossed her radius went into an uncontrollable rage, like they couldn't help themselves. Violence poured out of their souls. Not just men, but boys. Not just boys, but kids. Not just kids, but toddlers.

"I always suspected something was wrong, but I didn't know," she says. Her eyes are pleading for something. Forgiveness? "Do you believe some people are born evil?" she asks.

The detective looks at her with pity. "Tell me."

II.

FOURTEEN YEARS AGO

SERA, AT BIRTH

She didn't cry. She opened her eyes and looked and looked and looked and looked. She was beautiful.

All babies are beautiful.

SERA, AT THIRTEEN WEEKS

She didn't cry.

Not ever.

SERA, AT EIGHTEEN MONTHS

Sera's first word was "light." Her sister's had been "mama."

SERA, AT NINETEEN MONTHS

Kareena and Patrick fought all the time now. Maybe it was the strain of having two kids instead of one. When it had been just Calliope, things had been easier. If Patrick was too tired, Kareena would take over, maybe take Callie to the playground or to a Mommy & Me movie. Or if

Kareena was the tired one, Patrick took Callie to Kids Paint! at the museum, or tricycling around the neighborhood.

Now, though, there were no breaks.

And Callie was different, too. Needier. Shier. Fearful. It was like she'd disappeared into her own skin as soon as Sera was born. Like she was crouched down and afraid, hiding inside herself and watching. Watching her baby sister.

One night after both girls were asleep, Kareena dared to say the words she'd been thinking for nineteen months.

"Honey," she said to Patrick. "Honey, Sera is so—" Here she struggled to come up with the right word. So many to choose from: "Strange." "Unusual." "Different." She forgets now which word she did choose.

"Sera's so _____, isn't she?"

"All babies are _____," he said, and rolled away from her in bed. Before Sera, they used to curl around each other and chat themselves to sleep. Her head on his shoulder. His hand on her thigh. Not these days, though. Most nights he was silent. Most nights he slept with his back turned to her. He was tired. He was *always* tired.

Kareena told herself that things would go back to normal once they adjusted to being a two-child family. Ever since Sera arrived, they felt outnumbered. No, "outnumbered" was the wrong word. Outgunned.

SERA, AT TWO YEARS, ONE MONTH

The playground was a war zone, and Kareena hated going. Toddler boys were little shits. The four- and five- and six-year-old boys played war games over and over again. They used dull grey pirate swords or sharply pointed sticks. The more invested ones had bright plastic guns.

Kareena wondered about the parents of those boys. They cared enough to make sure the guns were brightly colored and couldn't be mistaken for real ones, but didn't care enough not to give them guns in the first place.

Had she hated going to the playground with Callie when she was younger? Kareena didn't think so. Maybe it was because Callie always avoided the warring boys. She chose the slide, the swings, the sandbox. Kareena was proud of her for avoiding them. *Good instincts, my little girl*, she thought.

But Sera was different. Sera watched and watched and watched the warring boys. She devoured them, eyes bright. Hungry. Kareena was sure Sera would hurtle herself into those boys if she could. If only Kareena would let her go, she would join them, become their general.

"Bang, bang, Mama," Sera says after. "Bang, bang."

SERA, AT TWO YEARS, FIVE MONTHS

Where do those blue eyes come from? Kareena wondered. She thought they'd have changed to brown by now. Both Kareena's and Patrick's eyes are brown. Callie had started off with blue eyes, but they were brown now, too.

In family photographs, Sera looked like a visiting relative. Distantly related.

SERA, AT TWO YEARS, TEN MONTHS

Callie said it hurt to hold her sister's hand. Kareena told her she didn't have to hold it if she didn't want to.

SERA, AT THREE YEARS, TWO MONTHS

Kareena and another mom were standing at the edge of the preschool yard, watching their kids play. It was one of those moments of peaceful anonymity before the children realized their parents were back again to pick them up after another ostensibly joy-filled day at school.

This was a thing that Kareena liked to do—watch her child without her knowing she was being watched. Other parents liked to do it, too, she noted. What did they hope to learn? Maybe that their kid was generous. That she said *please* and *thank you*. That she shared and took turns. That their kid did these things even when not under parental supervision.

Maybe it was simpler than that. Maybe in those anonymous minutes before they were once again *known* to their children, the parents hoped they could tell what kind of person their child would become. Good. Or evil.

Kareena needed this covert watching. She lingered longer on the periphery than the other parents. *Just one more moment out of sight,* she thought. One more moment and she'd gain some insight into the psyche of her *strange*—or was it *unusual*?—or was it *different*?—second child.

Now, standing with this other mom, Kareena tested the waters. *Were other kids like Sera?*

"Second children are so different from the first, aren't they?" she finally said out loud.

"Yes!" The other mom nodded, hand punctuating the air. "Yes, they really are."

Kareena felt a moment of hope. Maybe she wasn't all alone. Maybe *all* second children were—what word to use, what word?

But no. She would ask this question again and again over the next few months to different moms. She asked at preschool drop-off in the mornings, the other mom rocking back and forth, second child perched on her hips. She asked on the playground, the other mom diligently pushing the second child in the baby swing—the one that looked more like a harness. The differences were always harmless—about eating or sleeping. "Well, little Maximilian was always such a good sleeper, but this little one? *She never sleeps!*" Or: "Sophia is a *very* picky eater, but Madeline eats absolutely everything."

The differences were superficial, nothing to worry about, not really. Not like with Callie and Sera.

Once, someone came close to expressing what Kareena herself was feeling. This was one of the poorer moms, one who could no longer afford their preschool—the rates had gone up again.

"Compared to my first, my second kid has a nasty temperament," she'd said. Had that mom used the word "nasty"? That might be

Kareena's word. Probably the other mom had said something more innocuous and forgiving. Something more *loving*. Probably she'd laughed affectionately as she said it.

No one ever said what Kareena suspected. Not only was her second child different. She was somehow *wrong*.

SERA, AT FOUR YEARS

For her birthday, Sera wanted guns and soldiers and swords. She preferred the ones that looked real. Patrick wanted to indulge her, but Kareena did not. Instead, she bought her bright plush dolls with too-big eyes. Sera built forts with pillows, used her Barbie car as a tank, called in air strikes with her walkie-talkie, sent those dolls to war.

SERA, AT FOUR YEARS, TWO MONTHS

Her eyes never did turn brown. She never had any baby fat. She was always all angles and sharp places. So many differences. Hard where Callie had been soft. Fair—pale hair, pale eyes, pale skin—where Callie had been darker, richer, warmer.

Sera was fearless, but not in a good way.

There were things in this world to be afraid of, and Sera was afraid of none of them.

And then came the day that changed everything. The three of them—Kareena, Callie, and Sera—were walking home from the park. Winter was on the horizon. The days got dark earlier, and the mile-walk home longer and lonelier than in the summer.

Patrick was at work. He was *always* at work. To get to the park, they had to leave a very nice neighborhood and cross through a less nice one. Not that it was bad, but it had dead zones. Dead zones like the one they were approaching now.

The street ended in an abandoned parking lot on one side and a narrow, dark alley on the other. A few blocks beyond this dead space, the neighborhood once again became safe, inviolable. But for now there was the parking lot and the alley and two little girls who were too slow and a man who Kareena could swear she'd seen watching them at the park. Now he was half a block behind them and there was something about him, and that something was not good.

Kareena picked Sera up and told Callie to pedal faster on her bicycle. Callie frowned her little worry frown and, instead of pedaling, got off the bike. She held tight to Kareena with one small hand and pulled the bike along with the other.

"Get back on the bike, honey," Kareena urged, trying not to look back at the man, but looking back all the same. He was closer.

Callie refused, but not because she was being bad, but because she was worried. Her little Callie understood danger, but not what to do about it, and Sera—well, who knew exactly what Sera understood?

Should they run? Was she just being paranoid? Kareena looked back again, and the man met her eyes and he was closer, and they both knew that he would catch her and her girls and do to them what he would.

Kareena adjusted Sera's position on her hip so she only needed one hand to hold her. With her other hand, she grabbed Callie and pulled her away from the bike. They could always buy another one.

"Run with Mommy," she said, and Callie obeyed.

They ran. They just had to make it to the other side. Had it always been this dark on this street at this time of year?

Sera wiggled in her arms. "Put me down," she cried. "Put me down."

Kareena was the kind of mother who tried not to yell. She was careful to explain her reasoning when denying something or the other. She never told her girls that they were bad, just that they had bad *behavior.* She almost never yelled. But she wanted to yell now. She wanted to slap their faces so they understood that she was serious.

What she wanted most of all was to put Sera down and pick Callie up and run.

Sera would be fine.

The thought flew away as quickly as it came, but the shame of it almost killed Kareena as she ran. Sera stilled in her arms, as if she'd heard her mother's thought.

"Put me down, Mama," Sera demanded. And Kareena did, but before she could capture her hand again, Sera twisted away and ran in the wrong direction.

Kareena screamed because now she could see that the man was definitely a bad man. Not just bad behavior. No. He, himself, at his core was a bad man. She screamed as Sera ran toward him and Callie screamed, and Kareena could not think what to do.

"Bang, bang," Sera said loudly as her little legs brought her closer to the man.

He stopped moving.

"Bang, bang," she said again as she stopped a foot away from him.

He pulled out a knife.

Sera lifted her small hands into the air and raised her little voice so that it strained around the edges. The knife was still in the man's hands, and Sera was so close to him. Too close and her skin was pink, pinker than it had ever been, and even her hair seemed less pale. And the man held the knife and Kareena screamed and Callie screamed and Sera said "Bang, bang," and the bad man plunged the knife right into his own heart, and then he twisted the blade.

⁂

In the weeks after, they all went to counseling. The counselor said they would learn to accept, adjust, and recover as a family. Patrick nodded—conciliatory and vaguely guilty—through these sessions.

Kareena wanted nothing to do with acceptance. She wanted to forget. She wanted Callie to forget how the blood had soaked the man's blue shirt.

"Blue and red make purple," Sera had said sometime later.

Kareena wanted to forget about the small spot of blood that had landed on Sera's nose. Sera had smeared it across her face with her palm. She sucked at the palm before Kareena could get out a wipe. She looked less pale than she usually did.

SERA, AT FOUR YEARS, THREE MONTHS

"Are you sure you're remembering correctly?" the woman FBI agent asked in every interview in the weeks to follow. "Your daughter said 'bang, bang'?"

"Yes."

"And then he stabbed himself?"

"Yes."

"And twisted the knife?"

"Yes."

"Are you sure?"

Yes. Yes. Yes.

The agent told her that they were lucky. They'd been trying to catch that man for a very long time. He killed girls and their mothers in brutal ways. It was good he was dead. Kareena agreed.

She wondered if she'd imagined Sera tasting the bad man's blood.

SERA, AT FOUR YEARS, THREE MONTHS

Sera asked, "Do you have the light, Mama?"

Kareena said, "I don't know what you're talking about."

SERA, AT FOUR YEARS, SIX MONTHS

Kareena was shocked. *All* the parents were shocked when they learned that Mr. Jordan, everyone's favorite kindergarten teacher, had been fired.

"He slapped a child?" This shrieked question was from one of the preschool moms.

The parents had been summoned to an all-hands community circle meeting.

"What kind of school are you running here?" demanded one of

the dads. He was the CEO of some company or another and spoke as if life were a contentious board meeting with dissenting stockholders everywhere.

Mr. Jordan had been Callie's favorite teacher when she was in kindergarten. He was everyone's favorite teacher. And now he was gone.

Sera had been in his class for only two months.

SERA, AT FOUR YEARS, EIGHT MONTHS

The parents were shocked anew. Another beloved teacher—another teacher of Sera's—fired. CEO Dad pulled his son from school.

SERA, AT FIVE YEARS, TWO MONTHS

Patrick had his first affair when Sera was one year and nine months. It ended when she was two and seven months. Another one began at three years, four months and ended just two months later. This third one, though—begun at three years, nine months—seemed like something real.

When did things first start going so wrong between them? Kareena wonders. Was it the exact moment that Sera was born? They'd had a fight a few hours after her birth, right there in the hospital room. She couldn't remember what it was about.

There was a time when Kareena bragged about her and Patrick's relationship to anyone who'd listen. "We never argue," she'd say. "We're best friends. We communicate. We love each other, but we also *like* each other." Other couples were jealous of their relationship. She could see it in their eyes, and it made her feel satisfied and a little superior.

Now she understood a little of what those lesser couples must've felt. She'd like to meet the old Kareena and the old Patrick again. She'd tell them to be gentle with each other even when they were sleep-deprived. She'd tell them to be careful with their words. Some things once heard can't be unheard.

She'd tell them not to have a second child, not under any circumstances.

SERA, AT SIX YEARS, THREE MONTHS

Kareena didn't love Sera as she should. Not as much as she loved Callie. She tried to, but she didn't.

And Sera knew it.

SERA, AT SEVEN YEARS, ONE MONTH

Patrick remarried. Since the day he walked out on Kareena, he hadn't seen either of his daughters. He thought it for the best. He couldn't explain it, but thinking of them, thinking of Sera, made him angry.

SERA, AT SEVEN YEARS, TEN MONTHS

Sera said, "The light makes people angry."

Kareena closed the door in her face.

SERA, AT NINE YEARS, THREE MONTHS

Having a second child had been Kareena's idea. She'd always pictured herself as a mother of two children—sisters. They would play princess dress-up and go away to summer camp and share secrets and have crushes on the same boy and cry together and be the maids of honor at each other's weddings and love each other, love each other, love each other.

But Patrick thought one was enough.

"We're so happy now," he said. Callie was one and a half at the time and they'd finally hit their stride as parents. But Kareena could not help what she was, what she wanted.

"Callie needs a playmate, a sister," she said to Patrick.

"I don't want her all alone when we die," she said, upping the stakes.

Eventually, Patrick relented.

For a long time, Kareena hoped the sisters would grow close. But they didn't. Callie wilted in Sera's presence. She made other girlfriends. She had playdates and sleepovers and dance parties and treated them like they were her sisters. Kareena didn't blame her.

SERA, AT FOURTEEN YEARS, SEVEN MONTHS
She made three friends at school—the first she'd ever had. Sure, they were the girls no one else wanted as friends, but it was something. Kareena was grateful. Maybe Sera would finally become normal.

SERA, AT FOURTEEN YEARS, NINE MONTHS
Sera was sick, and no one seemed to know how to fix her.

SERA, AT FOURTEEN YEARS, ELEVEN MONTHS
Kareena watches Callie's body burn. She screams and she screams.

III.
PRESENT DAY

A life is a series of past moments, all of them leading you to the present one. The moment doesn't have to be an event. It can be a sudden insight that changes how you see yourself in the world. These moments serve to clarify you, to sharpen who you really are for yourself and for others. Here are mine:

I am born. I try to cry but find I can't.

I do not look at all like the rest of my family. My mother doesn't like this.

A white light lives under my skin. I ask my mother if she has it, too. She doesn't answer.

My mother does not love me. But she wants to.

I want to be more like Callie. I want to make strangers glad. I want them to ask me: *What's your name, pretty girl? How old are you? Oh my gosh, where did you get those cute shoes?* But they don't ask me questions. Instead, they say: *You're so quiet.* They say: *Smile. Be more like your older sister.* The more perceptive ones say: *You like to watch the boys fight.*

I make the bad man kill himself. My mother is afraid of me.

I want to be normal. I am the only one with the white light. It leaks out of me, and bad things happen.

It's my fault Mr. Jordan slaps Sammie so hard that he gets all red and swollen. I make people angry. And afraid. I don't know how to stop.

It's my fault Mr. Kelly screams so loud and so long on the playground. His heart is crowded with anger and fear. I did that, too. I don't know how to stop.

My father loves someone more than he loves my mother. My mother loves Callie more than she loves anyone.

My father leaves us and does not come back.

I dye my hair brown. I wear brown contacts. My mother still does not love me. She cannot.

I deny what I am. For a while, I am successful.

I am sick all spring. The doctors don't know what's wrong, but I do. I finally learned how to keep the light under my skin.

I hold the light in. I make a friend. My hair thins, falls like straw around my feet.

I hold the light in. I make another friend. My lips crack to blue.

I hold the light in. I'm too sick to attend school. My skin bleeds color.

Callie gets strong as I get weak. Still, I hold the light in. It burns me from the inside. All spring they—Callie and our mother—wait for me to die.

The light won't let me die. I burn. I burn. I burn.

Callie comes back from camp. It's the first summer she's ever been away from home. Away from me. She comes into my room and she looks better than I've ever seen her, beautiful.

Our mother says, "The doctors haven't been able to fix her."

Callie says, "Maybe it's better this way."

Our mother nods.

Callie comes close to my bedside. Ordinarily, she would never come this close, but I am helpless now with the light trapped under my skin. She says, "I was happy this summer without you." She says it sharp and fierce, like a stabbing.

I've never heard her sound so strong. I hold the light in for her. I want her to be happy. But then she puts her hands over my nose and my mouth. Our mother does nothing. I can't breathe, and I think, *Yes. Let me die.* Callie can finally have our mother back. My bones burn, but the light is stronger than me. It will not let me die. And then I finally understand what I am, and it's a relief. I give all the light to my sister. I let it pour from my skin to hers.

I watch as she turns pale. Finally, she looks like me. I watch as she turns to ash. My mother is still screaming when I leave the house.

☙❧

I am on the highway now, and everything turns to ruin. I don't know how to stop. I no longer want to.

We are born into our natures. It's not a thing we can help. I know that now but didn't always.

I am the curse of men.

I am War.

And this world is mine.

STEPH SINCLAIR AND KAT KENNEDY'S VILLAIN CHALLENGE TO NICOLA YOON:

Gender-Flipped God of War

THE BAD GIRLS' GUIDE TO VILLAINY

BY STEPH SINCLAIR AND KAT KENNEDY

In this male-dominated world, everything is harder as a woman—especially when you're trying to crush the world under your fine pair of sky-high stilettos, combat boots,[1] or whatever type of footwear you find best for disenfranchising humanity. Struggling to claim dominion over the huddled masses is one thing, but struggling with body image, self-image, interpersonal relationships, and even where you fit in with the world is another. So whether you're the God of War like Sera, who thrives on chaos, or a morally ambiguous deviant like us, our feel-good guide for villainesses[2] is here to help.

Dive in and be ready to answer the question "Who's the baddest bitch of them all?"

---

1. Sera found them particularly useful in stomping out opposition. Stomp, stomp, stomp.
2. All references to villainesses are fictional and represent no likenesses to people, animals, aliens, supreme beings, ghosts, zombies, the reincarnated, overlords, underlords, etc., dead or alive.

- The body that's going to conquer hearts and minds
  - What do you wear when you're on your way to inflict panic and fear in the hearts of civilians? A red satin bustier? Standard-issue military fatigues? Guess what? It's not important! Even if your heart of hearts leads you to wear rhinestone jeans or a fluffy pink unicorn onesie, that's okay. You be you. You can leave your enemies lying in a pool of their own blood no matter what you're wearing. Unless you're planning on wearing a cape. NO CAPES!
  - Oppress others, not yourself or your body. There is no perfect body or body type. You know what you should spend your time perfecting? Your war strategy.
  - Your body is a wonderland of terror and fear-inducing proportions. Forget the strictures of the male gaze. Dress to impress or cause extreme distress. If other people's bodies are temples, yours is a war machine with built-in booby traps, baby.

- You know what's humble? Pie! YOU ARE NOT A PIE!
  - Internalizing other people's expectations leads us to feel like we should be humble, ladylike, and civil. Be the villain you want to be and repent to no one. Not your family, not the neighborhood watch, not the military trying to shut you down.
  - Can you be too bossy? No, of course you can't, because you're The Boss! You're a leader, who demands the attention and respect of all who lay prone at your feet.
  - Are you asking too much? Are you giving enough to other people? What kind of guide do you think you're reading? You're a villain! Taking and expecting everything is Villainy 101. Live it, breathe it, bask in the bloodlust haze of glory.
  - Should you be sweet and innocent? Ha. If people are underestimating your feminine power, that's their mistake and

your opportunity to strike. Don't let it get to you. Their reaction may be initial mockery, because how dare a woman strike fear into the hearts and minds of men who laud themselves as gods? But the end result will always be the same: them begging for mercy and you giving exactly zero fucks. Yes, revenge is indeed sweet . . . and deadly.

- Nobody puts Villainess in a corner.
  - Everyone internalizes the expectations that their family places upon them. "Be good like your sister, do your homework, walk the dog. Smile and be nice!" What is this smile? You only smile when your plans come to fruition. Listen, what we're respectfully advising is that you take those expectations and you shove them down the throats of every single muppet who tried to make you be less of what you are.
  - Parents, family, and friends tell you that you can be whatever you want to be. But what they really mean is whatever you want as long as it fits in their neat, little box. And for a woman exercising her command, that box is restrictive as hell. Destroy that box and the horse it rode in on. Light it on fire for good measure. Nuke it from orbit. It's the only way to be sure.
  - Forget what the world and society and your family want you to be. You know why? Because you are going to shape and remold that as you exist in your perfect form upon the ruinous remains of the earth.

- I came in like a wrecking ball.
  - Relationships are totally unnecessary—the only relationships you need are with your minions and your weapons of mass destruction.[3]

---

3. But if, like Sera, you are forced to deal with family and friends, her solution to set them on fire may be the best one. Unless they're more useful as cannon fodder.

o You don't have room in your heart, because you don't actually have a heart. What you have is a gaping black chasm in your chest and an insatiable thirst for domination. Tears and nightmares fuel your hate fire.

o You may be asking yourself, "Where do I fit in if I have no friends or family?" On top of the world, laughing maniacally. Look, people have spent hundreds of years asking why women are out of the kitchen. Unless you're making a sandwich bomb, don't even dignify this with an answer. Not only are you capable of taking the world in your bloody fists, you deserve to, and everything that comes with it.

o You've earned this. Own it, be it, believe it. Then crush it in a fiery death along with everything else.

So whether your plan is to drill to the center of the earth and unleash hell, or blow up the moon, or just simply walk into the middle of a city and unleash your God of War powers, remember: villains are a dime a dozen. It takes true determination to outshine and outgun the rest. You can either choose to let the world dominate you, or you can dominate the world. And if it were up to us, when we're looking into the soul-dead, murderous eyes of our foe—we want a powerful, badass woman looking right back at us.

Briefly. Before she slits our throats.

Acknowledgments

It goes without saying that publishing is a team effort, and Team BYLTHM is huge. A big thank-you to my incredible agent (and overall extraordinary human), Joanna Volpe, without whom this anthology wouldn't exist. Yiiiii! Thank you to Sarah Goldberg, Jackie Lindert, Michael Kelly, Danielle Barthel, Kathleen Ortiz, Suzie Townsend, Hilary Pecheone, Devin Ross, and everyone at New Leaf Literary & Media for killing it every day. #TeamNewLeafAllDayEveryDay.

Thank you a million times to Bloomsbury for your unwavering support: Cindy Loh, thank you for your enthusiasm, your vision, and for bringing this project to life. A thousand emojis! Much gratitude to Hali Baumstein, Lizzy Mason, Erica Barmash, Cristina Gilbert, Diane Aronson, Christine Ma, and Rebecca McNally and the Bloomsbury UK team, as well as to Jessie Gang and Jacey for the book design gorgeousness.

To everyone who contributed their writing, I am honored to have worked with you; thank you so much for your time and efforts: Renée Ahdieh, Benjamin Alderson, Sasha Alsberg, Whitney Atkinson, Tina Burke, Soman Chainani, Susan Dennard, Sarah Enni, Catriona Feeney, Jesse George, Zoë Herdt, Kat Kennedy, Samantha Lane, Sophia Lee, Raeleen Lemay, Marissa Meyer, Regan Perusse, Cindy Pon, Christine Riccio, Victoria Schwab, Samantha Shannon, Adam Silvera, Steph Sinclair, Andrew Smith, April Genevieve Tucholke, and Nicola Yoon. The bookish community is magical, and I'm so thankful to be a part of it.

Also, a special shout-out to my critique partner, Tina Burke. Thank you for being in the writing trenches with me, for the critiques and the writing days and über support.

God blessed me with an incredible family. Thank you to my rock, my husband, Lenny Nicholson, who is everything. You see the little dictator in me, and still you love. Thank you to my parents, Mi Suk and Charles Edward Rogers, for all of your love and sacrifice, and for making me who I am. You fed my love of books from the beginning, you gave me my treasured *Complete Brothers Grimm Fairy Tales* aka The Real Deal, and you constantly renew my faith in humanity. Thank you to my Sissy Poohs, Angela M. Rogers. You really are the best sister in the universe. To my in-laws and my family and friends, thank you and I love you.

Finally, thank you, dear reader, for picking up this book and taking the time to cut open a few black hearts.

CONTRIBUTORS

AUTHORS

Photo © Chuck Eaton

RENÉE AHDIEH

Renée Ahdieh is a #1 *New York Times* and *USA Today* bestselling author of books for young adults, including *The Wrath and the Dawn* and *The Rose and the Dagger*. She is a graduate of the University of North Carolina at Chapel Hill. In her spare time, she likes to dance salsa and collect shoes. She is passionate about all kinds of curry, rescue dogs, and college basketball. The first few years of her life were spent in a high-rise in South Korea; consequently, Renée enjoys having her head in the clouds. She lives in Charlotte, North Carolina, with her husband and their tiny overlord of a dog.

Photo © Ameriie

AMERIIE

Ameriie is a Grammy-nominated singer-songwriter, producer, and lifestyle bon vivant. The daughter of a Korean artist and an American military officer, she was born in Massachu-setts, raised all over the world, and graduated from Georgetown

University with a bachelor's in English. She began writing at the age of seven, stories of fairies and pirates and witches and phantoms. She lives mostly in her imagination, but also on Earth with her husband, her parents and sister, and about seven billion other people. When she isn't writing or creating music, she talks books, beauty, and more on her YouTube channel, Books Beauty Ameriie. You can also visit her at Ameriie.com.

SOMAN CHAINANI

Soman Chainani's first novel, *The School for Good and Evil*, debuted on the *New York Times* bestseller list, along with each of its two sequels, *A World Without Princes* and *The Last Ever After*. The series has been translated into twenty-five languages across six continents and will soon be a major motion picture from Universal Pictures.

A graduate of Harvard University and Columbia University's MFA film program, Soman has made films that have played at more than 150 festivals around the world, and his writing awards include the Sun Valley Writers' Fellowship.

He lives in New York City.

You can visit Soman at www.somanchainani.net.

SUSAN DENNARD

Susan Dennard has come a long way from small-town Georgia. Working in marine biology, she got to travel the world—six out of seven continents, to be exact (she'll get to you yet, Asia!)—before she settled down as a full-time novelist and writing instructor.

She is the author of the Something Strange and Deadly series as well as the *New York Times* bestselling *Truthwitch* and *Windwitch*, the first two books in the Witchlands series. When not writing, she's usually slaying darkspawn (on her Xbox) or earning bruises at the dojo.

She lives in the Midwest with her French husband, two spoiled dogs, and two grouchy cats. Learn more about her crazy thoughts and crippling cookie addiction on her blog, newsletter, Twitter, or Instagram.

SARAH ENNI

Sarah Enni has come a long way from her first writing job, a journalism gig covering the radioactive waste industry. She now writes young adult novels and also produces and hosts the *First Draft* podcast, where she encourages other writers to spill their juicy secrets. She lives in Los Angeles with her cat, Hammer, and is very likely eating tacos right now.

Photo © Kirsten Hubbard

MARISSA MEYER

Marissa Meyer is the *New York Times* bestselling author of the Lunar Chronicles series and *Heartless*. She has a BA in creative writing from Pacific Lutheran University and an MS in publishing from Pace University. She lives in Tacoma, Washington, with her charming husband and their delightfully mischievous twin daughters. Visit her at marissameyer.com.

Photo © Julia Scott

CINDY PON

Cindy Pon is the author of *Silver Phoenix* (Greenwillow), which was named one of the Top Ten Fantasy and Science Fiction Books for Youth

Photo © Vania Stoyanova

by the American Library Association's *Booklist* and one of 2009's best Fantasy, Science Fiction and Horror by VOYA; *Serpentine* and *Sacrifice* (Month9Books), which were both Junior Library Guild selections and received starred reviews from *School Library Journal* and *Kirkus*, respectively; and *WANT* (Simon Pulse), a near-future thriller set in Taipei. She is the cofounder of Diversity in YA with Malinda Lo and on the advisory board of We Need Diverse Books. Cindy is also a Chinese brush-painting student of over a decade. Learn more about her books and art at http://cindypon.com.

VICTORIA SCHWAB

Victoria "V.E." Schwab is the #1 *New York Times* bestselling author of more than a dozen books for children, teens, and adults, including *Vicious*, the Shades of Magic series, and *This Savage Song*. When she's not wandering Scottish hills or tucked into French cafés, she can be found in Nashville, Tennessee.

SAMANTHA SHANNON

Samantha Shannon was born in west London. She started writing her first novel at the age of fifteen. She studied English language and litera-ture at St Anne's College, Oxford. In 2013, she published *The Bone Season*, the first in a seven-book series, fol-lowed by *The Mime Order*. Both were international bestsellers and have been translated into twenty-eight languages. The series continues with the much-anticipated third book, *The Song Rising*. Film rights have been optioned by Imaginarium Studios and 20th Century Fox. Samantha Shannon has been included on the *Evening Standard*'s 1000 power list.

Photo © Margot Wood

ADAM SILVERA

Born and raised in the Bronx, Adam Silvera is the *New York Times* bestselling author of *More Happy Than Not*, *History Is All You Left Me*, and *They Both Die at the End*. He is tall for no reason and lives in New York City.

Photo © Taggart Lee

ANDREW SMITH

Andrew Smith is the award-winning author of ten young adult novels, including the critically acclaimed *Grasshopper Jungle* (Boston Globe–Horn Book Award and Michael L. Printz Honor); *100 Sideways Miles* (National Book Award semifinalist); and *The Alex Crow* (California Book Award Silver Medal). He is a native-born Californian who spent most of his formative years traveling the world. His university studies focused on political science, journalism, and literature. He has published numerous short stories and articles. He lives in Southern California.

Photo © Nate Pedersen

APRIL GENEVIEVE TUCHOLKE

April Genevieve Tucholke is the author of *Between the Devil and the Deep Blue Sea*, *Between the Spark and the Burn*, *Wink Poppy Midnight*, and the upcoming *The Boneless Mercies*. She also curated the horror anthology *Slasher Girls & Monster Boys*. She has received five starred reviews, and her novels have been chosen for the Junior Library Guild, Kids' Indie Next picks, and YALSA Teens' Top Ten. When she's not writing, April likes walking in the woods with her two cheerful dogs, exploring abandoned houses, and drinking expensive coffee. She has lived in many places around the world, and currently resides in Oregon with her husband.

Photo © Sonya Sones

NICOLA YOON

Nicola Yoon is the #1 *New York Times* best-selling author of *Everything, Everything*, which is now a major motion picture, and *The Sun Is Also a Star*, a National Book Award finalist and Michael L. Printz Honor Book. She grew up in Jamaica and Brooklyn and lives in Los Angeles with her family.

BOOKTUBERS

Photo © Fiona Cue Photography

BENJAMIN ALDERSON (BENJAMINOFTOMES)

Benjamin started his channel, Benjaminof-tomes, in 2012, which has now led to his running his own micropublishing company called Oftomes Publishing. He enjoys his Greek grandmother's cooking, *RuPaul's Drag Race*, and endless supplies of music. You can find him in a coffee shop drinking an iced latte and reading.

Photo © Jenna Kilpinen

SASHA ALSBERG (ABOOKUTOPIA)

Sasha Alsberg is the #1 *New York Times* best-selling coauthor of *Zenith: The Androma Saga*. When Sasha is not writing or obsessing over Scotland, she's making YouTube videos on her channel, Abookutopia. She lives in northern Texas.

Photo © Jenna Clare Photography

WHITNEY ATKINSON (WHITTYNOVELS)

Whitney Atkinson is a full-time English major, part-time booktuber. She enjoys peeling dried glue off the tip of the bottle, being sassy, reading until three a.m. on school nights, raspberry sweet tea from Sonic, beards, and that one breed of guinea pig that's really fluffy. She hopes to one day move to New York City and work in publishing among all of her favorite authors (which is quite a hefty list).

Photo © Tina Burke

TINA BURKE (CHRISTINAREADSYA and THE LUSHABLES CHANNEL)

Tina was raised in Southern California by a boisterous Lebanese family, whose favorite words ("let me tell you a story") spurred a lifelong love of storytelling. After earning a BA in neuroscience, she moved to the East Coast for her PhD program. When she's not reading or thinking about her next research story, she can be found writing fictional stories.

Photo © Catriona Feeney

CATRIONA FEENEY (LITTLEBOOKOWL)

Catriona is an Australian booktuber who has been making bookish videos on her channel, LittleBookOwl, for over five years. When not reading books for pleasure, she is either looking at them longingly on her shelf or studying them at Macquarie University. Catriona is the young adult ambassador for the Sydney Writers' Festival and has been a panelist for Sydney Supanova and Sydney Writers' Festival.

Photo © Karen George

JESSE GEORGE (JESSETHEREADER)

Jesse George started his YouTube channel JessetheReader in 2012 and has been sharing his love for books on the internet ever since. When he's not nose deep in a book, he's traveling, spending time with his family, or making memories with his friends.

Photo © Christine Riccio

ZOË HERDT (READBYZOE)

Zoë Herdt lives in Orlando with her two dogs and in a room that is bursting with books. She is currently double majoring in English and advertising at the University of Florida. You can find her gushing about fictional characters on her YouTube channel, readbyzoe.

Photo © Jenna Clare Photography

SAMANTHA LANE
(THOUGHTS ON TOMES)

A Midwestern girl currently living on the East Coast, Samantha has been uploading bookish videos on her channel, Thoughts on Tomes, three times a week since 2014. She is currently the moderator for *Top 5 Wednesday*. When not discussing fictional characters online, Samantha can be found playing video games, marathoning episodes of *Buffy the Vampire Slayer*, or napping with one of her pets.

Photo © Byoung Lee

SOPHIA LEE (THEBOOKBASEMENT)

Sophia Lee is currently a student at Vanderbilt University, although she's really from South Texas. When not studying, she likes to share her love of books on her YouTube channel, thebookbasement. Sophia's interests include reading, writing, cinema, music, and medicine, and she hopes to eventually figure out what order to put those in.

Photo © Kyle Stuart

RAELEEN LEMAY (PADFOOTANDPRONGS07)

Raeleen is a twenty-two-year-old Harry Potter nerd from British Columbia, Canada. She spends her days working at an independent bookstore, and her nights hanging out with her cats, Simon and Luna. She also met Daniel Radcliffe one time and it was magical.

Photo © Sasha Alsberg

REGAN PERUSSE (PERUSEPROJECT)

Regan Perusse studied at the University of Texas, where she majored in advertising, history, and student loans. Besides working in the "real world," Regan also vlogs on her YouTube channel, PeruseProject, where she talks about all things bookish. In her free time, she enjoys hanging out with her pug, Chicago Bears football, and fangirling.

Photo © Jesse George

CHRISTINE RICCIO (POLANDBANANASBOOKS)

Story enthusiast Christine Riccio is from New Jersey. She graduated from Boston University with a degree in film and TV and now lives in Los Angeles. On her YouTube channel, PolandbananasBOOKS, she makes comedic book reviews, vlogs, and sketches. She's on a quest to encourage more humans to read.

Photo © JLowe Photos

Photo © Brian Bird Photography

STEPH SINCLAIR AND KAT KENNEDY (CUDDLEBUGGERY BLOG AND CHANNEL)

Stephanie Sinclair is one of the evil masterminds behind Cuddlebuggery, a blog that features critical, yet entertaining reviews of YA novels. Previously, she's written for YA Books Central and Tor.com, where she cowrote the YA Roundup alongside Kat Kennedy. When she's not inhaling books, she can be found knitting baby hats or taking a million pics of her cats.

Kat Kennedy has two great loves, a good drink and a good read. She's been blogging about books, particularly young adult novels, since 2012. It was only a matter of time till she wrote her own. Kat writes about fearsome girls who save the world.

She cofounded Cuddlebuggery with Stephanie Sinclair and was a sometime contributor to Tor.com.

She lives in Sydney, Australia.